$\mathcal{B}$EYOND *the*
BROKEN STATUES
MODERN GREEK SHORT STORIES

Beyond the Broken Statues

Modern Greek Short Stories

Translated by

Nicholas Kostis

COSMOS PUBLISHING

Book design by Mary A. Wirth
Cover painting by Basil Maros (1897-1954); *Figure with Columns*, 1948, oil on cardboard, 46 x 35.5 cm. Reproduced courtesy of Leonidas Tsirigoulis, the owner of the painting.

Library of Congress Cataloging-in-Publication Data

Modern Greek short stories.
    Beyond the broken statues : modern Greek short stories / translated by Nicholas Kostis with an introduction by Peter Bien.
        p. cm.
    Originally published: Athens : Odysseas, 1993 in English with the title Modern Greek short stories.
    Includes bibliographical references.
    10 digit ISBN: 1-932455-12-4 (pbk. : alk. paper)
    13 digit ISBN: 978-1-932455-12-0
    1. Short stories, Greek (Modern)—Translations into English.   2. Greek fiction.
Modern—19th century—Translations into English.   3. Greek fiction, Modern—20th
century—Translations into English.   I. Kostis, Nicholas. II. Title.
    PA5296.E5M63 2006
    889'.3010802—dc22

                    2006010433

First Published in 2006 by:
Cosmos Publishing Co., Inc.
P.O. Box 2255
River Vale, NJ 07675
Phone: 201-664-3494
Fax: 201-664-3402

email: info@greeceinprint.com
website: www.greeceinprint.com

In the memory of my mother,
DIONISIA KOSTIS

"... beyond the broken statues and the tragic columns ..."

CONTENTS

TRANSLATOR'S NOTE

The present book attempts to fill a lacuna in contemporary letters. While the poetry of Cavafy, the Nobel Prize laureates Seferis and Elytis, and the novels of Kazantzakis have long been available in English, modern Greek prose in general, and the modern Greek short story in particular, have not yet reached a wide English-speaking public. The primary aim of this anthology is to present in English translation and in chronological order representative authors who illustrate the development of this genre in Greece from the beginning of the mid-1800s to 1970. For despite the long interval of literary silence that may have occurred during four centuries of Turkish occupation, with the advent of the nineteenth century Greek literature entered the cultural mainstream of Western Europe. The short story in Greece developed concurrently with its counterparts in France, Germany, Russia, and other countries throughout the world, undergoing the same influences. Since literature is also the product of an individual country with its own political and cultural history, it is only natural that the short story in Greece possessed its own distinct characteristics. The stories chosen for this volume, therefore, bring to the reader a greater understanding both of the Greek temperament and of its special contribution to consciousness and literature.

INTRODUCTION

Greece's population is about 11,000,000, just about the same as Ohio's. In the century represented by these stories-roughly 1890 to 1990-Greece produced two Nobel laureates in literature, George Seferis and Odysseas Elytis. It also produced at least three others—Kostis Palamas, Nikos Kazantzakis, and Yannis Ritsos (not to mention a fourth who lived in Egypt, Constantine Cavafy—whose stature was grand enough for a Nobel Prize. Interestingly, with the exception of Kazantzakis, all of these figures were poets. The marvelous literary renaissance enjoyed by Greece in the twentieth century, paralleled only by the equally marvelous renaissance in Ireland, was strongest in verse. The short story, the form collected in this volume, was assiduously produced in Greece but as never accorded the recognition given to poetry and, later, to the novel.

Conversely, the only world-class literary figure produced by Ohio was Sherwood Anderson (1876-1941), whose collection of short stories "Winesburg, Ohio," published in 1919, is an American classic, although it did not secure him a Nobel Prize. All of his tales are set in the same place: Winesburg. Nicholas Kostis's volume is very different in that it offers stories by many authors that stretch across numerous decades in time and numerous regions in place. But very one (even if set in Egypt) is Greek in subject matter as well as language.

The variety is large. For example: A man sees a phantom in his dreams but the phantom turns out to be real. A man dying of cancer at the young age of forty pours out his chagrin. A rich woman during the second world war finds that her husband has joined the enemy and become an informer. A disgusting sex-mad expatriate tries to seduce every woman he can find, even when he is moribund. A soldier, aged twenty-two, returns home on leave to a mother who continues to think of him as a baby and therefore cannot abide his smoking (and worse). A hunchbacked girl somehow exists all alone in Athens. A teenaged young woman joins the resistance in Athens during the Occupation, is betrayed, and executed by the Germans. A man who has fought in the Albanian campaign prospers after the war, marries well, fathers children, makes a lot of money, but suddenly feels empty and wishes that another war would break out. A woman remembers being punished by her mother when she was a small child. A man returns to Greece after ten years abroad to find that his best friend is now a recluse and supposedly, but not really, insane. Visitors to Mycenae connect that site and its history with their own tragedy in the Asia Minor Disaster.

The settings—mainland, islands, Athens, Mycenae, Alexandria, Port Said—are just as diverse as the subjects. Most important is the variety of people. We read about the rich and poor, honest folk and scoundrels, males and females, children and adults.

The book encapsulates Greek life in the hundred years covered. For this reason a beginning student may find this collection more valuable than a novel or poetry by a single author. Furthermore, these stories are very easy to read. The translation is smooth and idiomatic, retaining a certain Greek flavor but at the same time imparting a tone that native speakers of English will find entirely familiar.

Beyond the Broken Statues: Modern Greek Short Stories offers an instructive, stimulating, and sometimes disturbing entree to a remarkable culture.

PETER BIEN

BEYOND *the* BROKEN STATUES

MODERN GREEK SHORT STORIES

EMMANUEL ROIDIS

(1836-1904)

Psychology of a Husband from Syra

I am ashamed to admit it. Eight months have passed since I was married and I am still in love with my wife, whereas the primary reason for having married her was that the state of being a lover was not at all to my liking. I do not believe that there exists another more agonizing sickness. I had no appetite, no sleep, nor any desire to work or to amuse myself. Except for Christina, I found all else tasteless, unsalted, uninteresting, and tedious; I remember how one day I made everyone in the restaurant laugh when I complained that the salted tuna fish was unsalted. My relatives were opposed to this match because she had nothing and I, for that matter, not very much—my ancestral home, an income of three thousand drachmas from two warehouses, and a position that paid me one hundred and sixty drachmas. How could we possibly live on that, especially since the young woman, despite being deprived of a dowry, was an only child, who was pampered and who liked the best society, good times, jewelry and dances.

Everything I had been warned against, I was discovering to be true! I cannot even say in my defense that passion blinded me; nor is there, I believe, an individual more positive than I. Others in love imagine the pleasure of possessing their beloved to be so great a happiness that, unafraid of being duped, they buy it at any cost. I, however, was not romantic. I was not dreaming of anything extraordinary, only for things to return to the normal state in which they were before I fell in love. I recalled that blessed condition with the burning desire with which a sick man remembers the time when he was healthy. I wanted Christina purely and simply to enjoy her, to have my fill of her, to grow tired of her, and to begin afterwards—as before—to eat, to sleep, to take walks and to play cards at the club. Even so, I would not have decided to marry her if an uncle of mine, an old man who we all thought to be penniless, seeing him dress like Diogenes and eat like an ascetic, had not happened to pass away during those days as a result of privation and hardship. Having suffered for some time from a chest ailment, he had requested of me a hundred drachmas to pay for the doctor and medicine. Only instead of using the money for such purposes, he had preferred to add it to another five thousand, concealed inside the straw mattress on which he was found dead one morning. His misfortune made me reflect that it would be foolish of me to continue tormenting myself from lack of sleep and appetite, seeing that I had the wherewithal to be cured. I married Christina as someone takes quinine to rid himself of a fever.

Though I was impatient, I was obliged, because of common superstition and our bishop Lykourgos, to wait until the end of May before marrying her. Immediately after the wedding, we went to Kea for our honeymoon. There I can say that I experienced happy days. The island was quite green, our summerhouse comfortable, the food excellent, the weather lovely and Christina even lovelier. What made me prefer her to all the other girls is that she alone had none of the usual virginal faults that generally made me loathe maidens. She was neither skinny, nor anemic, nor bashful, nor too young. In fact, I believe she was slightly older than I, somewhere between twenty-six and twenty-eight, with a dark complexion, tall, broad shoulders, a full bosom, a lively glance and extremely elegant shoes. So that the totality of so many gifts may not seem incredible, it is enough for me to add that she was from Smyrna.

We remained at Kea for the entire summer and my recovery was progressing remarkably well. I believe that I discovered the dictum "Blessed are they who possess" long before Bismarck. Sentimentalists view such possession as an imperfection and marriage in general as the tomb of love. But I could have no such complaint since I had married with the intention of burying love; with the desire not for extraordinary pleasures, but for peace of mind. And each day, I was succeeding in becoming more peaceful. In the morning we bathed in the sea; in the afternoon we went on long walks or on boating excursions. I returned exhausted, ate like a wolf, and having said to Christina whatever I had to say to her, slept straight through until morning. I no longer had dreams, except for one, which I was also able to interpret as a symptom of my complete recovery.

The evening was warm and we had gone out on the balcony after supper for a breath of fresh air. I cannot recall a more brightly shining full moon, nor such a scintillating sea, nor more sweet-smelling exhalations from the forest and gardens. Christina, too, was most charming in her white waist-less gown, or *peignoir* as it was called, over which her loose hair flowed down to her knees like an overflowing black river.

She looked at the sea, humming the cavatina in the fashion of the time, "Hernani, Hernani, come and abduct me," when suddenly she stopped modestly, straining her ear to the song of the nightingale that resounded from the neighboring garden. All this was very poetic, to be sure, but at dinner I had eaten too much tuna fish, which being difficult to digest, I had washed down with two or three glasses of the sweet wine of Kea. I was overcome with sleep, therefore, and dreamed...neither of songs of the nightingale, nor of black tresses, nor of moonlight, but that I was back in Syra at the club, and that I was winning three hands in a row from Aloisius Katzaitis, an expert piquet player. After such a dream, it would be wrong of me to doubt that I was thoroughly cured. The following week we returned to Syra, after a four-month stay at Kea, and after I had regained my former peace of mind, all my prose, and two *okas** of additional weight—as I ascertained upon weighing myself on the scales at the customs house when we disembarked.

Most assuredly I would have laughed at the time if someone had told me that in a few days I would be much more in love and miserable than before my marriage. The initial cause of the relapse was a

---

* Weight measurement.

dance given by the mayor in honor of the visiting minister of the Navy, who was also his guest. That dance was being held prematurely and unexpectedly and there was little time for the women of Syra to make themselves ready. They were all in a state of agitation. For three days, Christina ran to the shops, and on the fourth day our entire house was converted into a sewing workroom. There were pieces of material, linings, accessories, brassieres and shoes to be tried all over the place. I could not find anywhere to sit down. In the evening I had to wait until nine o'clock, or even later, before the seamstress cleared the dining table so that we might sup on salad or some fried sprats. Our sole and indeed encyclopedic servant had also been ordained as a dressmaker and had no time to cook. It would, however, be unjust of me to complain about this since the evil was generalized. It is the prevailing custom in Syra to fast—in addition to Christmas, Easter, and the other important holidays—on the eve of big dances as well. Most annoying of all was Christina's unceasing preoccupation and the assorted pieces of paper in which she wrapped her hair at night. From the day we received that cursed invitation, it was as if I did not have a wife.

However great my abhorrence for such preparations, I must admit that Christina's adornment was utterly successful—a deep crimson silk dress with a long train, and on her head the last relic from her mother's jewel case, a kind of antique diadem made of rubies, whose purple flames harmonized marvelously with the jet-black color of her hair. Adorned thus, she reminded me of Semiramis, Phaedra, Cleopatra, Theodora, and those other heroines who used to trouble my sleep when I was a schoolboy.

The house of the mayor was large, but even greater was his fear of overlooking even the least significant leader of his party, whether he was a pastry-cook, a skipper, a tanner, or some other storekeeper. Consequently, there were a great many people present and, as always happens in Syra, the male dancers outnumbered the women by three to one. They waited for the women at the front door with dance-cards in their hands and followed them up the steps, pleading for a dance. Upon our entrance, at least fifteen of them rushed toward Christina, who I admired for the courage and readiness with which, in this assault upon her, she distributed, like holy bread, a glance and a smile to each claimant. This distribution continued without intermission for the duration of the entire evening. I was the only one for whom there was nothing left, even though the adventures of the dance brought her in close proximity to me two or three times. Not being in the mood to dance and burdened by my annoying thoughts, I was searching for some familiar face in the crowd when I discerned, clinging to the wall like a tapestry, Miss Kleareti Galaxidis, a forty-year-old spinster who I liked very much—not, of course, because of her overripe beauty, but because of her kindness, her affability, her simplicity of manner and dress and her apparent lack of every claim to conquest and coquetry. She also danced exceedingly well whenever she happened to find a partner. I was on familiar terms with this old maid, but as a friend, nothing more than that; and she also seemed pleased to converse with me, to give me advice about my health or about household economies, and occasionally to send me aniseed zwiebacks, so that I might appreciate her excellent art of baking. In view of this, my surprise is understandable when, instead of extending her hand to me as usual, she responded to my "good evening" with a cold, almost hostile look.

"Aren't you dancing tonight?" I asked without thinking, forgetting that this was not entirely dependent on her desire.

"No, sir."

"Why, since you're our best dancer? How strange."

"There are still stranger things."

"Won't you tell me what?"

"There are certain men who, having assured a young woman for years that it would be impossible for them to love any but a sensible, quiet, modest woman who is a good housekeeper, then go out and marry a spendthrift, a coquette, and a scatterbrain who had love affairs with everybody and continues to do so even after her marriage."

From this I was forced to conclude that Miss Kleareti was not as kind as she appeared, nor her attentions, advice, and dispatching of zwiebacks as disinterested as I had supposed.

This unexpected revelation of the marital pretensions of an old maid, who could have been my mother had she married at the proper time, was, of course, ludicrous. But that evening my nerves were on edge and instead of laughing, I did not consider it beneath me to take vengeance by answering, "I don't recall ever having had such a conversation with a young woman."

Miss Kleareti bit her lip and turned her back to me. But her phrase, "had love affairs with everybody and continues to do so even after her marriage," did not stop resounding in my ears like the hissing of a serpent. The truth of the matter is that Christina was overdoing it. As I continued to spy on her, I observed that the distribution of her glances and smiles was not occurring as evenly and impartially as I had at first supposed. A far greater share of them were going to an elegant, blond young man than to the others. The man, having received two dances, remained behind her while she danced with someone else, then continued to have an endless conversation with her during the intermission of the quadrille. The strange thing was that this man was entirely unknown to me, whereas the inhabitants of Hermoupolis all know each other like monks in a monastery.

I was in great perplexity when my old friend Evangelos Haldoupis, the most intelligent but also the most perverse person in Syra, brazen as a monkey and more cynical than Diogenes, came and sat beside me. To avoid people's gibes, he had contrived to laugh louder than anybody else over his late wife's numerous and glaring infidelities. On his office wall he had hung pictures of Hephaistos, Agamemnon, Menelaus, Bellisarios, Henry IV, and himself alongside "his illustrious confrères." Throughout the duration of his five years of married life, not once did a complaint ever slip from his lips, nor a reprimand, nor a reproach, nor a remark of any kind, but only irony, mockery, and smiles so venomous that for many the question remained whether the deceased actually died from cancer or from the causticity of these innuendos. At any rate, immediately after the period of mourning, he announced that he was again an eligible bachelor. However, out of fear, as he said, that his wit might become depleted should he have to use it as inaptly as before in defense of his honor, he had already made three stipulations with regard to the future Mrs. Haldoupis—that she be ugly, dumb, and rich. This much-sought-after triad of attributes he had found joined in the person of Miss Panayota Tourlotis, a kind of young hippopotamus whose bulk had frightened away all the other fortune hunters.

This strange man, after observing me for several moments with annoying persistence, asked, "What's wrong? Your face is as somber as the mountains of Youras."

"Nothing," I replied. "My head aches slightly."

"And it aches all the more because you didn't heed my words when I told you that Christina was not for you; that she has too much blood running in her veins and bears a certain physical resemblance to my late wife. I see that her old friend Karolos Vitouris is next to her," he added, pointing to the blond youth who was continuing to speak with her. "They seem to have a lot to talk about."

"Her old friend?" I asked. "How is it that I don't know him? This is the first time I've ever seen him."

"For the reason that he only returned from abroad the day before yesterday. Five years ago, before you settled in Syra, he was madly in love with Christina, who he was not allowed to marry because he lacked the means to support her. He gave way to such despair that he wanted to commit suicide, and he might have, if my wife had not taken it upon herself to console him. He was, I believe, her first lover. I caught them red-handed in the garden of Koimos one day when I had gone there to call on Anika. My wife soon tired of him because he was overly sentimental. Furthermore, it appears that he continued to remember yours. Then they sent him to France to forget them both and to study pharmacy in order to follow in his father's footsteps. But it looks as though he was unsuccessful in finding an herb for forgetfulness. Notice how his eyes are devouring Christina. My advice to you is to watch him and not to bring your wife to dances very often."

"I will follow your advice."

"Don't forget that if you appear jealous or if you upset her or attempt to restrain her, it is still more certain that you will end up paying the piper."

"What should I do, then?"

"Even I don't know. Since you didn't follow my advice, the best I can recommend to you now is to imitate my example and regardless of what happens, not take it to heart. To remember that the thing in itself is of no importance. And also to hang the pictures of Agamemnon, Hephaistos, and Menelaus on your wall."

I stood up abruptly, fearing that I would not be able to resist the temptation to spit in that rascal's face. At that moment a cotillion started, which seemed endless to me. Thank God that it also came to an end and people started to leave. I went to get my wife's fur coat, I bundled her in it, and we were walking toward the door when three dancers blocked our way, contending that the gallopade finale was yet to be danced and that my wife had promised it to all three. She could not remember. The simplest and customary way to accommodate their demands would have been for her to say that she was tired and to dance with none of them. Instead, she suggested that they draw lots. Chance, or perhaps some sleight of hand, favored Vitouris, and my martyrdom was prolonged for another hour. I must admit, though, that the music of that gallopade, composed by the orchestral director and violinist Patsifikos, was extremely beautiful and the rhythm so lively that it placed wings on the feet of both the mayor and the other equally venerable citizens of Syra. The tray with warm wine being passed around brought the general liveliness to a peak, and I alone sulked in a corner as I watched Christina whirling around in the arms of Karolos. Haldoupis attempted to approach me again to pour his venom into my wound, but the look I gave him, I suspect, was so fierce that he considered it wiser to show me his back. We were almost the last to leave, and when we entered our bedroom, the clock was striking five.

The strange thing, or rather what seemed strange to me even though it was only natural, is that everything I suffered at that cursed dance from the calumny of Haldoupis and the conduct of Christina, instead of moderating my feelings, made me love her or at least desire her still more ardently than on the day I decided to marry her in order to cease desiring her. Aside from jealousy and ten days of abstinence, what contributed to the intensification of my desire was also the extraordinary sumptuousness of her inner attire—her silk brassiere, her embroidered petticoats, her satin shoes, and the intoxicating fragrance of iris and the oil of lavender. The fortunate inhabitants of large cities may acquire all these whenever they like with one or two twenty-five–cent pieces, but for the less fortunate inhabitants of Syra they are extraordinary things that we enjoy only when a big dance happens to take place, just as we try sweets, champagne, and stuffed turkey only at Christmas and Easter. When, therefore, I approached Christina, I must surmise that my eyes were "eloquent," as our authors of light literature succeed in writing and who I was wrong, it seems, to mock for this. Before I had time to open my mouth, Christina hastened to reply to my glance, "I'm worn out, ready to drop, you wretched boy. Please leave me to myself tonight."

I bid her goodnight with a sunken heart and withdrew to my own room. I should say, however, that she was not to blame for that separate room. It was I who upon our return had suggested it as more aristocratic and for the very reason that I had become overly satiated at Kea. Aside from everything else, people in love also possess this additional peculiarity: they are unable to comprehend that they can become hungry when they are satiated or that they can become satiated when they are hungry.

On the following morning she was still asleep when I left for my office at about eleven o'clock. Upon my return, I found her seated at the piano, good-humored and animated.

"Listen to how lovely this gallopade is," she said to me. "I, who am unable to play anything without the score, heard it once and remember it all."

As she spoke, she started playing the thrice-cursed gallopade from yesterday's dance, whose tune reminded me of my ordeal.

"I'm slightly dizzy," I answered abruptly, "and the music annoys me. Please leave it for another time."

She looked at me, somewhat surprised, closed the piano and went to lean against the window. A short while later I saw her greeting someone with a great deal of charm and amiability.

"To whom were you talking?" I asked with as much indifference as I could summon.

"The dance teacher, the elderly Kouertzis."

I hastened to the window in the adjacent room and indeed saw the elderly Kouertzis passing by, but he was leaning on the arm of the young Karolos Vitouris. Why, then, had she mentioned only Kouertzis, when in all probability the lion's share of her greeting had gone to his companion?

That year was an extraordinarily happy one for the people of Syra who, once their accounts were balanced, became dance fanatics out of joy. In the space of a single month, eleven large and small dance evenings were held. Christina did nothing but prepare herself all day long, tire herself all evening long, and rest during the following day; nor did I do anything but accompany her, stay awake, be a prey to anxiety, be jealous, spy, and dream of Hephaistos, Menelaus, and Vitouris. The last continued to pass under our windows at frequent intervals. Fortunately the customs of the island do not permit visits, except on the first of the year and on the nameday of the master of the house. A gentleman's calling on a lady on a workday and during work hours would have been no less scandalous in Syra than breaking into a harem. There remained, however, the dances and daily meetings on the ships and in the public square. Aside from them, I happened on two or three occasions to see my wife coming out of the pharmacy of Vitouris. Yet I could not consider this reprehensible, or even suspicious, since this is where the high-class women of Syra procured their creams and perfumes. But this reflection did not prevent me from being agitated and anxious.

What tormented me and worried me more than anything else, however, was that I rarely succeeded in seeing Christina alone and tranquil. Not even a field marshal on the eve of a decisive battle could have been as preoccupied as she. Rapid excursions to the stores were succeeded by consultations with her girlfriends. Sometimes she was upset with the seamstress who had failed to keep her promise, at other times with the one and only hairdresser in Syra, Anastasis, because he had been late in coming, or because the wicked man had dared to propose combing her hair in the afternoon, seeing that he did not have time in the evening. After all this came exhaustion from the dance, sleepiness immediately upon our return home, her profound slumber until noon, and my own tormenting sleeplessness. I was unable even to remain quietly in my bed, let alone sleep. Just as visions of springs, lakes, and green meadows torture the traveler in the desert, so was I tortured by the memory of those happy days at Kea, of the solitude, of the tranquility, and of Christina stretched out for hours at a time on a Turkish divan, in a white housedress and with a book in her hand. And what I remembered with an even greater burning desire were not so much the pleasures of the honeymoon as the ensuing serenity and equilibrium of the mind and senses, which allowed me to delight in the other pleasures of life. Whereas now the concentration of my desires on a sole object, because of jealousy and abstinence, had transformed me, the sensible man from Syra, into a kind of Traveler or Erotokritos reciting plaintive monologues.

One night, unable to bear it any longer, I opened the door that separated our rooms without making any noise and took several steps in the direction of my wife's bed. The room was lit, as usual, by a blue votive lamp in the iconostasis. That blue light, imparting a dreamlike hue to reality, had also been my invention during the happy days at Kea. Her fatigue and sleepiness upon our return had been so great that she had left all her things lying about. Her dress on a corner of the sofa, her hoopskirt on the floor, her brassiere on the edge of the bed, her garland on the bust of Korais, and scattered all over the seats were her fan, her corsage, her gloves, and her decorations from the cotillion. Her favorite cat was asleep on her white burnoose, and the stones of her bracelets and necklace sparkled on the marble mantelpiece. The room resembled a temple to the goddess Disorderliness. Yet it was not possible for that chaos, all of whose components were so beautiful, to be unsightly. To Christina's other qualities, I must also add that she was accustomed to sleeping with one knee bent and her hand behind her head, like the ancient statue of Hermaphroditus. At that moment she was probably dreaming of her triumphs at the Club as I surmised from a smile, so similar to those she distributed among her dance partners, formed by her slightly parted lips. I advanced another step. But suddenly my feet froze in their tracks at the thought that, should I awaken her, that sweet smile would be succeeded by a grimace of displeasure, a yawn, an "ugh!" and her turning her back to me. Nor would such a reception be entirely unjustifiable since she had gone to bed only an hour ago and already the dim light of the winter morning was visible through the cracks of her window. I withdrew on tip-toe, closed the door, and resumed my walking and monologue. When I thought how easy it would be for that woman to make me the happiest of men by caring a little less for parties and flirting, I felt the urge to strangle her. But there was little danger of this. I do not believe there exists a softer heart than mine in the world. If I myself had to slaughter the chickens I eat, I believe I would prefer to nourish myself on bran as they do.

I implore those who are inclined from the above to consider me a fool, to reflect how difficult is the position of he who is as powerless as a lover to beg without becoming ridiculous, or as a husband to demand without becoming odious. I feared both designations to such an extent that, if Christina happened to ask me why I was not eating or why I was out of sorts, I would answer by falsely accusing my stomach, or my head, or my teeth, or even my nerves, attempting to conceal my real pain, as if it were a crime. In fact, I knew very well that a woman is capable of forgiving everything, infidelities, insults, beatings, and everything else, with one exception—that someone should love her more than she deserves. If a man is foolish enough to admit to a woman how much he is suffering because of her, there is nothing left for him to do but to part from her on the same day or to throw himself in the sea with a rock tied around his neck.

Two days after that painful sleeplessness, upon returning from my office somewhat earlier than usual, I saw Christina change countenance and hasten to conceal a piece of paper she was holding behind the mirror. My mind immediately went to Vitouris, and my suspicion that the letter belonged to him was confirmed by my wife's increasing uneasiness and confusion. Nor, in this instance, was it any longer possible for me to apply my system of putting up with everything in silence for fear of worse since in all likelihood that letter contained proof that there remained nothing worse for me to fear.

The impending explosion was averted by the abrupt opening of the door, the diffusion of the fragrance of musk and the impetuous entrance into the room of the lively wife of our mayor, coming by to show my wife her new coat with galloons made from the tufts of birds. Christina was obliged, whether she wanted to or not, to receive her while I, on the pretext that I wanted to leave the ladies by themselves to talk about their own interests, removed myself to the adjoining room after I had overtly taken the envelope from behind the mirror. My hands trembled as I opened it. Instead of a letter from the romantic Karolos, however, I found inside three invoices from Poulos, Giannopoulos, and Geralopoulos for silks, hats, veils, ribbons, and other articles, whose total came to two thousand seven hundred drachmas. The sum, of course, was sizable, but much greater was the relief I felt in the face of proof that I had been wrong to consider myself a confrère of Haldoupis. My joy was comparable to that of a condemned man whose death sentence has unexpectedly been commuted to a simple fine. I was under the influence of this feeling when, after the departure of the visitor, Christina approached me somewhat timidly, abashed, and thinking that she absolutely had to offer some explanation and appease me. Instead of any remarks or complaints whatsoever, I hurried to embrace her with all my heart, saying, "Don't be upset." She was greatly surprised. Obviously it was difficult for her to guess why I would consider as deserving of amiabilities and kisses her act of squandering six months of our income in the space of a few days.

A little later, she went to prepare herself for our evening walk. But the sky unexpectedly became overcast; lightning flashed, and it began to rain in torrents. I was still seated by the window of our small drawing room, looking at the yellow cataract that was falling from the heights of Upper Syra, sweeping along in its muddy current orange peels, broken bottles, old shoes, and the carcasses of chickens and rats, when, suddenly, that panorama was supplanted by a deep darkness that spread over both my eyes. The eclipse was caused by the hands of Christina, who, in despair of going out, had returned without making any noise and, seeing me absorbed, found amusement in blinding me. This reminded me of past happy days. Thanks to that God-sent violent storm, we at last found ourselves alone and undisturbed for the first time since our return. When she consented to remove her hands, the expression in my eyes was, I imagine, again so "eloquent" that it brought a slight blush to her cheeks. She then smiled, turned, and passing by the door with the lock, went to sit down on the sofa and beckoned me to come sit next to her. At that very moment, while I was sinking in a sea of sensuality, the raging storm was at its peak. The rain had become a deluge, the wind blew away roof tiles, and claps of thunder rumbled repeatedly. Whether I was inclined to or not, it was my fate to be romantic. Burning desires and nocturnal monologues were succeeded by a locking of the door and a stretching out on the divan under the hissing of the storm. My resistance against predestination thus seemed futile, and it was far preferable that I allow things to remain as they were. I must also confess that my opposition to romanticism had diminished considerably in the space of a single hour.

In fact, comparing the quiet, daily pleasures at Kea with the sensual shudder that seized me when, after a ten-day exile, Christina beckoned me a short while ago to come next to her, I arrived at the conclusion that the degree of bliss one is able to experience at the side of a woman is exactly proportionate to the anxiety, jealousy, abstinence, and all the other torments preceding it. Only he who has gone through such purgatory may then receive the privilege of entering the sanctuary of supreme sensual pleasure, the doors of which cannot be opened to us by a modest maiden, nor by an affectionate husband, nor by a well-beloved mistress, but only by a coquettish, capricious, and not always kind woman.

The dances continued, but not Christina's special favors to Vitouris, which had disturbed my sleep. She already seemed to prefer the black whiskers and broad shoulders of our swaggering garrison commander to the sighs and blond tresses of the sentimental youth. After a few days, however, she found the commander uncouth as she compared his manners, worthy of a Greek, with the exquisite courtesy, grace, and wit of the newly appointed consul from France. Yet even his reign was not of long duration. The elegance of his Parisian dress coat was soon eclipsed by the splendid uniform and decorations of the commander of the English squadron. Then came the turn of the Italian improviser, Regaldi, who, on tour through the East to gather laurels and dollars, did not view those in Syra with a scornful eye. It amused her to keep this old swan of Novara in Syra for an entire month and to besot him to the point that, not content with all the acrostics he wrote in her album, he also recited from the stage a hymn, "To the Siren of the Aegean," greatly shocking the citizens of Syra and particularly those who did not understand Italian. But I was already calmer as I watched the favorites succeeding one another like phantoms of a mythical lamp.

It would, in fact, have been difficult for a person attempting to conquer the entire world to find time to love anyone. I gradually came to consider the unconstrained coquettishness of my wife as a security against a major calamity, as a kind of lightning-rod or, as Haldoupis might have said, a "cuckold-guard." The only thing that continued to worry me was that she had little time left for me. I had despaired of seeing her in a state of calm before the Lenten season, so impatiently awaited by me, when the festivities were unexpectedly brought to a halt by the death of the elder Monsieur Lìonis So-and-So, related somehow to everyone in the dance set of the island. I believe that not even those millions of nephews who were his heirs followed the funeral procession with greater gratitude than mine for his consenting to die.

Good things, like bad, rarely come alone. A few days after my deliverance from the nightmare of the dances, checking out the five lottery tickets of Hamburg, which I had inherited from my late uncle, in the Sweepstake Winners Sheet, I was astounded to see the number 14,517. It was the third winner and worth fifty-five thousand florins, or slightly more than three hundred thousand drachmas in Syra! I ran breathlessly to announce the good news to Christina, who fortunately was out visiting. I say fortunately because her absence gave me time to think that she would be far more grateful to me and would give me greater reward if, instead of knowing I was rich, she believed me eager to please her beyond the resources at my disposal. Thus, without breathing a word to anyone, I left three days later for Vienna on the pretext that I was going there to consult a medical specialist for the nonexistent stomach disorder that I had used as an excuse for two months to conceal my psychic torments. From Vienna I hopped over to Hamburg and, after collecting my winnings and investing them in negotiable securities, I returned three weeks later, bringing back to Christina twice as many adornments as she had asked of me. Observing her surprise and delight as she opened the box, I thought, congratulating myself on my hypocrisy, how much cheaper my gifts would have seemed to her had she known of the unforeseen generosity of fate. An indispensable condition for harmonious cohabitation with a coquettish woman is to conceal carefully from her two things: nine-tenths of one's love and at least half of one's wealth.

Having no inclination whatsoever to dazzle the people of Syra, I preferred silence and well-nigh secrecy to any display of my increased prosperity. I resigned from my position, claiming that I could earn more by working for myself and, under the pretext that two of the ceilings leaked whenever it rained, I renovated my entire house. I entrusted the wall paintings to an Italian refugee by the name of Orsati, a former set designer at the theater La Scala. He was especially successful in decorating Christina's bedroom, which he transformed into a veritable Oriental chamber, in imitation of that of Zaira in Bellini's opera of the same name. The resemblance was completed by means of heavy drapes from Prussia, a divan covered with gold-embroidered fabric from an old pontifical uniform, a Persian brazier, benches with mother-of-pearl inlay, and a silver-plated Byzantine font, transformed into a magnificent flower vase. All these things had been procured by the interior decorator during an excursion to Naxos, where substantial remains from Franco-Turkish luxuries may still be found; and he succeeded in unifying these diverse elements so aesthetically and with such a precise knowledge of the rules governing the contrast of colors and the diffusion of light, that they enchanted rather than dazzled the eye. This same invaluable man helped me to filch through outbidding—or, as the people from Syra say, "yoking" —the Milanese cook of the bishop of Upper Syra, whose ravioli, shrimp soup, and Lenten capon were renowned throughout the Cyclades. The sadness and indignation of the prelate were such that he felt it his duty to lodge a complaint against me for "proselytism" with the ambassador.

The embellishment of her nest to some extent curtailed Christina's endless fluttering outside it. I attempted to encourage this penchant for domesticity by offering her anything I thought would divert her: camellia plants, a stamp collection, an upright piano, a stereoscope, a voice teacher, and an Angora cat. She accepted them with immense gratitude and appeared enthusiastic for a while. One day, however, after asking the price of the silver tea set that I had offered her on her birthday, she exclaimed somewhat plaintively, "What a shame to have spent so much money. With those six hundred drachmas, I could have had a velvet dress made."

"Have the dress made too," I replied.

She jumped for joy, kissed me on both cheeks, and ran out to order it. Her passion for adornments appeared to be incurable, but fortunately I did not lack the means to please her. I thought it only fair, nevertheless, to use her to increase my own pleasures as well. To this end, I gave her a subscription to *Chronique Elegante* and *Vie Parisienne*, from which she was not slow in learning that true luxury of daily attire consists not in covering, as do the aristocratic women in Syra, cotton camisoles and chintz petticoats with satin and moiré, but rather in concealing chemises valued at a hundred francs, silk stockings, embroidery, and laces under simpler material. Adorned like this in her gold-trimmed bedroom, whose every ornament and every fold of fabric had been arranged by an experienced craftsman in accordance with its intended use, while the aloe burned in a gold censer and the blue votive lamp disseminated its sapphire light, Christina resembled an idol in a temple. Nor did I confine myself for long to the blue light alone; but like Darwin in the matter of the germination of plants, so was I also desirous of testing the effect of every color of light on the imagination and senses. Rose was mellow and blue-green was most poetic, but incomparably more rousing than either was the light shining through the golden glass of the antique ecclesiastical votive lamp.

An appropriate initiation into the divine mysteries before the entrance to this temple was, of course, the pontifical dinners that the Milanese cook served us. In appreciation of her pious devotion to the canons and traditions of the orthodox culinary art, I need only mention that the time required for boiling eggs was determined with precision by the recitation of two Ave Marias, and that she was the first to teach her favorite fisherman to kill the red mullets with a needle as soon as they came out of the net, before the spasms of a long agony had time to make the meat bitter. She boiled the gurnet with all kinds of aromatic herbs in the juice of unripe oranges; and to the turkeys, or as the people from Syra call them, "turkey cocks," she fed nutmeg for three days prior to slaughtering them. But her masterpiece was capon magro, or Lenten capon, an invention of Father Klimentos Gagkanellis; that is, fish garnished with shellfish, mussels, shrimp, and all kinds of other seafood. Even though I am from Syra, I am neither a glutton nor a big eater; I appreciate good meals above all for the cheerful state of mind which attends them, making us forget our troubles and causing us to see all the pleasures of life through a magnifying lens. Such a cheerful state of mind, it seems, is the aim of those who smoke opium and hashish. The latter have the advantage of being within easy reach and inexpensive. All the same, the morbid stimulation derived from them is far removed from that bliss generated around a sumptuous table by the simultaneous gratification of all our senses—the warmth of the hearth, the reflection of light on the silver and crystal tableware, the fragrance from the flower vase, the sea aroma of oysters, two or three glasses of aged wine, and the presence of a young woman whose face gradually becomes flushed and whose eyes sparkle.

The winter brought back the dances with all their annoyances and anxieties. These were diminished considerably, however, by my increasing confidence each day, not in my wife's love or virtue, but in her coquetry and egoism, which were capable of dissuading her from every kind of dangerous foolishness. Christina did not belong, of course, to the species of turtle doves and pigeons, but rather to that of peacocks. Her desires seemed limited to dazzling the women of Syra with the magnificence of her dresses and attaching to their hems a whole flock of admirers. Of these, the visiting officials were fortunately birds of passage and slightly molted by age, while the sentimental phrases of her youthful contemporaries bore a strong resemblance to the love couplets in which candy-makers wrap their sweets. Then, too, as modest as I was, I could not help having confidence in my own exceptional qualities as a husband—acquiescence, hypocrisy, patience, abstinence from every claim, and the willingness to pay every bill.

It is true that I suffered greatly when I saw her rubbing her bare shoulders on the gold epaulets of a naval officer, or withdrawing into a corner and for a long while speaking in whispers behind her fan; and even more when, immediately upon our return home, she said, "Goodnight." But experience had taught me to examine things from both viewpoints. The other viewpoint was that, if she had behaved better toward me, I definitely would have loved her much less, since only by suspicion, jealousy, and anxiety can passion be maintained at a peak. My former prosaic opinion, limiting happiness to deliverance from such tortures, had changed entirely when I came to understand the extent to which they contribute to the heightening of sensual pleasure. It would be unjust and somewhat ungrateful of me, therefore, to complain against my wife for behaving precisely as she should behave to make her kisses sweeter. If I had a wife every day, I would not have a mistress with extraordinary attributes at intervals.

I was thinking of these things while smoking on the balcony after dinner one warm evening during Lent and I was finding fault with those who complained and proclaimed that the world is badly made for the reason that roses have thorns. Instead of becoming indignant thereof, I thought it would be a dark ingratitude not to praise God, taking into consideration that I was not yet thirty, that I had an income of thirty thousand drachmas, thirty solid teeth in my mouth, the stomach of an ostrich, a wife capable of incarnating the dreams of a Sybarite, and a cook who Talleyrand would have envied. I saw my life stretching out before me in a long array of fine dinners, diaphanous clouds of lace, sparkling black eyes, and votive lamps of every color.

GEORGE VIZYINOS

(1849-1896)

My Mother's Sin

We had no other sister except for Annio.

She was the spoiled darling of our small family and we all loved her. But of all of us our mother loved her the most. At the table she always sat Annio by her side and gave her the best of whatever we had. And whereas she dressed the rest of us in clothes that had belonged to our late father, she usually bought new ones for Annio.

She didn't pressure her even in her studies. If Annio wished, she attended school; if not, she stayed at home. Something that we would not have been allowed to do under any circumstances.

Such exceptions were bound, naturally, to give rise to destructive jealousies among children, especially among tiny tots such as my two other brothers and I were at the time they occurred.

But we knew that inwardly our mother's affection was impartial and equally divided among all her offspring. We were certain that these exceptions were nothing more than exterior manifestations of some deeper allegiance to the only girl in our household. And not only did we put up with the attentions shown her without a complaint, but we also contributed to increasing them as much as we could.

For Annio, besides being our only sister, had unfortunately always been sickly and frail. Even the youngest member of the household, who, having been orphaned in the womb, was entitled more than anyone else to reap the fruit of maternal caresses, relinquished his rights to his sister, and the more willingly because Annio became neither domineering nor haughty for all that.

On the contrary, she was very sweet to us and loved us all dearly. And—strangely enough—the girl's tenderness toward us, instead of diminishing as her illness progressed, increased.

I remember her big, black eyes and her arched, closely spaced eyebrows, which appeared all the blacker as her face grew paler—a face by nature dreamy and melancholic over which a sweet joy spread only when she saw us all gathered around her.

She usually kept the fruit that the women from the neighborhood brought her as a "tonic" under her pillow, and divided it among us when we returned from school. But she always did this secretly because it angered our mother, who disapproved of our devouring what she desired her sick daughter to at least have tasted.

Nevertheless, Annio's sickness grew steadily worse and our mother's attentions became more and more concentrated on her. My mother had not left the house ever since our father died. For, having been widowed very young, she was ashamed to take advantage of the liberty that, even in Turkey, is accorded to every mother having many children. But from the day Annio became confined to her bed, she cast modesty aside.

Someone once had a similar sickness—she would run to ask him how he had regained his health. Somewhere an old lady harbored herbs with miraculous medicinal powers—she would hasten to buy them. Some bizarre-looking stranger had arrived from somewhere, or one who was renowned for his knowledge—she would not hesitate to solicit his help. The "learned," according to popular belief, are all-knowing. And mysterious beings in possession of many supernatural powers are sometimes concealed beneath the appearance of a poor traveler.

The fat neighborhood barber visited us at his own invitation and as if it were his right. He was the only official doctor in our region. The moment I saw him, I had to run to the grocer's because he never approached the sick girl without first gulping down at least fifty drams of raki.

"I'm an old man, my good woman," he would say to our impatient mother, "I'm an old man and if I don't 'wet my whistle,' my eyes can't see well."

And it seems he wasn't lying. Because the more he drank, the easier it was for him to discern the fattest hen in our yard in order to take it with him when he left.

Even though my mother had stopped using his medicines for some time now, she still continued to pay him regularly and uncomplainingly. First so as not to displease him and second because he often comforted her by maintaining that the progress of Annio's illness was satisfactory and exactly what science had the right to expect from his prescriptions. The latter, unfortunately, was all too true. Annio's condition advanced slowly and imperceptibly, but always toward the worse. And this prolongation of the unseen illness transformed my mother into another person.

For any unknown disease among the population to be considered a natural disorder, it must either yield to the rudimentary medical knowledge of the region or lead to death within a short time. As soon as it persists and becomes chronic, it is ascribed to supernatural causes and is characterized as "the work of the Devil." The sick person sat on a cursed spot; he crossed the river at night at the very moment when the Nereides were celebrating their secret and licentious rites; or he stepped over a black cat which was really the Devil in disguise.

My mother, who was more devout than superstitious, at first viewed such diagnoses with horror and she refused to execute the spells suggested for fear of committing a sin. Anyhow the priest had already read the exorcisms of evil over the sick girl, for any eventuality. But she presently changed her mind.

As the sick girl's condition deteriorated, maternal love triumphed over the fear of sin, and religion was compelled to cohabit with superstition.

Next to the cross on Annio's chest, she hung a charm inscribed with mysterious Arabic words.

Holy water was followed by sorcery, and after the priest's prayerbooks came the witches' spells.

But all was in vain.

The child continued to grow worse, and our mother became

increasingly unrecognizable. You might have thought that she had forgotten she had other children as well.

As to who fed us boys, who bathed us, and who mended our clothes, she did not even care to know.

An old lady from the neighboring village of Sofidi, who had already been living under our roof for many years, looked after us as much as her Methuselah-like age would permit.

There were times when we didn't see our mother for days on end.

Sometimes she went to some miraculous site where she would tie a strip from Annio's dress in the hope that the evil would also be tied up far from the sick girl. Other times she went to churches in neighboring villages that happened to be celebrating a saint's day, carrying with her a yellow candle molded with her own hands and exactly as tall as the sick girl. But none of these things were of any use. Our poor sister's illness was incurable.

When all means had been exhausted and all remedies had been tried, we then reached the last refuge in such circumstances.

My mother lifted the wasted girl in her arms and carried her to the church, while my older brother and I loaded ourselves with the bedding and followed behind. And there, on the damp, cold flagstones, before the icon of the Virgin Mary, we made up the bed and laid upon it the sweetest object of our concerns, our one and only sister.

Everybody said that she was possessed by the Devil. My mother no longer had any doubts about this and even the sick girl began to sense it.

She was, therefore, to remain for forty days and nights in the church before the Holy Altar, in the presence of the mother of our Savior, entrusted entirely to their mercy and compassion, so that she might be saved from the satanic affection lurking within her and gnawing so mercilessly at the tender tree of her life.

Forty days and nights. Because the terrible perseverance of the demons can resist only so long in the invisible battle between them and divine grace.

At the end of this period, the evil is defeated and retreats in disgrace. There is no lack of tales according to which the afflicted feel in their organism the awful writhing of the final battle and see their enemy fleeing in a strange shape, especially at the moment when the

priests pass by carrying the holy vessels and chanting the "With Fear."
Fortunate are they, if at that time they have strength enough to
endure the shocks of the struggle. The weak are crushed by the magnitude of the miracle taking place within them. But they have no
regrets about this. For if they lose their life at least they gain something far more valuable. They save their soul.

Despite all this, the likelihood of some such occurrence deeply
disturbed our mother who, as soon as we set Annio down, began to ask
her with great concern how she felt.

The sanctity of the place, the sight of the icons, and the fragrance
of the incense had, it seems, a beneficial effect on her melancholic
spirit, for after the first few moments she livened up and began to ban-
ter with us.

"Which one of the two do you want to play with?" my mother
asked her tenderly. "Christaki or Georgi?"

The sick girl cast a sidelong but expressive glance at her inter-
locutor and, as though chastising her for her indifference toward us,
answered slowly and thoughtfully, "Which of the two do I want? I
don't want either without the other. I want all the brothers I have—
all."

My mother was touched to the quick by shame and fell silent.

A little while later she also brought our youngest brother to the
church, but only for that first day.

In the evening she sent the other two away and kept only me by
her side.

I still remember what an impression that first night I passed in the
church made on my childish imagination.

The faint light of the lamps in front of the iconostasis, barely
enough to illuminate it and the steps in front of it, rendered the darkness around us still more awesome and frightening than if we had
been completely in the dark.

Whenever the flame of a candle flickered, it seemed to me that
the Saint on the icon of the opposite wall had begun to come to life
and was stirring, straining to wrench himself from the wood and
descend to the floor, in his broad, red robes, with the halo around his
head and with his watchful eyes on his pale and impassive face.

Or again when the cold wind howled through the tall windows, noisily rattling their small panes, I thought that the dead buried around the church were climbing up the walls and trying to come inside. And, trembling with terror, I sometimes saw opposite me a skeleton stretching forth his fleshless hands to warm them over the brazier that burned in front of us.

And yet I did not dare to show even the slightest apprehension because I loved my sister and considered it a great honor to be constantly near her and near my mother, who undoubtedly would have sent me back home the moment she suspected I was afraid.

So during the following nights as well I suffered those horrors with forced stoicism and eagerly carried out my duties, trying to make myself as agreeable as possible.

On weekdays I lighted the fire, fetched water, and swept the church. On feast-days and Sundays during matins, I led my sister by the hand and helped her stand under the Gospel that the priest was reading at the Beautiful Gate. During the service I spread the woolen blanket on which the sick girl fell face down, so that the priest carrying the sacraments might pass over her. At the conclusion of the service, I brought her pillow to the front of the left door of the Inner Shrine so that she might kneel on it until the priest laid his stole on her and made the sign of the cross over her face with the Spear, muttering, "By thy crucifixion, Oh Christ, tyranny has been destroyed, the power of the Enemy has been crushed, etc." And throughout all this my poor sister followed me with her pale and melancholic countenance, with her slow and uncertain steps, attracting the compassion of the churchgoers and invoking their prayers for her recovery—a recovery that, unfortunately, was slow in coming.

On the contrary, the dampness, the unaccustomed cold and, yes, the horror of those nights in the church were not long in having a harmful effect on the sick girl, whose condition now began to inspire the worst fears.

My mother realized this and began, even in the church, to show a grievous indifference to everything that was not related to the sick girl. She no longer opened her mouth to anyone except Annio and the Saints to whom she prayed.

One day I approached her unnoticed while she was weeping on her knees before the icon of our Savior.

"Take whichever one you want," she was saying, "only let me keep the girl. I can see that it is sure to happen. You have remembered my sin and are determined to take the child in order to punish me. I thank you, Lord!"

After several moments of deep silence during which her tears could be heard dropping on the flagstones, she sighed from the depths of her heart, hesitated a little, then added: "I have brought two of my children to your feet...let me keep the girl!"

As I heard these words, a shiver as cold as ice raced through my nerves and my ears started to buzz. I could not listen to any more. When at that moment my mother, overcome by dreadful agony, fell helpless on the marble floor, instead of running to her aid, I took advantage of the opportunity to flee from the church, running frantically and screaming at the top of my lungs, as if Death itself were threatening to seize me.

My teeth chattered from fright and I ran and kept on running. Without realizing it, I suddenly found myself at a great distance from the church. I then stopped to catch my breath and dared to turn and look behind me. No one was chasing me.

I began, therefore, to come to my senses little by little and to reflect.

I recollected all my gestures of tenderness and of endearment toward my mother. I tried to recall whether I had ever offended her, whether I had ever wronged her, but could not. On the contrary, I found that ever since that sister of ours had been born, not only had I not been loved as I would have wished, but instead had been pushed aside more and more. Then I recalled, and it seemed to me that I understood why, my father had made a practice of calling me his "wronged one." I was assailed by a feeling of injustice and started to cry. "Oh," I said, "my mother doesn't love me and doesn't want me! Never again will I set foot in the church! Never!" And I headed home, dejected and desperate.

My mother was not long in following me with the sick girl. For the priest, roused by my cries, had entered the church and when he saw the sick girl, had advised my mother to remove her.

"God is great, daughter," he said to her "and his grace extends over the whole world. If he is to heal your child, he will heal her just as well in your home."

Unhappy the mother who heard him! For these are the standard words with which priests usually turn away those about to die, so that they may not give up the ghost in church and desecrate the sanctity of the place.

When I saw my mother again, she was more disheartened than ever! But toward me especially she behaved very sweetly and gently. She took me in her arms, fondled me and kissed me tenderly again and again. You might have thought she was trying to appease me.

That night, however, I could neither eat nor sleep. I lay in bed with closed eyes, but strained my ears attentively at the slightest movement by my mother who, as usual, was keeping watch by the sick girl's bedside.

It must have been about midnight when she began moving about in the room. I thought she was making the bed to go to sleep, but I was mistaken. For a little while later she sat down and in a low voice started to chant a dirge.

It was our father's dirge. She used to chant it very frequently before Annio fell ill, but this was the first time I had heard it since then.

The dirge had been composed for my father's death, at her orders, by a sunburnt, ragged Gypsy, well-known in our area for his skill in composing extemporaneous verses.

I can still see his black, greasy hair, his small, blazing eyes, and his bare, hairy chest.

He was seated inside the gate of our yard, surrounded by all the copper utensils he had collected for tinplating. And with his head cocked to one side, he accompanied his mournful tune with the plaintive sounds from his three-stringed lyre.

My mother stood before him with Annio in her arms, listening attentively and weeping.

I was hanging on to her dress tightly and hiding my face in its folds because, as sweet as those sounds were, the face of their grim chanter terrified me.

When my mother had learned her mournful lesson by heart, she untied the corner of her veil and took from it two coins—at that time we still had plenty—to give to the Gypsy. She then served him bread and wine and whatever leftovers there were. And while he was downstairs eating, my mother on the floor above was repeating the dirge so as to fix it in her memory. And it seems that she found it very beautiful, for just as the Gypsy was about to depart, she ran after him and presented him with a pair of my father's trousers.

"May God forgive your husband's soul, bride!" the bard called out in surprise and, loaded with his copper utensils, walked out of our yard.

This dirge was the one my mother was chanting that night. I listened and let my tears flow silently, but dared not move.

Suddenly I smelt the fragrance of incense.

"Oh!" I thought. "Our poor little Annio has died!"

And I leapt up from my bed.

I then found myself before a strange scene.

The sick girl was breathing heavily, as usual. Next to her a man's suit was laid out, arranged as if to be worn. To its right was a stool covered with a black cloth, upon which rested a vessel full of water with a lighted candle on either side. My mother was on her knees burning incense over these objects and carefully observing the surface of the water.

I must have turned yellow from fear. For when she saw me, she hastened to calm me.

"Don't be afraid, my child," she said mysteriously. "They're your father's clothes. Come, you also pray to him to come and heal our Annio."

And she made me kneel down next her.

"Come and take me, Father, so that Annio will get well!" I cried out choked by my own sobs. And I cast a reproachful glance at my mother to show her that I knew she was praying for me to die instead of my sister. I didn't realize, foolish as I was, that by so doing I was plunging her into the depths of despair. I believe that she forgave me. I was very young at the time and unable to understand her heart.

After a few moments of deep silence, she again burned incense over the objects in front of us and concentrated all her attention on the water in the large vessel on the stool.

Suddenly a small butterfly spiraled above it and touched it with its wings, ruffling its surface slightly.

My mother bowed reverently and made the sign of the cross, just as in church when the priest passes with the sacraments.

"Cross yourself, my boy!" she whispered, deeply moved and not daring to raise her eyes.

I obeyed mechanically.

When that small butterfly had disappeared at the back of the room, my mother sighed with relief, rose cheerfully and contentedly, then said, "Your father's soul has passed by!" all the while following the flight of the butterfly with a look of affection and devotion. Afterward she drank from the water and had me drink some as well.

I then remembered how in the past she used to have us drink from that vessel as soon as we awakened. And I recalled that whenever my mother did this, she was lively and gay all day long as if she had enjoyed some great but secret happiness.

After she had had me drink, she approached Annio's bed with the vessel in her hands.

The sick girl wasn't asleep, but she wasn't entirely awake either. Her eyelids were half-closed and her eyes, or as much of them as appeared, emitted a strange brilliance through their thick, dark eyelashes.

My mother carefully raised the girl's thin body, and while she supported her back with one hand, she offered the vessel to her wasted lips with the other.

"Come, my love," she said to her. "Drink some of this water so that you'll get well."

The sick girl did not open her eyes, but it seems that she heard the voice and understood the words. Her lips parted in a sweet and lovable smile. She then sipped a few drops of that water which was indeed destined to cure her. For as soon as she swallowed it and she opened her eyes and tried to breathe, a slight sigh escaped her lips and she fell back heavily against my mother's forearm.

"Our poor little Annio! She has been set free from her torments!"

Many had reproached my mother, saying that while unrelated women had lamented loudly over my father's corpse, she alone had shed plentiful but silent tears. The poor woman had done this out of fear that she might be misunderstood, that she might go beyond the boundaries of modesty befitting young women, because, as I said, our mother was widowed very young.

She was not much older when our sister died. But now she did not give the slightest thought to what people would say about her heart-rending lamentations. The entire neighborhood rose up and came to console her. But her grief was frightful, it was inconsolable.

"She'll go mad," whispered those who saw her bent over and lamenting between the graves of our sister and father.

"She'll leave them to the winds," said those who encountered her in the street, "abandoned and uncared for."

And time was needed, the admonishments and reprimands of the church were needed, for her to come to her senses, to remember her surviving children, and to assume again her duties at home.

But then she realized the state to which our sister's long illness had reduced us.

All our money had gone for doctors and medicine. She had sold many woolen blankets and kilims, works of her own hands, for insignificant sums of money, or had given them as compensation to the charlatans and sorceresses. Still others had been stolen from us by them and their ilk, taking advantage of the lack of surveillance that prevailed in our house. In addition, our food supplies had also been exhausted and we no longer had anything to live on. Instead of discouraging my mother, however, this gave her twice the energy she possessed before Annio fell ill.

She moderated, or, more accurately, concealed her grief; she overcame the timidity of her age and sex and, taking the mattock in hand, hired herself out as a day laborer, as if she had never known a comfortable and independent life.

For a long time she supported us by the sweat of her brow. Her earnings were small and our needs great, yet she refused to allow any of us to lighten her load by working alongside her.

Plans for our future were made and examined every evening by the hearth. My older brother was to learn my father's trade, so as to take his place in the family. I was destined, or rather wanted, to go abroad and so forth. But first we all had to learn our letters, we had to finish school. Because, as my mother used to say, "uneducated man, unhewed log."

Our economic difficulties reached a peak when a drought descended upon the land and food prices rose. But our mother, instead of despairing about how she would feed us, increased our number by one with a strange girl who, after long-drawn-out attempts, she succeeded in adopting.

This event transformed our monotonous and austere family life, introducing new and abundant liveliness into it.

The adoption ceremony already took on a festive air. Our mother put on her "best clothes" for the first time and led us to the church clean and combed as if we were about to receive communion. After the service was over, we all stood before the icon of Christ and there, in the midst of the surrounding crowd, in the presence of her natural parents, my mother received her adopted daughter from the hands of the priest, after having first promised in the hearing of all, that she would love and raise her as if she were flesh of her flesh and bone of her bone.

The child's entrance into our house was made no less impressively and in a triumphant manner. The village elder and my mother led the procession with the girl, then we came. Our relatives and those of our new sister followed as far as the gate of our yard. Outside the gate the elder raised the little girl over his head with his hands and displayed her for several moments to all present. He then asked in a loud voice: "Which one of you is more kin or relation or parent of this child than Despinio Michaliessa and her kin?"

The girl's father was pale and stared grief-stricken ahead of him. His wife, leaning on his shoulder, was weeping. My mother was trembling with fear that some voice might be heard—"I am"—and thwart her happiness. But no one answered. The child's parents then embraced it for the last time and left with their relatives, while ours came inside with the elder and received our hospitality.

From that moment on, our mother started to lavish upon our adopted sister attentions such as none of us perhaps had received at her age, and in far happier times. And while I, shortly thereafter, was a homesick wanderer in a foreign land, and my brothers were sleeping in artisans' workshops and undergoing the hardships of apprenticeship, the strange girl reigned in our house as if it were her own.

My brothers' meager wages would have been enough to relieve my mother, and for this reason they gave them to her. But instead of spending the money to ease her own load, she used it to provide her adopted daughter with a dowry and continued working to support her. I was far, far away and for many years was ignorant of what was happening at home. Before I was able to return, the strange girl had grown up, been educated, been given a dowry, and married off as if she were a real member of our family.

Her wedding, which appeared to have been deliberately hastened, was a real "cause for celebration" for my brothers. The poor fellows breathed a sigh of relief at getting rid of this added burden. And they were right to feel this way. Because that girl, apart from never having felt any sisterly affection for them, in the end showed herself ungrateful to the woman who had cared for her with a depth of affection few legitimate children have known.

So my brothers had good reason to be happy, and they also had good reason to believe that our mother had learned her lesson.

Imagine their stupefaction, therefore, when a few days after the wedding they saw her enter the house tenderly hugging a second girl in her arms, this time in swaddling clothes!

"The poor thing!" exclaimed my mother, bending lovingly over the infant's face. "It wasn't enough that it was orphaned in the womb, but its mother also died and left it in the street!" And, as if in some way pleased with this unfortunate coincidence, she triumphantly displayed her booty to my brothers, who were speechless with surprise.

Filial respect was powerful and my mother's authority great, but my poor brothers were so discouraged that they didn't hesitate to point out tactfully to our mother that it would be better if she gave up her plan. But they found her unyielding. Then they openly displayed their displeasure and denied her the management of their purse. All in vain.

"You don't have to bring me anything," my mother said. "I'll work and provide for her the same way I provided for you. And when my George returns from abroad, he'll give her a dowry and marry her off. Don't you doubt it! My boy promised me! 'I'll provide for you, mother, both you and your adopted child.' Yes! That's what he said, bless him!"

I was George. And I really had made that promise, but much earlier.

It was during the time that our mother was working to support our first adopted sister as well as us. I used to accompany her during school vacations, playing by her side while she dug or weeded. One day we stopped work and were returning from the fields to escape the unbearable heat, which had almost made my mother faint. Along the way we were caught in one of those torrential rainstorms that occur in our part of the country after having been preceded by a hot spell or "sizzler" as our fellow countrymen call it. By now we were not far from the village, but we had to cross a stream that had turned into a raging torrent. My mother wanted to put me on her shoulders, but I refused.

"You're weak from having fainted," I said to her. "You'll drop me in the river."

And, gathering up my clothes, I rushed headlong into the stream before she had time to hold me back. I had more confidence in my strength than I should have had because before I had time to think of pulling back, my knees gave way, I lost my footing, and I was knocked down and carried away by the torrent like a nut shell.

A heart-rending cry of horror is all I remember of what happened after that. It was the voice of my mother who had thrown herself into the stream to save me.

It is a miracle that I was not the cause of her drowning along with my own. For that stream has a bad reputation in our parts. And when they say of someone that "the river took him," they mean that he drowned in this particular stream.

And yet my mother, faint as she was, exhausted, and weighed down by her provincial clothing, which alone might have drowned the most skillful swimmer, did not hesitate to expose her own life to danger. For it meant saving me, even if I was the child that on another occasion she had offered to God in exchange for her daughter.

When she reached home and set me down from her shoulders, I was still dazed. This is why, instead of attributing the mishap to my own lack of foresight, I attributed it to my mother's working.

"Don't work any more, mother," I said to her while she was putting dry clothes on me.

"And who will take care of us, my child, if I don't work?" she asked with a sigh.

"I will, mother, I will! "I answered with childish boastfulness.

"And our adopted child?"

"Her too!"

My mother smiled in spite of herself at the imposing stance I assumed while offering this assurance. Then she put an end to the conversation by saying, "Well, provide for yourself first and then we'll see."

Not long after this I left to go abroad.

Most likely my mother scarcely paid any attention to that promise. I, however, always remembered that her selflessness had granted me for a second time the life I owed her from the first. This is why I kept that promise in my heart, and the older I grew, the more seriously I thought myself obliged to fulfill it.

"Don't cry, mother," I said to her as I left. "I'm going off to make money. Don't you doubt it! From now on, whatever happens, I will provide for both you and your adopted daughter. But I don't want you to work any more, do you hear?"

I did not yet know that a ten-year-old boy cannot support himself, let alone his mother. Nor did I imagine what frightful adventures awaited me and how much sorrow I was yet to subject my mother to on account of that separation through which I had hoped to lighten her load.

For many years, not only did I not manage to send her help, but not even a single letter. For many years she roamed the streets asking passersby if they had seen me anywhere.

Sometimes they told her I was living in misery in Constantinople and had turned Turk.

"May those who invented that story eat their tongue!" my mother said in reply. "The one they're talking about can't have been my son!"

But after a short while, trembling with fear, she would shut herself up in our iconostasis and, weeping, pray to God to lead me back to the faith of my fathers.

At other times they told her I had been shipwrecked on the shores of Cyprus and, clothed in rags, was begging in the streets.

"May fire burn them," she would reply. "They're saying it out of jealousy. My boy must have made a fortune for himself and is going to the Holy Sepulcher."

But after a short while she would go out into the streets, questioning the traveling beggars and going wherever there was rumor of a shipwrecked person, in the mournful hope of discovering in him her own child, with the intent of giving him her few savings, as I received them abroad from the hands of others. And yet, whenever it was a question of her adopted daughter, she forgot all this and threatened my brothers, saying that when I returned from abroad I would put them to shame with my generosity and that I would give her daughter a dowry and marry her off with pomp and ceremony.

"Huh? What do you think! My boy promised me! May he have my blessing!"

Fortunately those evil tidings were not true. And when after a long absence I returned home, I was in a position to fulfill my promise, at least with regard to my mother, who was so frugal. As for her adopted child, however, she did not find me as eager as she had hoped. On the contrary, as soon as I arrived, I expressed my objections to keeping her, to my mother's great surprise.

In point of fact I was not strictly speaking opposed to my mother's soft spot. I found her partiality for girls in agreement with my own feelings and desires.

There was nothing I desired more upon returning home than to find a sister whose cheerful face and loving attentions would drive the lonely sadness from my heart and efface all the hardships I had suffered abroad from my memory. In exchange I would have been eager to tell her about the wonders of foreign lands, about my wanderings and accomplishments; and I would have been only too pleased to buy her whatever she desired, to take her to dances and festivities, to give her a dowry, and finally to dance at her wedding.

But I imagined this sister as pretty and likable, educated and intelligent, cultivated and skilled in crafts—in short, endowed with all the virtues possessed by the girls in the lands where I had lived until then. And instead of all this, what did I find? Exactly the opposite.

My adopted sister was still small, emaciated, ill-formed, ill-natured, and above all slow-witted, so slow-witted that she inspired my antipathy right from the start.

"Give Katerinio back," I said to my mother one day. "Give her back if you love me. This time I'm speaking in earnest! I'll bring you another sister from the City! A pretty girl, an intelligent girl, who will one day be an ornament to our house."

I then described in the most vivid colors what the orphan I would bring her would be like and how much I would love it. When I raised my eyes toward her, I saw to my astonishment that large tears were flowing silently down her pale cheeks, while her downcast eyes expressed an indescribable sorrow!

"Oh!" she said with an expression of despair. "I thought you would love Katerinio more than the others, but I was mistaken! They don't want any sister at all, and you want another. And how is the poor thing to blame because God created her as she is? If you had a sister who was ugly and stupid, would you for that reason throw her out into the street and take another who was beautiful and wise?"

"No, mother! Of course not!" I answered. "But she would be your child, just as I am. Whereas this one is nothing to you. She's a total stranger to us."

"No!" my mother shouted, sobbing. "No! The child isn't a stranger! She's mine! I took her from her mother's dead body when she was three months old, and whenever she cried I would put my breast in her mouth to fool her, and I wrapped her in your swaddling clothes and lulled her to sleep in your cradle. She's my child and she's your sister!"

After these words, which she uttered in a forceful and imposing manner, she raised her head and fixed her gaze on me, awaiting my answer defiantly. But I did not dare say a word. She then lowered her eyes again and continued in a weak, sorrowful tone, "Eh! What's to be done! I wanted her better, too, but my sin, you see, has not been atoned for yet. And God made her like this to test my endurance and to forgive me. I thank you, Lord."

As she spoke these words, she placed her right hand on her breast, raised her eyes full of tears to heaven and remained thus in silence for several moments.

"You must have something weighing on your heart, mother," I then said with a certain trepidation. "Don't get angry." And taking her cold hand in mine, I kissed it to mollify her.

"Yes!" she said decisively. "I have something heavy, very heavy, inside here, my child. Until now only God and my confessor have known of it. You are learned and sometimes talk like my confessor and even better. Get up and close the door, then sit down that I may tell you about it. Perhaps you will even comfort me a little, perhaps you will take pity on me and bring yourself to love Katerinio as if she were a sister."

These words and the manner in which she pronounced them threw my heart into great confusion. What could there be that my mother wished to confide to me and not to my brothers? She had related to me all her misfortunes during my absence. I knew all of her prior life like a fairy tale. What could there be, then, that she had kept from us until now, that she had not dared to reveal to anyone except God and her confessor?

When I returned to sit beside her, my knees were shaking from a vague but powerful fear.

My mother hung her head like a condemned person who faces his judge in full awareness of some terrible crime. "Do you remember our Annio?" she asked me after several moments of oppressive silence.

"Of course, mother! How could I forget her! She was our only sister and she died before my very eyes."

"Yes!" she said with a deep sigh, "But she wasn't my only daughter! You're four years younger than Christaki. A year after him, I had my first daughter.

"It was around the time when Fotis Mylonas was planning to get married. Your late father delayed their wedding until I had finished the term of confinement after delivery so that we could give them away together. He also wanted to take me out into society, so that I could enjoy myself as a married woman since your grandmother had not allowed me to enjoy myself as a girl.

"The marriage took place in the morning, and in the evening the wedding guests gathered at their home. The violins were playing, people were eating out in the yard, and the wine jug was passing from hand to hand. And your late father, entertaining as he was, was making merry and tossed me his handkerchief to get up and dance. As I watched him dance, my heart opened up to him, and being young, I also loved to dance. And so we danced, and the others danced on our heels. But we danced better and longer.

"When it was nearly midnight, I took your father aside and said to him: 'Husband, I have a baby in the cradle and can't stay any longer. The child is hungry; I'm full of milk. How can I feed it in all this crowd and in my best dress! Stay if you still want to enjoy yourself. I'll take the baby and go home.'

"'Eh, very well, wife!' he said, may he rest in peace, and he patted me on the shoulder. 'Come dance this dance with me, and then we'll both leave. The wine has begun to go to my head and I'm looking for an excuse to leave myself.'

"After we had danced that dance as well, we took to the road. The bridegroom sent the players to escort us half the distance. But we still had a long way to go before we reached the house for the wedding took place in Karsimahala. The servant walked ahead with a lantern. Your father carried the child and also held me by the arm.

"'You're tired, I see, wife!'

"'Yes, Mihalio, I'm tired.'

"'Come on, just a little more effort until we get home. I'll make up the bed myself. I'm sorry I made you dance so much.'

"'It doesn't matter, husband,' I said to him. 'I did it to please you. Tomorrow I can rest.'

"And so we arrived home. I swaddled and nursed the baby while he made up the bed. Christaki was sleeping with Venetia, who I had left to watch him. A little while later we also went to bed. There, in my sleep, I thought I heard the baby cry. 'The poor thing!' I thought, 'it didn't get enough to eat today.' And I leaned over its cradle to nurse it. But I was very tired and couldn't hold myself up. So I took it out and laid it next to me on the bed and put the nipple in its mouth. At that point I was overcome by sleep again.

"I don't know how long it was until morning, but as I felt day breaking—'I'd better put the child back in its place,' I thought. But when I went to pick it up, what should I see? The child was not moving!

"I woke your father up. We unswaddled it, we warmed it, we rubbed its little nose, nothing! It was dead!

"'You smothered my child, wife,' said your father and burst into tears. Then I started crying and wailing too. But your father put his hand over my mouth. 'Shush!' he said to me. 'Why are you screaming so, you ox?' That's what he said to me, may God forgive him. We had been married three years and he had never said a harsh word to me— but he did then. 'Eh? Why are you screaming so? Do you want to wake the neighborhood so that people can say you got drunk and smothered your own child?'

"And he was right, may the dust that covers him be blessed. Because if people had found out, I would have had to tear open the earth and enter it out of shame.

"But what's the use! A sin is a sin. When we buried the child and returned from church, then the great mourning began. Then I no longer cried in secret. 'You're young, you'll have others,' they told me. But time passed and God gave us none. 'There!' I would say to myself. 'God is punishing me, because I proved myself unworthy of protecting the child he gave me.' I felt ashamed in the presence of others and I feared your father because all that first year he pretended not to be sad and he consoled me so as to give me courage.

"Later, however, he started to grow silent and pensive. Three years passed without my being able to enjoy a meal. But after these three years, you were born. I made many offerings of thanks.

"When you were born my heart returned to its proper place, but it did not find peace. Your father wanted you to be a girl and one day he told me as much: 'This one is welcome too, Despinio, but I wanted it to be a girl.'

"When your grandmother went to the Holy Sepulcher, I sent twelve shirts and three gold coins with her to procure a paper of pardon for me. And just look! The very same month that your grandmother returned from Jerusalem with the paper of pardon, I was pregnant with Annio.

"Every so often I would call the midwife. 'Come here, Madame, and let's see. Is it a girl?' 'Yes, daughter,' the midwife would say. 'A girl. Don't you see? You can't fit into your clothes!' And I was beside myself with joy when I heard this!

"When the child was born and really did turn out to be a girl, then my heart returned to its proper place. We called it Annio, the same name the dead girl had, so it would not seem that anyone was missing from the house. 'I thank you, oh Lord!' I said day and night. 'I, the sinner, thank you because you lifted my shame and expiated my sin!'

"And Annio became the apple of our eye. And you were jealous and nearly died from envy. Your father called you his 'wronged one' because I weaned you too soon, and he scolded me sometimes because I neglected you. My heart ached when I saw you wasting away. But, you see, I couldn't let Annio out of my hands! I was afraid that something might happen to her at any moment. And your late father, regardless of how often he scolded me, he, too, could not bear to have a drop of rain fall on her!

"But the little darling, the more attention she received, the less healthy she became. You might have thought that God had regretted giving her to us. The rest of you were rosy-cheeked and lively and mischievous; she was quiet and silent and sickly. When I saw her like this, so very pale, the dead child came to my mind, and the thought that I had killed it began to take hold of me again. Until one day the second one also died!

"Whoever has not experienced it himself, my child, cannot know what a bitter cup that was. I had no hope of having another girl. Your father had died. If there had not been some parent to give me his girl, I would have taken to the hills.

"It is true that she didn't turn out good-natured. But as long as I had her and cared for her and fondled her, I felt she was my own and I forgot the one I had lost, and I calmed my conscience.

"As the saying goes, a strange child is a torture. But for me this torture is a consolation and an alleviation. Because the more I'm tormented and exasperated, the less God will punish me for the child I smothered.

"For this reason—and may you have my blessing—don't ask me now to send Katerinio away in order to take a good-natured and industrious child."

"No, no, mother!" I cried out, unable to stop myself from interrupting her. "I ask for nothing. After all that you've told me, I beg your forgiveness for my heartlessness. I promise you that I'll love Katerinio as if she were my own sister and that I'll never again say anything disagreeable to her."

"May you have the blessings of Christ and the Virgin Mary!" my mother said with a sigh, "because, you see, my heart pities the poor thing and I don't want people to speak ill of her. How do I know? Was it destiny? Was it God's doing? No matter how bad and unintelligent she is, I assumed responsibility for her and that's that."

This confession made a profound impression on me. Now that my eyes were opened, I understood many of my mother's actions, which at times had seemed superstitious, at other times entirely the result of an obsession. That terrible misfortune had influenced my mother's entire life, all the more because she was simple and virtuous and God-fearing. The consciousness of sin, the moral necessity of atonement, and at the same time the impossibility of atonement— what a horrible and relentless Hell! For twenty-eight years now the unfortunate woman had been tormented without being able to calm the pangs of her conscience, either in bad fortune or in good!

From the moment I learned her grievous story, I concentrated all my attention on lightening her heart, trying to represent to her on the one hand the unpremeditated and involuntary nature of the sin, and on the other God's infinite mercy and His justice that does not return like with like, but judges according to our thoughts and intentions. And there was a time when I believed that my efforts were not without success.

Nonetheless, when after another absence of two years my mother came to see me in Constantinople, I thought it well to do something more impressive in her behalf.

At the time I was a guest in the most distinguished house of the City, in which I had occasion to become acquainted with the Patriarch, Ioachim the Second. One day while we were walking alone in the thick shade of the garden, I disclosed the story to him and implored his assistance. His high position and the exceptional authority with which his every religious pronouncement was invested were bound to inspire in my mother a belief in the absolution of her sin. That not-to-be-forgotten old man, praising my religious zeal, promised me his earnest cooperation.

Thus, shortly afterward, I conducted my mother to the Patriarchate to confess to his Holiness.

The confession lasted a long time, and from the Patriarch's gestures and words I realized that he was obliged to employ all the strength of his simple and clear rhetoric to arrive at the desired result.

My joy was indescribable. My mother bade the venerable Patriarch farewell with sincere gratitude and came out of the Patriarchate so happy, so buoyant, as if a great millstone had been lifted from her heart.

When we reached her lodgings, she took from her bosom a cross, a gift of his Holiness, kissed it and began to examine it carefully, slowly sinking deeper and deeper into thought.

"A good man, the Patriarch. Don't you think?" I said to her. "Now, I imagine, your heart has at last returned to its proper place."

My mother did not reply.

"Have you nothing to say, mother?" I asked her after some hesitation.

"What can I say, my son!" she answered, still full of thought. "The Patriarch is a wise and holy man. He knows all God's intentions and wishes, and he forgives the sins of the whole world. But what can I say! He's a monk. He's never had children, so as to know what a thing it is to kill one's own child!"

Her eyes filled with tears, and I remained silent.

ALEXANDROS PAPADIAMANTIS

(1851-1911)

Dream on the Wave

I was a poor mountain herdsman, eighteen years old, and still ignorant of the world. Without realizing it, I was happy. The last time I
felt happiness was that summer of 187-. I was a handsome youth; and
would see my prematurely stern, sunburnt face reflected in the
streams and springs, and exercise my tall, supple body on the crags
and mountains.

The following winter old Father Sisois, or Sisonis, as our peasants
used to call him, took me in with him and taught me to read and write.
He was a former teacher, and to the end of his life everyone addressed
him in the vocative, "O Schoolmaster." During the years of the
Revolution he had been a monk and a deacon. Afterward he had fall-
en in love with a Turkish girl, as it was rumored, abducted her from a
harem in Smyrna, had her baptized, and married her.

Immediately after the restoration of order under the ruler
Capodistrias, he had taught in various schools throughout Greece,
and the reputation he enjoyed under the name of "Sotirakis the
teacher" was not negligible. Later, after he had provided for his family, he had remembered his obligation from the past, donned the cassock once more—this time as a simple monk, since he was barred
from being ordained as a priest—and lived out the remainder of his
life in repentance in the cenobite monastery of the Annunciation.

There he wept over his sin, transforming it into a minor offense by his many good deeds, and they say that he was saved.

After learning my first letters from old Sisois, I was sent by the monastery with a scholarship to a divinity school in the provinces, where I was immediately placed in the upper class, then to the Rizarios divinity school in Athens. Consequently, I was nearly twenty when I began my education and was thirty when I took my departure from the university, coming away with a degree in law, a licentiate.

You must realize that I did not achieve success. Today I still work as an assistant in the law office of a prominent lawyer and politician in Athens whom I despise—I know not for what mysterious reason, but in all probability because he is my patron and benefactor. I feel restricted and awkward, nor can I take advantage of the position I hold with this lawyer, a position resembling that of a courtier.

Just as a dog tied in his master's yard by a short rope can neither bark nor bite outside of the arc circumscribed by the radius of that rope, so I, too, cannot say or do anything more than is allowed me by the confined authority to which I am subject in my superior's office.

The last year I was still a natural man was that summer of 187-. I was a handsome youth, a brown-haired herdsman, and I would take the goats of the monastery of the Annunciation to pasture on the coastal mountains which rise steeply from the craggy shoreline, above the sovereignty of the north and the sea. This entire expanse, known as Harbor Furl from the ships which, whipped by storms, lower sail and put into port, was mine.

My towering, rockbound coastline, which contained within its confines Platana, Big Beach, and Vine Branch, faced the northeast wind and unfurled toward the north. I, too, felt closely allied with these two winds which blew in my hair and made it curl like the bushes and the wild olive branches, bent by their inexhaustible wind and the lashes from their eternal blowing.

All these were mine: the thickets, the ravines, the valleys, the entire seacoast, and the mountains. The field belonged to the tiller only on the days when he came to plow or sow, made the sign of the cross three times, and said: "In the name of the Father and of the Son and of the Holy Spirit, I sow this field to provide food for all strangers and travellers, and the birds in heaven, and so that I, too, may reap the rewards of my labor!"

Without ever plowing or sowing, I reaped a share of it. I emulated the hungry disciples of our Savior and practiced the precepts of the Deuteronomy without knowing them.

The vineyard belonged to the woman in need only during the hours when she herself came to sprinkle sulphur and cut back the vines, to fill her basket with grapes, or to harvest it, if there was anything left to harvest. The rest of the time the vineyard belonged to me.

The only rivals I had in the use and harvest of it were the salaried employees of the town hall, the field guards, who, under the pretense of guarding peoples' orchards, had every intention of choosing the best fruit for themselves. They certainly cared nothing about my well-being and were formidable rivals.

My main haunt was higher up, beyond the radius of the olive groves and vineyards, but I often crossed the border. There, further up, between two ravines and three mountain peaks, grown over with wild shrubs, weeds, and brushwood, I would take the goats of the monastery to pasture. I was an "adopted son," receiving as a salary five drachmas a month, which was subsequently raised to six. In addition to this salary, the monastery also gave me swaddling bands for sandals and lots of large pieces of dark bread or "flat cakes," as the monks called it.

The only permanent neighbor I had when I descended to the edge of my domain was Mr. Moschos, who belonged to the lesser nobility and was very eccentric. Mr. Moschos lived in the country in a small, lovely castle with his niece Moschoula, whom he had adopted because he was a widower and childless. He had taken her in, an only child and an orphan from the womb, and loved her as if she were his own daughter.

Mr. Moschos had acquired his wealth from his business enterprises and travels. Possessing extensive property in that area, he persuaded some of his poor neighbors to sell him their fields.

In this manner he purchased eight or ten adjacent fields, built a wall around them all together, and thus created what in our parts was a large estate, stretching for hundreds of acres. The cost of building the enclosure was considerable, perhaps as much or more than the property was worth, but this didn't worry Mr. Moschos, who wanted to have his own separate kingdom, as it were, for himself and his niece.

At the edge of his property he constructed a tall, two-story house in the shape of a tower, cleaned and gathered up the scattered springs, dug a well, and installed a winch for irrigation. He divided the property into four sections: a vineyard, an olive grove, an orchard with a great many fruit trees, and vegetable gardens surrounded by a stone wall or melon fields.

He settled there and lived permanently in the country, rarely going down to the town. The estate was on the edge of the sea, and while its upper wall reached the top of a small mountain, the waves almost splashed its lower wall whenever the north wind blew vigorously.

Mr. Moschos had for companions his pipe, his string of beads, his hoe, and his niece Moschoula. The girl was about two years younger than I. As a child she would leap from rock to rock, dash from cave to cave, gather shells down along the shore, and chase after crabs. She was as hot-blooded and restless as a shore bird. Beautiful and dark-complexioned, she reminded one of the sunburnt bride in the Song of Solomon who was made to guard the vineyards by her mother's sons: "How beautiful you are, my love, how beautiful you are! Your eyes are doves." Her neck, bright and beaming beneath her chemisette, was far whiter than the skin of her face.

She was dark-haired, rosy, golden like the dawn, and resembled the small and frail kidless she-goat with glistening hide that I had named Moschoula. The western window of the tower opened onto a thicket, which became denser beyond the top of the mountain and which was marked by bushes, fragrant brush, and hard, clayey soil. This was the beginning of my domain. I would frequently descend as far as there and put to pasture the goats of my spiritual fathers.

One day, I don't know how, as I was taking my usual count of the goats (all together there were fifty-six that year; in other years the number varied between forty-five and sixty), I realized that Moschoula, my favorite goat, had remained behind, for she was not among those counted. I counted only fifty-five. If one of the other goats had been missing, I would not have noticed right away which one it was, only that one of them was missing. But Moschoula's absence was conspicuous. I became frightened. Had an eagle carried her off?

In those somewhat lower regions eagles do not deign to visit us often. Their main starting place was high up toward the west on the pure white, rocky mountain, which, was appropriately called the Eagle's Nest. Still, it did not seem entirely unusual or unbelievable to me that an eagle might have suddenly swooped down, smitten by the charms of Moschoula, my goat.

I began shouting like a madman. "Moschoula! . . . where is Moschoula?"

Nor had I noticed the presence nearby of Moschoula, the niece of Mr. Moschos, who happened to have her window open. The wall surrounding the property and the house adjoining it were about five hundred steps away from the spot where I was standing with my goats. When she heard my shouts, the girl got up, leaned her head out the window, and called out.

"What's the matter? Why are you shouting?"

I didn't know what to say; nevertheless, I answered. "I'm calling my goat, Moschoula. It's got nothing to do with you.

When she heard my voice, she shut the window and disappeared.

Another day she saw me again in the same spot from her window. I was lying down in the shade while my goats were grazing and I was whistling the tune from a mountain song familiar to herdsmen.

I don't know what came over her, for she called out to me. "Do you always sing like that? I've never heard you play the pipe. A herdsman without a pipe, I find that strange!"

I did have a pipe (or flute) but was not bold enough to play it, knowing that she would hear me. On this occasion I felt honored to play for her sake, though I cannot say what she thought of my skill as a flutist. I only know that as remuneration she sent me a few dry figs and a goblet full of grape juice turned into syrup.

One evening, when I had taken my goats down to the shore along the rocks where the tidal flow formed thousands of graceful coves and alcoves, where in some places the rocks, cunning and bending, shaped themselves into piers and in other places into hollowed-out caves, amid the winding and meandering of the water, which made its way, murmuring and dancing in unruly splashes and sprays, like a stuttering child that jumps up and down in its cradle and longs to be picked up and dandled by the arms of the mother who touched it—when, as I said, I had taken my goats down to "get a taste of salt" as I often did, I beheld the seashore in the magnitude of its joy and magic, and I yearned for it, and longed to plunge in and swim. It was the month of August.

I led my herd a little ways above the steep rock between two crags and onto a footpath that was marked out on its ridge. I had come down it and intended to return by it to my fold in the mountains that night. I left my goats there to feed on samphire and dittany even though they were no longer hungry. I whistled to them softly so that they would be still and wait for me. They heard me and lay still. Seven or eight of them were he-goats with bells and I would hear tinkling from a distance if they grew restless.

I turned back, again climbed down the steep slope, and reached the sea below. Just then the sun had set and the almost full moon began to shine, low-lying, as though only two reeds above the mountains of the island opposite. The rock I was on faced northward, and beyond the other promontory to the west, on my left, I could see a fold of purple from the sun that had just set. It was the train of the royal purple gown that trails behind, or perhaps the carpet that, as they say, his mother spreads for him when he sits down to his supper.

To the right of the large, crooked rock was a small sea cavern, strewn with white, crystalloid shells and bright, multicolored pebbles, which looked as if it had been arranged and decorated by sea nymphs. A footpath began right at the cavern by which one could climb the side of the steep coast and reach the lower gate of Mr. Moschos' enclosure, one wall of which girded the shoreline for hundreds of meters.

I immediately threw off my shirt and trousers and plunged into the sea, washed my body and my hair, then swam for a few minutes. I felt a sweetness, an ineffable magic, imagining that I was one with the wave, that I shared its liquid, salty, cool nature. I never would have felt like coming out of the water, I never would have had my fill of swimming, had I not been anxious about my herd. However obedient the kids were, however well they hearkened to my voice to lie still, they were only kids, as stubborn and unreliable as small children. I was afraid that some of them would break away and flee. Then I would have to run looking for them in the dark, in the gorges and mountains, guided only by the sound of the bells on the he-goats! As for Moschoula, to make sure that she would not run off again, as she had once before, when an anonymous thief (oh! if only I could lay my hands on him) had stolen—the fool—her gilt bell with its red collar from her neck, I took the trouble to tie her with a short rope to the root of a bush, a little above the rock at whose base I had left my clothes, before plunging into the sea.

I leaped out of the water, slipped on my shirt and trousers, and took a step uphill. Once on top of the rock, whose base was washed by the sea, I would have untied my little Moschoula and, two hundred or more steps further, I would have rejoined my herd. That climb up the slippery precipice was like a game to me, like those contests among the neighborhood children who compete with one another by jumping from the lower to the higher rungs of a marble staircase.

That moment, just as I was taking my first step, I heard a loud splash, as though a body had fallen into the water. The sound came from the spot where I knew that Moschoula, Mr. Moschos' niece, sometimes descended and bathed in the sea. I, the satyr of the mountain, would not have risked coming so close to her border, had I known that she was also in the habit of bathing at night by moonlight. I was only aware that she was in the habit of bathing in the morning at sunrise. Taking two or three steps without making the slightest noise, I climbed up the slope and leaned with the utmost caution in the direction of the cavern, concealed behind some bulrushes and the top of the rock, and saw, in fact, that Moschoula had plunged naked into the water, and was bathing.

I recognized her right away in the honey-colored and silver moonlight that was diffused over the endless, calm sea, making the waves dance like phosphorescence. When she plunged into the sea, she had sunk entirely beneath the surface and wet her hair from whose locks the water flowed like a stream of pearls as she emerged. She happened to be facing in my direction, playing and floating as she flitted here and there. She swam well.

If I wanted to leave, I would have to stand upright for a moment on top of the rock, bend over behind the bushes to untie my goat, and vanish—holding my breath and not making the slightest sound or rustle. But the moment during which I was making my way to the top of the rock would be enough for Moschoula to catch sight of me. It was impossible for me to leave without being seen, for Moschoula was looking in my direction.

My form, tall and bathed in the moonlight, would be outlined for a moment on top of the rock. The girl would see me there since she was facing this way. Oh! How startled she would be! She would be frightened and rightly so, she would cry out, and she would accuse me of wicked intentions. Then woe to the young herdsman! My first impulse was to cough, thus making known my presence immediately, and then to yell out: "I just happened to be here, I didn't realize ... Don't be frightened! I'll leave at once, my young lady!" I can't say why, but in my awkwardness and timidity I didn't stir. No one had given me lessons in social graces up there in my mountains. I drew back, again climbed down to the base of the rock, and waited. "She won't be long," I thought. "She'll have her swim, then she'll get dressed and leave. She'll leave by her footpath, and I'll leave by way of my cliff." I then remembered Sisois and Father Gregorios, the confessor in the monastery, who had often exhorted me to avoid the temptation of women at all times.

Aside from waiting, there was no other means of escape unless I was determined to dive into the sea as I was, clothes and all, and swim in very deep waters the entire distance westward from the shore where I was standing, from here where the girl was bathing, to the main inlet and the sandy beach, since in all that distance of a half mile the coastline was completely inaccessible, all rocks and precipices. Only at the spot where I was standing did the water from the sea form a cradle amid the caverns and rocks.

I would have to abandon my goat Moschoula to her fate, tied up there on the rock, and as soon as I reached the beach in drenched clothes (having been forced to swim with my clothes on), dripping with brine and foam, I would have to walk two thousand steps back by another path to where my herd was, and descend further down on the precipice to untie my goat Moschoula. By then the niece of

Mr. Moschos would have gone away without, of course, having left any trace along the shore. If I carried out this plan, it would be a huge undertaking, a real feat, and would require more than an hour. Furthermore, I couldn't be sure that my herd would be out of danger. There was no alternative for me but to wait, and to hold my breath. The girl would not suspect my presence. Anyhow, my conscience was clear. I very slowly climbed back up to the top of the rock and, hidden behind the bushes, leaned over to look at the young lady as she swam.

She was a delight, a dream, a marvel. She had moved five or six fathoms away from the cavern and was floating. Now she was facing east with her back to me. I saw her dark yet dimly glitter ing hair, her slender neck, her milk-white shoulders, her wellshaped arms—all hazy, honey-colored, and dreamlike in the moonlight. I made out her supple hips, her loins, her calves, her feet, between the light and the shadows, as they dipped into the water. I imagined her bosom, her breasts, graceful and rounded out, receiving the gentle breeze and the divine scent of the sea. She was an inspiration, an apparition beyond belief, a dream floating on the wave, she was a nereid, a nymph, a siren, floating as a magic ship floats, a ship of dreams...

Nor did the thought even occur to me at that moment that, if I were to step onto the rock, either stooped over or standing up, with the intention of leaving, it was almost certain that the girl would not see me, and I would have been able to get away without any difficulty. She was facing east, I was to the west, behind her. Not even my shadow would have disturbed her. Since the moon was in the east, it would have fallen to the west, behind the rock and to this side of the cavern.

I stood there agape, in ecstasy, no longer thinking about earthly matters.

I am unable to say that no sly and at the same time childishly foolish thoughts came to me, a curse in the guise of a blessing: "If only she were suddenly in danger! If only she began to scream!

"If only she saw some garfish at the bottom of the sea and thought it was a monster or a shark, and yelled for help!"

The truth is that I could not get enough of watching the dream floating on the wave. But at the last moment, oddly enough, my first thought returned ... that I should dive into the water, head in the opposite direction, swim all the way back to the beach, and flee, flee from temptation!

Once again, however, I could not get enough of watching the dream. Suddenly the voice of my goat brought me back to the demands of the real world. Little Moschoula suddenly began to bleat!

Oh! This was something I had not foreseen. I could remain quiet myself, but unfortunately I could not easily impose silence on my goat. I knew nothing of makeshift muzzles for animals—a box-thorn full of branches in the mouth, esparto grass around the snout, or some other such means—since I had not yet learned to steal live things, unlike the unknown enemy who had stolen her bell, but had not cut out her tongue to prevent her from bleating. But even if I had known of them, I would not have thought of them.

I ran frantically to clasp the palm of my hand over her snout, to stop her from bleating. At that precise moment I forgot all about the girl swimming for the sake of the girl herself. Without stopping to think that there was danger of her seeing me, I got up and, still half-bending, stepped onto the rock in order to reach the goat.

At the same time I was also seized by fear because of the love I harbored for my poor goat. The rope with which I had tied her to the root of the bush was very short. What if she had become embrangled, what if her neck had gotten entangled and twisted in it, what if there were danger of the poor animal's being strangledI

I don't know if the girl heard my goat calling as she bathed in the sea. But even if she had, what was strange about that? What was there to be afraid of? There was nothing unusual in her hearing an animal cry as she swam just a few yards from shore. But that one moment when I stepped on top of the rock was enough. Whether or not the girl heard the goat calling—though it seems that she did, because she turned her head in the direction of the shore—she saw my dark shadow, the outline of my form, on the rock among the bushes, and let out a half-stifled cry of fear.

I was overcome with terror, emotion, indescribable sadness. My knees buckled under me. Out of my mind with fear, I managed to find my voice and cried out: "Don't be afraid! ... it's nothing ... I won't harm you!" In my panic I wondered whether I should dive into the water and go to her rescue or run away. Perhaps my voice would reassure her more than if I remained and ran to her rescue.

At that very moment, though there was nothing unusual in this coincidence in that all the coastal waters there were frequented by fishermen, a boat hove into sight coming from the southeast promontory across the way, which formed the right bend of the bay. It seemed to be sailing slowly in our direction, under oars, but its presence, instead of reassuring the girl, increased her terror. She let out a second cry of still greater anguish. In a flash I saw her sink and disappear in the wave.

There was no time to hesitate. The boat was more than twenty fathoms away from the agonized girl; I was but five or six fathoms away. At the same instant I dived headlong into the sea, clothes and all, from the top of the rock. The water was deeper than the height of two men. I nearly touched the bottom, which was sandy, free from rocks and stones, and thus posed no danger to me. At the same moment I came to the surface and rose out of the foamy wave.

I was now less than five fathoms away from the spot where she had gone under, where eddies and swirls formed and twirled in the frothy sea and would have been the watery and instantaneous grave of the luckless girl—the only traces ever left on the sea by a living creature in the throes of death! With a few powerful strokes and maneuvers, I was next to her in no time.

I saw her beautiful body struggling below, closer to the bottom of the sea than to the foaming wave, nearer to death than to life. I went under, grabbed her body in my arms, and came up again.

As I enveloped her with my left arm, it seemed to me that I felt her faint, warm breath on my cheek. I had arrived in time, thank God! Nevertheless she showed no clear signs of life. I instinctively shook her with a vehement motion to enable her to breathe, buoyed her up on my back, and swam using only my right hand and legs, swam strenuously to shore. My strength increased miraculously.

I could feel her body clinging to me. She wanted to live. Oh! Let her live, and let her be happy! There was not a selfish thought in my mind at that moment. My heart was full of self-sacrifice and selflessness. I would never have asked for a reward!

How much longer will I remember the soft, delicate body of that chaste girl that I once felt against me for a few minutes of my otherwise useless life! It was a dream, an illusion, an enchantment. How different that ethereal touch was from all the selfish embraces, from all the false friendships and vulgar, mundane loves of the world. That burden in my arm was not a weight, but a pleasure and a consolation. Never had I felt lighter than while I held that weight. I was a man who had succeeded for a moment in holding in his arms a dream, his very own dream.

Moschoula lived. She didn't die. I rarely saw her after that, and I don't know what she is doing now. Possibly she is a simple daughter of Eve, like all the others.

But I paid a ransom for her life. My poor little goat, whom I had abandoned for her sake, genuinely became embrangled. She became hopelessly entangled in the rope I had tied her with and choked to death. My sadness was tempered by the thought that I had sacrificed her for the girl's sake.

And I, thanks to the auspices and charity of the monks, went on to become an educated man and a lawyer. This was to be expected, since I had attended two divinity schools. Was it perhaps that one and only incident, that dreamlike remembrance of the girl bathing, that prevented me from taking religious vowsI Alas! It was precisely that remembrance that should have led me to become a monk. The venerable Sisois was right in saying that "if they wanted to make me a monk, they should never have sent me away from the monastery." The few letters that he had taught me were enough, and indeed more than enough, for the salvation of my soul!

And now, when I remember the short rope from which my goat Moschoula choked to death, and then I think of that other rope in the parable, with which the dog is tied up in his master's yard, I wonder whether the two were not closely related, and whether they were not "the pledge of our inheritance," as the Scriptures say.

"Oh! If only I were still a mountain herdsman!"

IOANNIS KONDYLAKIS

(1861-1920)

How the Village Became Greek

He had heard from his father many times the story of how they had sold everything in Modi and moved to the mountain town of Akaranou. The reason for this was, if you'll excuse the term, a Turk and, begging your pardon, a pig, as he was apt to say to express his hatred for that Turk in particular and for Turks in general. In those days, the town of Modi was still under Turkish rule. It had a small number of Christians among its inhabitants, but they were humble people, from the lower regions, that is, tillers of the Turkish soil, in return for which they received thirty-three percent of the yield. Virtually slaves. The only one with some human dignity and pride left, seeing that he possessed a considerable fortune and did not have to work for the aga, was his father, Michalis Alefouzos. But it was precisely because he entertained independent opinions and his spine did not bend easily that the Aga Kerim, the richest and most powerful Turk in Modi, a fanatical and tyrannical man who wanted the Christians to realize they were alive only by virtue of the tolerance of the Turks, could not stomach him. This is why whenever Alefouzos passed by and greeted him with a simple "good evening, Aga Kerim," he shook his head, and followed him with a threatening look as he moved away. One day he said to another Turk who happened to be present, "That Alefouzos, I swear to God, is a rebel. He holds his head high and is no *rayah*.*"

When the Egyptian sovereignty somewhat alleviated the condition of the Christians in Crete, Alefouzos, encouraged, did something daring. He bought a hog and was fattening him for Christmas. A hog in Modi! A hog in the Aga Kerim's town, in fact right next to his farmhouse! Damn it! Fuck your mother, you infidel!

The first grunts of the pig sent a shudder through the Turkish village and made the hair of many Turks stand up. A meeting of the agas was held at Aga Kerim's and it was decided that the rebel Alefouzos should be driven out of the village or murdered. But prior to any other action, the pig had to be killed. The situation was intolerable. Why, just yesterday, while Aga Kerim was smoking his chibouk in his yard, he saw it poke its stinking face through the half-closed gate. Damn it! Fuck your religion, you infidel!

"Some day, I swear to God, it will come right up to our window and say good morning to us!" said another aga.

"It wriggles its way into any opening it can find. Mou! Mou!"

"Listen, you agas, I must kill this pig," said the Turkish-Albanian *bouloubasis*, a sort of police sergeant, who represented authority in the village and who approved all their prior decisions.

The following day, as he passed Alefouzos' house, he pulled out his pistol and killed the pig.

"Hey! Why don't you keep that wild animal tied up inside instead of letting it crawl between our legs? Damn it! You'll get into trouble," he said to Alefouzos' wife who, upon hearing the pistol shot, had appeared anxiously at the door.

Alefouzos was a stubborn man and a week later he brought home another hog, bigger than a plane tree.

"Good heavens, Michalis, are you asking for death?" she said to the only Christian in the village. "Don't get under their skin or they'll kill you!"

"They won't kill me," Alefouzos replied calmly. "The time of Turkish military occupation is over."

But the time of Turkish military occupation was not over to the

* Enslaved Greek.

extent that he supposed. The *bouloubasis* murdered the other hog as well, alleging by way of excuse that it had knocked over his narghile. Alefouzos realized that if he persisted in buying pigs, he would be helping the Albanian Turk to improve his target practice.

Aga Kerim, seething with rage, one day vented his anger in the street when he came face to face with Alefouzos, "What do you mean by such improper behavior! Are you going to start bringing pigs to our village, you infidel?"

"It's not improper behavior, Aga Kerim," Alefouzos replied in a reverent but firm tone. "Begging your pardon, but our faith tells us to eat pork."

"Your faith! There...take that for your faith!"

And he simultaneously lifted his chibouk and brought it down on Alefouzos. The latter, however, avoided the blow and held the Aga's arm in check.

"How dare you lift a hand to me, you Christian dog!" shouted Aga Kerim and began to beat him frenziedly. Other Turks rushed to the scene, and Alefouzos was immediately carried home, unconscious and covered with blood. A month later, going out one night to feed his oxen, he was shot in the arm by an unidentified person. He was in peril for his life and remained bedridden for a long time. Convinced that the Turks had decided to do away with him, he was forced to sell out and take refuge in the mountain village of Akaranou.

His son Stamatis had heard this story from his father many times and ever since he was a child he had been storing up hatred in his heart against the Turks—particularly the inhabitants of Modi—and dreaming of revenge. Kerim had died, as had the old man Alefouzos. Let those two settle their scores in the next world, where assuredly they had also transported their hatred. But just as Alefouzos had left behind a son, so had Kerim also left behind a son, Aga Arif. These two would settle the family accounts. Arif was quite different from his father. A kind man who loved wine and good times, he was on very good terms with Christians and Turks alike and divided his time between Modi, where he had a wife and children, and Chania, where he had mistresses and drinking companions. His sole occupation was to amuse himself and to borrow or sell whenever his income failed to meet his needs.

Stamatis had inherited from his father a love of work and a particular rancor toward the Turks in Modi. He was about the same age as Arif, a young man of thirty-five with an enormous physique, a blond, rough beard and eyes full of liveliness and ruse.

One day the inhabitants of Modi suddenly learned that Stamatis Alefouzos had bought back the paternal property, and that a few days later he had installed himself in the paternal house next to Arif's farmhouse. One of his first concerns was to bring from Akaranou a pig with six or seven piglets, which were so noisy and restless that you might have thought the town was full of hogs. And it really was full of them, for all the Christians in Modi who were without one bought one, and all who had them tied up set them free to roam through the town and the surrounding fields, to visit the Turkish coffee house occasionally, and to wander into the Turkish yards—to the great indignation and horror of the Turkish ladies—where they turned the agas' vegetable gardens upside-down.

Now there were no more *bouloubasis* and the era of the Turkish military occupation had receded so, that it was in danger of being forgotten. From being a Turkish village, Modi was transformed into a Christian village because during the last revolution many of the Turks had killed themselves or had stayed put in Hania. And the Christians from the mountain villages stepped into the place of the Turks, imitating the example of Stamatis and buying Turkish property for sale. Stamatis rejoiced as he watched the Christian population of the village increase and the Turkish one diminish. One day, smiling sarcastically, he said to Arif:

"Eh, Aga Arif, if only your late father was alive to see what the village has become!"

Arif scowled. "What has it become?" he said in a choked voice.

"Why, Greek. I say! Just look! Just look!"

And with a triumphant gesture he pointed to an approaching herd of young pigs which were following their slow-walking mother. Arif, however, unlike his father, observed the young pigs without spitting or cursing. "If your father was alive," Stamatis added, "he would explode with anger."

But seeing that Arif, instead of losing his temper, looked rather sad as a result of his teasing, the vindictiveness of Stamatis abated.

And he abandoned a retaliation that he had been planning for a long time—to send the son of Aga Kerim his finest piglet as a gift on the day of Baram.

Perhaps Stamatis was never more pleased, however, than on Christmas Eve, when Modi reverberated with the cries of slaughtered pigs. To express his elation he sacrificed two of them. As he disemboweled them, he grinned from ear to ear and kept saying, "Only today have I realized that Modi has become Greek."

He always clung to the idea that, despite the apathy Arif exhibited, inwardly he was exploding with anger. Nor was it a matter of small consequence to slaughter two pigs before his very door! But a few days later, Arif, returning from Hania, stopped on horseback before the door of Stamatis.

"Good evening, neighbor," he said at the sight of Stamatis. "Bring me some wine...I'm in a good mood tonight."

Stamatis started to go for the wine when Arif stopped him. "And a tasty snack."

Then he leaned over from his horse and said in a low voice, "A piece of...sausage!"

C. P. CAVAFY

(1863-1933)

In Broad Daylight

I was sitting one evening after supper in St. Stephen's Casino at Ramleh. My friend Alexander A., who resided in the casino, had invited me and another young man, an intimate friend of ours, to have supper with him. Since it was not an evening with music, very few people had come, and my two friends and I had the entire place to ourselves.

We were talking about various things and as we did not belong to the very rich, the conversation turned quite naturally to money, to the independence it provides and to the pleasures that attend it.

One of my friends was saying that he would like to have three million francs and began describing what he would like to do and, above all, what he would like to stop doing if he possessed this large sum.

I, being slightly more modest, would have been satisfied with an annual income of twenty thousand francs.

"Had I wished," Alexander A. said, "I would now be who knows how many times a millionaire—but I didn't dare." These words struck us as strange. We knew our friend A.'s life well and could not recall that the opportunity to become many times a millionaire had ever presented itself to him. We assumed, therefore, that he was not speaking in earnest and that some pleasantry would follow. But our friend's face was very grave and we asked him to explain his enigmatic remark.

He hesitated a moment—but then said, "If I were in other company, finding myself unexpectedly among so-called 'evolved people,' I wouldn't explain myself because they would laugh at me. But we are slightly above so-called 'evolved people,' that is, our perfect spiritual development has again made us simple, but simple without being ignorant. We have come full circle. Thus, naturally, we have returned to our starting point. The others have remained midway. They do not know, or even surmise, where the road ends."

These words did not at all surprise us. Each of us had the highest regard for himself and for the other two.

"Yes," Alexander repeated, "if I had dared, I would be a multi-millionaire—but I became frightened.

"What I am about to tell you happened ten years ago. I did not have much money then, as now, or rather I had no money at all; but in one way or another I was going forward and living moderately well. I was staying on Shereef Pasha Street in a house that belonged to an Italian widow. I had three well-furnished rooms and a personal servant, not including the good services of the proprietress, who was at my disposal.

"One evening I had gone to Rossini's. After I had listened to enough foolish talk, I decided halfway through the evening to return home and go to sleep. I had to be up early the next morning, having been invited on an outing at Aboukir.

"When I arrived in my room, I began, as was my custom, to pace up and down, thinking about the day's events. But seeing that they were of no interest, I became sleepy and went to bed.

"I must have slept one and a half or two hours without dreaming because I remember that at about an hour after midnight I was awakened by a noise in the street and remembered no dream. I must have fallen asleep again at about one-thirty, when it seemed to me that a man of medium height and no more than forty had entered my room. He was wearing black clothes, which were quite old, and a straw hat. On his left hand he was wearing a ring set with a very large emerald. This struck me as out of keeping with the rest of his attire. He had a black beard with many white hairs and there was something strange about his eyes, a look both mocking and melancholic. On the whole, however, he was a rather ordinary type. The sort of man one frequently encounters. I asked him what he wanted of me. He did not reply right away, but looked at me for a few moments as if with misgiving or as if scrutinizing me to make sure that he had not made a mistake. Then he said to me, in a humble and servile tone of voice, 'You are poor, I know. I have come to tell you a way to become rich. Not far from Pompei's Stele, I know a spot where a great treasure lies hidden. I myself want no part of this treasure—I will take only a small iron box, which is to be found at the bottom. The rest will all be yours.'

"'And of what does this great treasure consist?' I asked.

"'Of gold coins,' he said, 'but above all of precious stones. It comprises ten or twelve gold coffers filled with diamonds, pearls, and, I believe'—as if he were making an effort to remember—'with sapphires.'

"I wondered then why he did not go by himself to take what he wanted and why he needed me? He did not allow me to voice my objections. 'I know what you're thinking. Why, you're thinking, don't I go take what I want by myself? A reason that I cannot tell you prevents me. There are certain things that even I cannot do.' When he said 'even I,' it was as if a radiance came forth from his eyes and transformed him into an awesome magnificence for a second. But he immediately resumed his humble manner. 'Thus you will do me a great favor by coming with me. I absolutely need somebody and I choose you, because I desire your well-being. Meet me tomorrow. I'll be waiting for you from noon until four in the afternoon in the Small Square, at the café near the blacksmiths' shops.'

"With these words he vanished.

"When I woke up the next morning, there was at first not a trace of the dream in my mind. But after I had washed and sat down for breakfast, it returned to my memory and seemed quite strange to me. 'If only it had been real,' I said to myself and then forgot it.

"I went on the country outing and had a very good time. We were quite numerous—some thirty men and women—and in unusually high spirits, but I will spare you the details for they have no bearing on my subject."

Here my friend D. observed, "Nor is it necessary. For I, at least, am familiar with them. Unless I'm mistaken, I was on that outing."

"Were you? I don't remember you."

"Wasn't that the outing Marcos G. organized before finally leaving for England?"

"Yes, that's right. Then you remember how much we enjoyed ourselves. A happy time. Or rather, a time gone by. It comes to the same. But getting back to the gist of my story—I returned from the fête quite tired and quite late. I barely had time to change clothes and eat before going off to some friends, a family, where a card-playing evening party was under way and where I remained, playing until half past two in the morning. I won a hundred and fifty francs and went home very pleased. Consequently, I went to bed with a light heart and fell asleep instantly, the day's fatigue not being a minor factor in this.

"No sooner had I fallen asleep, however, than something strange happened to me. I saw a light on in the room and was wondering why I hadn't turned it off before going to bed, when I saw coming from the back of the room—my room was quite large—from the location of the door, a man who I recognized immediately. He was wearing the same black clothes and the same old straw hat. But he looked displeased, and said to me, 'I waited for you this afternoon, from noon until four at the café. Why didn't you come? I offer to make your fortune, but you're in no hurry? I will wait for you again at the café this afternoon, from noon until four. Don't fail to come.' Thereupon he vanished like the last time.

"But this time I woke up terrified. The room was dark. I turned on the light. The dream had been so real, so vivid that it left me astonished and shaken. I was cowardly enough to go see if the door was locked. It was locked as usual. I looked at the clock. It said half past three. I had gone to bed at three.

"I won't conceal from you, and am not in the least ashamed to admit to you, that I was very frightened. I was afraid to close my eyes, lest I go back to sleep and see again my fantastic guest.

"I remained seated in a chair, my nerves strained. At around five, day began to break. I opened the window and watched the street as it awakened slowly. A few doors had swung open and a few very early milkmen and the first bakers' carts were passing by. The light somehow calmed me and I returned to bed and slept until nine.

"When I woke up at nine and recalled the trepidation of the night, the impression began to lose much of its intensity. Indeed, I was amazed that I had become so upset. Everybody has cauchemars and I had had many in my life. Besides, this was hardly a cauchemar. It is true that I had had the same dream twice. What of it? To begin with, was I certain of having dreamt it twice? Couldn't I have dreamt that I had seen the same man previously? But after examining my memory carefully, I dismissed this notion. I was certain of having had the dream two nights ago. Yet what was strange about that? The first dream, it seems, had been very vivid and had left such a deep impression on me that I had it again. Here, however, my logic had a hitch in it. For I did not recall that the first dream had made an impression on me. Throughout the previous day I had not thought of it for an instant. During the outing and reception in the evening, I thought about everything except the dream. What of it? Doesn't it often happen that we dream of persons whom we haven't seen for many years or whom we haven't even thought of for many years? It appears that their memory remains engraved somewhere within the spirit and suddenly reappears in a dream. What, therefore, was strange about my dreaming the same thing in the space of twenty-four hours, even if I hadn't thought of it during the day? I further told myself that perhaps I had read about a hidden treasure, and that this had secretly worked upon my memory, but regardless of how much I searched, I was unable to discover any such passage.

"Finally I grew tired of thinking and began to dress. I had to attend a wedding and my haste and the concentration of my thoughts on what I would wear drove the dream from my mind altogether. I then sat down to my breakfast and, to pass the hour, I picked up and read a periodical published in Germany—the Hesperus I believe.

"I attended the wedding where all the fashionable society of the city had congregated. At that time I had many acquaintances and, because of this, after the ceremony I repeated an endless number of times that the bride was very pretty, only slightly pale, that the groom was a fine young man, as well as rich, and the like. The wedding ended around eleven-thirty in the morning. When it was over, I went to Bulkeley Station to see a house that had been recommended to me and that I was about to rent for a German family from Cairo who were planning to spend the summer in Alexandria. The house was in fact airy and well laid out, but not as large as I had been told. All the same, I promised the proprietress I would recommend the place as being suitable. She thanked me profusely, and to arouse my pity she related all her misfortunes to me—how and when her late husband had died, how she had even visited Europe, how she was not the sort of woman who rents her house, how her father had been the doctor of I don't recall which pasha, etc. This obligation fulfilled, I returned to town. I arrived home at one in the afternoon and ate with a hearty appetite. After I was through lunch and had drunk my coffee, I went out to visit a friend of mine who resided in a hotel near the Paradise Café, so that we might arrange something for the afternoon. It was the month of August and the sun was scorching hot. I was walking down Shereef Pasha Street slowly to keep from perspiring. The street, as always at this hour, was deserted. I encountered only a lawyer with whom I was transacting business relevant to the sale of a small lot in Moharrem Bey. It was the last piece of a rather large ground plot that I was selling bit by bit, thus covering part of my expenses. The lawyer was an honest man and this is why I chose him. Only he was talkative. Better he had cheated me a little than pestered me with his rambling. He launched into an endless harangue on the slightest pretext—he talked to me about commercial law, Roman law, dragged in Justinian, mentioned old lawsuits of his from Smyrna, praised himself, explained a thousand equally irrelevant things to me, and all the while held on to my clothes, something I abhor. I was forced to endure the chatter of this ridiculous person because every so often, when the course of his babbling ran dry, I would inquire about the sale, which was of vital interest to me. These efforts were taking me out of my way, but I stayed with him. We passed the sidewalk of the Stock Exchange on Consul Square, we passed the small street that connects the Big and the Small Square, and finally by the time we reached the center of the Small Square, I had obtained all the information I wanted and my lawyer, remembering that he had to pay a call to a client who lived in the area, took his leave of me. I stood for a moment and watched him retreat, cursing his babbling, which had made me go out of my way in so much heat and sun.

"I was about to retrace my steps and walk to Paradise Café Street when, all of a sudden, the idea that I should be in the Small Square struck me as odd. I asked myself why, then remembered my dream. 'This is where the famous owner of the treasure told me to meet him,' I thought to myself and smiled, and mechanically turned my head toward the site of some blacksmiths' shops.

"Horrors! There was a small café, and there he sat. My first reaction was a sort of dizziness and I thought I was going to fall down. I leaned against a stall and looked at him again. The same black clothes, the same straw hat, the same features, the same gaze. He was staring at me intently. My nerves stiffened so, that I felt liquid iron had been poured into me. The idea that it was midday—that people who were unconcerned and under the assumption that nothing extraordinary was happening kept passing by, while I, only I, knew that the most horrible thing was happening, that a ghost was seated over there, possessing who knows what powers and arising from what sphere of the unknown, from what Hell, from what Erebus—paralyzed me, and I started to tremble. The ghost did not lift his gaze from me. I was now overcome with terror lest he stand up and approach me, lest he speak to me, lest he take me with him, and what human power could come to my defense against him! I flung myself into a carriage, giving the driver some remote address, I don't recall where.

"When I had somewhat collected myself, I saw that we had almost arrived at Sidi Gabir. A little calmer, I started to examine the matter. I ordered the driver to return to town. 'I'm mad,' I thought, 'surely I was mistaken. It must have been someone who resembled the man in my dream. I must go back to find out for certain. In all probability he's left, and this will be proof that it wasn't the same man, because he had told me that he will wait for me until four.'

"With these thoughts I arrived at the Zizinia Theater; and there, summoning all my courage, I ordered the driver to take me to the Small Square. As we approached the café, I felt my heart beating to the point of snapping. I had the driver stop a short distance away from it, pulling his arm so violently that he nearly fell from his seat,

because I saw that he was drawing very near to the café and because…
because the ghost was still there.

"I then began to subject him to close scrutiny, trying to find some
dissimilarity with the man in the dream, as if the fact that I was sitting
in a carriage and subjecting him to close scrutiny—something anyone
else would have misinterpreted and demanded an explanation for—
were not enough to convince me that it was he. On the contrary, he
returned my gaze with an equally scrutinizing gaze and with a countenance full of anxiety for the decision with which I was faced. It
seemed that he intuited my thoughts, as he had intuited them in my
dream, and to dispel any doubts as to his identity, he thrust his left
hand toward me and showed me—showed me so clearly that I feared
the driver would notice—the emerald ring that had impressed me in
my first dream.

"I screamed in terror and told the driver, who now began to feel
uneasy about his client's health, to drive to Ramleh Avenue. My only
aim was to get away. When we reached Ramleh Avenue, I told him to
head for St. Stephen's, but as I could see that the driver was hesitating
and mumbling to himself, I got out and paid him. I stopped another
carriage and had it take me to St. Stephen's.

"I arrived there in a dreadful state, entered the main hall of the
casino and, seeing myself in the mirror, was appalled. I was as pale as
a corpse. Fortunately the main hall was empty. I fell onto a divan and
began to think of what I was going to do. To return home again was
impossible. To return to that room where he had entered as a supernatural shadow, he who shortly before I had seen sitting at an ordinary
café in the form of a real man, was out of the question. I was being
illogical for, of course, he had the power to hunt me down anywhere.
But I had already been thinking incoherently for some time now.

"Finally I came to a decision. It was to turn to my friend G.V., who
at the time was living at Moharrem Bey."

"Which G. V.," I asked, "That eccentric who spent his time studying magic?"

"The very one—and this played a part in my choice. How I managed to take the train, how I arrived at Moharrem Bey, looking right
and left like a madman in fear that the ghost would reappear next to
me, how I stumbled into G. V.'s room—I remember only faintly and

with confusion. All I remember distinctly is that when I found myself with him, I started to cry hysterically and to tremble all over as I related my horrible adventure to him. G.V. calmed me and, half-seriously, half-jokingly, told me not to be afraid; that the phantom would not dare to enter his house, or that, even if it did, he would chase it away at once. He was familiar, he said, with this type of supernatural apparition and knew how to exorcise it. He further implored me to believe that I no longer had cause to be afraid because the phantom had come to me with a specific purpose—the acquisition of the iron box which, apparently, it was not in his power to obtain without the presence and aid of a human. He had not achieved this purpose, and must have already realized from my terror that there was no longer any hope of achieving it. He undoubtedly would go on to persuade someone else. V. regretted only that I had not informed him in time to intercede, so that he himself might have seen the phantom and spoken to it; because, he added, in the History of Phantoms, the appearance of these spirits or demons in broad daylight is extremely rare. But I found none of this reassuring. I spent a very restless night and the next morning I woke with a fever. The doctor's ignorance and the excitation of my nervous system were the cause of a cerebral fever from which I nearly died. When I somewhat came to, I asked to know what day it was. I had fallen ill on August third and assumed that it was the seventh or the eighth. It was the second of September.

"A small trip to an island in the Aegean hastened and completed my convalescence. I remained for the entire duration of my illness in the house of my friend V., who cared for me with that kindheartedness you both know. He was annoyed with himself, however, for not having had character enough to dismiss the doctor and to cure me through magic, which I also believe, in this instance at least, would have cured me just as quickly as the doctor did.

"See, my friends, the opportunity I had to become a millionaire—but I didn't dare. I didn't dare, and I don't regret it."

Here Alexander stopped. The deep conviction and utter simplicity with which he had related his story prohibited us from making any comments about it. Besides, it was twenty-seven minutes past midnight. And since the last train for town left at twelve-thirty, we were obliged to bid him goodbye and take our leave hurriedly.

ANDREAS KARKAVITSAS

(1865-1922)

The Prince

Crushed by the weight of years, the King of Livorno has no appetite for honors, no hand for scepters. The years, like a wood-fretter, have thrust him into old age, decaying old age, and deadened his ambitions. Snow is falling on Mount Olympus! Pure white hair, trembling legs, his heart a barren tombstone. New life—tumultuous, illusory, and brave—scatters all around him, flees, and disappears like gurgling water under a withered forest oak. How is he to experience it and where is he to pursue it? Impossible! He calls his son, his unique and cherished descendant, beseeches him in a dying voice and with dim eyes: "Dear and precious boy, come and take them. Don the mantle, shirt of iron; put on the crown, wreath of thorns; hold the scepter, goad of your country—reign and govern. Govern as father and as king!"

The prince answers him unrelentingly: "I address you as father and worship you as king. Neither do I want nor will I take anything. A wicked mermaid stands by your side. You do not rule a kingdom; you do not govern a people. Either I banish the mermaid or I perish."

Thereupon he takes a schooner with a red sail, equips it fully, and goes out on the open sea. Not only is the prince graced with youth and courage, but he also possesses knowledge. Not only does he take with him deadly arms, bows and arrows, swords and iron clubs, but also nourishment, food and drink for trickery. He takes meats—whole oxen. He takes loaves of bread—entire ovens of it. He takes wine—thousands of barrels encircled with strips of tin. And he sets sail straight for the island.

"Either I save my people or I perish," he says with determination.

The sailors call her the mermaid, but she resembles a salamander, an undulating, all-blue salamander. A rockstrewn desert island lies among the diaphanous waters of Livorno. Up there the Arabs are hidden—four bloodthirsty and inhuman Arabs, demons of the world, the terror of seamen. They are a father, his two children, and a nephew. The father is cruel, the children heartless, the nephew ferocious. They recognize neither law nor God. Their sole possession is a well-equipped and fast-moving fishing boat. Ensconced there, they lie in ambush day and night before the open sea. And as soon as they see an ill-fated ship, they swoop down on it! Who can escape? Who dares resist? They pirate the goods, eat the people, sink the ships. Perverse hobgoblins of the sea.

Many courageous young men set out to do battle with them. Many princes wish to bring honor to themselves by the Arabs' death. Of all who venture forth, however, none has time to regret his action. The ungraceful island, as if planted with herbs of forgetfulness, bestows everlasting sleep upon them, exposes their bones as altars to the burning heat. And the beastlike Arabs, ever fierce and indomitable, remain there as a threat to the seafaring world.

Meanwhile the prince of Livorno is speeding along, laden with hopes and full of inventiveness. The prayer of the people becomes air and swells his red sail. The tears of the sea join the blue wave and lash out in front of his skiff. It is nighttime when he arrives at the criminals' den. He unloads all the provisions. He unpacks the meats—whole oxen. He unpacks the loaves of bread—entire ovens of it. He unpacks the wine—thousands of barrels encircled with strips of tin. He unpacks and spreads everything out on the seashore, then hides with his schooner in a small harbor out of sight. Will the insatiable demons be satisfied with his provisions?

At the break of dawn the Arabs descend to the seashore. They see the meats and loaves of bread, they see them and ask who could have sent them. Somebody, of course, who trembles at the mention of their name, who fears their shadow. But their craving for the food is greater than their astonishment. They sit down, eat, and stuff themselves. They also see the wine, they smell it. Their thirst exceeds their astonishment. They pounce on it and gulp it down, struggling to quench their thirst.

"Let's not drink this ruse, uncle, and not know what's happening to us," the nephew at one point says to his uncle.

But the old man, who is a fool, smacks him in the face, putting his chin out of joint. Then he pounces again on the wine, as do the two boys, as does the nephew, too, in order to forget his pain. Gulp gulp, they drain the casks. They drain the casks, gorge their stomachs, muddle their minds. They break into song, begin to dance, and continue to dance until they fall sprawling on the sand, numb bodies. The black demons are now dead to the world!

The prince then abandons his hiding spot, looks fearlessly at the Arabs, and smiles. He wastes no time, binds them securely, weighs them down with heavy chains, loads his schooner with ballast, and rapidly reaches Livorno.

"My people have been saved!" he reflects joyously during the entire voyage.

The old king is lying on his all-gold throne, paralyzed with fear and despair. Surrounded by solitude, inhabited by despair. Twelve pale bodyguards assist him and shining arms protect his precious life. But he anxiously awaits only one arm, one symbol—his son. Before him the flawless crystal of the window reveals the tumultuous harbor below—a multitude of sails and tackle, a boundless sea plowed by a thousand skiffs. The skiffs, however, are mute for him; the sentries do not give him the longed-for sign. The mermaid, it appears, has kept his beloved son; he will remain alone, his illustrious throne without a descendant forever!

Suddenly the door springs wide open and a golden ray, the prince, enters.

"I address you as father and honor you as king," he says, kneeling before him. "I now assume everything and unburden your life. I don the mantle, shirt of iron, I put on the crown, wreath of thorns, I take the sceptre, goad of my nation. I govern as father and as king."

The old man has barely embraced his son when fierce and adverse shouting is heard outside. One might have thought the barren island, thrown into a turmoil, had encircled the palace.

"Revenge! Revenge!" resounds again and again in the sky. The populace disarms the guards, breaks down the doors with axes, climbs the carpeted stairs, tears the silken curtains to shreds, smashes the vases, arrives raging mad before the king. "Let me ask you, father and equitable judge," it says to him. "How is he who disobeys the quarantine punished?"

"With death."

"Sign."

The king obligingly places his gold seal on the death sentence. The crowd then recounts to him the prince's deed. Uncontrollable cholera was destroying the surrounding towns and the city was under quarantine. Yet the prince did not wait to be sure he was free from infection, but came straight to the palace. He may have brought the sickness into their very houses.

"I am grateful to you!" the king says with tears in his eyes. "The prince is my son, the law also is my son. The prince has wronged the law, the law will lose its prince."

They take the unique and cherished descendant, dress him in flowers, and the merciless blade of the populace cuts down the royal tree from its root.

The Arabs are standing now in the middle of Livorno, turned into marble, with heavy chains around their necks. The old man first, stretched out face down on the flagstones, opens his thick lips like a ravine, exposing his teeth as though wanting to gulp down the open seas. His two sons, lying on their backs, lift their eyes painfully to heaven as though asking for mercy. Next to them the nephew, his jaw dislodged, makes dreadful faces as though still in pain. And above them all stands the prince, the conqueror and martyr, revealing joy and sorrow on his beardless face.

The noble victim has criminals for a throne. New life—tumultuous, illusory, and brave—still scatters all around him, flees, and disappears like gurgling water under a withered forest oak. And from time to time a trembling voice, belonging perhaps to the people, perhaps to the king, crushed by the weight of years, swells to a lamentation and calls the prince: "Dear and precious boy, come and take them. Don the mantle, shirt of iron; put on the crown, wreath of thorns; hold the sceptre, goad of your country—reign and govern. Govern as father and as king!

GREGORIOS XENOPOULOS

(1867-1951)

The Madman with the Red Lilies

When I returned to my homeland, after having lived abroad for ten years, among the first persons I asked to see was my friend Popos.

The answers I received were evasive: "I don't know...I haven't seen him in years...he never leaves the house...it seems he's sick...surely you remember that the fellow was always a bit of a hypochondriac?".

A neighbor, Sior Nionios, with deep-felt, if somewhat hypocritical sorrow, spoke to me more straightforwardly.

"My dear, your Popos is mad."

"Mad?...a long time?"

"Oh, for some years now."

"What drove him mad?"

"Nobody knows, my dear. But why else do young people go mad?"

"And he always remains in the house?"

"Yes, he hasn't crossed his threshold since the night—two or three years ago as I said—when he came out shouting that the garden was on fire. (This was told me, I didn't hear him myself.) Since then, however, he's been calm and has not been heard from again."

"The poor man, I would so like to see him."

"Hmm! That would be difficult, dear boy! He doesn't allow a living soul in his house, except for the priest Menego, whom he summons every so often and who reads the 'Te Deum' to him in his garden."

"In his garden?"

"Who knows…he probably imagines it's a cemetery. My dear, he uprooted all the sweet-smelling plants—you remember what an enchantment that garden was—filled it with red lilies, and slaves over them all day long. Now that they're in bloom, you should see the madman's garden from my window. It will make you shudder. Honestly, you'd think it was on fire. What a wild sight!"

"Does he live alone?"

"That poor Angelica, his nurse, is with him. She loves him like a son, but God alone knows what the negress puts up with in there, even though she doesn't say a thing. The old man, you know, kicked the bucket."

"But doesn't he read? In the past he was devoted to books."

"Books upon books! That house, my boy, is a regular university! Then again, who knows what he's up to? You don't suppose that creature Angelica ever breathes a word, do you? Regardless of what you ask her, she replies, 'He's fine.' She is goodness incarnate to put up with all that! You can even ask Father Menego."

"Do you think, Sior Nionios, that he won't receive me if I ask to see him?"

"It's out of the question! All the same, as a friend who's just returned, you can always try. What have you to lose?"

I felt compelled to try. Popos was once a close and dearly loved friend, and this strange conversation rekindled my love just as much as my curiosity. I wanted to see him. My imagination repeatedly conjured up before me the garden with the red lilies, and I was seized by the longing to explain, if there were some way to do so, the mystery. Then, too, I thought my visit might be beneficial to him. There was the possibility that it would awaken in him our former, intimate friendship, and that he would make some kind of confession to me which would comfort him. There was the possibility that he would reveal to me what he had never revealed to anybody else, being reticent, distrustful, as always, and destitute of close friends.

I headed for his house and, seeing it again the way I had left it, the friendly little house where as an adolescent I had spent so many enjoyable hours, I was deeply moved. It was completely unchanged on the outside. The same pale, yellow walls, the same white cornices, the same green grilles, the same brown door with the small latch and three stone steps. I climbed them and rapped on the door with the same lively and cheerful knock as in the past, when every afternoon I would stop by for Popos and we would go to Pseloma. And just as then, a grille now swung open instantly and the head of the negress Angelica, wrapped in a black kerchief, popped out.

"Who is it?" she asked, somewhat surprised at seeing a stranger.

"It's me, Angelica. Don't you recognize me?"

"No. Who are you?"

I told her my name and Angelica immediately began to act as if she were crazy.

"How about that! Just imagine! Welcome, master! Welcome, my joy! Well, well, my darling, lovely boy! What a delight!"

Her voice gradually grew weaker until I again heard it loud and clear behind the door. She hastened to admit me, "Come in! Hurry and come in, master. Come in so that I may rejoice at the sight of you. Dear me, how could I possibly recognize you...you were a little boy when you left and have returned a man!"

I went in and the door closed at once. I repaid with the utmost sincerity Angelica's effusiveness, and as she led me to the room on the ground floor, the *metzao*, I made so bold as to ask, feigning ignorance, "Is Popos here?"

She did not seem eager to tell me the hows and whys. Who knows what hope may have been inspired in her, seeing me unexpectedly this way.

"He's here...he's here, master!" she said. "Oh, how happy he'll be to see you! Wait a moment, darling, while I go and inform him...Sit down...I'll be right back!"

She drew up an armchair, made me sit down, and ran upstairs, as sprightly as a young girl.

I waited a considerable length of time and had time to look around carefully.

No, the inside of the house was not as I had known it ten years ago. The entrance, the *basia*, had been stripped of the lovely flower pots that had formerly embellished it, the plaster negro who had stood outside the door of the drawing room was missing, the wallpaper had faded and was torn in places without having been replaced, the furniture looked still older and neglected. Perhaps it was my frame of mind that was ten years older, perhaps it was even prejudice on my part, but it seemed to me that something mournful and mysterious was hovering over the interior of this house, which had never been cheerful.

This is why, in a sense, I was not unduly surprised when I saw Angelica returning, sorrowful, discouraged, tearful, her face pale. She stood before me, clapped her hands in distress and, keeping them joined, looked at me silently.

"Well, did you tell him?"

"Woe is me! Pity me, master, pity me!"

"But what did Popos say?"

"Ah, our Popos is not well! May God take pity on me and lift his hand, otherwise even I don't know how he'll end up. How difficult he's become! How strange! And here I, poor creature, thought he would be pleased and would come running with open arms...seeing that you were such good friends...and after so many years...instead he's telling me this and that!...What didn't I do for him, what didn't I say to him! It did no good! He won't, he's unwilling!"

"Well, what can we do about it? Have patience!"

"Patience is merely a word, master...That the child I raised with great pains should end up like this! What an affliction! That he should shut himself up in here like this and not see a living soul, a young man with such learning, such wealth, from such a family, who today would be the pride and glory of the land! Woe to me, woe to me! What a great misfortune has fallen upon me! Oh, my sad destiny!"

Angelica was crying now, the kind little old lady who from her youth had devoted herself to this family with all the affection of the mother that had disappeared upon bringing Popos into the world, was crying—kind Angelica, who had no other hope in her old age than to see the child she had raised the way she had dreamed of him, the way he was depicted in the old lullabies she used to sing to him when he was an infant.

Weeping and with the deep-felt pain of a maternal heart, the unhappy nurse told me everything. She spoke to me about his shutting himself up in the house, about his persistent misanthropy, about his permanent melancholy, about his alarming sleeplessness, about the garden with the red lilies, about Father Menego's 'Te Deums.' She further told me that Popos had left the management of his estate to his son-in-law, that he did not want to have anything to do with it or with him for that matter. She returned again to the subject of the red garden, without my asking her to, and told me that Popos had dismissed the gardener and cultivated it himself, that he spent entire hours there, many times even the night, and that now his passion, his mania, was the lilies, which had grown big and were strangling everything in a wave of red.

"What about his books, Angelica?"

Angelica sighed.

"Ah, the books! It seems to me that those *limbra* destroyed my poor boy's head. He opens them, even now he reads, but after the lilies..."

"May I see the garden?"

"Heaven forbid, darling! He'd kill me if he found out that I had taken someone there. Anyway how could I? He keeps the key to the outside door in his pocket. He's even raised the walls all around."

I remained at the house about a half hour and during all this time Popos was neither seen nor heard. I said goodbye to kind Angelica and left, my heart wrenched by one of the keenest of the many disappointments I had suffered in my country, where so many changes, so many catastrophes, so many ruins of dear memories awaited me.

I was in despair at the thought that I would never see Popos—and better had I not seen him!—when on the next day a child came to the house and left the following letter for me:

"My friend, I'm deeply sorry that I was not in a condition to receive you yesterday. You will make me extremely happy by coming and having lunch with me tomorrow at noon. We'll have a cozy chat. There is so much we have to catch up on! Do come, I'll be waiting for you."

It was signed Popos.

This seemed no less than a resurrection to me. It was the identical and peculiar handwriting of Popos as I knew and remembered it from our schooldays, from his exercise books, from the few letters we had exchanged during the first year of our separation. For a moment I thought that anybody whose handwriting was still this steady and unshaky could not be as mad as he had been portrayed to me.

The extent of my misapprehension was about to be revealed to me the very next day. I went to Popos' at midday. Angelica opened the door for me with indescribable joy; the table was set for two, I entered the *metzao*, Angelica went upstairs to announce my arrival, then came downstairs in despair and lamenting more plaintively than on the day before yesterday. Once again Popos was not in a condition to receive me! Tomorrow, he beseeched me to come back tomorrow.

"Don't be offended by him, my child," Angelica finally said to me, "and please come back tomorrow. Who knows! Now that he's taken it upon himself, he may see you. I saw right away that he wanted to, that he was pleased...but unhappily that devil shows his tail every so often! Woe to me! ...and he was so well today at dawn! Come back, master, come back tomorrow."

I went back. Angelica opened the door for me with apprehension, yet the table was again set for two. Would Popos receive me this time, or would he perhaps behave toward me the same way? I would never know for I had taken another decision. Instead of sending Angelica up to him, this time I climbed the stairs myself, knocked on the library door, and before hearing distinct words denoting permission to enter, I impulsively threw open the door and rushed into my friend's arms.

He showed no surprise, stood up, embraced me, kissed me, and without uttering a word, made me sit down next to him on the small divan.

I then looked at him. What a transformation! Framed by a long, jet-black beard and thick, bushy hair, his face with its large, aquiline nose looked gaunt, ascetic, and extremely pale. Only his deep-blue, liquid, dreamy eyes had preserved their youthful glow and that strange, indeterminate expression. Had I seen him out of doors only his eyes would have enabled me to recognize him.

"Well, how do I look to you?" he said with a melancholic smile.

"Quite frankly, I was always thin and bony, but now I've gone to an extreme. And they say that exercise is beneficial. If you only knew how much I exercise every day! Just imagine that I cultivate the garden myself. But what's the use! I've aged. After all, I'm forty now..."

He fell silent and stroked his heard with the long, sinewy fingers of his emaciated hand.

I whispered something, but he paid no attention to it. His mind was elsewhere.

Suddenly he lowered his eyes and asked, "Have you heard that I'm mad?"

I laughed loudly.

"Ah," he said with a certain reproach, "don't pretend. I know that you've heard it. Even if no one else has told you, you must have heard it from my son-in-law, who has the goodness to spread it about. But don't pay any attention to words. No, I'm not mad. And to prove to you that I'm not—and it's necessary to prove it to you because I can see that you're uneasy—I'm going to read you a little something I finished recently. Do you want me to?"

"Not if it's to prove to me that you're not mad! If, on the other hand, you wish to read it simply as a reminder of the old days, then you'll be doing me a favor."

"Fine, then let's assume it's to remind us of the old days!"

He stood up and approached his table. It was the same table that was familiar to me, in the center of the large room, surrounded with walnut bookshelves filled with books. Popos was a man of letters, one of those men of letters whom only the lovely Seven Islands possess—or at least possessed—one of those men of letters who inherit (often together with a title) their father's library and love of books, who read more than they write, who publish an article or poem in some local magazine once every five years, and who cultivate letters not to acquire renown or riches, but rather because of an imperative need in their soul, because of a desire for beauty and truth. They are patient, unassuming, studious people. Whatever free time is left them after the administration of their property and the fulfillment of their social obligations, they spend shut up in their library. They know the classics by heart, possess a knowledge of their contemporaries, are abreast of the latest ideas; and when they die, as unknown as they lived, they leave behind their manuscripts—one a translation of Petrarch, another an essay on Engels, still another a history of his region.

The "little something" that Popos now wanted to read me was nothing other than a translation of the fifth canto of Dante's *Inferno*, the story of the celebrated Francesca. While he was looking for the large, leather portfolio—the same one that was familiar to me—I had time to glance around in the library, to which I was no stranger, and there, at one end of the room, on top of a tall, narrow desk, I saw something that made me shudder—a vase with fresh, red lilies.

He wasn't mad; fine. But what about those flowers? And the vision of the red garden again passed before me—the lilies, the lilies inside it that grew big and strangled everything in a wave of red. My initial anxiety seized me again and I expected to hear an unrecognizable and incoherent Francesca, the raving of a madman, the reverberations of a lunatic asylum.

Popos sat down, assumed a pose familiar to me and, in a voice equally familiar to me, began to read. The introduction consisted of a commentary on the excerpt, several theories pertaining to certain difficult lines and an explanation of that unexplainable *amor che a null' amato amar per dona*. It was all rational, judicious, and scholarly.

When he finished reading the introduction, Popos called Angelica and asked her to bring us some mastic brandy. Oh, what joy shone on the nurse's small face wrapped in a kerchief when, on the two occasions she came in, she saw us quietly seated there "reading" as in the old days! She looked at me and for a moment I thought that her kind eyes were tearful.

I listened to the story of Francesca, lying on the small divan, my eyes raised and fixed steadily on the red lilies. And as long as those harmonious verses unfolded, slowly and passionately, as long as my friend's deep and thunderous voice was imbued with life, as long as the atmosphere around me was inundated with passion, music and beauty, every dissonant thought was neutralized, I forgot all recent events, I returned to bygone times and it seemed that he and I were the friends of ten years prior. No, nothing had changed. Not only was he not crazy, but he also had scarcely changed. I can say that I listened to him, that I saw him, as in the past. And those lilies in the vase ceased to alarm me with their wild color. One might have thought that at this particular moment they were in harmony with the poetry that was caressing me and I saw before me nothing other than the red lilies of Florence.

"That's it!" Popos said with the final verse. "What did you think of it?"

"A masterpiece!" I replied with candid enthusiasm. "Until now there has never been a translation of Dante like that."

"Hmm! Would you like me to give it to you, my dear, so that you may have it published in Athens? Your countrymen amuse me! Don't worry, I'm not mad. I believe you are no longer doubtful."

"Oh!"

"You're the ones who are mad, you people from the Seven Islands, I must say, parading in the public square in order to be judged by the population of the Peloponnesus! What a bore, old chap! . . . What are you staring at? My lilies? Surely you've heard about them as well; it's not possible that you haven't. Never mind, I'll tell you the story behind them. I'll tell you everything. You have a great deal to hear. This is why I sent for you and this is why I hesitated to see you. One moment my mind was made up, the next it wasn't. Will you forgive me for letting you leave yesterday? Ah, you will forgive me, won't you? You're my oldest friend, and believe me when I say that I never had and never will have another like you. Indeed, of late I see no one. They must have told you that as well, didn't they?"

And he sighed.

"I'll tell you about that as well," he continued. "I'll tell you everything. Now let's go downstairs and have lunch. Poor Angelica is waiting for us."

We descended.

The dining room had a large window and a glass door facing the yard. In the middle of the opposite wall of the yard was the door to the garden and among the iron rails, a strange painting was visible, four alternating areas of vivid and different colors—at the very bottom dark gray, above this green, above this red, and at the very top blue. It was a section of the garden.

I had this spectacle directly opposite me during the entire dinner. Ah, how can I ever forget that dinner! The food was ordinary; the conversation with Popos commonplace, insignificant, and unrelated to his story; and there were no incidents, no perturbations of habit. And that red, bleeding strip of garden in front of me, which I looked at occasionally, no longer made upon me the impression I expected. Only Angelica's behavior was something unbelievable. It was enough. She served us with alacrity, with willingness, with the love of a mother who is breast-feeding. "My darling" and "my dear" could be heard continuously. And so great was the joy that inundated her at the sight of Popos being kept company, conversant, laughing, cheerful—oh, how long it had been since the unhappy nurse had witnessed such festivity!—and that at every moment caused her to overflow with such awkwardness and exaggeration in her words and movements, that it nearly made her ridiculous. I would have smiled if I had not felt my heart contracting for this very reason, if the mad, comic joy of the little old lady had not possessed something infinitely melancholic, which brought tears to my eyes.

～

When dinner was over, Popos stood up hastily. We sat down in two armchairs in front of the window and near a round table where coffee was steaming in two old, strange-looking cups. We lit our cigarettes. Angelica left us, closing the door behind her. We were alone.

My friend remained silent for several moments, observing with his dreamy, deep-blue eyes the balls of thread formed by the smoke. Suddenly he turned to me abruptly and said, "Do you remember Vasiliki?"

I shuddered for I realized that he was making a painful effort, that he needed courage to pronounce that name. It was undoubtedly the beginning of the confession I was waiting for.

"Yes, I remember her."

In fact, I remembered her very well. A fresh, black-eyed beauty with a silver voice and a tall, slender body. The daughter of a merchant—not among the most prominent—from Rougas Square, she had lived in Vourla in a new house with a small garden facing the sea. A terrace overlooked the garden and in the old days the three of us—Vasiliki, my friend, and I—had often sat on this terrace under the shade of a pergola tree and in the fragrance of jasmine. After a while, the three of us were reduced to two, then to one. Nor did this last long. I remember hearing, before going away, that Popos had fallen in love with another woman.

Whether or not he had heard my answer, he again sank into his reverie. I had to awaken him, "By the way, what ever became of Vasiliki?"

"She died!" Popos replied.

He said it in such a deep tone of voice, with such bitterness and despair, that without wanting to, I also considered it a great misfortune and repeated sorrowfully, "She died?"

"Yes, but that's not the worst...the worst is that she was seriously in love with me, and I took the matter lightly."

"But...I seem to have heard that she had married."

"It was I who allowed her to marry. I also committed that crime! But how was I to know! Ah, how was I to know? I was accustomed never to believe in women...or in anyone else for that matter! I didn't believe her...and now I'm the unhappiest man in the world! 'Oh! Please don't let me marry the person they are forcing upon me,' she wrote me on the eve of her ill-fated marriage, 'please don't, because I will die.' There! She said it and did it."

"Did she commit suicide?"

"No, no, something worse, something more heart-breaking: she died from languor, from bitterness and from unhappiness in the hands of someone coarse, someone mean, someone whom she was unable, not only to love, but even to endure. Oh, my God! My God! It was I who committed that crime! I who delivered her into his hands, with my eternal hesitations and my eternal suspicions. I remember the last time I saw her, when she returned here with her husband—she had been living abroad—in order to die. A corpse, the poor thing had become a skeleton in a years' time. People stared at her with open mouths. Could that be Vasiliki? And all the while I was happy and carefree. Oh! that grief-stricken look she gave me. A burning knife entered my heart and has remained there ever since. There it remains and will remain until I die. Why, I'm raving...But let me tell you the whole story from the beginning so that you'll understand—if any man alive could ever understand my pain, my guilt, my misfortune!"

He then attempted to tell the story from the beginning, but was unable to preserve the order of events, repeatedly turning it into delirium, into lamentation, and interrupting it with sighs and cries. Why did I want to hear this story anyway! Did it not, as a result, reveal to me more vividly the pain in his soul? Was there need, moreover, for me to see the letter she had left him as she was dying and in which she assured him that she loved him to the very last moment, for me to understand all the guilt that had accumulated in my friend's heart because of his awful and irreversible destiny?

As I listened to the wailing of that passion, as that futile repentance pierced my heart, the form of Vasiliki rose vividly in my imagination. I beheld in a new light now a certain number of her salient characteristics attesting to her determination and steadfastness, and I found it natural and undeniable that she had loved Popos with such strength. I recalled our encounters on the terrace in the small garden, I remembered every characteristic and every detail surrounding us at the time—the rocks along the seashore, the circular parapet and wooden staircase of the terrace, the white façade of the house amid the greenery of the garden. And I don't know why, but the red area of the picture before me now began to attract me more and to appear, how shall I put it, more intimate, more in harmony with the story I was listening to, just as previously, upstairs, the red lilies in the vase with the story of Dante's Francesca. Suddenly it came to me!

"Tell me," I turned and said to Popos, "weren't there red lilies in Vasiliki's garden?"

"Oh, what a memory!" my friend shouted with amazement. "Yes!... there were...the ones you're looking at are also from there. 'Those red lilies are beautiful,' I said to her one day while we were still involved. 'Don't you have any in your garden?' she asked. 'No.' 'I'll send you some bulbs.' And she did. To be frank with you, I barely noticed them. My late father took them and planted them. A short while later, however, the garden was full of them. Wherever you turned, you saw red lilies. And I who had forgotten about them—ah! I had forgotten everything—was surprised one day and asked my father, 'Where did all these lilies come from?' 'They are from those Vasiliki sent us the year before last. Have you ever seen such fecundity?' It was really quite astonishing. No other flower took root in our garden the way those lilies did. They possessed such energy and strength that they choked everything and prevailed all by themselves.

You might have thought she had sent to me all her love as seeds and it had put forth shoots and spread and overflowed—great and eternal like the sea. Well, after she died, I no longer allowed any other flowers in the garden. I threw them all out so that the red lilies would reign. I cultivate them myself—ah! All that I didn't do when I should have—and from spring straight through summer one can see a boundless wave of crimson in the garden, as if all the love that had come to be buried here was alive again and pouring out of the tomb."

"Buried?" I repeated in spite of myself, frightened by the nuance Popos gave to the word.

"Yes, buried. Come and see."

He went out into the yard and I followed him. He unlocked the outside door, all the while keeping the key in his pocket, and we went into the garden. First a small, graveled passage, which was unplanted and surrounded by walls, and after that, open and free, the entire expanse of the garden.

I was struck with awe from the first glance. What a far cry from the garden I knew! Somewhat steep, long, and narrow, it appeared even narrower among the walls, which had been raised deliberately now to conceal the view. There was nothing visible all around except the immediate lid of the sky. It was something deserted, oppressive, and cramped despite being endlessly long. The sparse trees had thin trunks and few leaves. Only an enormous cypress tree—the cypress tree I remembered—rose jet-black down at the other end next to a large, low marble table that we called a *trapeza*. There was nothing else but bushes and lilies. Above the green and yellow sword-shaped leaves appeared the blazing, deep-red, countless flowers forming that bewitching lagoon of blood that rolled its silent waves upward. These waves, which seemed to follow a law of their own, aroused in me an overwhelming sensation of strangeness, of the supernatural. And that redness, which in some places grew pale and in others became crimson—for there were withered lilies here and there as well—presented me with an image of torrents of blood, one on top of the other, here fresh and alive, there cold and dead. This astonishing vegetation had its own life apart and truly seemed like a symbol of the great love that had sowed it.

Both of us were silent as we walked quietly along the footpath in the middle, following the waves. It brought us straight to the tall cypress tree I remembered.

"It's here!" Popos said to me in a voice that was barely audible and with a grievous movement, as if he were showing me a tomb.

I looked, and among the biggest and most beautiful lilies in the entire garden, I saw the marble *trapeza*. I drew nearer and there, on top of the marble which resembled a tombstone, I read carved in big letters:

VASILIKI

"Here is the grave," Popos said to me. "All that you see here is the tomb of my love. She is asleep in the garden that she herself enriched. What more could she desire?"

And a fierce smile of bitterness, irony, and repentance flashed across my friend's face, then died out.

Afterward he plunged into the silence of grief.

I dragged him away from the place he called a "grave," took him by the arm, and we again followed the footpath. I sought to console him but only found empty words:

"Filling the garden with her lilies and erecting a cenotaph in her name is an idea worthy of your beautiful, poetic soul. You did not know and are not to blame. No, my friend, you are not to blame. Stop all this guilt, mourning, and unhappiness. Don't go to extremes. It seems to me that the time has come..."

I left off what I was saying. The red lilies, the ones closest to us and surrounding the small path, seemed to be looking at me with irony.

And Popos, as though anxious for me to be silent, promptly said, "You know, I often bring the priest, who reads the 'Te Deum.'" He squeezed my hand. I became alarmed.

When we reached the outside door and before we went inside, he took hold of me, leaned over, and squeezing my hand still tighter, in a muffled voice, and with a facial expression that only a madman might assume, whispered in my ear, "What you saw is not a cenotaph. She herself is asleep under there. I abducted her one night from the cemetery!"

STRATIS MYRIVILIS

(1890-1969)

The Little Hunchback

Today I watched a rachitic girl walking down Stadiou Street toward Omonoia Square. She was all dressed up and her make-up was carefully applied. She had large, black eyes and thick, shiny hair. Her head seemed disproportionately large in relation to her tiny body. This, of course, was also owing to her neck, which was missing, crunched between her deformed shoulders. It seemed to me that I had seen this girl before, that I had encountered her somewhere, and I tried to recall the circumstances. But when I remembered, I realized that personally she was a total stranger to me; however, the manner in which she was walking in front of me brought back to my memory the deceased Little Hunchback. She used to climb the hill on Sina Street every afternoon and disappear in one of the poor houses on Leontos Sgourou Street, the worm-like outgrowth of Sina Street where this upper-class road ends.

It is strange to what an extent all rachitic girls look alike, like twins. All of them have an oblong face with beautiful, dark eyes, black eyebrows and a large, fleshy mouth. They are shorter than average, their head is stuck to their shoulders without the intervention of their neck and their thighs are joined to their sternum without the inter-vention of their waist. Behind their back and in front of their bosom they have an abrupt bulge, as if they were concealing there, under their clothes, a large box with sharp angles. They try their hardest to strut and this further emphasizes the broken line of their back. All of them wear exceptionally high heels. They share still another trait— they are frightfully coquettish. Painted, well groomed, their hair just done. A tragic and sad dilemma ensues, whether to hurl accusations against an unkind nature that drove these wronged creatures to walk with their peculiar gait among the beautiful and supple girls who come alongside them with a light, triumphant step and hurriedly pass by, looking at them strangely out of the corner of their eye, just as they would glance at some bizarre cartoon in a magazine. Every time I see them I feel a sense of protest seething inside me. How is it possible that a Power who we believe puts the finishing hand to goodness, yet who at the same time has the sadistic cruelty to wound a young woman in such an inhuman manner, exists somewhere?

The girl I was observing on Stadiou Street was also a real coquette, which made you wonder. Dressed in the latest fashion, her hair done at the hairdresser's, made up, her nails recently painted, she was descending with an air full of self-confidence, whether real or feigned I cannot say. She confronted courageously, almost defiantly, the glances cast at her by the passersby. Every time she encountered a mirror in the window of some pastry shop, she lingered for a moment, inspected her elegance, and set forth with greater self-confidence.

Thus, this girl brought back to life before me the unfortunate Little Hunchback from my old neighborhood at Lykavittos. She was exactly like her, only her attire was shabbier, though just as ostentatious. She must have worked somewhere, perhaps in one of those narrow, badly lit offices on the side streets which extend from University Street to Stadiou Street and where poor, withered girls, bent over cold typewriters, make boring lawyers' transcripts. We get glimpses of them in the winter behind opaque windows, heating their ink-stained hands by blowing on them.

The Little Hunchback, mounted on her high heels, would climb the hill on Sina Street with slow, weary steps. She always wore cheap, clean gloves, tried to stretch upright as much as she could, and stared at us with her large, black, almond-shaped eyes. Behind those extraordinary eyes sat imprisoned a proud, embittered, and combative soul that faced the world from within its desperate solitude without lowering its gaze. She passed among people without greeting anybody, then disappeared into one of the yards of the poor neighborhood lying at the foot of Lykavittos. She took refuge behind an old, faded outside door, beneath whose wooden doorstep greenish water from washtubs flowed continuously. No one around there knew her name, nor did she speak to anyone, and everyone called her "the Little Hunchback." How old could she have been? Perhaps fifteen, perhaps twenty-five. It is difficult to say with rachitic girls. They all seem to be the same indeterminate age. She, too, had large, brilliant eyes and a large, heavily painted mouth. She always passed beneath our windows at the same hour and when the weather was sunny she went out on Sundays and strolled at a gentle pace in the golden light of Lykavittos. Always stretched upright, all alone, silent, and all dressed up. When the weather turned cool, she wore a gray coat with a fur collar which made her look shorter. Then you might have thought she had a mandolin concealed behind her back.

Young couples flock up there, among the delicate pine trees of Lykavittos, all year long, and the chirping of kisses never ceases night or day. The Little Hunchback passed all alone among the happy couples without disturbing them with indiscreet glances. She stood for a little while on the rocks of Saint Sideris and watched the sunset in silence. Finally she again descended the countless steps of the upright street and, erect and steel-like, headed for her dismal yard with the filthy gutter. A little while later, an old gramophone could be heard from the depths of the yard, playing the same records over and over. A "Musical Moment" by Chopin, the end of the "Ninth" with the "Ode to Joy," a dance by Brahms, the "Moonlight Sonata," and an aria from "Le Prophète" with the deep voice of Chaliapin. The record of Chaliapin must have been scratched, for the needle stuck momentarily in the middle of the groove. She would reposition it and Chaliapin would resume. From the pieces being played, I strained to comprehend her reclusive soul. Had she chosen them herself, I wondered, or had they simply fallen into her hands by chance?

The men and women of the neighborhood observed her as she went out dressed in this ostentatious manner, with inquiry and amazement in their eyes. "Look how coquettish the Little Hunchback is. Why is the Little Hunchback coquettish?"

It was heartless of them, but you could not say that the question was unnatural, for her little body was a cruel joke on the part of the Creation. Every time I saw her, I imagined a large beautiful doll to which a mad and wicked giant had given a headlong blow with his fist. Its skeleton had snapped and the wires inside the collapsed body had given way, half of them bending forward, the other half bending backward. The head had sunk into the chest as far as the chin, breaking the shoulder bones. The wires attached to the legs near the knees had also given way. Yet the doll preserved its colorful and youthful clothes, its glossy curls, its freshly ironed collar and its elegant, immaculate little pumps. It had not, moreover, noticed the havoc played upon it, and now its head, neck-less, was again turning to the left and to the right between the two humps, and its big eyes with their long eyelashes were looking all around in wonder. Why all these affected and showy clothes? What was this broken doll asking of the world and its Creator? What did it feel in its crushed little heart and why were its bright eyes looking at the sunset that way among the erotic couples on Lykavittos?

God knows.

Then, suddenly, one day the Little Hunchback died.

It was a freezing New Year's Day, the north wind was tormenting the pine trees on Lykavittos, the children in the street were blowing into cheap paper trumpets, and the Little Hunchback died. Suddenly and unexpectedly. On the evening of the previous day she went into the house, well-dressed and made-up, closed her bright eyes, and died.

We found out about it in the neighborhood two days later, when she failed to come out again to go to work and when that deep voice of Chaliapin singing "Le Prophète" was not heard again.

"Have you heard? The Little Hunchback died?"

"Really? How did she die?"

No one knew, just as no one knew how she had lived. Was it consumption? Was it suicide? Was that perhaps why they had not yet buried her? They were waiting for the doctors to come, to open up the broken doll, to see what was inside that crushed breast. Was it shavings or warm human entrails all cut up by sorrow? Later they said no, this was not the reason why there had been a delay of two days in burying her. It was simply because she lived all alone without a soul in the world to care for her or to pay for her funeral. And now they were waiting for the Municipality to take her away; the Police Department had notified it, but because it was New Year's Day, the Municipality was closed, etc.

Finally on the third day the hearse arrived. It was a black automobile covered with dust, belonging to the Municipality, and with a cheerful driver who kept blowing the horn. "Coming through! Coming through!" They stopped at the end of Sina Street because the hearse was too large to make its way up the narrow streets. A priest and a policeman were also present. The policeman was a handsome young man with a small moustache and cheeks red from the cold. He kept smoking and ogling the pretty girls in the neighborhood who were poking their heads out the half-closed windows. The priest, indignant, kept muttering to himself. The children had gathered in front of the door and were speaking softly, "They've come to take away the Little Hunchback…"

A little while later, they brought her out in a cheap wooden box. It was small like a child's casket and large like the box of an expensive doll. The handsome policeman lifted it under his arm without exerting much effort. He was looking in the direction of the windows and smiling bashfully. All the women crossed themselves as the corpse passed by, each one turning to the next and saying, "Good gracious, my dear, how small the Little Hunchback was. A wee bit of a thing…"

Her crumpled body truly was unbelievably small, lying on her back as she was. And it kept moving about inside the box on account of her double hump, which wouldn't allow her back to stretch out and rest and the lid to close. Then they opened the rear door of the black automobile, shoved—"wham!"—the small casket inside and closed the two small doors again.

The priest sat next to the chauffeur and was again muttering what this time seemed to me like death blessings, for he had removed a cross from his cassock and was holding it. There was not enough room, however, for the policeman, who grabbed hold from the outside, standing on the running board of the automobile. When the engine started up and the black automobile rushed down the slope of

Sina Street, the policeman's gray cape could be seen fluttering behind. The neighbors crossed themselves again and said, "God have mercy on the Little Hunchback."

An old lady, whose head was shaking uninterruptedly, asked while crossing herself, "What was her name, my girl?" They all shrugged their shoulders; nobody knew. For years she had repeatedly passed along Leontos Sgourou Street, yet no one knew her name. The next day the Municipal Department came and dismantled her house. Beneath the disinfector truck, in between its wheels, the dirty water from the washtubs was flowing again.

I wish I could write a very beautiful and sad song about the Little Hunchback on Leontos Sgourou Street, about all the Little Hunchbacks who pass by all dressed up on their high heels, their painted lips stubbornly sealed, their beautiful eyes provocatively open. It would be a tender song, relating even how God greeted the Little Hunchback from my old neighborhood when she appeared before His throne with her little hands crossed over her deformed breast, caressed by no man. And even how the Creator faced the blazing, enigmatic flame in her almond-shaped eyes. This poem would have to relate how God descended from his throne, took the Little Hunchback by the hand, caressed her hair, and with one word corrected her breast and back so that from now on she too would be a beautiful doll for all eternity. Just that. And the angels with their golden and blue wings would begin playing the "Musical Moment" by Chopin on their violas and mandolins, and her embittered, painted little lips would smile for the first time. I was unable to write it and sat down and wrote instead this small story, small like the Little Hunchback.

ELIAS VENEZIS

(1904–1973)

Mycenae

M any years ago in faraway Anatolia, surrounded by perennial trees and isolated from the world, Katerina Pallis, a noble woman of the region, had withdrawn with her little boy to live on the property of her ancestors. She was still very young when her husband died, their son had just been born, and she assumed alone the task of preparing this child for true manhood. From the time he was little, she taught him to love the earth and the sun, to respect the labor of others, and to believe that a conscience is vindicated only by one's deeds. When he was a child, she would lull him to sleep with legends that told of distant lands, of places lashed by strong winds and tempests, of seafaring men who battle all their lives against the cold and the water and the phantoms of the sky. Their gaze is capable of rending the night, and their ear of seizing sounds brought by the wind from miles away. They worship the lightning that inscribes fire on the dark; they have rough hands and, like their bodies, their hearts are also lashed by violent winds. But in the hour of Judgment, those hearts come forth pure and spotless because they performed their duty in life, having fought hard and suffered much.

This is how young Philip was raised. When he was old enough to understand and ask questions, Katerina Pallis spoke to him about his father. This was also like a legend that lasted many nights. In a warm voice, she attempted to bring back to life the form of that unknown father, which slowly assumed shape out of uncertainty and came, serene and sacred, to enter their midst.

And when Philip became older still, and his mother thought he was ready to be told, she then spoke to him about Greece. It was winter, the trees in the forest wailed, and the starving jackals howled. Huge logs burned in the fireplace, the air was thick, and the heat rose in small waves toward the high ceiling while the child, wide-eyed, listened to stories about the gods of Olympus, about the ravines and islands of Greece. They were strange legends, all the ones describing those gods, manlike creatures, who played with the joy of life, hunted in the forests, fell in love and suffered. There was nothing cruel or ascetic about them, they were all-powerful, they governed the wind, fire, and lightning. Of man's splendor there was only one thing they did not possess: the splendor of death. They were immortal; that is, never once at some mystical hour did they experience the terrifying shudder, the sign from the other world, that which gives men the right to be helpless, great, and alone: the chill of the grave.

Beneath such gods lived the mythical heroes of the land of Greece: Agamemnon and Clytemnestra and Iphigenia. When, at one time, evil men from parts of Asia came and abducted Helen, queen of Sparta, then the brave young men of the realm became very angry.

They said, "This cannot be; we must take back our queen!" And all the women said to their husbands, "Do not forsake our queen all alone to the barbarians! She is a woman and is as helpless as a reed!"

The brave young men then armed their wooden sea crafts in order to set out on an expedition to the distant land of Troy. The spirits of the winds, however, were not well disposed; the sails would not swell and the ships stood stuck to the beaches of Greece. The prophet consulted the spirits, and they replied that they desired the sacrifice of a maiden. Iphigenia, the maiden with the black hair and black eyes, the first maiden of the land, heard it and said, "This is my destiny."

She went of her own will and offered up her girlhood of sixteen years as a sacrifice to the spirits of the winds. Then a favorable wind blew, the sails swelled, and the ships set forth.

Katerina Pallis narrated the story of Mycenae to her son in this manner. The child became wrapped in thought as he listened to the marvelous legend, trying by himself to understand the significance of the sacrifice, the motive of the courageous acts, the power of the calm. Outside, the night was black as pitch and starless; the jackals howled; the earth of Anatolia, not depleted and virginal, was nourishing the worms and the seeds.

"Ah, when will spring come?" begged the boy. "Will we go to Greece then?" he asked, and his voice trembled, for within this journey that he had been promised for the spring lived all the legends and dreams, the adoration of gods and men, the sacred earth.

"Let spring come!" his mother reassured him. "Then we will go to Greece."

Spring came; Katerina Pallis took her son and they went to Greece. It was afternoon when they arrived at Mycenae. They were climbing the uphill road leading to the Acropolis of Mycenae on foot when they grew weary. They looked around them. There was nothing to see. Only the barren earth and Sarra, the austere mountain that covered the site of the tombs.

"Is it much farther?" the child asked his mother.

"I don't believe so," answered Katerina Pallis. "If you want, we can sit down."

Then they saw a herd of goats, led by a young herdsman, descending around the bend in the deserted road.

"Let's ask the herdsman," said his mother.

When he came closer, she asked, "Is it still a long way to Mycenae?"

The young herdsman looked puzzled.

"Mycenae...?" he asked. "I don't know of any Mycenae near here!"

"How about all this land around here...what is it?" Katerina Pallis asked again.

"Ah, here?...This is the pastureland of my grandfather Kakavas!"

The boy from Anatolia then laughed with all his heart. "See, mother!" he said. "And here we are looking for the tombs of our ancient kings!"

But Katerina Pallis became even graver and hastened her step.

It was then that he appeared at the top of the road.

An old man was descending, with heavy movements, erect and serene. His white beard wrapped his face in small ringlets, his cape was thrown over his shoulders, he was wearing a white, billowing kilt made of wool, and his face, baked by the sun, looked like bronze. A light wind was blowing and ruffling his hair, but his steady gait gave the finishing stroke of serenity to the entire image. He was a living incarnation of the ancient figures of the land as recounted in books and statues.

"Look, look, Philip!" the mother said to her son. "See how Greece lives on…"

"It's true, mother! It's true…," he also said, deeply moved. "How strange it is…"

In the simplest manner, with an old herdsman who appeared and inscribed his image on the evening landscape of Mycenae, the legends of Olympus started to assume a vivid form—the expedition to Troy and Agamemnon and Iphigenia, the sacrificial daughter with the black hair.

The old man approached, waved his rod in the air, then lowered it and rested it on the ground. But he did not lower his head like the villagers and herdsmen in Anatolia. He looked them right in the eyes, his body straight as a tree.

"Welcome to our land!" he said. "You must be strangers." This time Katerina Pallis did not ask if it was Mycenae. She merely said, "We are strangers, old man! Where are the tombs of your ancient kings?"

The old man, gesturing slowly, pointed behind him.

"Just beyond Sarra!" he said. "There is where you will find them!"

There, as night fell and the sea of Argos disappeared from their sight, there they found them. First they saw the large, arched, royal tomb of Agamemnon and they went inside. The earth, to preserve it these many thousands of years, had gathered above it, becoming a hill, sprouting grass and trees, bringing forth flowers until its hour should come to emerge again and be worshipped by men. Darkness and profound calm prevailed within. On a small altar, where the sanctuary or the place for offerings must have been, Katerina Pallis found a few dry twigs. They set fire to them, then waited and watched. Nothing. How desolate it was! Except that every once in a while, a little water dripped from the dome. The earth above gathered it, held it inside itself, sanctified it, and later allowed it to pass down through the hard rocks of the dome and confer upon the serenity of the tomb a sound—a message from the world and from eternity.

"How alone the great king is in here...," the boy murmured. Katerina Pallis pulled him away and they went out. They passed by the humble tomb of Clytemnestra. The boy said they ought to enter there also, but his mother refused. What could she say to him about Clytemnestra and about her horrible deed? What should she say to him? No, she refused.

"Let us go to the Acropolis," she said, and headed toward the uphill path.

When they reached the Gate of the Lions, a fear seized the boy's heart. He took hold of his mother's hand.

"Are you afraid?" Katerina Pallis asked. "The citadel has been deserted for thousands of years. The dead do not speak."

She spoke thus even though she was well aware that in Greece the dead do, in fact, speak.

Here the atmosphere was happier, simpler. There were no vaulted monuments. The graves were only slightly below the surface of the earth. Wild flowers, yellow and red, grew here and there.

The child bent down to pick one. Later, when they descended from the Acropolis, he asked to enter again the tomb of Agamemnon. And there, on the ashes of the altar, on the ashes of the burned twigs, he placed it with affection, a message of the joy from the outside world, so that Agamemnon would not be alone.

What a long time has passed since then, what a great many years!

Katerina Pallis is journeying again on foot, this time alone, all alone, climbing the road to Mycenae. Now it is not spring, as it was then. Heavy clouds hang over the Acropolis of the tombs. And she is dressed in black. Mourning seals her pale face and her hair is white. Of all that she lived for and brought up, nothing remains. Everything was left back there, in the catastrophe of Anatolia. There, the brave young man, who from the time he was a child she had prepared to become a true man, to respect the labor of others, and to believe that a conscience is vindicated only by one's deeds, had also perished. What is the meaning now of the legends she used to tell him about in faraway lands, about places lashed by strong winds and turbulent seas, about men with pure hearts who all their lives battle against the cold and the water and the phantoms of the sky. What is the significance of all that now...

Katerina Pallis entered the tomb of Agamemnon. The same tranquility, identical to that of so many years ago. The same desolation and the silence of death. There are no longer any ashes on the small altar, nor any twigs as before. Only water from the earth drips slowly from the dome, slowly, at irregular intervals.

"My son..." the mother softly says. "My boy..." she says again, and remembers the humble flower the boy brought from outside to place on the altar so that Agamemnon would not be lonely.

"So that Agamemnon would not be lonely..." she murmurs. "And you, my child, where might you now be...?"

With her white head bowed, with slow, weary steps, she goes outside. She looks around. She casts her eyes nearby, on the other, humble tomb where Clytemnestra rests. They remain there. Remain. And then, only then, does she see, truly see, that tomb for the first time. She humbly directs her footsteps toward it. She goes inside. How silent it is in here as well, the silence of death! Slowly, the light disappears, time disappears, only shadows stir in the air. And from inside there, from the depth of the shadows, forms slowly emerge and become clearly discernible. There once lived a hardhearted king. He was called Agamemnon. The people in his kingdom moaned and groaned under his tyranny and poured out rivers of perspiration so that he could accumulate countless riches in his castle. His power and tyranny stretched as far as the eye could see, over the entire plain of Argos. At one time, travelers who had gone astray happened upon these parts. From their mouths Agamemnon learned that at the other end of the sea, toward Anatolia, in a wealthy land, Priam reigned, hoarding countless treasures in his castle—gold and much copper, herds of livestock and women the color of wheat and with sparkling eyes.

Agamemnon's mind became inflamed. Without delay, he sent messages to the neighboring kings of the Arcadians and they decided to at once launch the expedition to Troy. The entire army gathered on the beach of Aulis to embark. But a favorable wind would not blow. They waited for days, for weeks. Finally the prophet consulted the stars. And the stars said that if the angry gods were to be appeased, Agamemnon must offer as a sacrifice Iphigenia, the maiden with the black hair and black eyes. The king hesitated for a moment, but for a moment only. Then he thought of the herds of livestock and the gold and the copper and the slaves in the distant land, which was at the other end of the sea. His mind became muddled and he no longer hesitated. He sent a message for his wife to come, bringing his child. And there, beside the calm sea, he surrendered with his own hands the maiden with the black hair, Iphigenia, to the executioner. The wind then blew, taking with it the fast-moving ships and the lamentations of Clytemnestra. And the land was filled with her wailing and curses.

For years, Clytemnestra waited for Agamemnon to return from the foreign land, for years she brooded over her dreadful revenge. One of her slaves stood sentry every day, from dawn to dusk, to sight the much traveled ships. Until one day the slave arrived breathless and fell at her feet, bringing the momentous news, "He's coming! Agamemnon is coming!"

Clytemnestra withdrew to her chambers; for a long time she remained alone, praying to the gods. She did not cry. She only beseeched them to come to her aid in this sacred hour when a mother would perform her supreme duty. Next, she calmly went out to the Gate of the Lions, determination flashing in her eyes. She sent for Aegisthus to stand by her, should her hand tremble at the last moment.

Agamemnon arrived, dragging behind him herds of slaves and cattle from the plunder of Troy. Next to him, Cassandra, Priam's daughter, followed barefoot. Clytemnestra led him to the bath. She gave him aromatic oils with which to anoint himself and, as soon as he had bathed, she threw a large sheet over his face. And at the same time as he was drying himself, Clytemnestra raised the axe and split his head. Afterward she sent for Cassandra. And she butchered her with her own hands next to the blood-stained body of Agamemnon, as he had butchered their child Iphigenia next to her.

Night is falling when Katerina Pallis emerges from the tomb of Clytemnestra.

The weather is oppressive; the black clouds collide with one another in the sky. They touch the top of the naked mountain, Sarra, and hasten away from it, as if there were danger that it might detain them. Its bulk rises dimly, a dark divinity that waits.

Katerina looks around her. After a time her bitter gaze falls to the ground with calm resignation—the refuge of people who have suffered greatly.

Then she sees it at her feet. It is a poor, lonely, yellow flower of the earth. How is it able to endure there, in the dreadful solitude, how?

She bends down and plucks it. Afterwards slowly performing the same action her son performed so many years before—before they took him from her hands—but now in a different spirit, she comes and lays it on the deserted tomb of Clytemnestra, so that a mother, the mother of Iphigenia, will not be alone.

M. KARAGATSIS

(1908-1960)

The Boss

At that time, namely some thirty years ago, I was an employee in the store of a Cephalonian in Port Said. From morning until night we sold to the Arabs all the worthless objects that Europe would no longer condescend to buy. For me to describe what was in that store would be labor lost. Redingotes from 1860, rubber shoes, celluloid collars, taffeta crinolines, women's blue stockings, English hunting suits from the Victorian age. Whatever your heart desired, whatever your liveliest imagination hankered after was to be found in the store of Gerasimos Gerasimatos. Everything except contemporary articles.

Just dusting that limitless storehouse made us spit blood every day. Then, too, selling was difficult. The Arab is distrustful, stingy. You have to wrangle with him, to yell, to shout yourself hoarse before persuading him to open his purse. Yet those were wonderful years. I was a boy of twenty, full of strength, zest, and youth. When, after seventeen hours of work, I dropped into bed, sleep descended on me like lead. The next day I would wake up fresh, cheerful, ready for the sweatshop.

The boss entered the store every morning at seven. He had no home and had his bed set up at the back, in the storehouse—a hole consisting of two rooms that faced a filthy back street of the Arab quarter. He rarely slept in the store, however, for he had concubines in the city and spent the night in their arms.

Upon his arrival our good mood of the morning, our laughter and our songs were cut off as if with a knife. Everyone shrank into his corner in anticipation of the storm that was not long in bursting. The boss, stooped and with trembling legs, advanced slowly, glancing to the left and to the right with his distrustful and apoplectic look. When he reached the office, which was located at the back of the store, he removed his Panama hat and always hung it on the same hook on the wall. But every morning the hook had been removed by some crafty hand. The old man could not see it. His body, hunched over from dissipation and rotted by sickness, was incapable of stretching. Feeling his way, he extended the hand holding the hat toward the spot where the hook was supposed to be; and when the hat, not encountering a prop, fell to the floor, the old man's anger exploded into unrepeatable insults.

"What son of a bitch, what son of a whore removed the hook again? May the devil possess him!"

We hid behind the showcases and laughed furtively. Because, deep down, this crazy brawler was a decent man who wronged no one.

In the late afternoon he went out in front of the store and exposed his half-paralyzed legs to the sun. His tempestuous life, filled with sensual pleasure of every sort, had unhinged his nerves and reasoning. There were moments when he was utterly debilitated with a lifeless and inexpressive look in his eyes. Yet at other times anger made him raving mad. He howled, shouted, beat his breast. Then he sank into a depression fraught with sighs and hiccoughs.

He sat in the sun for hours, spitting endlessly, and the sidewalk in front of him became covered with disgusting spittle. Afterward he murmured something or other, spoke incoherently, and amused himself all alone with visions from his sick imagination.

When some woman entered the store, he became another man. He got up, attended to her himself, wooed her, tried to steer her in the direction of the office, to push her toward the store house. The Arab women laughed at his antics, but many times they accepted his shameless caresses. Whenever he shut some wanton woman in his room, we would gather outside the door and listen to his groans, as well as to the insults of the woman who refused to tolerate his strange perversions. When it was all over, he would come out of the room in a state of total exhaustion. Lifeless and senseless, he would drag himself as far as the sidewalk and cover it with spittle.

He had neither friend nor relative in Port Said. It was rumored that he had some cousins or nephews in Cephalonia, but perhaps he didn't get along with them. He never spoke of his homeland.

"I live alone in the world," he used to say sometimes when his mind was clear. "What do I ask of other people? I have never had a friend, nor loved a woman. Yet I have enjoyed life more than anybody."

The store had a thriving business, especially when *Baram** came and we made a mint of money. Everyone in Port Said said that the boss was very rich. He had deposited eight thousand pounds in Egyptian Credit alone. This was separate from the promissory notes—state loans, stocks in the Suez and French renter—that were locked in the store safe. As the true Cephalonian that he was, however, he lived wretchedly and miserly, always ill-dressed, dirty, and starving in the two sunless rooms of the storehouse.

His sole expenditure was women. In that domain he squandered lavishly and absurdly to satisfy his lascivious old age. Every so often the women go-betweens in Port Said came by to fix him up with whatever new fruit had cropped up in the flesh market. He locked them in his room, and in hushed tones they began bargaining endlessly over the price and the particulars. He did not let a single one slip by. Greek servants whose heads had been turned by pimps, French actresses who were selling their bodies, Hungarian artists from cabarets, Jewish women, incognito, who pretended they were high-society ladies, and whatever other fruit happened to fall on this transient city of sailors and adventurers. But his weakness was Arab women—young, unripe girls with adolescent, boyish bodies. He had his personal mediators who were on the lookout for tender young things in the squalid Arab quarters, and whenever they brought him some choice morsel he paid well—paid well enough to shut the

* A muslim holiday.

mouths of their parents. For, more often than not, the girls returned home exhausted by his strange caresses, in a stupor and half-mad from his strange carnal pleasures.

He had left the store to the Lord's mercy. Except for his dirty dealings with the female pimps, he was not in a condition to discuss any other business matters. But he was fortunate. For years he had an employee, Dionysius, who had demonstrated that he was a real work-horse. It was he who was in charge of the store, who placed the orders, paid the bills, and kept the ledgers. Every evening he gave an account of the cash-box to the old man. Gerasimos did not harangue him, for despite being a dotard, he was aware that Dionysius managed the shop well. He never insulted him. As the Cephalonian dog that he was, however, he never once spoke a kind word to him. Dionysius, nevertheless, sweated and slaved, administering the store as if it were his own. He was the first to awaken and the last to go to bed. Neither Sundays nor holidays existed for him. Nor friend, nor wine, nor woman. And all for five pounds a month.

With the arrival of summer, the roads of Port Said became inflamed. Work became torture in the terrible heat. Inside the dark and airless store, our lungs struggled in vain to inhale a fresh breath. All day long we swam in perspiration and at night the mugginess sat like a nightmare on our weary chests.

The one who suffered more than all the others was Dionysius, who had become pale. In the afternoon his hands would perspire and burn. Some draft must have hit him, for he started coughing. Still, he did not complain, alleging some slight indisposition that he would get over on his feet. And he continued to work hard, as always.

One night I felt someone shaking me in my sleep.

"What is it?" I asked, barely awake.

"For God's sake! Turn on the light quickly!"

It was Dionysius, whose bed was next to mine.

I found the matches under my pillow and lit the spermaceti. In the trembling flame, I saw Dionysius seated on his bed, coughing and spitting blood in a handkerchief.

I became frightened and woke up the others.

What were we to do? In the initial confusion we were unable to think clearly. Suddenly I remembered that across the way from us lived a doctor, Dr. Laurency. I dressed hurriedly and went to inform him to come at once.

Dr. Laurency was a fifty-year-old Frenchman, kind, ruddy-complexioned, and with a gray, drooping mustache. He came straightaway. After reassuring the sick man that it was nothing serious, he ordered complete rest and ice packs on his chest.

When the boss, returning the next morning from his paramours, learned the particulars, his face dropped a mile.

"That worthless creature got sick? Damnation! May the devil possess him! Now who's going to look after the store? Not me by any chance? I'm an old man and unfit for such work!"

All morning long he grumbled, spit, and cursed "that vile devil who had made the best lad in his store consumptive."

At midday the doctor returned and examined the patient at his ease.

"It's nothing serious," he said. "Only you must return to your village, to lovely Cephalonia, for three months. Don't tire yourself, eat plenty, and you'll get well."

When the boss learned what the doctor had said, he became furious.

"You're not going anywhere!" he told the sick man. "There's nothing wrong with you. Besides, what will you do in Cephalonia? Are you going to abandon the store just like that and without reason?"

In vain did Dionysius plead with him, complaining that he would become consumptive, that he would die. The headstrong old man would not listen to anything. He flatly refused to grant permission for a trip or, what was crucial, to give him any money.

Dionysius, in despair, went and told his grief to Dr. Laurency. The latter took out his wallet and offered him twenty pounds.

"My boy," he said to him, "go back to your homeland and rest for three months. Afterward, when you return, come directly to me; I will employ you at eight pounds a month."

Dionysius left without saying goodbye to the boss. When the old man learned what had happened, he flew into a rage. Foaming at the mouth with frenzy, he opened the middle drawer of his desk. Inside were various weapons, which were strange, peculiar, and harmless. One-barreled and two-barreled pistols with flint, revolvers, repeating pistols, stilettos, penknives, two-edged knives, and yataghans. The old man selected an enormous, frightful, and rusty saber. Holding it, he went out and stood in front of the door of the store. And he began to howl, to curse, to foam, and to threaten Dr. Laurency that he was going to rip out his guts because he had turned the head of his best employee.

This went on for months. Every morning Gerasimos, brandishing his saber, menaced the doctor. Laurency, looking through the window, laughed at the antics of this madman. The Arabs, who congregated at the disturbance, joined in with inarticulate shouts while jumping up and down hysterically.

In time he got over this mania as well. Unable to manage the store, he appointed me as supervisor. Only I was not weak like Dionysius. I knew what I wanted and was fully aware of my capabilities. Furthermore, the boss had deteriorated considerably; the light in him had gone out completely. He dragged himself as far as the door of the store with great difficulty to expose his hunched body to the sun every day, until one day he took to his bed for good. His legs became paralyzed and he was unable to hold his water. I sent for Dr. Laurency, who came, as always, jovial and ruddy-complexioned.

He examined Gerasimos, then shook his head.

"He does not have long to live," he said to me. "Two or three months at the most. Doesn't he have any relatives here?"

"Not a single one!"

"I do not advise your taking him to the hospital. It would be better to engage a nurse for him."

I made him as comfortable as I possibly could in the small, sunless room, and found a servant—a kind of nurse—to take care of him. She was a girl from Karpathos, no more than twenty years old, inexperienced and intimidated.

She nursed him as best she could, feeding him, giving him drink, and changing his sheets, which he dirtied continually with his filth.

Most of the time he lay in bed half-unconscious, sleepy-eyed, tongue-tied, blurting out nonsensical and mixed-up words, groaning, and filling his covers with spit. He was repugnant.

When, however, he occasionally came out of his mental stupor, his eyes slowly searched the room and arrested themselves on the girl who stood shyly huddled in the corner. His mouth babbled something or other, his lips feigned a laughter of sorts, then he sank again into his former torpor.

❧

This had gone on for several days when, unexpectedly, the boss showed some improvement. His reason cleared. He revived slightly and began to talk. We were all pleased and thought that he had escaped death. Dr. Laurency, however, was not of the same opinion.

"Don't be fooled by what you see," he said. "He's a dead organism and will die anyhow."

We cared for him as best we could. Only how can you perform household work in a dark storehouse drowned in the sweltering heat of the African summer?

The girl from Karpathos tried harder than any of us. With the recovery of his senses, the boss's whims and demands became indescribable. He was always calling her, always asking for her—sometimes to give him water, sometimes to straighten his bed, and still other times to empty the mechanism that had been attached to him because of his inability to control his urine. Lecherous and shameless, he exhibited his naked body with a diabolical smile. And he screamed with laughter, as if being tickled, when the blushing and embarrassed girl was obliged to touch his paralyzed body with her hands.

From this point on a war began. A revolting war of shameless life and wanton death. Every time the nurse bent over the boss's bed to attend him, his half-paralyzed hands, fortified by the demon of his entire life, sprang up unrestrained, propelled by unconscious memories of sexual desires. Grabbing her, he would pull her on top of himself, fondle her breast, and shove his hands under her dress. The girl, embarrassed and totally inexperienced, would not utter a sound but would press her lips together and struggle desperately to escape from the desiccated fingers that were torturing her flesh. Afterward she would shut herself in her room. Humiliated and inflamed with disgust, she did not wish to exhibit her martyrdom to anyone.

The more the days passed, the more the half-rotted beast lost all reasonable restraint, accompanying his indecent gestures with words, cynical provocations, and insane, brazen laughter that left the nurse speechless. How often, entering the hot and dirty room unexpected-ly, did I not save her from his hands, to which the imminence of death granted the rigidity of a harpoon! The young woman thanked me with a faint smile, then shrank into a corner, exhausted and embarrassed by the obscene display of eroticism before her ignorant eyes.

I was afraid that, unable to endure her disgust, she would drop everything and walk out on him. But she was alone and destitute in Port Said and did not know where to go or what to do. Her stoicism was admirable as she sat in the asphyxiating room, next to this mad-man on the point of death, in surroundings where at every moment her sensitivity, her female dignity, and her virginal shame experi-enced pangs of mortal humiliation.

Whenever I could steal a few moments from my work, I rushed to the storehouse, trying to lift her spirits and bolster her courage. I told her funny stories; I chatted with her; I did everything I could to make her forget, if only for a moment, her martyrdom.

I succeeded to some extent. Her frightened eyes became calmer, her lips smiled.

"Courage!" I would say to her. "Courage, my girl! In a few days the filthy dog will croak and your troubles will be over."

She looked at me with sorrow and anxiety. "Will they be over or just beginning? Where will I go? What will become of me?"

I did not reply for I knew that she was destitute and alone in the world. A cousin of hers, a sailor, had brought her to Port Said to find work for her—her family in the village had died out—entrusting her to me as he put her ashore.

"Look after her!" he said to me. "I'm placing her in your hands."

Thereupon he left as a stoker on an English cargo ship headed for Vladivostok, Siberia, and other such godforsaken places. Who knew when and if he would return. In the battle waged by the expatriated Greek to earn his livelihood between the equator and the North and South poles, man does not count, the individual is not worth a brass farthing. Everyone is preoccupied by his own sorrows, troubles, hunger. Would the stoker from Karpathos, stuck like a beefsteak to the ship's boiler and burning up, a wage earner plowing the seas and oceans of the world for his morsel of bread, ever remember that he had a cousin working as a servant in Port Said? What would become of this inexperienced creature after she left the bedside of Gerasimos Gerasimatos? What bed would she fall on—and this time for good? One must be aware of the ports of transit-trade, with their taverns for thirsty sailors and their "houses" for men who have dried out in the furnace of the Indian Ocean and the Red Sea for thirty or forty days with only the anticipation of women; one must have witnessed the underworld of hashish smugglers, of dealers in white flesh, of cynical Levantines who make money with money and pistols; then one would understand the drama of a destitute woman.

Feeling my hard Cephalonian heart grow heavy whenever she looked at me with her frightened eyes, I would take her hand and feign laughter to bolster her courage.

"Don't worry," I would say to her, "God will provide!"

Within me, however, I did not believe that God "provides" anything whatsoever for girls who remain unprotected in Port Said.

One night while I was asleep in the loft, drenched in perspiration, I was awakened abruptly by a noise. At first I thought my ears had played a trick on me, that it was nothing. I sat up in bed and reached for the pistol under my pillow. The others around me were all sleeping peacefully.

The noise continued, distant and indeterminate. It sounded like chairs being dragged or someone groaning.

Without turning on the light, I slipped on my trousers and groped my way down the stairs, the pistol still in my hand.

When I reached the store, I stopped and listened stealthily. The disturbance was coming from the storehouse, where the boss was confined to his bed. I smiled with relief, put the pistol in my pocket, and went to see what the matter was.

As I opened the door, a strong odor of urine struck my nostrils. The lamp was lit.

I was startled upon seeing the patient's bed empty. But, lowering my eyes to the floor, I beheld another sight that, were I to live a thousand years, I will never forget.

Gerasimos had climbed out of bed and, with all the remaining strength of his paralyzed body, had managed to tumble down to the floor. Then, with his hands and feet, with spasms and convulsions, and like a repugnant giant worm, he had dragged himself as far as the door of the room where the nurse slept.

Before going to bed, however, the young woman was in the habit of locking her door. Terrified from previous similar attempts, she would drag an entire wardrobe and position it behind the door.

When Gerasimos reached the front of the barred door, he pleaded, cried, threatened. When the door remained shut, however, he decided to break it down.

He must have pushed for entire hours. Where did that paralyzed, half-dead human wreck find the strength? What all-powerful demon fortified his dead muscles and revived his broken sinews?

By the time I entered the storehouse, he had succeeded in breaking the lock. While pushing, he knocked over the small wardrobe and the crash it made as it fell had awakened me.

Beside himself with joy at his accomplishment, he was dragging himself on the floor, struggling to make his way through the small opening in the door. The mechanism had slipped from his legs and the spilled urine was inundating the room. His naked, senile limbs were moving slowly, like the tentacles of an octopus. He was laughing and guffawing, delighted with his accomplishment, gasping for breath, hiccoughing, swimming in his urine and phlegm.

My insides were churning. With two kicks I sent him rolling far from the door. Then, taking him in my arms, I threw him on the bed.

He said nothing. He merely threw me a glance full of hatred, a glance that would have made my blood run cold if anger were not making it boil like molten lead.

I made my way through the half-open door into the young woman's room in order to calm her.

The poor thing was standing in a corner, petrified with fear, staring in the direction of the door with dazed eyes. Underneath her long nightgown her entire body was shaking. Her breathing had frozen in her parched throat.

I took her by the hand and laid her on the bed. I feigned laughter in my desire to bolster her courage. I reassured her. I gave her a sip of water to drink. But the nervous crisis suddenly burst. An abatement, a flood of tears after the immensity of the fright. She buried her head in my chest, as if asking for help in the face of life's tragic revelation. And she was crying, sobbing like a baby, in an outburst of helpless despair.

I comforted her like a baby, laughed, told her funny stories, caressed her combed out-hair.

Suddenly, I realized that this child was a ripe, beautiful woman with a body watered with the juices of her twenty years. From her hair my hands descended to her neck, caressed with desire her naked arms, plunged trembling into the opening of her nightgown.

She was no longer crying. She simply closed her eyes and waited...

I meshed my lips with hers, squeezing the slender body that abandoned itself in my arms. And as a warm gust of wind extinguished the candle, I rolled over with her on the bed.

It was an African summer night, warm and languid. The moon, rising in the sky, illuminated the small room. A cricket chirped in the palm tree of the adjoining garden. Beyond, in the canal, a ship was whistling.

I loved her with all the vigor of my twenty-two years, with all the eroticism of my until-then loveless life. Her body was a revelation to me, her lips a spring of unutterable happiness.

We remained there until morning, abandoned to what was for both of us our first discovery of love. Instinct taught us how to caress, secretly revealed to us sensual pleasures of which we were ignorant. And when beyond in the east, dawn appeared, pure and blue, we heard with a heavy heart a song full of Oriental grief, echoing in the now-quiet back streets of the very white city.

The sun had nearly risen when I got up. Walking softly, I left the room, when a strange sight stopped me.

Gerasimos for a second time had climbed out of bed. He had dragged himself as far as the open door. And there, quiet and mute, he had observed our lovemaking. Death had found him in this position. His gaping eyes were fixed on the disorderly bed with insatiable lechery. A smile of supreme bliss was frozen on his mouth. And his flesh, aroused for the final time, remained as a gruesomely shameless symbol of his entire life.

Thirty years have passed since then. I am now fifty years old and all that is left to me is the remembrance of that wonderful time of my youth. The remembrance...and a tomb. A white tomb in the small cemetery in Port Said where the girl from Karpathos lies sleeping for the last time. My wife.

STRATIS TSIRKAS

(1911-1979)

Blackout

It was almost dark, but the indecisive girl continued writing on the iron plate of the gate door.

She was on a deserted street in Alexandria, in a neighborhood made up entirely of machine shops, garages, and factories. At one moment she paused. The thought, "This business has to come to an end, it can't go on forever," made her hand numb. Then she reflected, "As soon as the inscription's finished, I'll see what I'm going to do." And she started writing again, slowly and in her finest penmanship, which they were teaching her in school.

Voula G. Drakou

Age 10+1/2

Fourth Grade...

At that moment she heard steps. A lady appeared, making the turn in the road and coming hurriedly straight at her. Voula, with a slight feeling of guilt, dropped the hand that was writing. She turned her head and looked in the direction of the wall, waiting for the lady to go away.

The latter, however, said as she walked past her, "Why are you loitering about, child? It's gotten dark. A fine predicament you'll be in if you're caught in a blackout all alone in a neighborhood like this."

Then Voula did something improper. She puckered up her mouth like an old lady. "Nya! Nya! Nya!" she blurted and in the end she even stuck her tongue out at her!

The lady made an about-turn and came closer. "You can be sure she'll report me," Voula reflected, and with her sleeve she hurriedly started to erase her name from the iron plate. At the same time she shielded her eyes with the reverse side of her hand, expecting a slap in the face as well.

But now it was the lady who did something unexpected. Drawing her face very near, with the two fingers of her left hand she pulled the flesh under her eyes, while at the same time with the index finger of her other hand she pushed her nose upward, and her beautiful, heavily made-up face became ugly, as ugly as that of a Chinese woman.

"Oh! Oh! Oh!" she said to Voula. "I'll bet you can't do that!"

Voula, unable to contain herself, burst out laughing. The lady also laughed.

"Shall we go now?" she said to Voula.

"All right."

"Is your home in this direction?"

"No, but it doesn't matter. Let's go anyway."

"What do you mean, 'it doesn't matter'! You must have been going somewhere. Little girls your age aren't allowed to wander about all alone. Either you were on your way home or you were sent somewhere. Where?"

Voula became alarmed.

"Nowhere," she replied. "I can't go back home. I have to go somewhere else first. And I don't want to go there, I can't, I can't, I won't..."

She hugged the lady's legs right then and there and started crying against her stomach. It was the month of May. The lady was dressed lightly and wasn't wearing a corset. She was simultaneously soft and hard. And she smelled nice.

"What's come over you, my child? This is something else again. Come, don't cry, you've stained my dress, can't you see?" But the girl had become hysterical. It was already getting dark and the isolation of that neighborhood was enough to terrify anyone. Then the lady hailed a taxi going by and took Voula home with her.

It was a magnificent house in the center of the city, the area where doctors and lawyers reside. In the elevator, Voula was still crying.

"Shame on you, shame on you, that's enough! What must the barber who can see you be thinking?" said the lady.

She paused outside the door and, along with her key, removed a handkerchief from her small bag. She tidied up Voula's face, wiping her nose and eyes carefully, waited a little until she was through sobbing, then opened the door.

They entered a large hall. A gentleman, seated brazenly with one leg straddling the arm of a chair, was smoking a pipe. He was listening to the radio.

"Hello," the lady said to him.

"Hello," he replied moving his leg negligibly.

He appeared to be her husband or brother. The lady hesitated in case the gentleman should ask, "Who's the little girl?" He, however, was staring at the ceiling with a smile on his face and smoking his pipe, puff, puff.

"Let's go, Voula," said the lady and took her to her room.

"My God, how beautiful! All mirrors and silk," Voula exclaimed. The lady fondled her hair, made her sit down on a small sofa, and offered her some chocolates.

"Come now, Voula, tell me what's wrong. Start from the beginning and don't hurry. If you have to go home, we'll go together. If you don't, you'll sleep here tonight and tomorrow we'll see."

For a long time, Voula kept wrapping and unwrapping the end of the lady's handkerchief around her finger. Then she gave the following account.

"The doctor's to blame for everything," she said. "If he hadn't come this morning, nothing would've happened. The Directress comes in unexpectedly and says to us: 'Girls, today we have a medical examination.' 'Oh! Oh! Oh!' we cried out terrified. Afterward they made us go into her office one by one. My turn also came. The doctor saw these red spots around my neck and became alarmed. 'Take off your smock, my child,' he says to me. 'It's nothing, Sir,' I say to him. 'It's from fleas.' 'What do you mean, from fleas?' the Directress says, jumping up with embarrassment. 'Not here, Miss, at home,' I say to her. 'Ever since my mother took in a tenant, I've been sleeping on the floor in the room. The bed's not big enough for all three of us. And the floor boards have fleas, do you understand?' 'But where does your mother sleep?' the doctor asks. 'In the bed,' I say to him. 'With the tenant.' 'What? What?' he shouts and stood up. The Miss had turned scarlet and was touching her cheeks. The supervisor said, 'Good heavens,' and remained with her mouth wide open. They collected my things helter-skelter and sent me home. 'Go tell your mother that I want to see her tomorrow morning without fail,' the Miss said to me, irritated. 'I won't allow you in the class unless your mother presents herself first, do you understand? These fleas are a serious matter. You could get sick and infect the other children.' But I knew that it wasn't on account of the fleas."

"And where is your father, Voula?" the lady asked, waving the cigarette she had lit.

The little girl seemed to falter, then said, "He's a soldier."

"Ah!" sighed the lady. "What happened next?"

"I went home. 'Here's what happened at school, mommy,' I said. What followed is incredible! She all but killed me. She beat me. She cried. She screamed, she roused the whole neighborhood. She tore her robe from top to bottom. She beat me again. And she cursed and cursed... 'I won't go, I won't go,' she said. 'Those hypocrites, those thieves, those murderers,' she said. At noon she let me go hungry. 'I was the cause of everything,' she says, 'with my stupidity.' In the afternoon her anger wore off a little. 'Come here,' she says to me. 'Do you know where the house of the Directress is?' 'Yes,' I reply, thinking she would take me and we would go there together. 'Then listen,' she says. 'You will go and tell her exactly what I'm going to say to you, do you understand? Miss, you will say, my mother wishes to inform you that there is no need for her to come see you. Mother says that if you had been in her situation, you would have done the same. It's not her fault, she says, if her husband got mixed up with Bulgarians in the army and turned traitor and along with him all the others also turned traitor and have now been placed behind bars...' 'Hush, mommy, hush, you're lying, I say to her.' 'Nonsense! Can't you hear what everyone's saying, what the newspapers are writing? Would the Council have cut off our allowance if it were lies? Would I have taken a strange man in my house to help us make ends meet!' 'Hush, hush, hush. My daddy's a hero!' I say to her. 'More nonsense,' she says to me. 'He was a hero at Alamein in '42; he even received a medal and made us proud...But two years went by, Bulgarian informers infiltrated our army and made traitors of them all. With their demands for unification and other such foolishness...What business do they have getting mixed up in all that? Are they the government?' 'So daddy isn't a hero?' I say to her. 'Not at all?' 'Not in the least,' she says. 'He's an informer. And any girls having a father who's an informer would do well to tell their mother to exchange him as I have done. That's what you should say to the Directress...'"

At this point Voula stopped because she heard laughter behind her. She turned around and saw the gentleman with the pipe leaning against the open door. There was an air of indifference about him, as if he were not with them. He simply pretended to stare at the ceiling and he was smiling. But the lady had also changed. She stood up from the sofa—not right then but several moments earlier—nervously put out her cigarette on a small plate, and clenched her teeth. Her face assumed the air of a great lady and she looked at Voula with hostility, as if she were in some way to blame.

"Stand up," she said to her abruptly.

Voula, startled, stood up. She tossed the handkerchief she was holding onto the sofa. But the gentleman came between them.

"It's not the poor child's fault, *Dear*," he said to her.

He didn't say it with compassion, though, but coldly, as if he were laughing at someone who wasn't present in the room.

"How am I to blame?" the lady *Dear* replied. "I thought I was witnessing an ordinary event..."

"And you dragged home the enemy!" the gentleman interrupted her. "You nearly warmed this red scorpion in your bosom. 'Present-day philanthropy' and other such rubbish!"

Now it seemed that the person the gentleman was laughing at was present in the room.

"A good whipping, that's what they need, a good whipping..." he continued, looking at Voula with eyes capable of killing. Voula understood nothing.

At this point *Dear* started a conversation with the gentleman. Voula surmised that they were discussing her father "who at any rate is an out-and-out rascal" and her mother who, the lady was saying, "perhaps believes the things she says, perhaps possesses sound principles..."

"Sheer romanticism, *Dear*, sheer romanticism," the gentleman again interrupted her. "Don't you see the 'offensive intent' of the message to the Directress?"

Dear fell silent, clenching her teeth. Afterward she seemed to have come to an abrupt decision. She called the servant and told him to accompany Voula downstairs as far as the street door. Without as much as a goodnight or a caress or anything at all. And Voula suddenly found herself in the pitch dark of the magnificent street. She walked haphazardly until she found her bearings. She bumped into a low wall and hurt her nose, felt the pain, and started to cry.

She was crying and moving ahead, trying to find her way and cursing. The wall, the darkness, Hitler. And when she found the road that led to her house, she took it without hesitation but didn't stop cursing. First, the doctor who sure knew how to choose the day on which to show. The Directress who made such a fuss over a few red spots. Those darn fleas. The boarder who had driven her out of her bed. The Council who had cut off their allowance. The lady *Dear* who at one moment was all sweetness and kindness and at the next mean and driving her away like a beggar. The gentleman who didn't seem to like anyone, anyone in the world, and who only knew how to laugh at others. Her mother...Oh, not her mother, nor her father. Her father was a hero, a hero of Alamein! How thrilling was the day the Directress entered the classroom with the newspaper and announced, "Girls, the father of Voula Drakou is a hero!" How Voula's chest puffed up, what a proud air she assumed, and how her report cards began to improve after that...How can she now go and say, "My daddy's not a hero, not in the slightest bit"? But supposing it's a lie, supposing it's not true. Mommy says that daddy's an informer, but if it was true how could she still love him? Because she does love him, she does, even though she says the opposite. Even the tenant says so. At night in the dark, when mommy asks in a low voice, "Wait, has the child gone to sleep?" and they begin to wrestle, and the tenant kisses her until he makes her hurt, squeezes her until he crushes her, tortures her, and she groans under her breath, holds back, holds back, then suddenly cries out, "George, my bones, you're hurting me"—the tenant's name is Michalis, whereas George is the name of Voula's father—and the tenant curses both George and mommy and she comes to him and asks him to forgive her, she unintentionally let it out again, she says, you see it was so many years, Michalaki, and she cries, and he gets up and opens the window and the stars are shining in the sky and he lights a cigarette...

DEMETRIS HATZIS

(1913-1981)

Margarita Perdikaris

E tu onore di pianti, Ettore, avrai
Ove fia santo et lagrimato il sangue
Per la patria versato, e finche il Sole
Risplendera su le sciagure umane.

And you, Hector, shall be honored by lament
wherever blood shed for the fatherland
is held sacred and is mourned, and for as long as
the Sun shines over human misfortunes.

UGO FOSCOLO, I SEPOLCRI (*The Graves*)

When the Germans shot her at the beginning of the summer of 1944, shortly before the liberation, Margarita had not yet turned twenty. Her thin body endured all the hardships of prison with unbelievable resistance; her mouth remained sealed despite all the tortures it was later learned that they inflicted on her. And as she stood before the firing squad, she smiled with that sad smile peculiar to the Perdikaris family. This last bit about the smile was related by the priest who, by his indispensable presence at executions, sanctions in the name of Caesar the rendering of the soul to God. It was he who related that when they raised their guns, little Margarita waved her hand and uttered an incomprehensible good night. In fact, she didn't say good night but, to be precise, "good night now…"

She was the first woman in our city to die in such a manner. Until this time women there knew only how to die in silence from sickness and old age on their bed or mattress; they died in childbed or post-childbed or from the affliction of poverty, a bad marriage, or separation from their husband and children who were living in a foreign country—the kinds of things everyone finds quite natural. As for the women of her own race, the Perdikari women died from the torments of old age, nervous breakdowns, and heart attacks—old maids for the most part. The last of their line, Margarita, also died unmarried.

It had been two years since she finished Teachers College in Athens where they had sent her to study, it being her turn and an old family tradition. Upon her return, she was assigned to a teaching post in the city and resided with the others in the old, two-story house, where the last remnants of this memorable family of Perdikaris lived, all together and clinging to a great and unapproachable nobility. No one knew—even they could not have said—what sort of nobility it was, when they possessed it, and when they actually lost it. Nevertheless, our community was forced to acknowledge that in this matter the Perdikaris had never taken a false step, never beaten a retreat, never made a concession.

Their women still wore their hair in the old-fashioned style, pushed back and up and gathered very tightly—in a "duck" as it was called, because the tightly tied bun that jutted out behind actually resembled the head of a duck. They still dressed in their noble short pelisses of black brocade, with a wide braiding of grayish fur that descended from the collar all around the lapel down to the hem and all around, and with a pinched, narrow waist.

These women, without ever finding fault with anyone overtly—they disdained such behavior in their inferiors—knew exactly how to express their contempt for upstarts, sinners, and conceited persons by slightly protracting their thin lips, with the result that everyone found it preferable to be afraid of them. They were a species of sacred geese that belonged to the capitol for the preservation of the virtue of our city.

The men also wore black, both in winter and in summer. They never set foot in the cafés, frequenting only the pharmacies, the offices of the notaries, and the Office of Charities of the holy

Cathedral—as did the old-timers. None of them worked. Thus, they were able to remain aloof from every kind of vulgar contact with the lower classes and to scorn everything contemporary—men, knowledge and things. All three of them had a small pension of sorts, and the family lived in perfect dignity with what little means it still possessed.

Quite justifiably, therefore, each of them figured among the bastions of society and traditional class order. The Cathedral clique always included a Perdikari on the ballots of the parish councils, and in time these austere and faultless men had become a permanent factor in the management of our city's philanthropic foundations. Separate from this were their services in behalf of "aid" distributed to the poor and which always bore—this had practically become a custom—the signature of one of them, usually that of the doctor-philosopher, Pericles Perdikaris, who was thought of as the leader of the family and was church warden of the holy church of Saint Antony, the modern martyr and miracle-worker. In this very church, certain difficult questions had arisen with regard to who should receive the oil and gifts the worshippers brought to the saint—that is, should the Cathedral receive them, or the rectors of the parish, or the direct descendants of the saint? It was acknowledged by everyone that Pericles Perdikaris had brought order to these perplexing issues. Still more generally, it was acknowledged as his prerogative and obligation not to have any occupation or care in life other than this exalted mission—the exercise of philanthropy in the city.

For this very reason there was a great to-do when Margarita was caught. Everybody had difficulty believing that the pampered last child of the Perdikarises could have been such an important and, indeed, such a trustworthy agent in the Resistance movement. She herself had never shown any sign or committed any action that might have singled her out from her other relatives during the two years she had lived with them. A puny, withdrawn, infinitely lonely creature with sorrow written all over her face, she seemed more frightened of others than concerned about the future of mankind. People therefore tried immediately to link the affair to the local cliques and when some exposed the clique of the Metropolite, while the metropolitans in turn speculated about her, various rumors spread throughout the city.

Margarita cut them short. It was learned that this unsalvageable creature had told the Germans straightaway that she was a Communist,
that her associates were also Communists, and that they would torture her in vain to make her betray them. As for the Perdikarises, she
claimed that they had no notion of what was hidden in the cellar of
their house. Scoundrels, speculators, and the others who were always
abreast of what went on disassociated themselves from her. They
understood. Margarita didn't belong to their world. There was nothing in it for them. They abandoned her, therefore, with the satisfac-
tion that the Germans wouldn't delay shooting her, just as deep down
they desired to see them do to all the accursed, disinherited children
who had multiplied—at least exterminate them before they left.

All that remained was the mystery of how it came about that they
caught her, of how they discovered her, that is, down there in the
Perdikaris catacomb. It was quite evident that someone had betrayed
her. This is why, as people said, the constables who went to the house
headed straight for the cellar, as if knowing in advance. There they
found the small duplicator, a few bundles of paper and tubes of ink—
a small, illegal printing machine. Margarita had placed everything in
a large, old trunk that had been abandoned there years ago and covered it on top with a lot of ragged old clothes. The spiders hung from
the ceiling, the wood-fretter moths slowly gnawed the forgotten
trunk, the clothes moths ate the useless clothes. No one else ever set
foot down there. How, then, were they able to find Margarita out
unless someone had betrayed her?

She had never been seen without the family's black attire. She grew
up in it; she died in it. Except that in the summer, returning from
Teachers College for vacation, she would arrive these last few years
wearing a large, white pique collar, which ended in a bow at the front
of her neck, and whose narrow ribbons hung down to the cleavage of
her bosom onto the black dress. Her hair parted in the middle and
tied tightly behind—a little more and it would have resembled a
"duck"—her large, sorrowful eyes beneath a slightly curved forehead,
her long legs, and the ungraceful attire—everything projected an
image of awkwardness and modesty that bordered on the ludicrous.

"So the sniveling brat is back," the girls in the city would say slan-
derously and surreptitiously on the first days of summer, as they
began their indefatigable promenades in groups up and down the
public walk.

She was always all alone and never approached another girl—
neither her former schoolmates, nor those in her neighborhood, neither rich girls, nor poor girls. Her return in the summer created the
most difficult problems for the family. Margarita knew nothing of
their life, the veritable life of the faultlessly dignified family of
Perdikaris inside that two-story house that appeared to be crumbling
little by little. And because things turned out as they did, with her
departing from their midst as soon as she began to grow up, they now
found it difficult to initiate her. Without even understanding how,
they found themselves entangled within their very own house in a lie
that kept their life in the dark.

The rest of the time, in the winter, Aunt Katerina could get up
early in the morning, place a wet rag on a board, and pound vigorously with the *kiftenteni*, the large knife for chopping meat, so that the
neighbors would hear and think that they had again bought and were
cooking meat in the Perdikaris household. In reality they could go
without eating and they could even hurl insults and spit at one another. Naturally, Margarita was not supposed to witness any of these
goings-on. As early as the beginning of spring, they all began to think
about what would happen in the summer when "the child" returned,
preparing her clothes, her room, her bed, and seeing to it that the
money that would be needed was raised.

Pericles continued to believe that Aunt Katerina, his sister and
senior, still had some gold hidden away. She should, therefore, hand it
over for the sake of "the child," and hand it over this very minute, and
hand it over to him—so that he might have peace of mind.

Thereupon Katerina would scream, "You've gone through everything I had, everything, cursed family," and she would raise her hands
as high as her hump allowed her to curse them one more time.

Buckets of tears would begin to flow from her eyes again, because
he was reminding her of such things as money and gold. Her husband,
Kanavos, a name of repute, had returned on one occasion from Vlahia
with a sack of sovereigns—a sack, not a pouch, mind you—only to

have the Perdikarises pounce on him as if intending to flay him to the bone. The poor man had been stunned for he was both generous and a little timid; and, overcome with despair, he had taken one look through the window and thrown the sovereigns into the street where the poor had gathered and taken them—"if only to avoid your begging and whining. You devoured the man, and what a man, like a plane tree, and you're still making demands on his wretched wife that you widowed and have cooped up in here and..."

The doctor-philosopher Pericles barely became angry with these accusations of hers about the past, which were moreover somewhat exaggerated. Bringing the conversation back to the here-and-now, he reminded Katerina that at present he was the one who had to carry her on his back, until such time as God took pity on him and raised her up.

"Lies, lies!" Such injustice always made Katerina furious. "You're the one living off me with the money you take from the Metropolis—and don't ever go back there!"

"Ssh!" This remark made him shudder and he glanced round the room, terrified that someone might be listening.

It was true that his basic source of income in life was the city's philanthropic foundations. Every time benefits were distributed among the poor, he also pocketed a round sum. Not on his own behalf, naturally, but for widowed Aunt Katerina; for cousin Fotine who, poor thing, was an old maid; for Antigone, Margarita's mother, who was still waiting for her pension. There were no written receipts for these sums of money—aid to such distinguished individuals was considered a confidential secret and the responsibility of his Reverence. In exchange Pericles Perdikaris, under no one's supervision, signed the inflated statements that were handed to him.

Aunt Katerina knew all about these things and in circumstances such as these she always remembered to demand her share in order to silence Pericles. Their daughter-in-law Antigone, Margarita's mother and also a widow, soon butted in. Uncle Stephanos, whose hand was paralyzed, always had the knack for further aggravating their squabbles, and his daughter Fotine, the old maid, again began sniveling about her relatives' utter heartlessness toward the two "girls," that is, her and Margarita. The only person who didn't become involved in these squabbles was Uncle Vasilis. By means that were completely secret and unexplainable, he managed, without a cent to his name, to be drunk all the time.

The raving and deception in which the entire family lived had found in Margarita the pretext it needed. The life and happiness of Margarita were the life and concern of all of them collectively and of each of them separately. In her name they found an ethical and logical base from which to criticize, insult, spit at, and curse one another all winter long.

With her arrival in the summer, war raged in the house—but silently now, underhandedly, behind her back, behind doors, so that "the child" would not hear, so that "the child" would not see, not suspect anything. Should she go out, they never let her go alone—one never knows what others might say to her—someone was always present to accompany her. Should she stir ever so slightly even within the house, disappear somewhere for a little while, do anything out of the ordinary, they all became alarmed and were thrown into a state of confusion. She often saw them break off a conversation, conceal something hastily, and alter their demeanor in her presence, quickly pasting a blissful smile on their lips for her benefit.

From the very first day after her return every summer, this prepared lie wrapped her, swaddled her, choked her. She never opened the door on any one of them, never went into the kitchen, never wandered about in the house, never asked for anything—and she, too, smiled at everyone. Most of the time she would shut herself in her room, place a chair next to the window and sit there, without crying and without reading. This wilted, girlish form at the window of the Perdikaris' dilapidated mansion became a familiar sight to the neighbors and passers-by every summer, all summer long.

Every day, evening arrived heavy and numb for all in the house, like the termination of a difficult and useless effort—one more day.

"Has she finally gone to bed?"

"Yes..."

They would calm down then, and before turning in they would go off to her room, one by one, to see her.

"Good night," Uncle Pericles would say protectively, half opening the door.

"Good night," she would likewise reply.

"Good night, dear Margarita," Uncle Vasilis would say, stammering slightly.

"Good night, uncle."

"And don't read at night...your eyes...as a rule you shouldn't read."

"As a rule I shouldn't read?"

"Only astronomy."

"Astronomy?"

"Good night, my darling, gentle little child blessed by God," would be heard two minutes later from Aunt Katerina, her body shaking all over.

"Good night, aunty."

"Good night" as well from Uncle Stephanos with the paralyzed hand, who always looked right into her eyes as if trying to detect whether they were concealing something.

Hurriedly, as if casually passing by, Fotine in like fashion would utter her "good night" dripping with honey.

Yet another "good night" to her after which she would wait. "Who's still missing?"

"Dear Margarita, good night to you," her mother, last of all, would say in a tone of sovereign forcefulness.

"Oh, good night," she would say again and count them. "Have they all stopped by?"

Then she would turn off the light and open her eyes in the dark.

"Good night now," she would say all alone, and a sad smile would etch itself on her lips.

Every night before going to sleep, she would count the days still left before she returned to school. Returning in the fall, she had grown accustomed to being all alone there as well, and sorrowful, her eyes wide-open, as if they were trying to find something, to explain something, and a flame burned inside them. The other girls knew that she was capable of self-restraint and silence, that she never became angry or obstinate, that she was never forgetful, neglectful, or procrastinating. Nor did Margarita ever play. Only occasionally at night in the dormitory, when the others started screaming and throwing pillows, she would shout to them with her hands folded behind her head: "Good night now."

This was Margarita's distraction, her sole distraction. And all the girls were amused by it and laughed when they heard it. The dormitory resounded with the same shouts until the proctor arrived, stood at the door, turned off the light, and also said to them no more than once: "Good night now…"

The others then quieted down, delighted with Margarita's pleasantry, while she remained with her hands folded behind her head.

When she completed her schooling and returned to live with the Perdikarises, then everything came out into the open, by itself and with the utmost rapidity. It was unnecessary for the others in the house either to speak about the real state of things or to provide her with explanations. Just as it was unnecessary for her either to ask questions or to be surprised. It was as if she had known everything from the beginning, always. And there was something else as well—it was as if things had to be this way and only this way.

The Perdikarises pounced on her small salary, the sole steady income in the household. She made no attempt to fend them off and let them have it all in the belief that doing so would be best both for them and for her. But this only became the cause of further confusion and turmoil. Once again their wheel of life turned around her, only this time inside-out. The hysterical love of old was now claiming, with the same hysteria, its reward.

Her mother, first, demanded straight-out that she not give anything to any of the others, that she hand her salary over to her on a regular basis to enable the two of them to support themselves and also to provide her with a dowry. Uncle Pericles protested to the Almighty himself against the selfishness of his daughter-in-law and claimed that, as head of the family, he should remain Margarita's real guardian. And, indeed, all the more so because he had received specific instructions in this matter from her father before he passed away. Thereupon Aunt Katerina, who had no claims on "the child," insisted—since her brother was that kind of person and was seeking to devour her salary, and since her daughter-in-law Antigone was such a viper—that instead of "the child" the two of them should pay her the equivalent value of the three gold rings she had sold to pay for Margarita's education. Cousin Fotine started crying night and day because of her relatives' lack of compassion and went to Margarita's room every evening where she would remain until she had succeeded in making her cry as well. Fotine's father, Uncle Stephanos with the paralyzed hand, was the only one who asked nothing of Margarita. He preferred to pilfer her pocketbook from time to time, invariably providing an incontestable alibi, with the result that all the others became implicated and the turmoil, which he always savored with delectation, increased. Lastly, Uncle Vasilis, the wise astronomer, settled his problems directly with Margarita. He explained to her paternally that he was neither self-serving nor at odds with the family, and that he had neither roots nor needs in this world. For he lived only in the realm of the spirit. All he needed was something for his daily raki, a mere trifle that she could give him in private without causing a fuss. In this way—and this was the dark secret of his life that he was revealing to her because he loved her so—he, poor devil, would escape the clutches of that bastard. By this he meant the gravedigger, with whom together at night he dug up and robbed corpses, but who in the end gave him nothing. The gravedigger kept him under his thumb by indulging him with this small amount of raki while cheating him out of the rest of the money.

What the other girls at school called home, Margarita at the age of seventeen saw collapsing altogether on top of her, along with whatever may have been bound to it—kinship, love, compassion. Amid the never-ending family rows, everything else was crumbling bit by bit. She learned about her father, with whose grandeur and wisdom her mother until now had nourished her daughter's soul. The pharmacist, Gregorios Perdikaris, had been the most loathsome pederast in a city that was not short of them—priests, bishops, storekeepers, and other upright and respectable citizens. In his final years he had sunk so deeply into his vice that they were forced to shut down his shop and keep him locked up in his house. It was rumored that Kanavos, Aunt

Katerina's eminent husband and the bearer of sovereigns, had killed a man in Vlahia. Perhaps he hadn't killed anyone, but this is what they went around shouting in the house. In his absence Aunt Katerina had defiled her body with a young Turk. Perhaps this hadn't happened either, but in moments of heightened tension the Perdikarises threw it in her face. Uncle Pericles still lugged home his share of Saint Antony's oil. Uncle Stephanos was syphilitic as a result of his passion—even while his wife was still alive—for the most disgusting whores. Other horrid and somewhat veiled accusations were made against Fotine. Uncle Vasilis, in all frankness, may have been the one human being among them, for he had a heart when he wasn't obsessed with astronomy, drinking, and hatred for the gravedigger.

The virtue of the Perdikarises was sinking into the greatest depravity. Margarita heard about the thefts in the Cathedral, in the churches, in the town hall, about the dishonesty that prevailed everywhere. Church, justice, government, public authorities, and palatial residences, everything was collapsing, her entire universe, the one she knew and of which she was the child.

At first she cried a great deal. Every day and every night. Both secretly at school sometimes and together with the others at home when they started crying after a row. And by herself at night. She foresaw that her life would never escape the fate of the Perdikarises—sickness, madness, deception. She further foresaw that she would not even be entitled to the unhappiness of ordinary people. She had to clench her lips, live like the others, and pretend that she accepted all those traditional class principles she saw being torn to shreds. Otherwise, a still worse sentence awaited her in this small provincial city should she deviate the slightest bit—ridicule. This is why, both in the city and at school, no one ever saw her do anything that might set her apart from the other members of the family.

Little by little, day after day, she elaborated an idea in her mind, fused it, organized it, all by herself, day after day, night after night, tear after tear. Everyone in life has one joy, one hope, one love, one illusion. She had nothing. Thus there was not a creature in this world more orphaned than she. She was unsalvageable as a person, insignificant as a woman, with a limited mind and a timid soul, without any talent and without a friend in the world, and swaddled in a thousand strings that she knew she never would, or could, cut in time. Hers was a destiny she could do nothing to change, to soften, to elude, to delude, to delude herself—nothing. All she could do was to stare it straight in the eye.

Absolute despair...to this realization she now attached her existence along with the justification for her existence. And she sucked in the poison of lofty pride at being able to look her life and destiny straight in the eye "with the now fearless pride of infinite orphanhood," as the poet said.

At that time, the great and terrible World War was raging all around her. There, too, people were hungry, they were cold, and they all had some close relative who had died—someone who died every day—to mourn. That there should be so much suffering in the world at first astonished Margarita. It seemed as if people were brought closer to her now by their own troubles, their pain, their fears. And she felt uneasy, as if they were coming to encroach upon the sacred ground of her solitary despair. She wasn't one of them; she didn't want them as her companions in despair. She set herself apart, in her own pain and destiny, from all the others, with their troubles that seemed temporary to her and that she considered unworthy, with their tears that were no more than cowardly tears. She would have liked to remain alone as before. Without fear and without hope, as before.

Yet the wave of misfortune and destruction was encircling her from every direction, reaching her daily. The children at school brought her its echo every day with their frightening news. There were many whose parents, siblings, or other relatives had already been baptized with fire—they died of starvation, were killed fighting, were killed by the Germans, were taken to concentration camps; others left, disappearing suddenly—and the children wouldn't say where. But they trusted her, told her everything—wanted to tell her everything.

"Yes, Margarita...my father said so." And tiny as she was, they didn't call her teacher but simply Margarita.

They told her their woes, how they had no bread at home, how they had no fire. They brought news of the Germans who were killing, who had killed anew both yesterday and the day before—and news of who had been killed and who had been captured by them. The children also talked about the villains, those in the black market who were getting rich on the hunger of the people; about the bigwigs and patricians in the city and how they too were on the side of the Germans. They were no longer sitting back with their hands crossed on the unshakable throne of their ancestral class, but had also gone out on the attack, some secretly, others with the hands of the Germans, still others openly. Every edition of the Bugle advocated killing them all off. Antigone agreed wholeheartedly, preferring the blond, well-nourished Germans to the puny prefects of the Greek state. As a result of the empty jargon of the mob who dared to speak out, our well-known Captain Liaratos had again turned fanatic, becoming chief of the Security Battalions in the city and parading up and down in front of the German command. The children knew everything, knew all the news about the guerrillas in the mountains, knew all the Resistance songs. And they, too, shared the hope of mankind for a better world once the war was over.

Margarita listened to them as they spoke and smiled, sadly at first. Afterward, little by little, if they were very frightened, she would say something to comfort them—she told them what they wanted to hear. If one of the children was unhappy, she took it and soothed it, she hugged it, and she listened to its little heart beating next to hers. If, on the other hand, they were happy and shouted and made fun of the Germans, she still had to be with them. And once, unable to do otherwise, she announced in the classroom that she also shared the same hope as all men regarding "this war which is finally coming to an end and the Germans are now being crushed everywhere and will be crushed forever and will leave from there as well and then…"

That day she returned home shaken. Inside the small room where she had come to know her own martyrdom, she crossed her hands and for the first time, she thought about the unhappiness of people in the four corners of the world—both then and in the past and always. And about hope, and how it blossoms and becomes man's will that life move forward. And whether she, too, didn't nurture some tiny hope within the great hope of mankind. Foolish thoughts. Yet they kept running through her mind…

The Perdikarises' backyard was adjacent to that of the Stournases. A humble breed of people, poor day-laborers, they had never been deserving of more than a "good morning" from them. The father, a cobbler, had been dead for years. The mother had accepted char work to raise the two orphans he left her, until she also died. Their daughter, Angelica, who was the same age as Margarita, had grown up with her. They attended elementary school together and were always together thereafter until Margarita went away. After that they were no longer allowed to see one another again.

The dry party-wall in the yard had crumbled and the Stournases' chickens were straying into the Perdikarises' yard. Angelica would leap over the barrier every so often, supposedly to gather them together. She wanted to see Margarita again. At the sight of her, Margarita would dash downstairs and, finding herself in the yard as well, run toward her with open arms.

"Margarita!" came a voice from above. Someone among them had been spying upon her again.

"Yes?" Her hands fell like wilted flowers and her eyes, full of tears, turned toward Angelica.

"Come upstairs for a moment, darling."

"Tomorrow, Angelica, agreed?"

"Tomorrow," Angelica replied and was also sad.

This happened every summer.

Upon returning one afternoon from school, Margarita went and stood in front of Angelica's door. Her heart was beating loudly and she hesitated several moments, undecided, before knocking. No one came to open the door. Bowing her head, she turned around and went home.

Night after night she had thought about it, about why she would go and why she would go now. She had worked out how she would explain the visit to her and had tried hard to conjecture how Angelica would behave toward her, how she would receive her, what she would say to her, what would happen after that. In her mind everything assumed the importance of a momentous event. It was not merely a first step toward others. It was this and something more, and everything taken together was something much more. Angelica's brother,

Nicholas Stournas, was one of the leading Communists in the city. During all these years, he had first been in exile, then in a concentration camp. Margarita knew this. And here she was now on her way to knock at their door.

But no one let her in, no one came to the door to let Margarita in. She returned on another evening, and again no one let her in. Wasn't Angelica inside, or had she seen her, but no longer wanted to have anything to do with her? Once again Margarita abandoned herself for a short while to her former despair. She allowed herself to sink into it again, to find again the serenity of nothingness. But she became alarmed at no longer being able to find it. The crumbling dry party-wall that separated her from that house, the door that didn't open to her, Angelica who didn't wish to have anything to do with her, Nicholas who was a Communist, and the people all around them who were wretched while harboring this great hope in their hearts—all tormented her day and night. From now on, it would be much worse for her. Alone, all alone again, and without her despair.

One evening, returning from school, she went up to her room, put down her bag, and sat down waiting for night to fall. The others in the house went to sleep; she went down to the yard. It was raining. She leaped—she finally leaped over the crumbling dry wall—and entered Angelica Stournas' yard. In the window a small light was shining, red as if blood-stained, sweet. As she stood in the rain and watched it, everything seemed like a dream. She tapped on the window with her finger.

"You came?" the other said and took her hands, as if she had been waiting for her all along.

Nothing else happened.

Little by little, night after night, along with their former girlhood friendship which was reawakening, they took heart together inside the small room with the red light. After Margarita was through teaching, she would walk a few extra steps every evening and first pay her a short visit. On these occasions they spoke anew about the news the children were bringing to school, about the war, about the fronts, about the great insurrection of the masses, about Russia. Nicholas was always at the center of these concerns, at the forefront of their thoughts. Angelica rejoiced in all these happenings with a satiated heart, Margarita with an insatiable thirst—sometimes until late into the night.

"You had better not go out through the front door," Angelica said. The police had their eye on her.

They went out into the yard together and Margarita again leapt over the crumbling stones. When, with the defeat of the Italians, Nicholas escaped, as did others, from exile and returned clandestinely to live in the city, Angelica let her into the secret—by the spring of 1944 she had nothing to hide from her.

"You know...I also told Nicholas..."

"Told him what?"

"About you, naturally."

"About me?"

"Yes, I told him..." she paused and looked at her with her honest, innocent eyes—"I told him...that you were one of us."

Margarita reached out and took her hands.

"Yes," she said hastily, as if she were tearing out her heart. Afterward she leaned her head on Angelica's large bosom and let her tears flow.

That night she slept in a never-ending dream of chases and escapes, in places that were unfamiliar, bleeding, calm, savage, beautiful, with people who wept, groaned, shouted, fell down and stood up and laughed and shouted for joy, millions of people all around her. The form of Nicholas came and went and came again among them. At some point, apparently, he stopped and looked at her.

"Is that you, Margarita?"

"Yes."

"One of us?"

"Did Angelica tell you?"

He took her by the hand and they disappeared into the dream, among the millions, hand in hand.

She had not seen him for years and remembered him as a little boy with a large, shaved head, barefooted and holding a big chunk of bread in his hands. When she awakened in the morning, she had a lingering impression that she was holding this head in her arms. Still half naked, she jumped up and without knowing why looked at herself in the mirror. Perhaps she wasn't all that ugly...Inside the spring day, the dream held her tightly, her body was jolted every so often, fear invaded her heart. Was it such a big thing, then, that she was "one of us"?

"And what did Nicholas say, Angelica?" she asked that evening.

"As a matter of fact, he did say something. And he also said something about you..."

It turned out that Nicholas would be leaving and Angelica would be going with him—to the mountains. So that was it, she would be going with him. And that other matter, "Do you want to come with us? Nicholas said you may if you like."

"No," she replied hastily, as if prepared with her answer. "I will remain here..."

She paused for a moment. There was a lump in her throat. She clenched her teeth and knitted her eyebrows. Her entire face became sad.

"No," she repeated. "I will remain here where nobody knows me. I can accomplish a great deal. Ask him to send me..." She refrained only from pronouncing his name. Angelica, drawing her into her arms, let her tears flow. Margarita didn't cry.

❧

Later, in the night, the two of them together lugged the small duplicator to the cellar. One evening before they left, Angelica called Margarita to their yard. The man with the large head was standing next to her. Margarita felt her hand trembling in the large, warm hand that was squeezing it hard. He saw her eyes, two big eyes which were shining in the dark.

"So then, it's good-bye, Margarita..." She said nothing.

"When we return..."

His words seemed poor to her, not worthy of the occasion. "I don't need anything else..."

He let go of her hand, then placed both of his on her shoulders. It bothered her that he was taller than she. She stretched her entire body, reached up with her hands, which weren't trembling at all, and caressed his head. Holding her like this by the shoulders, he pulled her toward him and kissed her. Angelica, slightly off to the side, looked on and wept.

"Good-bye, comrade Margarita."

"Good-bye, Nicholas, my Nicholas. Good-bye, Angelica."

Later, a child no taller than a dwarf stands behind the crumbling dry wall at night and hands her a stencil. Along with the six phantoms that roam through the Perdikarises' two-story house during the day, another phantom now stirs in the night. The small duplicator operates silently, with only the whish of the organdy each time. It is enough for Margarita to hear again in her heart the same voice: "Goodbye, Margarita, comrade Margarita." She prepares neatly and nicely the package that the errand boy will come to fetch tomorrow evening— there at the dry party-wall. A child who smiles and winks at her.

"Okay Margarita."

"Tomorrow night."

"At seven?"

"No, come at seven-thirty."

"I won't be coming, the old man will come instead. At the corner of the school…"

During this time, cousin Fotine died of a heart attack in the throes of a hysterical fit. Uncle Stephanos, struck with apoplexy, also became bedridden. It was a time when the whole world was changing with Russia's victories on all fronts and the end of the war approaching. The family was beset by its own new complications: Fotine's inheritance and concern about Stephanos. Quarrels again came to a head. Although Fotine's inheritance amounted to next to nothing, and concern about Stephanos was equally insignificant, very little was needed to heat things up. After a great deal of haggling, it was finally deemed proper that Margarita should become Fotine's heir and that her mother should look after Stephanos. Margarita had no objection to any of this, none whatsoever, as she said. Just when it seemed that they were about to calm down, a new incident brought about the greatest upheaval. Aunt Katerina discovered that two pillows, a linen tablecloth and a porcelain vase were missing from Fotine's chest. She demanded, in the name of "the child" and with dreadful curses, that the stolen items be returned. All of them denied the accusation. Uncle Stephanos, being bedridden, remained beyond suspicion. From all the others, curses and insults crisscrossed, accompanied by the most dreadful oaths. Since nothing came of it, however, it seemed that eventually this matter was also being laid to rest.

The bedridden Stephanos, nevertheless, confessed privately to Katerina that the precious articles were stolen by someone in the house and that they were stolen after Fotine's death. He was absolutely certain of this; she had shown them to him herself shortly before her death. From his viewpoint, to be honest with her, he greatly feared for Vasilis.

Thereupon Aunt Katerina brought up the matter with Vasilis. "Why would I steal the pillows?" said the unruffled astronomer. "I only need a little raki and Margarita keeps me supplied."

"Keeps you supplied?"

"But of course," he said proudly. "She's a good girl."

"Fiddlesticks...Where does she find money to keep you supplied?"

"How should I know where she finds it? In any event she does."

Aunt Katerina then started searching throughout the house by herself and without the knowledge of the others. First she searched in Antigone's room. Not a thing. Then in Pericles' room. Not a thing there either. She again searched in Fotine's chest in case she had overlooked them. They weren't there. Twice more in Vasilis' room. They weren't there either.

"They're in this house, they are, they are...I know what I'm saying," Stephanos shouted.

She remembered the opening in the ceiling through which the carpenters climbed onto the roof and she took the ladder and climbed up to the partition between the ceiling and the roof, tearing her hands and nearly killing herself in the process. There was nothing there either. The sole result was that she had to keep her hands hidden so that no one would see them. And every day after that, from morning until night, she would sneak into the rooms of the others, looking under their beds and mattresses, under the stairs, under the piles of blankets and clothes—in every nook and cranny of the house.

When she discovered the small duplicator inside the chest down in the cellar, she was taken by surprise. She had never before seen anything like it and had no idea what it was. She was only certain that it didn't belong to the house. Whose was it? And these tubes? She unscrewed one, getting ink on her hands—what a strange object. She opened the packages—plain paper. A sheet of waxed paper impressed her the most—it was still intact. Margarita had received it the day before and intended to use it that same night.

The cellar was dimly lit. Katerina took the waxed paper, covered the other objects carefully, the way they were, and went upstairs. She locked her door, put on her glasses and set to work reading the letters. One or two lines sufficed—they mentioned the Allies, lashed out against the Germans. She stopped reading and did her utmost to understand, but understood nothing.

Suddenly it dawned on her.

"How should I know where she finds it? In any event she does."

"She does?"

She tucked the paper in her bosom, ran to find Pericles, took him and led him to her room.

"So that's the story with the sovereigns?"

"What sovereigns are you still harping on," he said tired of her questions. "Is that why you brought me here?"

"Stop pretending, Pericles. The sovereigns, I tell you..."

"Katerina, have you lost your mind? Just what sovereigns are you hanging on me?"

"You know very well, the English sovereigns."

He shook his head and stood up to leave, but she grabbed him by the arm.

"Pericles, I'm telling you that I know what's been going on. I saw with my own eyes."

He shook his hand free wanting to leave, believing the poor woman was out of her mind. But she took the waxed paper from her bosom and placed it before his eyes.

"What about this? Aren't these English sovereigns? You hide them from me and spend them by yourselves. Vasilis told me...you learn things from drunks."

Pericles took the waxed paper in his hands, secured his glasses and also started to read—he raised his eyes and looked at her again.

"Good heavens, what is this, Katerna?"

"Now go ahead and tell me that it's not your doing."

"I can't make any sense of it," he said looking at her and attempting to read further down at the same time. Katerina was taken aback by his manner.

"You really don't know?"

"No, I tell you. Where did you find this?"

"Come along."

She took him and they descended to the cellar. He stared in amazement, after which he raised his eyes and looked at her carefully.

"No, no, Katerina, these aren't sovereigns."

"Then what are they?"

"Bad business, very bad business...I don't understand." He took her hand. "Don't breathe a word to anyone."

"What are you going to do?"

"Just don't breathe a word."

He was so alarmed that she also became frightened.

"All right, I won't."

He took the waxed paper, folded it, and headed straight for the Archbishop's office where he requested through the deacon who was standing outside an entirely private audience. He went in, sat down, glanced at the door, and handed the paper to his Reverence. The latter read the first few lines, stopped, raised his eyes, and looked at him.

"Why yes," he said with indifference. "It belongs to the Communists, those they put out. Where did you find it?"

"To the Communists, Reverend Father, precisely."

"What of it? There are things like this circulating every day."

"Every day?"

"What's wrong with you, Pericles? What's this got to do with you?"

"Do you know where they're printed, Reverend Father?"

"Nobody knows who they are, nor their whereabouts."

"So, Reverend Father...yes, every day. Well I happen to know where they're printed."

The Archbishop lowered his eyebrows and looked at him carefully.

"That would be of the utmost interest. How can you possibly know?"

"Reverend Father, Reverend Father, these papers are printed in my house."

The holy father was unable to refrain from laughing.

"He's raving, Pericles Perdikaris has lost his mind."

Unfortunately not...he hadn't lost his mind in the least, and he related everything to him—about the pillows, about Stephanos, about Vasilis' brandy, about Katerina, about Margarita. And the longer he spoke, the more sullen the face of his Eminence became. At the end he said to him, "Leave this paper with me and don't worry. Only don't breathe a word to anyone."

Pericles left feeling relieved. His Eminence, however, was deeply worried. This affair could cost him dearly. The Perdikarises were close acquaintances of his—go try and explain that to the Germans. That very same midday he summoned the police commissioner to his office on an urgent national matter. He wished, as he said to him, to entrust it to him personally. In his opinion there mustn't be any trouble. Margarita would readily give him the names of the Communists and they wouldn't even have to disclose their source. The whole thing should be made to look like a triumph on the part of the police who had exposed the ring.

The police commissioner, in complete agreement and promising to act with secrecy and caution, kissed the venerable hand. Upon finding himself alone, however, he thought the matter over more carefully and chose to settle the whole business by himself directly with the Germans once the girl had revealed the names to him—just imagine though, my friend, where they went and hid the duplicator.

In the evening, Margarita did not return home. Pericles and Katerina divulged their secret to the others as well and they all began insulting one another again regarding their own concerns, the same old ones, all over again, and no one stopped to think that they might have delivered their "child" to death.

In the morning it was learned that Margarita had been taken from the Greek police station to the Gestapo. That same evening it was learned throughout the city that she was being tortured and refused to say anything. The line of interrogation began and ended with her. His Eminence had compromised himself in the eyes of the Germans and the police commissioner was angry with himself over his blunder. Why had he been so trusting and eager to arrest her—such a venomous monster?

Then even the Perdikarises understood—they had betrayed her to the Germans. It was the final act of their lives, to kill their own child. Very soon thereafter Uncle Stephanos was the first to die. The pillows and tablecloth were discovered under his mattress. The vase had been hidden by him inside his mattress where it had broken to pieces. Later, within a short period of time, the others also died— Katerina, Antigone, Pericles. Last of all, Uncle Vasilis, after having harrowed for some time, a derelict now, in the city's taverns, getting drunk, insulting the gravedigger, the Germans, the Archbishop, and weeping for his Margarita.

For her, everything ended very rapidly—tortures, interrogations, trial. She had, it is said, a smile on her lips during all this time, a light in her eyes that made them appear even bigger—even more beautiful. Your eyes were beautiful, Margarita!

At the final moment, in front of the firing squad, she turned her eyes toward the city, which was still covered in mist. A world of madmen, hysterical persons, degenerates, and bandits was crumbling, together with their dilapidated houses—the entire regime of decadence that had given birth to her. The family's sad smile rose to her lips and with her hand she made that ambiguous gesture described by the priest, as if she were dispelling the image.

"Good night now!"

"Fire!"

Behind the tall peaks of the Pindos mountains the sun is rising. Soon day will break. Nicholas and Angelica, the new world! The final thought returns to you as long as there remains a final spasm of life inside the open skull: "Build that better world!"

George Kitsopoulos

(1919–1996)

Comparisons

Miss Euterpe was a very carefree person. Not only now while she was vacationing by the sea, but also in the city where she worked, everyone had something to say about her cheerful laugh. She, in turn, selecting the most unusual comment about this laugh from among all those she had either heard or been told of, would remember it at an appropriate moment. The present situation provided her with just such an occasion. Feeling the need to respond to the commonplace compliment of the gentleman who often accompanied her on her evening walk, she allowed, as the occasion of every recollection requires, a moment of silence to pass before saying, "You know, Costas, someone once used to say to me that I possess the rarest jewelry in that my laugh always matches the dress I'm wearing. Don't you find that somewhat excessive?"

Costas, however, who for some time now had forbidden himself to find anything that concerned women excessive, made no objection. Instead, he took her by the arm. Just as the road leading to the promontory was about to end, he suggested that they sit down behind the rocks along the dark seashore. There, the August night offered Euterpe another opportunity for remembrance. She had once read somewhere with regard to shooting stars that they crack the vitreous stillness of the sky like diamond stones. Yet it didn't seem right to her to involve the writer in a moment such as this and she passed the observation off as her own. Costas, despite having read in the newspaper that shooting stars are insignificant pieces of dust from the universe, again evaded discussion.

"Costas," she asked him suddenly, "is it true that my eyes resemble…"

He threw away his cigarette and gently pulled her toward him.

"Your eyes don't resemble anything since they're your eyes," he replied and he kissed her.

First the hours, then the days passed swiftly thanks to their companionship. In the morning they swam behind the promontory facing the sea and then sat on the small sandy beaches between the rocks, Euterpe reading *Rebecca* and Costas hunting crabs. As she observed him thus, tanned and lying in wait with his harpoon in the cracks of the rocks, it crossed her mind that he resembled something. She never arrived at a comparison, however, because she knew that he didn't want to resemble anything. Nevertheless, this seemed to her slightly stupid on his part. How could she tell him that she liked him without finding some manner in which to do so?

In the afternoon, when they took the boat far from shore toward the spot where the sun was setting, and as she watched the waves changing color, like old taffeta ribbons, in each of their movements, she attempted to persuade him to look at beauty in her manner. He, however, observing her expression—you might have thought he was avoiding some danger—anticipated her.

"The setting sun is beautiful," he said to her with such seriousness that she felt the urge to shout that platitudes don't require pomposity.

It seemed, so she rationalized, that this peculiarity of his was the result of the way he had been brought up. He had told her, moreover, that he was an employee for a company that built roads and that he had to work very hard so that people might enjoy the convenience of driving with greater ease. Yet all this was said in an informative tone that resembled a newspaper ad announcing a competition for the lowest bidder. In other respects he was very kind and so strong that he would pick her up like a feather and, holding her, jump out of their boat onto the seashore.

Since he had never asked her if she loved him, she too avoided asking herself the question. Even so, she had observed that she didn't laugh as often as before, that there were moments when she realized her heart was constricting inexplicably and she felt very unhappy. Finally, one day, she burst into tears.

She hadn't cried since she was a student in grammar school, the time when she was told that she would no longer hear any more fairy tales because her grandmother had gone on a long journey to heaven. Strangely enough, her present tears were also provoked by a trip.

Costas had to be away on business in the city for several days. But this wasn't what distressed her. Quite the contrary. Although she looked sad when he said goodbye to her, deep down a brief period of solitude didn't seem like a bad idea to her. Besides, he had promised to write and as she waited she kept hoping that, on paper at least, he wouldn't be able to resist the temptation of a comparison.

Thus she was powerless to conceal her joy before reading his letter, just as she was powerless to conceal her tears after having read it. It was abominable, as unable to be swallowed as the lump in her throat from the sobs that were choking her. Even if he had written to her that she would never see him again, he would have hurt her less than with these two closely written pages of his that, from beginning to end, dryly described a streetcar.

What did she care if this streetcar had defective breaks and whenever it stopped its passengers fell on top of one another? What did she care if the conductor didn't have change for a twenty-drachma piece? What did she care if the smoke from the pipe of the man opposite him smelled horrible? It was he who was more horrible than anyone, he who had found the patience to devote himself to such meaningless matters and to close by signing as hers.

After Euterpe stopped crying without, as in the instance of her grandmother, being able to explain her tears, she wet two handkerchiefs and placed them over her eyes as compresses. But that afternoon, as she attempted to read *Romeo and Juliet*, she was unable to concentrate. A broken streetcar seemed to be passing above the railing of the Capulets' balcony.

Nevertheless, as often happens in stories that repeat themselves, a small and perhaps even disgusting detail from the preceding story suddenly acquires significance in the one that follows. Returning to the seaside, Miss Euterpe, less carefree after her rejection of a marriage proposal and a year older than last year, discovered her ideal.

She had thought it in keeping with her sentimental nature to go to the promontory on the same night as her arrival, to see again the small sandy beaches that formed inside the rocks. And she had taken her shawl, as the occasion required, because it would be chilly. She reached the end of the road as the sun was setting and she ran down the hillside. Only, when she stopped to look sorrowfully at her lost moments of love, she noticed a change that reminded her of something and made her laugh.

Someone was now living in last year's wilderness. They had erected a double tent out of faded green canvas and reeds that, because of the wheels and big windows they had painted on its outside, resembled the carriage of a streetcar. At first, influenced by the American films she had seen during the winter, her imagination made her hope for something improbable. But the man who eventually came out to see who was laughing was a complete stranger to her.

"Do you think my nest resembles a streetcar?" he asked her.

Surely, to be speaking of a nest, he must have intuited something, for being white, tall, and thin, he resembled a stork.

She did not say so then, but later. One evening when they had lit a fire to boil crabs, she mentioned the initial impression he had made on her.

"You weren't wrong," he laughed. "And stork that I was, I was amazed to see you in front of me like a baby that fortune had brought me."

"Don't these crabs resemble frogs that will be eaten by the stork?" she asked.

"You are undervaluing your worth with storks," he replied pensively. "For your beauty pheasants would willingly slaughter themselves for you to feast on them."

That same evening Euterpe, upon returning, ran to look at herself in the mirror. She wanted to see if she was all that beautiful. Although she knew that storks were slightly timid, she was troubled, for a month had passed and her new companion had not yet kissed her.

"August went by slowly this year and if you hadn't been here, it would have seemed endless," he told her as he noticed her looking at the first clouds.

"Yes," she replied.

"Naturally you're thinking that soon the storks will be forced to leave without…"

"Without saying what they're supposed to say?"

And yet the two of them had said so much, enough to fill many empty days. It appeared, however, that words had impeded their actions.

"You're a strange man," she ventured unexpectedly. "Why didn't you kiss me all summer long? Don't you like me?"

He turned and looked at her and for the first time something distant and dry appeared in his eyes, like a vitreous sky without falling stars.

"Fall is a very unwieldy season," he said afterward. "It resembles a ship that has been delayed and is hurrying to reach its destination before winter."

"Someone once used to say to me that a thing loses its value if one compares it with something else."

"That someone was right," he said, looking at her again.

And his eyes had now filled with a gray, impenetrable cloudiness.

"Serenity comes and looks at me sorrowfully like a girl abandoned in a dance hall. She extends her hands to me like the trees in the wind that takes away the birds in the autumn. She speaks to me and her words roll in my eyes like the inscrutable rain that dwells invisibly in the secrets of every season…"

Euterpe stopped reading his letter and looked at her watch. Outside, the first autumnal rain had begun to fall slowly and hesitantly. Nevertheless, to hear the raindrops resounding on the pavement, you would have to wait until after midnight when traffic from the automobiles and streetcars abates.

He was a good person, but unduly romantic, she reflected. And she would have lost herself in her daydreams if her small nephew, seated next to her in the bus that was taking them to the movies, had not been pulling at her dress to show her something.

"Aunt Euterpe, is that tree asking God for alms and does it look like a beggar?"

"That tree does not resemble a beggar," she replied. "It is a tree that has been pruned so that it will be greener when summer returns."

"You grownups don't understand," the young boy insisted loudly.

Two gentlemen seated up front laughed. She also laughed. And the laughter passed through her heart like a calm recollection from the dead summer.

GALATIA SARANTI

(1920–)

The Hand

The first time she saw it, it was stretched out, as if reclining. Abandoned, evidently, in a beautiful position. A white hand, slightly plump, without rings, and with clean, groomed nails.

It passed very slowly in front of the window all by itself, visible up to the wrist, then came and stood directly opposite her for a little while. Just long enough for the details—its whiteness, its stillness, its beauty—to impress themselves on her. Then it disappeared.

She started and rubbed her eyes. "I fell asleep," she said, laughing half-heartedly. "I fell asleep without realizing it." Her hands felt numb and her feet heavy. It was her arthritis. She stood up wearily. "You must walk," the doctor had said. "If you're in pain, you must walk." She went as far as her kitchen, therefore, without a reason and straightened something. Everything in there was very orderly, but she had to justify to herself in some way the doctor's order. So she straightened something and afterward returned and sat down again near the window.

There was bright sunlight and she was gladdened by it. The street was quiet. The school at the corner was barely audible. The pupils were in class. Later, during recess, all that would change.

As the bell rang, the children would come pouring out, the yard become inundated, the road overflowed. Boys, little boys, yelling, coarse, fierce, who kicked even the air, whistled, shoved one another. Fear seized you while watching them. They possessed impudence in their eyes and meanness in their voices. Once, a few of them had stood outside her window, gaping at her, laughing scornfully, and speaking drivel. She had pretended not to notice them, not to see, not to hear. She had been hurt, however. Without reason, of course. Still, she had been hurt. It was a grievance that arose long ago and welled up, welled up inside her as their bursts of laughter grew louder. How can such young children be so cruel? How can they chase squirrels with sling shots, tie tin cans to the tails of abandoned cats, make fun of unmarried old ladies? They can, though!

From then on, whenever she heard the bell, she even drew the curtains. She would go and sit in the back room and look at the flower pots in the yard. Some anemic asparagus, some uncared-for geraniums, and the cats—all the neighborhood cats that had claimed this small yard as their kingdom. The boys in front, the cats behind. The cats were preferable.

This was in the morning. In the afternoon her friend came. They knew each other from way back, since they were children, and were the same age. At one time in their lives each had experienced an unhappy love; each had had a sickly mother who died when she was extremely old; both had been employees in a company for years and were now retired. There was no marked difference between them. Only that she herself, everyone acknowledged it, had once been beautiful. Very beautiful. She even had pictures to prove it. Indisputable evidence. Her friend, however, poor thing, had never been beautiful and was secretly jealous. Now, of course, they were practically identical and her friend had no reason to be jealous. Nevertheless, even today she would subtly change the subject whenever they talked about the pictures—the evidence—or about old dresses and styles. Her friend liked to talk only of the present. Why, just yesterday evening she had said to her, "Do you remember a green jacket with a fringe all around that I used to have? Everyone told me how becoming it was on me. It matched my hair, blonde the way it was!"

Her friend, however, was unresponsive, not even saying whether or not she remembered it. She spoke instead about one of her own jackets, "I'm going to unravel my brown jacket and reknit it and you'll see that there will be enough wool left over for me to make night slippers!"

The jacket her friend intended to unravel was quite ordinary. In no way comparable to hers with the fringe all around! But she could not say so to her friend and hurt her feelings. The poor thing, she thought, is jealous of me! Yet she always behaved charitably and compassionately toward her. She forgave her. The poor dear had been so unattractive in her youth. Her hair had not been blonde, nor her skin soft. All the same, her friend was the only person she had left. Her legs were strong and she came regularly. Nearly every afternoon.

She told her friend about it that same evening.

"I had a dream. A white hand, all white, cut off…A beautiful hand. Strange dream, eh? I suddenly fell asleep right in the middle of the day…"

The other tried to understand. Anyhow, she liked to interpret dreams.

"A hand? Was it a man's or a woman's?"

"I don't know! It was a beautiful hand!"

"You're going to receive a letter!"

"A letter, from where?

"How should I know? A hand means news. That's what it means in dreams!"

She was listening attentively to her friend when suddenly, for the first time, she began to doubt if what she had seen had been a dream. Perhaps I wasn't asleep, she thought to herself. And she became frightened.

"Perhaps I wasn't asleep," she said softly. "I was at the window and saw it pass through the pane. It was strange!"

"If you weren't sound asleep, I can't interpret it for you. One can interpret what one sees in one's sleep. Everything else is imagination and can't be interpreted!"

That night, doubt became certainty. I wasn't asleep, she kept thinking to herself. Nor had I fallen asleep without realizing it. I was wide awake when I saw the hand!

She accepted it, as she said it, as something natural. Nor was she frightened. In fact, since she had insomnia, she began to think of the hands that had passed through her life. Perhaps one of those resembled the one she had seen, perhaps it was a distant memory of...Her father's hand was so faint in her memory that it failed to emerge even as a vague form. Her mother's hand, however, that she was holding onto was merely lifeless. Wrinkled, old, and lifeless. How truly sad all this that was happening to her really was. To have lived side by side for so many years and to be unable to remember it, the way it used to caress her, the way it used to scold her when she was a child...Fresh and plump...However hard she tried, it appeared before her only as lifeless—yellow, cold, lifeless. What she had seen, however, was a living hand, a warm, beautiful hand!

Next she thought of his hand, and her mind traveled far..."Miss, you know what my feelings are toward you. I'm asking you for permission to speak to your mother..." She had bowed her head, she was blushing. Oh, she had adored him for some time already. Her hands had turned cold and he was holding them tightly in his own. What were his hands like? They were a warmth without shape and color. A warmth and a fever at the same time.

What she saw may have been beautiful and well maintained, but it was also indifferent. She could vouch for that without hesitation. It was a calm, indifferent hand. It was not his!

He came to see her mother, he even brought flowers. Everything then was very tender and warm. It was spring of 1887...She was wearing a new dress made of batiste with a flowered pattern, and she had put on a bustle for the first time. She felt somewhat strange, somewhat silly. She had done her hair up, as was suitable for a young lady about to become engaged! Afterward the mobilization came...A train loaded with soldiers, pandemonium, heat...She had gone to the station secretly.

Her mother and her aunt had said to her, "It's not proper. You will say goodbye to your fiancé here!" This was certainly the appropriate thing to do and this is what took place. His hands were trembling slightly, she would never forget that, never, never...Then the train whistled. Handkerchiefs, caps, parasols waved...He shouted to her, "I'll return...I'll write to you!"

Neither did he return, nor did he write. He perished at the outset, having barely arrived at the front. What remained of him? A ring, a picture, two dried flowers, and his hands on the window of the train..."I'll return...Goodbye, till we meet again."

No, the hand she had seen wasn't his! The one she had seen wasn't waving goodbye. It was indifferent, still, and reclining. It wasn't his...

Afterward she forgot about it. Many days went by and she no longer thought about it. The sunshine returned just when no one was expecting it. The humidity disappeared, her arthritic pain abated. She and her friend began to go out on walks. They visited the park, sat on the benches, idly watched the babies in the carriages and the infants playing. The sunshine lasted like a miracle in the heart of winter. The two of them talked incessantly about the weather and further confided in each other. They took a bus, went even as far as Ekali. Always just the two of them. They ambled through the streets and took pride in and enjoyed—as though they belonged to them—the gardens bursting with green vegetation and pyracanths. They talked incessantly about the sun, its warmth, how good it felt! They resembled happy schoolgirls! It was not at all humid, not in the least, and there was lots of sun! Not a harsh sun as in summer! A compassionate sun, a tender sun. And flowers. What more could one ask for?

They ate in a small tavern and enjoyed themselves, drinking beer as well. "We'll come again," they said happily. The waiter sat down next to them and struck up a conversation. He told them his troubles. Many troubles. Could they all be true? They tipped him a ten-drachma coin and he was content. "We'll come back," they said to him.

But the weather suddenly became oppressive and they didn't go back. Remembering the waiter, however, with his troubles, the beer, and the beautiful gardens, they said, "In the spring when the warm weather returns, we'll go back."

Now it was raining, it was raining night and day, the way it's supposed to rain in the heart of winter.

On one of these dull days, the hand returned. It was something unbelievable. She bent over to pick up a fork she had dropped and saw it, as she remembered it, down on the floor. "The hand!" she said almost aloud, but without fear. "There's the hand again!"

As she picked up the fork, the hand also rose and stood next to the bread. "Now what shall I do?" she thought to herself. "I'll pretend I don't see it!"

She ate pensively, the hand present all the while, then cleared the table very slowly. Only she didn't gather up the crumbs, for she would have had to touch the hand and didn't want to. Yet she was neither upset, nor frightened. She slept peacefully, and when she opened her eyes the hand was still on her bedside table. Seeing it, she smiled.

In the evening she told her friend about it. "You know, the hand came back!"

"What hand?" the other replied.

"The one I told you about. It wasn't a dream. Look! Even now while I'm talking to you, it's up there on the table."

Her friend looked at her with alarm. Afterward she looked at the table.

"You're not in your right mind! I don't see anything."

"And yet it's there! When I go to bed, it comes too…There."

Her friend interrupted her abruptly, "Go to the doctor's. Do you hear me? Tell the doctor about it without fail…"

"Why should I tell the doctor about it? What harm is there in a hand? On the contrary, it keeps me company…"

Of course, that's what it is, company. Especially now that the weather had become oppressive and she was forced to keep the light on all day long, and the children no longer came out at recess, and the cats had sought shelter elsewhere. She began to look for it. When she opened her eyes, the first thing that came to her mind was the hand. What if it doesn't come today, she would think with anxiety. Seeing it, she would smile. Now and then, she spoke to it. About various things. Mostly about old times. It remained there, always like that, still and calm. Why be afraid of a hand…

One day her friend asked her with concern, "Did you tell the doctor about the hand?"

"No, why should I?" she replied, vexed.

"Why? So that he may give you something to calm you. At one time I used to see a fly, but it was caused by my eyes. Do you understand? Maybe your blood pressure has gone up."

"Nonsense! What harm is there in a hand? It's company for me."

She became angry. She became very angry. And when her friend left, she didn't ask her as usual, "Will you come tomorrow?" She had always been jealous. Jealous and ugly! And now she was jealous of the hand because she had nothing. She was ugly and her fiancé had not been killed in the war. He was married, he was living in Volos and he made fun of her. Yes, the more she thought about it, the angrier she became. Her cheeks were burning, her temples were throbbing. You're jealous, she was saying excitedly, I never again want to see you!

The hand was there, next to the Prayer Book. She looked at it with affection, and felt the need to caress it just once. She wanted to cry, to hold it tightly in her hands, and to tell it how lonely, how unbelievably alone, she was. The hand, you might have thought it was alive and had understood, moved and gradually came next to her. It touched her forehead, her cheeks, her neck. A lingering caress, all affection, all love, all eroticism. She held her breath from happiness. It was as though Easter bells, the bells of the Resurrection, had begun to ring. The room became filled with red burning pyracanths, and the burning sun inundated the room. A harsh August sun...

The grocer's boy found her the next day. He rang the bell and when no one opened the door to let him in, he placed his hand inside the small windowpane and pulled the latch. She was seated with her head slightly tilted back, smiling happily, and didn't seem to him like an old lady!

George Ioannou

(1927–1985)

The Teacher

She was returning in the night, worn out from night school, her bag with the copy-books in the right hand, a nylon shopping bag in the left, lonely and dejected, eager to enter her apartment, to turn on the switch, to diffuse light around her and within her, to turn the key from the inside and attach the chain, to listen for a little while to *Deutsche Welle*—as much as she managed to catch—and then to sit down at her small table and look at the agenda on the wall, her list of projects, that is, from Christmas to Easter, as written down by her, first, second, third, fourth, somehow to get her bearings and begin work on one of the programmed items. Nothing tonight either, never mind. Not even tonight…

As she approached, she discerned someone in a military cap waiting near her door and at first she was alarmed because in those days a military cap waiting outside your door was not a sign of something good; then she somehow regained her courage, somehow became excited at the thought that it might be a student of hers from among the policemen, from among those who looked her straight in the eye with such innocence, and that perhaps he had come to ask her something personal, something he didn't want the others to see or suspect. The upholders of the law are mysterious, being themselves oppressed and underground, boys full of sap that old fogies with the soul of a weasel or of a fox-skin torment and eventually subjugate.

But as she continued to approach, she reflected that this nevertheless was something, that it might result in something pleasant, if only a conversation, looking into eyes that sparkle, implore tacitly, delight in looking, and afterward jolting, warm handshakes, all promise and without expectation, of course, because she had sworn never to caress her students, she held her dignity and her position above all else, unless of course they had finished school and were coming now to confide in her, to speak to her in a manly fashion and with straightforwardness, and she, as if entirely prepared, as if she had her answers ready under an exceptionally fine skin however much she had been separating them to an absolute degree for some time now, or for that matter as of always, speaking to them forcefully, yet from a certain distance, and saying to them that yes, she had understood everything and that she herself had provoked it up to a certain point, because she enjoyed looking into their eyes as, moreover, into those of another and another and yet another, there are always three or four in every section, she had observed this in particular yet had never taken advantage of it, leaving it unfulfilled intentionally, not only because the young are superficial, but also because under such conditions the transference of the lesson is always conducted more advantageously as they exchange looks and become utterly artless and trusting with one another.

The young man at her door was smiling at her, this was evident, his white teeth were shining in the half light, the lines of his strong face were playing about, but he neither stirred nor spoke, awaiting her approach with certitude, certain of the pleasure his being exhaled on her and she, turning her head like a revolver, I mean like the roulette of a revolver, was totally incapable of hitting him, such lines, stature, smile—dear God, why do you torture me. This is what she was thinking.

When she was practically next to him, ah! then she remembered, he was her student, really her student, only a former one, from another period when she still nurtured dreams, and now he had come to find her since he also had been brought from the capital to train in the Military Academy before being assigned to some village to provoke the married women with the wriggling of his body inside its uniform and keep close watch on their husbands, to gain access to secrets in advance, to come upon one unexpected revelation after another.

Yes, she remembered him very well, having actually caressed him with her eyes, even though he was very young, quiet, and with a downcast head and wouldn't answer her when she questioned him at recess or on class outings; he merely sat apart and played rather sad tunes about loneliness on his harmonica, such a young boy, she would look at him, continually imprinting him on her flesh, because she actually had never before seen and would never again see, her experience bears witness to this, a boy so handsome and erotic in his very first puberty, and perhaps only Antinous, the rustic youth whom the emperor Hadrian adored and whose death tore him to pieces, perhaps that Antinous was as handsome, to have been carried off from Bithynia by Hadrian, who was roaming up and down the country, more in quest than anything else.

And now it was being disclosed that he too had noticed her glances, had been affected, had acknowledged them in any event, inasmuch as he was coming, now that he had matured, to become entangled with her, if she also so desired, and obviously she did, why else was she looking at him covetously, why else was she making so much of him, like no other woman, this also explains why that old tenderness remained in him, that undeclared, mute adoration that perhaps outstripped, outstripped all the others he felt rubbing against him, and that remained uneffaced in his soul. Then came the handshake, welcoming, and the light kiss that allowed her to catch the scent of his clothes, especially his uniform, and this probably is also how it occurred for him, inside her, however, the engulfing began again, that dark mystery of the odor of erotic bodies clad in khaki, doubtlessly not freshly washed, but surely not unwashed either, not terribly sullied, not loaded with common dirt, but slightly anointed with the erotic grease that the handsome body pours out, the one that encloses the well of perfection.

She turned the key as he stood behind her, they sat down and the light spread over them, illuminating for the first time not these two in particular but simply any two, since none other had penetrated her home, here for such a long time, having left her people, self-exiled for this and this alone, which she felt that they back there pruned with their love, their protection, their wakeful vigilance. And if only for something like this, she thought, for such a visit, for the unexpected in the night outside your door, a door entirely yours, it's worth living alone, exiling yourself, living forever outside family paradise. Suddenly she remembered her family and looked at the telephone through which they could intrude in a second to request of her a little tenderness once again, to hear that voice with its nuance of old love, even though she might be uttering apathetic, entirely commonplace words about this and that, about money, checks, clothes, and food, and certain presumably coded words about the unbearable political situation. All of a sudden the black telephone terrified her. Supposing they call me now, what will I say and, even more important, how will I say it? In the presence of another person how will I be able to produce those intimate, imperceptible tones from mouth to ear and inversely, how will I be able to when I realize that I'm also talking for the benefit of someone else who, even if involuntarily, is listening, is somehow participating, as I also am participating in this transmission, and without wanting to I become less responsive, less relaxed, and so anxious for it to end that I keep hurrying? How will they not detect that something has changed, that I'm not alone, that something's coming between us, and not be hurt? She thought and was temporarily transported to other worlds, but he understood instinctively.

All of a sudden the time went by, the infamous clepsydra dried up without their realizing it, they looked at their watches, which were accurate, neither slow nor fast, they alone were blazing backward and forward, each of them saying separately, "Dear God, let us remain like this, talking until morning." Sleep is something superfluous that takes away joy, images of beauty, touch, and play. She had once consoled herself this way when, from an overabundance of life and self-concentration, she was unable to sleep and was running to doctors, disgusting psychiatrists who, in order to do a little psychoanalysis at the same time, asked: "Are you by chance in love? Is there some disappointment?" In reality, everything was an absolute disappointment, but perhaps now she was being vindicated for so much deprivation, delay, hunger and thirst, starvation.

They started leaning sideways, closing their eyes, their bodies exchanging warmth from a distance, their hands and feet, after numerous illusions of having touched, actually touching with tacit acquiescence. She made up a bed on the floor, the single sofa was not wide enough for them, nor was it perhaps long enough for him should he stretch out, extend himself downward more than she. First she swept up the dust or small quantity of dirt with the vacuum cleaner until nothing remained, next she spread out sweet-smelling blankets that had not yet been used in the capital, that were unsaturated with the smells and pollution of Athens. White sheets and sparkling pillow cases suggestive of a wedding night. After that she lay down.

He then went to the bathroom, took a bath, brushed his teeth, shaved, doing everything at his ease and without any haste whatsoever, you might have thought that nothing mattered to him, that he had forgotten where he was, as though he were not the same person who earlier had been speaking and looking at her so gently, as though he were taking his time in order for her to go to sleep, so that he might also lie down next to her or spend the night in the bamboo chair, seated like an old man in front of the fireplace in which a flaming log is being consumed.

She, however, was unable to fall asleep, nor for that matter would she have done so had he lain down next to her, even quietly, she was simply thinking that they in any case can fall asleep in situations like this, what is it that goes on inside them and what, she wondered, was the meaning of his taking so long, for she had also observed this on another occasion, but because in that instance it didn't much matter to her, she had said outright, "What in heavens name are you doing, why are you taking so long?" and had received a supposedly witty answer, "Don't behave like a widow. There are things a man also has to do before going to bed." She waited patiently, curled up in her bed clothes, it was many years since she had slept on the floor, even though she enjoyed it, the hardness of the bedding gave her strength, nor did she understand why she perceived it as strength since, according to all she knew, people, and particularly women, generally complain bitterly when forced to sleep on the floor. Her thoughts kept turning to details like these, somewhat banteringly, in order to forget the awkwardness of her situation and for a moment she became frightened lest after grooming himself he should come out and announce his sudden departure. From the young, who in reality are children, one can expect anything.

At some point he appeared, his shirt sleeves rolled up, his collar reversed from shaving, his pants splattered with water, especially there, at the spot where they bulged, and as she looked up at him from below she was overcome with horror, he had put on his clothes again, to tell the truth he was debating whether to leave or to stay, but after looking down at her from above, obviously troubled, he said with determination, "I'm going to sleep with you," an indication that until this moment he had not completely made up his mind. He started taking off his clothes, first his shirt and boots, then his pants, remaining in his undershirt and shorts, white the way they're compelled to wear them in the military academies where they sometimes also inspect them, so they say, getting them up out of bed unexpectedly, lining them up in front of their bunks, and then passing by and examining their underwear there, at that spot, to see whether there is some trace of spermal emission, because they know from their own experience that a man's hand, especially that of a young man, goes toward his penis as soon as he gets into bed, and if he's alone and without sexual relations, it is not unusual for him to gratify himself, soiling, whether he wants to or not, his underwear in order to be able to get to sleep with some measure of tranquility, otherwise he twists and turns on his mattress like a lamb on the spit, not knowing what he's after, and the next day he feels rotten.

Suddenly he threw off his remaining clothes, quickly removing first his undershirt, then his shorts, and she had time enough to see something inconceivable, a molded, leavened chest, covered with hair distributed according to a plan, not disordered as with adults, but in rows, something like needlework with a secret meaning, and not hard so that it pricks you, as she soon found out, but silken, softened, slightly resistant upon contact—as much as necessary. The skin underneath was dark, as a result not only of the sun but also of its nature, as a result of youth and manliness, just as certain glands determine the color of the body by making that of the male, even without exposure to the sun, darker and browner, whereas that of the female is usually pure and white and has difficulty darkening from exposure to the sun.

Even the ancients paid attention to this detail on their urns—what had those incredible people not paid attention to—painting male bodies tan while making those of women white and somewhat bland.

He lay down like this beside her, but did not twine himself around her, neither making his arm into a pillow for her, nor bringing his fully developed palm toward her breasts, remaining instead at a distance from her body which was still in underclothes and writhing from the illusion of contact. "Let's calm down and go to sleep," he said and immediately began to breathe heavily and actually fell asleep. She didn't turn off the light, leaving it on so as to look at his face, his eyelashes, that hard, shining hair she dared not caress, since he had not given her permission to do so. She stayed awake like this, pleased with what was happening to her, nor was it negligible, still at times she felt as if she were going mad, how utterly absurd to be so close and not to be able to reach out, to caress him, to fondle him, if only gently, as in the old days when she had him as a student. "How did he grow up so fast!" she thought and she felt entirely like a mother with her infant. And seized with tenderness she turned over on her other side, forgetting the strangeness of the situation.

She didn't sleep a wink, nor did she stir again, she merely listened to his soft breathing until the alarm clock went off. Even then she didn't turn over to see his body in its entirety, respecting his dark wish, the far distance where with such dexterity he had repelled her. She was only aware that he was reaching out, half-seated, for his underclothes and putting them on one by one, that he was standing up with self-assurance, that he was fondling her hair for a moment in a single gesture, perhaps thinking that she was asleep, but also admiring her patience in this all-night martyrdom. After that in the bathroom and then back in the room, all-resplendent in his uniform, military jacket, soldier's cap, insignia, and decorations, all those priceless adornments that wisely emphasize daring and courage and inevitably provoke admiration.

"Saturday," he said as he left and she accompanied him to the door solely in order to see him, and looking at his muscular build and swaggering stride, she later became aroused as she thought about the beast next to which she had spent the entire night. "Anyone seeing him leave will think orgies took place in here," she said to herself as she locked the door behind him. But she already felt determined to submit to everything, to endure—yes, endure—everything, to be maligned, perhaps driven away, by the other tenants, for they would spread rumors that she was lulling to sleep lively, indeed very handsome, young men and, what is worse, an educated, cultivated woman like her who was at least forty. "We have wives and daughters, they mustn't be allowed to witness such goings-on," they would say. With these thoughts she went and buried herself on his side of the bed, in his warmth.

She was left waiting for Saturday, doing nothing other than staring at the projects above her desk, first, second, third, fourth. And her soul wept as she realized that everything was going to blazes, that she would be left neither time nor desire, that now she would walk with a rapid step, with the rhythm of those who do nothing except live.

In the evening at school when her students, her children, looked into her eyes, they no longer found her the same, that radiance, warmth, and persistence—yes, persistence—with which as she taught she looked at them here and there, was blurred, ailing. During recess her lambs, her darlings, were low-spirited, she hadn't looked at them today the way she usually looked at them, and they sensed it and huddled around her, to make sure that at least she wasn't angry on their account, probably just worried, some bad news. There's no telling what those wretched telephones are capable of bringing you out of the blue.

Until Saturday, not a sign from him. Neither a phone call nor any other message; with the return of Saturday, however, the same scene was reenacted, she returning with her bag, stooping slightly toward the side it was on, murmuring lines that were suited to this moment, "Gun, you are heavy and the Agarinos knows it," and he leaning against the right-hand side of her door post, a much broader grin on his face, not without a touch of mischief in his gaze where the other day's events could be read along with an imperceptible promise, and with a ready speech, which suggested that he had been struggling with himself all these days: "I don't know if I'm making you uneasy, but I decided to come to your place tonight." She shuddered upon hearing this, having been certain these past three days that he would come, that's why she had not taken any measures, such as asking him for his phone number or address, to prevent their losing contact.

They went inside thoroughly at ease, but as they did so she saw out of the corner of her eye that the people across the way were staring at them, that they had lifted the curtain slightly and were watching, and she said to herself: "I'm off to a good start, it'll be the same here as elsewhere." But she forgot all such thoughts as she watched him advancing down the hall, a slight snap in his movements, the bull-like nape of his neck, wide, triangular shoulders, bulging buttocks, extraordinary evidence of repeated thrusting in and out—pity anyone who doesn't know…Now what's this again, she thought, what a revelation, dear God, what unexpected life!

He sat down more naturally tonight, removed his military jacket, hung it up, drank some water that he himself took from the refrigerator, looked at her cheerfully, then said, "You know, I gave them your address and phone number, otherwise there's no spending the night here. They want to know where we spend our nights, supposedly to call us in case something comes up, in reality it's to watch us closely and keep us in check, to find out what sort of company we keep, about our love life, they're afraid, you see, of politics and love alike, maybe they're even jealous, nobody's certain about anything." She listened to him attentively, then smiled. But inwardly she didn't feel right somehow. "Look," she said to herself, "it's as if this boy were looking for trouble," and she decided immediately to speak to him plainly, something she had not considered necessary until now. Nor did she wish to hurt his feelings, inasmuch as it was quite evident that there where he was doing his military service, he had political leanings, or rather that his family did, that they belonged to some party because at his age, and all the more so in a village where even newspapers don't arrive on a regular basis, it was unlikely that he had yet formulated any political views, he must have been as innocent as in his lovemaking, even though he looked like a wild beast. From the time she was young, she had observed that privately all those to the right were more inclined toward sensual pleasure, quicker to consent, more passionate and steadfast in their relations, free from pronouncing theories and proclamations, whereas publicly, not as individuals but with their representatives, they affected austerity, in fact they even appeared dangerous, since for decades, rather for hundreds of years, they had possessed authority on their side, laws and courts and prisons; you might have thought that leftists would be the opposite, more liberal in their lovemaking; on the contrary, they were more cross-grained, more difficult, even though they weren't accustomed to proclamations and admonishments, both before and after their political disgrace.

"Listen," she said to him in order not to have it weighing on her conscience, "every so often they summon me to the Security Police, not to the police station, a branch office of the Security Police, or the like, but to the Security Police themselves, General Headquarters, where they make trouble for me, pound their fists on their chest and on their desk, tell me to sign various papers, and threaten me with dismissal. Just be aware that you can get into trouble by coming here. Not only will they discharge you, but you'll also receive a sound thrashing until you recite the hows and whys, and should they find you in my bed, there's absolutely no way you'll get out of it, schoolteacher and private lessons and other such justifications notwithstanding—what business do you have in her bed, they'll say to you, and since you provided them with my address and phone number, nothing could be easier than for them to come and prove it." As she spoke she felt as if a heavy weight had been lifted from her but not, of course, in its entirety; she could see that he was a mere boy, that it wasn't possible for him to fully discern the extent of the danger. He answered her calmly. "Listen. I'm aware of all that, so don't worry. It's what I was thinking about all these days while I was away from you. The danger doesn't faze me. Furthermore, we even share the same political beliefs." And he settled himself more comfortably on the couch.

He slept with her but didn't take off all his clothes as he had the other day, removing neither his undershirt nor his shorts. This was total isolation since even stark naked he was girded by some unapproachable plain. Now that courage was involved he designated more clearly where he would like their physical contact to stop. Accustomed as she was to privation, she would have found even this more than enough, provided she was given some explanation. But this hulk of a man in appearance, yet so young mentally, gave the impression that he was comfortably and permanently settled just as he was, that he didn't need anything more or less, and perhaps it didn't even cross his mind that the other creature lying next to him might be suffering deeply and at the same time might feel slightly offended by his preposterous inaction.

In reality, however, she who had been so deprived was not suffering. For this in itself was a great deal, besides being a privileged situation, with depth and mystery, not like those ordinary ones with motley young men who barely manage to lie down before they've already finished. Nevertheless, every so often her mind suffered, contained a blank space, sought an explanation.

She thought at first of having him sleep separately. He on the couch, she on the floor. He refused outright. Then she made him understand that he would have to rent a room somewhere else and could visit her whenever he liked. He could even spend his days at her place, during the hours she was away. He told her that he had also thought of that, in fact he was discussing the possibility with two or three of his friends who were also interested in renting off base, thereby having somewhere to stow their civilian clothes and to keep a couple of couches for some unforeseen event. This recitation shattered her and made her stop trying to return to her former isolation. She saw clearly where he was about to end up, in Plaka being picked up in some bar or at Omonia Square on the sidewalk. Thus she finally kept him near her, indifferent to the turmoil wrought on her life. Especially when one evening he telephoned her from inside the Military Academy and asked, "How's our home?"—she became oblivious to all else.

Now, however, because of her abnegations and sacrifices, she felt entitled to certain rights. She wanted to penetrate his secret and began to observe him carefully. She discovered that he telephoned in her absence, wrote down names or numbers on the note pad, then took the paper with him. Not wanting to search his pockets—besides, when could she?—she started to devise stratagems. She would place, let us say, a hard-lead pencil next to the telephone so that when he began to write, he bore down hard with it on the note pad. Afterward he removed the paper, but the imprint remained on the sheet underneath. Then, in his absence, she slightly sharpened the head of a pencil and darkened the back of the paper with scribbling to reproduce the numbers and names. The names without doubt belonged to women and the phones were situated in lower-class neighborhoods.

This information was obtained by her from the telephone exchange. She bought, for otherwise she had no need of it, a guide to the capital which enabled her to locate and walk past the houses to which the phones necessarily belonged. Poor houses in out-of-the-way neighborhoods, they seemed in no way unusual.

Instead of dissolving, the mystery thickened. Why, while avoiding her altogether, did he desire relations with other women? And do you suppose he went further with them, did he at least provide them with explanations, did he open up more about his sexuality? All this preoccupied her to such an extent that, without realizing it, she neglected her work at night school. Every evening her students sought her former, penetrating look in order to be caressed, to be compensated somehow erotically, inasmuch as while so many other children their age were on dates or even in bed at such an hour, they were seated at their desks trying to roll through another year, to obtain at long last that wretched piece of paper that would allow them to better their work status. They looked at her, looked at her again, repeatedly discouraged, aware that something was happening to her, that something in her life or in her feelings toward them had changed. And without saying so, they were all unhappy.

She would stay at home and think, not bothering to turn on the light, not thinking about anything specific, simply conscious of life. She was swallowing down her new situation like a boa and attempting, motionless, to digest it. This young man had changed her life, not only by his erotic substructure, but also by his manner of thinking, by the simplicity with which he did, or omitted to do, things that seemed to her could never be done differently. Outside in the street, the cars were passing by in a chain, only slowly, on account of the narrowness of her street. It was years since she had been aware of the light of the Town Hall flashing on and off—this too made of "neon" to remind her, you might think, of her age—and it was many more years since she had abandoned herself to the voices that sometimes rose to a pitch as people talked, sang, or muttered drunken words. She particularly liked the warm voices of the men from the capital, especially those who came from the south. She listened to them attentively as she watched from behind the curtains and, transferring them inside, she distilled them and what she felt was left and hers, she found warm, tempting, and charming.

Once in a while, at such moments, the phone would ring. Naturally it was him. He would inquire about her day, her work, ask her what she was doing just then, speak about his military duties. In the semi-darkness, his voice came across as warm and loyal. Sometimes he ventured something more: "Right now, while I'm on the phone with you, some woman [or even some man] is making advances at me. She's standing outside the phone booth and will say something to me when I step outside." But he hung up without saying what he himself intended to do, how he would confront the aggression, whether he would succumb or not. The truth is, though, that she also failed to ask any questions, certain that the young man would find some pretext to be evasive. In any event, for a moment she attempted to concentrate her thoughts on the scene of sexual aggression. The provocative, amorous looks, his smile of gratification and apparent wavering, finally the decisive continuation of his itinerary.

Afterward she sat and waited for him. Frequently she discerned light footsteps on their terrace. Some person or persons were walking softly, rather they were changing from one position to another. New to this house and unfamiliar with the surroundings, she started imagining that their terrace was the site of amorous rendezvous, and perhaps not for someone who was a stranger to the house, it would be difficult for a total stranger to assume such a risk unless he was in a completely desperate situation as regards a roof, or rather a bed, whereupon an individual is blinded and becomes absurdly daring, and the strange thing is that this courage—"defiance" as the ancients called it—emboldens the other as well, this is why at first she conjectured that it must be some tenant in the building who, for whatever valid reason, was taking refuge on the terrace, or a former tenant who, familiar with every nook and cranny, knew that the house did not have a superintendent or a dog and that there was little likelihood of encountering someone on the stairs, and was climbing on tiptoe to the top, resolving thus the problem of both a flat and his hot pants. She was trying to bridle her imagination, not to be carried away by nightmarish stories like the one that she had once seen at the movies, in which the satanic husband, wishing to drive his isolated and already half-crazed wife mad, would secretly climb to the attic of the house and there, manipulating a valve, would consciously lower and raise the gaslight. The story took place in England in the last century when lighting was still produced by gas with its nightmarish flame. She refused, therefore, to let her imagination run away with her as a result of similar stories and repeatedly drove them away, yet the footsteps in the night on the floor above were a reality that could only make her shudder. Seated in an armchair in the dark, absorbed by her loneliness where her thoughts were idling about, she could distinctly hear the sounds of creaking, which, she had no doubts about this, were erotic, and she felt even more deeply her isolation from life—that position of eternal expectation to which she had been condescendingly relegated.

At some point her door creaked, the key was turning in the lock—you might have thought in her heart—and he would appear, powerful and handsome. Upon removing his splendid military jacket (designed and embroidered with so very much erotic wisdom in order, of course, to emphasize strength and virility), however, he was not significantly dispossessed of the lines of his body, he gained rather, since now the curved muscles of his shoulders were outlined more clearly, as were his arms, his strong buttocks destined for sexual rapture, and his chest especially, puffed out near the top, dark, and with shining, ordered hair as she knew it from his nakedness toward which she forbade herself to turn her head. Every once in a while, together with all this beauty and the ease of his manners, the mystery leapt up. "Something's going on," she said to herself, "something's going on." But there was no way the young man could be caught, not even with the tape recorder she used to leave on while supposedly going to the grocer's to do her marketing. In his presence, moreover, she forgot about the steps, they ceased to concern her, you might have thought they didn't exist.

In any event, as a result of concentrating intently and repeatedly on the same things, something started to become clear. And this was the steps on the floor above. There was some connection between the young man and all those footsteps, and there was some connection between those footsteps and his entire strange behavior, his want of sexual appetite, the atmosphere of mystery he dragged around with him. That such a young boy should be capable of manipulating life and its shadings thus, of creating mysterious and impermeable spaces for moments exclusively his, seemed to her something unbelievable. Yet she saw it, or rather heard it, for she had ascertained with absolute certainty that as soon as the young man showed up at her place, the footsteps on the floor above ceased. This also constituted his miscalculation. Whereas he had organized everything admirably, he had not taken into account that his footsteps could be heard on the floor below. Thus his innocent face and even more innocent words were all wasted. The teacher had him at her mercy.

Eventually there were evenings when the young man declared that it wasn't possible for him to spend the night at her place. He claimed that he had to be at the Military Academy, in all likelihood there would be a check, things looked grim, something was up. The teacher, credulous and in love, believed him at first, and when she heard the iron outside door bang behind him, she believed him even more. As she was trying to fall asleep, however, she discerned again the sound of creaking. It can't possibly be him, she thought. Heaven forbid if it is, he'll have to spend the entire night up there because he has nowhere else to go, nor does he dare, of course, to come down here. And what in God's name is he doing up on the terrace, what can he possibly be doing at such an ungodly hour? In any event, the creaking stopped toward daybreak. He left or fell asleep in some corner— this is something else again. "Our Father who art in heaven..." the teacher was praying and surely her prayer was ascending at least to the terrace. She desired as much herself.

Still, she had to do something. There was danger of a scandal, first of a quarrel, then, after the usual gossip over the incident by busybodies, of a scandal. It was highly probable that some evening another tenant, more likely a woman, would go up to the terrace, suddenly confront the unknown young man, start shrieking, and cause the second coming. Then you'll hear moralizing, then you'll hear gibberish. They know everything, they've observed everything, but they're waiting for some such excuse. She had to do something, but had no notion of how to justify it, how to risk such an offense.

One evening it seemed that the young man was obliged to leave promptly, to return to his Military Academy where they were wanted, where they were on alert, there could be a check at any moment and some punishment doled out. He was dressing hurriedly, in a panic, and she slipped some money in his pocket for the taxi fare, thoroughly convinced this time. He dashed out and the heavy door slammed behind him. A little while later, however, again—yes, again!—the sound of creaking could be heard from the floor above. "It's not possible! It's not possible!" she said in despair, going in and out of her flat. There was something very serious afoot here and she invented ten stories per minute.

The most likely was that the young man was taking someone up to the terrace. They had a date, he met her, took her up there. So that's why the gentleman was in such a hurry. He was expected!

She grabbed the flashlight without thinking. Despair blinded her. "Imagine that!" she muttered as she climbed the stairs, "imagine that!" Opening the door to the terrace, she extinguished the flashlight and instinctively lightened her step—better to catch them red-handed and settle things once and for all. He was alone, however, with his hat lying on the parapet, his strong face bathed in moonlight, and that innocent look, rather, all his sensations, directed at the balcony door across the way where something seemed to be shining. She understood. Deeply moved, she stopped and looked at him. He was unbuttoned, erect, of course, and as he must have been looking at something, masturbating frenetically. She was unable to contain herself, approached rapidly, came next to him. At a loss, he reeled backward.

She practically had to drag him into her apartment. He refused to go inside, crying and beating his breast. She grabbed hold of him, tugging at him and pulling, afraid that some door might swing open at the racket. Then who would wipe her clean? He collapsed in a chair, crying. She let him cry, then knelt down in front of him and removed his boots. Now he really was hers, a man with a crack through which the grace of God had entered. He calmed down, fondled her hair gently. Such a young boy and he realized it.

And she, polishing his boots, said smilingly, "Come on, get undressed for bed, otherwise how will you be able to get up in the morning?" Then, as though chatting, "We have windows down here as well, there's no need for you to be cold on the terrace."

COSTAS TAKTSIS

(1927–1988)

Small Change

"I've spit! So watch out or you'll get it if you dillydally again along the way!"

She never really spit, only said that she had, but the intent of the threat was clear: you had to be back before the saliva dried. How quickly the saliva dried was determined by her, according to the circumstances, according to her mood. Sometimes it dried before you could say Jack Robinson; you went and came back faster than a bird, but the saliva had already dried, and she was waiting for you at the door with the strap in her hand.

At other times you returned from the errand she had sent you on, and at the sight of the house from the street corner, you began to tremble all over, something gave way in you, your knees turned to jelly, instead of going forward, your legs went sideways, backward, sideways, backward...You wondered, full of self-indignation, why you had been so distracted, what devil had made you take your time and gape at the kids dragging the blackbird by its leg, whether it was worth getting such a whipping for a diversion that had chanced along the way, in which you had not even taken part, and which, worst of all, already belonged to the past, whereas the hour of judgment, the moment of reckoning, was approaching inexorably with every step you took toward the door.

And yet your fears were often unfounded. You entered the house, trembling like a condemned man on his way to be executed, when suddenly, from the expression on her face, you realized that the saliva had not yet dried, your chest heaved with relief, and filled with love and gratitude, filled with ecstasy before this miracle, you looked at her, you would have liked to run up to her and kiss her, your guilt at having dillydallied went up in smoke, and suddenly you regretted not having dillydallied a little longer, indeed you even dared to tell her that the kids on the next street over had caught a blackbird and were dragging it by a string tied to its leg and kicking it like a ball; it was as if you were flagrantly confessing that you had dillydallied, as if you were provoking her to show you her cards, if she intended to beat you, to beat you right then and there so that you would be done with it. But she either ignored you completely or said something totally unrelated to your dillydallying and the blackbird: "Leave the bottle in the kitchen, and run across the way to Mrs. Christina and tell her to stop by for a few minutes. I want to speak with her."

In fact once in a while—though this happened rarely—when she was in high spirits, when the gentleman who had bought her the miniature gramophone at the International Fair had come the night before, or the gentleman who always brought the mussels and red caviar, at such times she even forgot to spit, and when you returned from the bakery, panting under the weight of the loaf that you had dropped three times along the way, not only did she not scold you, but she also took you in her arms and said: "Ah, what a joy for me to have a son, who has grown up and runs errands for me, my good little boy who, when I'm old, will take me from the shade and place me in the sun!" and she laughed with all her heart.

How wonderful life was on such days! The gramophone played continuously, and she sang along with it:

To a tango they danced on and on, hugging and embracing.

But as the record went round and round she kept looking all around...

In the morning Mrs. Roxane came from Tomba and washed the clothes, because she herself loathed doing the wash, or scrubbed the floor, she made the house spotless, it was a joy to look at it, or she came simply and solely to keep you company, to tell you fairy tales, because she herself had to step out, to go first to the lawyer's about the divorce, then to the dentist's, and from there to Modiano's to do the marketing. But if she stayed at home, she stared out the window in the afternoon, and called to the icecream vendor: "Mr. Prodromos, let me have two vanilla icecreams, and make sure the cone isn't hollow on the inside, what have you been up to, you rascal, we haven't seen you in days."

She bought two icecreams, one for Mrs. Roxane and one for you, she herself didn't eat icecream because of the dentist, though sometimes she couldn't stand to see you licking it while she ate none, and said to you: "Won't you give a tiny bit to your dear mommy who bought it for you?" And she placed the palms of her hands over her face and cried, "Boo, hoo, hoo!"

And you immediately ran up to her and held the hand with the cone high, even though you knew she was only pretending to cry, proud at being able to do something for her as well, but, come now, admit it, also watching with bated breath to see how much she was going to bite out of it, because when all was said and done the icecream was yours, she could have some too, but not all of it.

The evenings were even more beautiful when she was in a good mood. The place was fragrant with the scent of jasmine and honeysuckle coming from the yard of the house across the way, and there was something festive in the air, it was May Day, she put on your flower-printed pinafore with an elastic band round the trouser legs and sent you out into the street to play as long as you liked, so long as you didn't return dirty-faced. Afterward she placed the flower pots with the begonia, the hortensia, and the two rubber plants outside, next to the front door, and watered them, also pouring one or two buckets of water on the sidewalk to cool the place off, and then she too sat down on the doorstep, next to the flower pots, and started chatting with Mrs. Christina, or else she gathered together the big boys and girls who were in the third grade, and taught them how to play paper, rocks, and scissors—one, two, three—shoot! In fact once she got up and played jump rope, to show the girls how to jump, and didn't quit the game because she lost, but only when she was out of breath, and she burst into laughter, and said: "Leave me alone, you she-devils, I'm not for things like that, I've a son who's a big boy!"

Yet there were other days, entirely wintry, entirely overcast, when she was in a bad temper, when she smoked continually like a chimney and chewed her nails; on such days, not only were you not to dilly-dally in the street, but you were not even to play in the house with the gold cigarette wrappings, nor to speak. Because she said to you: "Be careful! Don't breathe a word today, or I'll tear you apart like a sardine!"

On such days it was better that she not send you out on an errand for you knew, regardless of how quickly you returned, that the saliva had already dried, and if the saliva hadn't dried, you had forgotten to buy salt: "What else did your mother tell you to get?" the grocer asked, but no matter how hard you tried, you found it impossible to remember, or you dillydallied along the way, you completely forgot that she was in a bad temper today, and you stood and watched the kids who were paying a penny to see the peep-show, they saw you clutching something in your fist, and said: "Come on over and wres-tle with me and I'll let you beat me," and they stole your change with-out your realizing it, only she, instead of going out and beating the children, beat you. "Have mercy on me, mommy," you shrieked between sobs, "have mercy on me, I won't do it again!" and you tried to hide behind her skirt, but the more you eluded her and the more you cried, the more enraged she became, she didn't like you to cry, or to beg, she wanted you to take your punishment like a man. "Either you're going to become a man and learn not to cry," she said foaming with rage and striking at random, "or I'm going to kill you right now once and for all, to mourn you and forget you, the world doesn't need any more cowards like that good-for-nothing father of yours—tell me, are you going to become a man? Say: 'I will become a man!' Say it or you won't get out of my clutches alive, today will be the end of you!" And you said: "Yes, mommy, I will. And I won't dillydally along the way again."

"And I won't dillydally along the way again!"

"'Nor will the street boys fool me and steal my change!'" "No, mommy, no!"...

"Now get out of my sight before I change my mind, go and wash your face, and not another word out of you!—I wish to God I had never given birth to you!"

On such days the gramophone didn't play at all, or else it played the same record continually...

Poverty, you begat more children than anyone...

And she went out in the evening without asking Mrs. Roxane to come keep you company, she put you to bed and went out, and she returned late, how late you didn't know, often you didn't even know that she was gone, but you must have been in your third or fourth sleep when you heard voices from far away; and for just an instant you opened your eyes and saw your angel nude, without wings, next to her bed, and then the oil lamp died out, the voices died out, and the darkness was like a heavy blanket over your eyes, and you fell like lead into your fifth sleep...

"Ah, mother! How many years have gone by? It has been thirty years since then, and I still haven't learned my lesson. I still haven't become a man, I still dillydally along the way, watching the children, the street boys still steal my change. And this is your greatest punishment. And my punishment as well—that I didn't realize, while there was still time, what you were going through then, and I wanted to avenge myself on you. But why the devil did you have to take it out on me? Couldn't you, after all, look the other way when I was ten minutes late or when I forgot to buy salt? And, if I remember correctly, the change that the children on the next street over had stolen from me was, for God's sake, mother, only six or seven pennies!"

MARIOS HAKKAS

(1931–1972)

The End of the Matter

So long as lips shall kiss
and eyes shall see
so long lives love
and love gives life to thee.*

A hospital room with practically bare walls. Only a small picture, the corner of a prison cell with a cloth band depicting Genoveva.** The furniture consists entirely of two beds with night tables, an old wardrobe, and a desk. My universe is becoming more and more restricted to this room. I'm in my forties, my prospects gloomy: metastasis, eventual generalization, the end near and inevitable.

I know nothing can save me. Never mind their telling me to stop smoking, a mere detail among the forces pushing me toward death. From the beginning something was leading me toward the worst, and now that the evil's spread, it's not meant for me, when you come right down to it I don't want to get well, let's just say I enjoy having my chest boil like a pot, a small cat purring in my arms, company in the night that assists me when I wake up.

My wife's asleep in the adjoining bed. I cough and am unable to spit up the phlegm. It's an engine that tries to go forward; for a

---

* This was written at the bottom of a poster depicting a statue of a female Indian goddess with six hands. (Author's note)
** A beautiful woman with long hair often depicted in Greek pictures and tapestries.

moment you think it's gotten started, but there's something wrong with it somewhere, the sound doesn't stabilize; you can hear it degenerating in the cylinder, gradually dying out. I try harder. "What is it?" my wife calls out startled in her sleep.

"Nothing. Go back to sleep." She turns over on her other side and goes on sleeping with a slight whistling at the end of her breathing.

A good woman. She takes care of me, brings the milk to my bed, sometimes I spill it all over myself, she bears me no grudges, straightens my pillows, picks up the tissue that for no reason I throw on the floor. Ten years of marriage have led to this tranquil relationship, neither one of us disgusted by the other's slaver, a feeling of tenderness and a sense of understanding. Often when she has a headache, "Come," I say to her, "come let me fondle you a little," and the pain goes away immediately or subsides.

Not that it was always like this. We went through many ordeals before arriving at this point. In the early years, war raged in our relationship and maybe I was at fault for not having made up my mind right from the start that I was married now; I kept playing hanky-panky, was assailed by her fits of nerves and tears, refused to give in, until at some point I surrendered; then illness came along and we fully regained our equilibrium.

Life's an endless adaptation and a contraction, until in the end you accept as your space this room, you search the ceiling and walls, trying to detect some stain on the whitewash, and are always amazed by what it resembles: a face, a thing, or the shape of some animal. The one and only picture is slightly crooked. Did I take my pill? I'm running out of Kleenex. The book I'm reading is insipid. I turn over on my other side. Maybe I'll be less uncomfortable.

At one time I used to think that if I lost my legs in a traffic accident I'd commit suicide. Now I'm panting, my knees have collapsed, every so often I stop to sit down, I'm without legs, and yet I persist in existing. I want to live as before, even though I've no strength, in the streets, without altering my pace at all, but it's slowing down and will flag at any moment, I won't make it up this hill, I want to lie down, I'm nostalgic for my bed, the room with the stains, the light that the shutters project on the wall.

I was betrayed by my body, white as a sheet; my face, drained of color; frothy sputum. My body's abandoning me, I've let go, I'm sinking. "Don't surrender," my wife shouts, and I make one final effort.

Now I'm in some hotel at Paddington, in another at Bayswater, elsewhere at Camden, everywhere, a plastic rug on the floor, a washstand next to the wall. Now I'm walking along Fulham Road, I'm at Brompton in front of a red-brick building. The woman doctor arranges my sparse hair, straight as leeks, with one hand while with the other she holds the x-ray; she projects it onto the lighted screen and her oblong face becomes even more oblong. "Unfortunately that's what it is," she's saying. "In any event I'm satisfied with its overall progress. It's growing of course, but quite slowly. I'm hoping it won't develop any faster."

I leave the hospital. At South Kensington station I see the newspapers with the latest headlines. "Lillian Board, twenty-two years old, Europe's leading athlete, winner of the four-hundred-meter dash, dies of cancer." "Dies" and I think of myself, no dice, as the escalator takes me to the bottom.

Later in Paris, at the Porte d'Orléans station, I read about her death. The newspapers were publishing old photographs of her at the starting line and others of her at the finish. There was also one in which she was walking; she'd just won the four-hundred-meter dash and was smiling at the flashing cameras, her face and her hair luminous, her inhaling chest teasing her shirt to the point of tearing it. I placed my finger on her chest and it went down immediately, a handful of dust now, the photographs are turning yellow, the flashing cameras are pointed elsewhere, her record broken, the loudspeakers silent. Thus the two of us are slowly being forgotten, wedged up there in the constellation Cancer (I saw it once in my sleep and was terrified, the same shape as the one the x-ray shows that I'm carrying around in my chest). I place my fingers on my chest again and again, grope myself repeatedly, at some point it no longer goes up and down, kaput, I barely manage with one final effort to cut the thread.

Nor could it have been otherwise, this was its natural development: it started out as a chickpea, became a five-drachma coin, later an egg, now it's the size of a fist. Hopes are unraveling.

There are some old cafés with high ceilings and marble tables; pensioners and veterans gather there to play cards, gambling Turkish delights. Occasionally the third player is absent because of the flu or else his urea's gone way up; they find another third player; then they're again reduced to two; one by one they disappear, quietly give up their place, get out of the game, and repose a little way outside the city. I also had hoped to end like this and it would have happened just about this way if this thing hadn't grown in my chest.

There's a certain café in Paris, Porte d'Orléans. A little old man sits in the corner leaning on his cane. He wears a jacket, a cap on his head, and a badge with a ship's helm on his lapel. In front of him stands a liqueur glass containing a yellow-colored beverage. From time to time he sips it. His chin has almost merged with his nose. The next day I go to the café earlier. He's at his spot. The day after that I get up at the crack of dawn. There he is again. I'm sure he'll be there even when I'm no longer able to go, even when I no longer exist to go, the old man will be at his spot even after you're gone, you can verify it in two or three generations, he wears a dark jacket with wide lapels, a blue cap on his head, and first and foremost that badge on his lapel. "Captain, hey captain, where do you ship us while you always remain behind? How do you manage things so that we're the ones to leave while you remain behind?" He has an inexpressive face, all wrinkles, the skin of a lizard, and his chin's about to touch his nose. Porte d'Orléans, the corner café facing you as you exit from the subway, not the one above, also on the corner and facing the subway (another exit), I'm still talking about the one underneath, called Café d'Orléans or maybe that's the name of the other one, I don't remember, or on the opposite corner, if necessary look on the other corner as well, there can't be more than four corners, and watch out for the exits because there are lots of them, don't get confused, otherwise he'll give you the slip, be careful or you'll lose him, in the end I don't think you'll find him and it was such a good opportunity, it seemed so simple at first and yet so difficult to find yourself face to face with the old captain.

I'm dragging myself through the streets of Athens, moving ahead by hanging on to the trees. There's nothing else for me to hang on to. Until now many leaned on me and I carried them.

Once, a jinn, naturally without my knowing at first that I was dealing with something of the sort, begged me to take it to the opposite side. I hoisted it on my back, but when we got there it wouldn't climb down. For years I walked with the jinn clamped to me and maybe that's why I'm slightly bowed. I don't know how I freed myself, I only know that the effort to do so resulted in this harshness in my face.

Now I too have to find someone to transport me. The unfortunate thing is that in my prime I drove away friends and ideas. I make a few phone calls, more often than not there's no answer. Those who finally do pick up the receiver falter when I ask them straight-out, "Are you there?" I'll walk alone but how will I make it the rest of the way?

I meet a girl, take her to a hotel. She has two large, hanging breasts. I grab hold of them, she starts screaming, whimpers, keeps saying, "Take me along." "Where to?" I ask her irritably. "Where I'm going I can't take anyone along." She insists, "Take me along," and offers me her breasts. I hurriedly put on my trousers and run out into the street. A burden. The question is, where am I going to rest mine?

I enter a church and hear an austere voice behind the icons: "Walk not in the dark…" "The 'land of the Dark'?"* I ask myself. "What has the land of the Dark got to do with it?" "…ἀλλ' ἕξεις ζωὴν αἰώνιον"* the voice continues but I don't understand why Alexis** is getting mixed up in this. Life everlasting, fine, but what's Alexis after? A riddle. That's what comes from getting entangled with metaphysics. I try to discover who's devising the enigma for me and notice a sign: "And I will put you to rest." No, one can do without that kind of rest. I know, my body in clover and they, it seems, will save my soul. The problem for me is exactly the opposite, if it's possible for me to save the body, I'm indifferent as far as the soul's concerned, in the cauldrons, in the pitch, may it never find peace, an invisible little dog announcing its presence with a little bell, frightening the travelers on deserted country roads at night until they take to their heels. I leave the church walking backward.

I go to a clandestine meeting, sit down in a corner, and try to forget about myself as I listen to the speeches of the others. For a while I manage to lose myself in the group, but the cough returns to remind

---

* Hakkas puns on the word σκοτία, which means both "dark" and "Scotland" (which I have translated in the text as the "land of the Dark").
** The author further puns on the Greek words ἀλλ' ἕξεις ζωὴν αἰώνιον: "but you shall have eternal life" and Ἀλέξης: Alexis.

me of my condition; it persists and they're annoyed by me; I'm unable to assimilate myself into the group, to become one with its goal, which when I no longer exist will continue even without me, an attempt at perpetuation through others. Alchemy. Either you exist or you don't, all the rest is consolation, this is also why the goal is so big so as to accommodate many, entire generations, each one yielding the banner to the next; secret meetings are prolonged, specific problems are resolved, others are discovered, people forget about themselves in all that; at some point they reach the end; "the others will continue," they reflect with absolute serenity and then surrender.

I take the floor and, half choking from coughing, manage to give the password, "Let he who saves himself be saved." Naturally no one embraces my opinions (a familiar story, as if anyone ever listened to me) and I'm forced to explain to them that I'm going to die for myself and for myself only, my goal isn't to die for some goal, so I'm going to live it up, this condemnation is my affair, unabashedly mine, and I'm not about to burden others with it. I leave and continue my peregrinations.

I stop to rest at a bar, in the loft, there where the stairs end. At the table next to mine a girl is slowly drinking her coffee. The waitress ascends with a full tray. I lean over and say to the girl confidentially, "Do you want me to make her trip and fall?" And before I've even finished speaking the sound of broken glasses is heard. I run toward the waitress.

"Forgive me," I say to her.

"For what?" she replies with surprise while wiping herself. "Why are you to blame?"

Naturally I'm unable to explain why and return to my seat. After this incident I feel quite strong, my cough's also gone, my feet are firmly planted on the floor of the loft. The girl looks at me persistently as if to say, "It wasn't right"; she's abandoned her half-full cup of coffee; she nervously places one leg over the other, shakes her hair that falls all over her shoulders like a torrent. I want to continue my role; it's enough for me that she not think I'm a juggler.

"I offer you a tuft of my hair" and I uproot as much as the palm of my hand can hold (anyhow the chemotherapy's causing it all to fall out; it remains in my hands when I yank it). She's exerting more and more charm over me. I'm prepared to offer her one of my eyes (and it's not a glass eye either); unfortunately I don't have a fork with me in order to poke it out. I want to give her everything I have on me in duplicate, except, naturally, a kidney since one's already been removed; in general anything of mine she wants she can have. It seems the attraction is mutual; I also exert a certain charm over her and I don't want her to think I'm a juggler, to have a false notion of me. Whatever I do, I do in accordance with the rules of objective reality; I'm not a good-for-nothing, at the very most a strange man.

"Are you coming?" I ask her without specifying whether I mean to my table, to the nearest hotel, or on that long trip. She approaches—tall, her legs well-shaped and endlessly long. I have always hankered after a tall woman. Those I happened upon were all three feet high, stocky, and had to strain their necks to look at me. I abandon my pathetic stance, strike a pose, finally smile (in my condition this is another sign of improvement). I feel a force flowing through my hands. I lift my fist and bring it down on the machine—one of those that measure how strong-armed you are. The small piece of wood inside pops up; everyone expects it to stop at sixty, at the most seventy, but it presses on, exceeds a hundred, and pops all the way out. Many look at me in amazement; others see my thin, shriveled-up hands and don't believe it. "For you, darling," I murmur and slip quietly away from the crowd. Smiling, she encourages me. Now the supernatural strength has reached my legs. I climb the mountain, practically running, the first to reach the top, light a cigarette, and wait for the others. "For you, darling," I repeat and she hugs and kisses me.

"I can perform a great many feats."

"Don't worry, you'll get well," she replies.

"But whether I get well or not, you won't go away, will you?"

"No, no," she reassures me. "I'll remain with you forever."

"Otherwise I'll carve you up, I'll disfigure you by making two slashes with the razor on your cheek. I'll inscribe my coat of arms on your flesh, an 'H,' so that you'll always be mine."

"I'll apply a thick layer of make-up and it won't show."

I then begin feeling her face with my fingertips. "It's not you." I dig my nails into her flesh. "It's not you." I scrape off the make-up and finally discover the scars. "It is you. Are you coming?"

"Where?"

"Everywhere, even to the pitch-darkness. In any event I at some point will walk in the dark."

"Yes, yes, to the land of the Dark. There's a special center of research for your sickness there. They're applying new methods. You'll get well, you'll see. They make your temperature go up to forty-one and a half by pouring oxygen and sun into your lungs."

"So then it's off to the land of the Dark?" I say, bewildered. "And how about Alexis, how does one explain Alexis? Not that I much care about possessing 'life everlasting.' I'm asking merely out of curiosity."

"Ἄ λέξεις, ἅ ἀναφορικὸ καὶ τὸ ῥῆμα στὸ μέλλοντα λέξω καὶ ἐρῶ, that is, 'only your words may attain eternity.'"

"So it's words and questions," I keep muttering.

"You must go on writing and perhaps your writings will live on after you."

Thus the combat with words continued, as did the other, the struggle with women, the two taking me beyond the boundaries of the world and hurling me into a state of high from which I thought I would never return, until I would in fact return to reality for a short while, attend to my sickness, and then depart again.

"I took him so as to raise him high up," the other woman said.

"So that afterward he'll come crashing down," my wife replied.

"It's a type of treatment," I interposed. I was lying in bed with my head propped up by the pillows, breathing with difficulty.

"We must raise his morale," the other woman repeated.

"Without any protection? What will he lean on?" my wife insisted.

"We'll attempt to raise the temperature," I butted in once more in an attempt to reconcile them. They were standing to the right and left of the bed, their eyes shining. "I'll reach forty, perhaps forty-one, the evil will burn up inside me, and then I'll gradually descend to my physiological limits."

"All I know," said my wife angrily, "is that you must step firmly; self-deception is not permissible."

"His elevation is necessary, otherwise he'll sink. He'll bury himself inside and after that he won't come out again."

"I'm going to keep him here where he is," my wife said stubbornly and made a movement to grab hold of the bed.

"On my way down I'll pass by here again, don't worry, in fact you would oblige me by restricting me to thirty-six point six in order to prevent my going much lower, whereupon the cure will have worked, only the patient..."

"It's not certain that on your way down you'll pass by here again. Your space is vast, your possibilities infinite. The problem is getting started; you're not going to be buried in this room," the tall woman said, and gave the bed a vehement shove; my wife tried to grab hold of it but I ascended by myself, barely managing to pull a sheet over me since I had nothing on, and floated to the ceiling. Below they were quarreling and had already come to blows.

"Leave," the tall woman shouted. "Stay," my wife retorted. I was about to cave in when I saw the small picture tilting and thought I would descend to straighten it. Afterward I caught the tall woman's hard look, as though she had understood, and she won me back.

"Where from?" I shouted at her as the sheet started to slip and there was danger of exposure.

She ran toward the window as my wife rushed after her, managing to open one of the shutters.

"It's not wide enough for me to get through," I hurled at her. My wife was firmly holding onto the other shutter. "Let's see which one is stronger," I thought. The tall woman pushed her forcefully and they both fell on the bed struggling.

"Leave," the tall woman shouted, gasping for breath, but I insisted on seeing whether my wife still wanted me, whether she would shout, "stay"; the other one, however, stopped up her mouth, from which only a moan was issuing. I made a small volplane and, opening the other shutter, started to go out when I heard the heart-rending voice of my wife: "Don't, she'll destroy you."

"It's for my own good," I hurled at her but was unable to stay longer to provide her with explanations; oxygen and sun were inflating my chest and I was gaining altitude.

On the second floor, my wife's brother was busy repairing a broken-down chair.

"Where are you going?" he asked me, stooped over.

"Regards to your wife," I said to him as I waved my hand cheerfully.

"Where are you off to?"

"Overhead. It's a new cure, a sort of space trip." .

He wished me "good luck" and went on with what he was doing. On the top floor, my sister's husband was reading a book. His hair was disheveled and his eyes red, probably from staying up all night.

"I wanted to go either up or down; I couldn't stand it any longer where I was," I tried to explain.

"I'm sorry, so sorry," he said hurriedly, anxious to get rid of me and return to his book.

"Please tell them to stop squabbling down below because I've given them the slip; even if I wanted to I couldn't remain," and I arranged the sheet over myself, bringing one end over my shoulder while allowing the other to hang down to my feet.

"I don't get involved in the family affairs of others. In any event I wish you a pleasant journey. If you don't return may I use your library for my research?"

"Naturally, and you have my permission to work on my opus," I shouted and left.

I was sinking into a white vacuum and becoming more and more lost. The tall woman and my wife had gone out into the yard and were staring overhead with tinted glasses; after that I buried myself in a cloud and could no longer discern anything; I don't believe even they could see me. Solitude enveloped me, I was slightly cold, why hadn't I also grabbed the blanket as I was leaving, my teeth were chattering, why did I take only the sheet, I wanted to exhibit the figure of a would-be Christ in space and now I was shivering, I huddled up like a small ball of thread and as the wind diminished I made an increasingly great effort to breathe. Inside I was aflame; the oxygen together with the sun was burning my entrails, opening windpipes that cigarettes had blocked years ago. The fever was rising in waves, going from violet to red and from light to dark blue, then gray; I realized I was advancing steadily toward the darkest colors; in the far distance I saw a variation of black approaching, it was an enormous centipede and it covered me, "it's already reached forty," I thought, it was crawling all over me, my entire body was tingling, I was shaking, jumping up and down, "what will make me reach forty-one and is the worst thing that could happen to me?"

I had gone beyond the six colors; only the seventh remained; my blood was seething, my heart beating like a frenetic jazz drum, when moving like an octopus the blackest black appeared; it seized me; I was getting lost; soon now I would be approaching the boundaries, only I mustn't go beyond them, just stand there and look at the other side. I was on the edge; my forehead, a spring, was emitting burning water; my hair was melting; I looked inside the pitch-blackness and with all my remaining strength shouted, "Eurydice, Eurydice"; there was no answer; not even the echo of my voice returned; it disappeared in the abyss; "Eurydice," I persisted, no longer able to hear even my own voice.

I continued to confine myself to the edge, but felt forces pushing me inside; it was with difficulty that I narrowly managed to keep my feet outside; the rest of my body had already gone beyond; "forty-one and a half," I heard someone next to me say when I whispered "Lillian Board" and heard my voice multiplied by tens of megaphones blending with the uproar from the stadium. "Lillian Board," I said more steadily and saw a light in the darkness speeding my way. It was her walking with the stride of a female stag, holding a torch some four hundred meters away and coming straight at me from above. I started to grow heavy with a propensity downward; I thrust my hands behind and fell gradually in the direction traced by Lillian's light. The darkness was waning. "Thirty-nine and a half," I heard, and everything around me was violet. "I'll take her home as well," I thought and turned around to see if she was coming. Now she was running in the opposite direction, growing smaller and smaller until she became a tiny dot; finally she froze there and remained a little star.

I continued to lose altitude and everything around me was whitish; clouds, possibly sheets, I thought. In the distance I seemed to see frightened houses leaning on one another and warming themselves. Afterward I discerned trees, bare acacias, and thought to myself, "deep fall"; as I headed there I distinctly saw the stone enclosure and, despite my attempt to remain outside it, finally fell inside; I landed right in a pit around which people were standing; a few were throwing flowers and covering my face; someone threw a handful of earth; they were dirtying my clothes and I thought for a moment of shaking it off, but I was unable to distinguish what were my hands and what was the sand, both flesh-colored, the color matched. Someone threw a handful of small pebbles; it seems there was no more earth; then someone else flung a big stone that hit me in the knee, paralyzing me with pain. A fair number of acquaintances were present. Way up front stood my wife with a black hat and mourning veil; further back the tall woman in a black skin-tight dress who aroused me as she tried to push her way through the crowd to reach me, making strange dance movements and showing off one after the other her bosom, her high rump and hips, her legs, oh my God, those endless legs of hers; her arms were waving as she approached and then leaned on me; she pulled me up amid a shower of stones; I grabbed hold of her, clung to her, searched for her mouth.

"This is not the time for that sort of thing," she said to me sternly. "Throw a few handfuls of earth so that we may cover him."

By now some were using shovels; others, to avoid getting dirty, were pushing with their feet to fill up the hole; three of them together were lugging an enormous stone; somebody else heaved a garbage can that was full. As a symbolic gesture I also threw a pebble and then went off with the girl. I climbed out of the enclosure and the tall woman held me protectively by the arm, as if to console me, to assist me; I immediately took advantage of the situation, suggesting that we go to a hotel.

"I have time," I said to her. "Now that they think I'm inside there," and I started looking for a taxi, "we'll lock ourselves in and no one will bother us." I became impatient again and as there was no taxi in sight I was forced to modify my proposal: "Over here, inside, behind the pine trees, quick," and was already unbuttoning my trousers, unable to contain myself any longer.

"You mustn't dissipate yourself on that sort of thing," the girl repeated sternly.

"But I'm not dissipating myself. It's a kind of rebirth."

"Channel your energies into writing."

"Words and love," I reminded her.

"First words, then love."

They told me they would make me well, hogwash, that I would be able to breathe, to move my hands, to go on walks from time to time, provided of course that I not waste my energy, especially on writing.

I replied by asking them if I'd be able to write even if I couldn't walk, even if I couldn't move my hands at all, even if out of necessity I couldn't breathe. They lifted their hands high, pointing vaguely in some direction. I went.

It was someone with a big white beard, holding a long string of beads that he was slowly telling. I explained to him that it wasn't a question, that I wasn't asking for any special favors, but since I began writing at a slightly advanced age, thirty and over, and since by the looks of things I won't get beyond forty, in other words seeing as I'll run out of time and I've got five or ten images in my head, so that they won't be wasted, strange thoughts that perhaps no one else after me will have, barely enough for one more book, and not a very big one at that, a little fatter than the previous one, all in all two or three inches thick. And above all it won't say anything against anyone. Against myself maybe, my nose which is rather large, this is noticeable as soon as I lose a little weight, my eyebrows which are turning blond and are no more than a bare suggestion, my eyes just like buttonholes, and yet the girls used to run after me.

The one with the big white beard kept staring at me. He was not surly, nor even pompous. Implacable, of course, and inside his gaze the abyss.

"You're an egoist as well," he says to me. "You don't come begging 'grant me a few years of life,' instead you ask the impossible of me, to violate my principles; you want to keep on writing even after your ballpoint pen has run out of ink. No, it can't be done. The sun will come out every day."

"Listen," I say to him, "don't irk me because I'll set to work and dash it off in two or three months, I'll write it on my knees and it can come out as drivel for all I care (the way you're handling things there won't be time for penmanship, a second, third, or tenth rewriting if possible or any other nitpicking, all superfluous details when you're crowding me for time). I'll write it regardless and it'll be against you, a provocation, how I accosted her and brought her next to the bed, how we fell on top of each other as though we were demented, and those garters of hers that wouldn't come off. Stop playing nervously with your string of beads, there are things you've never done and you can't even imagine what happened on the bed that night."

His face is dry, an infrangible wall, while I'm looking for some crack, some small contraction to slip through and pass safely to the other side until this book gets written; not permanently, not even for the average age span, perhaps for the next five years, which might very well be my most productive, a small exception to the big rule, a small exception, some drug that will arrest the tumor's growth for four or five years, not a cure, the danger of generalization ever-present, so that I'll always be scrutinizing his dry face, looking for some crack and, not finding it, withering away in a pool of perspiration until the final rattle likewise recorded.

The time will come when I'll go and prostrate myself pleading for one more day. As soon as I hear those around me whispering, "His race is run," their hands raised high and pointed in some vague direction, then I'll go back and beg if only for one more day, and if he's merciful he'll grant it to me even though in the meantime I've raked him over the coals.

My wife to the right and that other tall woman to the left will be washing my feet with a very expensive eau-de-cologne. A waste, certain individuals may think, just to prove that there were people who disapproved of me to the very end. All the same, this eau-de-cologne is indispensable because of the various odors I give off; vomit, urine that's leaked out, acrid sweat, the eau-de-cologne comes along and covers them all so that the girls on the cloth band with Genoveva won't turn away their faces, on the contrary, they also sprinkle the corpse in their own way. At the head of the bed, my mother's tearing out her hair, crying so plaintively that I can't bear to hear her. "More softly," I beckon to her and she begins a drawling dirge.

These three women form the first ring around me, assist me though still not reconciled with one another, my mother because my wife took away her son, my wife because my mistress took away her husband. Tomorrow someone else will take me away, thus enabling them to become reconciled. Ultimately I always belong somewhere, I was never able to exist as my own man. "Don't quarrel," I whisper, "they gave me a day's time and I had to beg even for that, I'm clenching my teeth to hold on to it, it's not entirely gratis, I have to make an effort as well."

It's a good thing I divided up my body accurately, a leg and a hand to each of them, the genital organs excluded because the eau-de-cologne itches there, the navel and chest bone the straight dividing line, the neck, Adam's apple, chin, and ridge of the nose the boundary stone, the intelligible line passes between the eyebrows and divides the forehead. I retain my hair in case one combs it one way and another some other way; I don't wish to be an object of ridicule. My wife of course gets the scar from the operation; she loses the heart, but that's how it should be, what with her always being to the right, and I want no misunderstandings about this.

I turn to look at the cloth band with Genoveva. She's always ready to mount her horse and ride off. "Wait," I say, drawing my final breath, "tomorrow we'll leave together." She resembles the girl I was in love with when I was fourteen; she too had loose, blonde hair somewhat like hers and the same rose-colored flesh. The Easter lamb was grazing in the forest and when the time came to slaughter it, the lass started wailing so, that they decided to spare it. I was in high school at the time and in the habit of reading in the forest (there was hardly any space at home with four persons living in one room and a kitchen in the Kaisariane quarter) and God still loved me because the lamb would trail after me bringing along the girl as well. It was still beautiful that spring under the pine trees, our steps in stride with the little bell of the lamb, little Genoveva, the lamb, and I rolling in the grass, the book cast aside and the sun smiling through the pine needles. Now and then God revealed a portion of his white beard—the frayed ends of a downy cloud in heaven that kept disappearing and leaving us the cloudless forest. Until one day I suddenly heard my mother's voice behind me: "You there, is that what you call studying?" Her hands were planted on her waist and she was emitting smoke and flames from her nostrils like a beast from the Apocalypse. The lamb fled frightened; the girl sat up and I saw her white panties slightly wet from fright. "And you, Jezebel," my mother says to her, "why are you turning his head? I'm going to tell your mother everything." When I returned to the forest the following day the little lamb was slaughtered and the loose hair replaced by tight pigtails. My mother was naturally satisfied because she had brought me to the path of God, as she used to say, though from that time on I no longer saw his face, as if he were persecuting me; at least insofar as girls were concerned he was always exposing me, and later when I found a girlfriend who would allow me to feel her breast (which was growing and was hard as stone; I didn't squeeze it, I only caressed it, passing my hand gently over it, and was amazed at not finding a nipple like the one I used to see women in childbed offer their infants, large and red like a marble), he again caught me with my hand in her bust and the wretched thing had become entangled in a strangely fabricated brassiere and wouldn't come out.

Now she's whimpering at the head of the bed and if I were to recall the events to her she would be quite capable of telling me that I'm in this predicament because of such sins and that I must, even if only at the last moment, repent. She recently purchased a large candle the same height as my body; she also bought a little silver man and was running off to Christ at Spata in the hope of saving me. I know now that she'll insist on my taking communion. I've no objection. Toward the end, however, when my time has run out and as I'm supposedly opening my mouth, I'm going to dip my fingers in the chalice and begin sprinkling the priest, my mother, my wife, and my mistress. Why? Just for the hell of it. When I asked for his protection he answered, "It can't be done." Why must I die at forty when others reach seventy and eighty? Never mind about me, all right, so be it, forty, but what about Lillian in her twenty-second year, why? Didn't she exercise? Didn't she have a proper diet? Or for that matter did she smoke? Who is he who gives and takes away and on Saturday dies? Justice.

I do not desire mercy, I do not desire mercy, dear God (the "dear God" a
sigh from the recesses of the heart and not an invocation).
For I have no sins for you to efface
transgressions for you to wash away
or crimes for you to cleanse.
I would have been the first to acknowledge my transgressions and
my crimes and they would have condemned me in my eyes for ever.

No person, no thing have I harmed and nothing deceitful have I done at the expense of another that I may justify your words and accept your judgment.

I refuse to believe that my parents are at fault and that my mother sinfully bore me in her stomach.

I seek but do not find the truth; what is secret and invisible always remains unknown to me.

Sprinkle me with oregano and the seed of myrtle, the dust of thyme, mildew from the mountain, and perhaps I will be purified, perhaps I will even become whiter than snow.

I hear music and rejoice; my weary bones exult.

See, see how my pure heart is reflected in my face and how my upright soul rises from deep within me.

Do not place your face as an obstruction; allow me to see even beyond it.

DINOS CHRISTIANOPOULOS

(1931–)

Rosa Eskenazi

O h! The half-mad old lady got lost again among the streets of boundless Athens. And her cop, like a madman, will again go from police station to police station until he finds her. Only then will his heart return to its proper place. He will affectionately take her back to her hut, and there he will try to bring her to her senses, he will feed her, he will clean her of excrement, and he will put her to bed like a baby.

She was the famous singer of the thirties, the diva of old popular songs. Her Bohemian picture (as a beauty of the Belle Époque) in all the record and gramophone shops used to drive the street urchins and slick lovers mad. She had everything—her husband a successful businessman in Thessaloniki, one of her brothers-in-law a politician, one of her sons an officer. And Rosa, nothing but goodness, assisting songstresses with money and medicine, finding young workers employment in some factory. Once, a few years before the war, she also befriended a policeman from Corinthia—or was it perhaps a secret idyll? Nobody knows.

Afterward came misfortunes, one on top of the other: war, hunger, the occupation. Rosa was no longer a diva, others were at the zenith in her place. Something also started to go wrong with her mind. Then her nearest of kin banished her to a small hut at the edge of Athens. A wretched old age, her chicken-coop full of rats and dung, and she relieving herself in her clothes, living in the wreckage of her former glory. Until her cop finally found her. He was now a trucker and the owner of a great number of trucks, but he refused to forget his former benefactress (or old love) and moved heaven and earth to find her. He wanted to take her to his home in Corinthia, to live there in great comfort, but the old lady would not hear of leaving her chicken-coop!

He alone attended her and nursed her, he alone did the household chores in her hut, fed her, washed and combed her hair, took her out on walks and whenever he went away on a long trip, he left her in the care of the neighboring women. This story, they say, lasted thirty years. And when Rosa died, stark-raving mad, he took her and buried her in Corinthia.

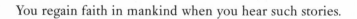

You regain faith in mankind when you hear such stories.

MENIS KOUMANTAREAS

(1931–)

The Bath

The heat began to press itself around the house. The windows, their shutters ajar, were sucking in light, and the doors, upright, were snoring through the cracks. The entire farm was steaming like a Turkish bath.

Harry stopped short, the toothbrush in his mouth, as a hand snatched it from him along with the tube of toothpaste. He was about to protest, to explain that where he was going there wouldn't be space for such luxuries, but the foam muzzled his mouth. The drawers in his room were panting with their tongues sticking out. His suitcase was swallowing up clothes, brushes, small scissors, hangers, shoes. The mother was stirring about, looking for and always finding something to feed the hungry beast. The perspiration was rolling down her, a veritable fountain of pearls, but before it dripped to the floor the thirsty air rushed forward and drank it. The old man in the corner was nervously turning the pages of his newspaper. In the sky a flash of lightning accompanied by thunderbolts from a summer downpour crouched, ready to leap like a spring.

Harry, the cause of all this agitation, was standing off to one side, silent and unparticipating. It could not be said that it was simply the languor of summer or the thought of the trip that was draining him.

It was also the workers, penknives folded in half, who were digging all around the farm, opening up ditches and trenches. The blows from their adzes were falling straight on his head, opening up passages which, instead of pale ore, brought forth tattered thoughts. It was the eyes of his old man that gave no sign of detaching themselves from his newspaper. It was also his mother who was watching for an opportunity, ready to assist him. For years now Harry had learned to bow his head before her, worshiping her like the Virgin Mary. Today, at the age of twenty-two, all that remained for him was to utter a curse and leave. But the pestle, which in his mother's hand was pounding parsley and garlic, was falling on him and finishing him off.

"You'll make a fine soldier," the old man said to him from his bench, the newspaper spread open in front of him. You might have thought he was looking at his son, but his gaze, boring a hole through him, ended by falling on a seascape hanging on the wall. Because of his sorrow at having abandoned the sea, his first love, in order to take a wife, grapevines, and plows, he had stopped looking at people, except when he was able to imagine their hands as oars and their smiles as etesian* winds.

"Watch out, you poor devil, or you'll be done for if you so much as hold a cigarette in your hand," his mother was admonishing him. "It can do no good, only harm." Dressed in black, with a work kerchief drawn tightly over her rectangular head, erect, stemlike, wrinkleless, and with a belly that cried out with fertility, she was holding him by the shoulders and shaking him. She possessed something of the vigor of the air that strips young trees of their leaves. Yet her eyes, black, uncut diamonds, gleamed with mysterious love. She still couldn't believe that Harry was leaving her. Her hands had grown accustomed to holding him, her mouth to speaking to him. The separation was something beyond her comprehension. However hard she tried to retain her dignity, her voice came out like that of a dog barking at the moon. She saw him as he departed behind the tomato plants and the beanstalks, disappearing behind the green crops and the oxen that were steaming like chimneys.

The house became empty at a single stroke. Only the dust

---

* Annual northerly summer winds.

remained, sunning itself on the furniture. Throughout the entire farm all you could hear was the sound of women's teeth cracking green almonds. You could also see the perspiration rolling in beads from the men's armpits. The sky stretched out, unconscious, on the horizon. Only an occasional evening breeze revived it, painting its anemic cheeks with cheap rouge. The days breathed with difficulty and the nights were filled with owls, mourning doves, and crickets. The sole oasis was the postman. The mother knew his route and would wait for him. And the longer he cut capers in the fields, joking and smoking cigarettes with the laborers, the more the mother kicked like a mule being saddled.

"Hey! Old chap. Did you get stuck like your stamps? Come a little closer. It's nice chatting, but I've been broiling in the sun waiting for you."

The old chap never turned a hair upon hearing such remarks. For years now he had been accustomed to silently enduring people's complaints. Rain or shine he went at his own pace and everyone went along with his ways. Only Harry's mother intimidated him. "Look, you poor devil, don't come empty-handed or else..." She didn't finish what she was saying, perhaps because if she told him that she would strangle him, it might not have been mere talk; she had moments when she was quite capable of anything. And as the old chap pulled the letter out of his leather bag, she would jump on him like a tigress being thrown raw meat in her cage. Only instead of tearing him to pieces, she would offer him a cherry drink in the kitchen. She, too, knew how to savor her joys to the fullest.

Private Parashos, Harry, son of Theodore and Antonia, 2nd Company, 4th Platoon Battery, Camp Syros: the old man barely read the letters. It was enough for him to run his fingers over them. Every time he touched the word Syros his hands grew numb. Gradually his desire for his son became anticipation—he loved him now like the sea, writing him off. He didn't resemble the mother. She never had her fill of reading Harry's letters. The first time she would drink them at one gulp; the second, she understood them; but only with the third reading did the words take root in her. And if you sometimes saw her with a ladle in her hand stirring vegetables in the saucepan, suddenly she groaned like a wounded beast and grazed the air as she passed until, like the runner who cuts the tape at the end of a race, she came and fell on the precious letter. She ended up knowing them by heart. The contact with the paper, however, remained irreplaceable, just as, while talking with a person one loves, one also wants to hold their hand.

And all the while that the old man was bent over on his bench, with the newspapers wrapped around him like a sheet, the mother went to and fro in the empty house, wearing only a baggy slip, uncombed, without make-up, unwashed, the image of despair. Around her the saucepans were piling up, mounds of dirt and burnt butter, and the smell of burning meat pricked your nostrils. The bedclothes were in disarray, the dresses unironed, the stockings undarned, the furniture buried in prehistoric dust that the impertinent spiders wrapped in a cocoon embroidered with flies. The photographs, only they, were arranged on the shelves, in rows and according to chronology, in the china closet, on the mantelpiece, on the tables, everywhere, beaming with the affection of the mother who kept them clean and always looking brand-new. "Harry in his cradle," "Harry when he was one," "Harry's first steps," "Harry in his bath," and here she would pause to delight in her son's little body, which was whiter even than soap. Her arm, dark and with tucked-up sleeves, loomed in a corner of the photograph, clutching the soft dough of the sponge with which it was scrubbing, causing every complaint and protest of the child to disappear. "Harry when he was six," "Harry on the farm," "Harry with his father," "Harry with his mother," and each time, deep down, she was secretly pleased that the little boy held his father's hand while looking elsewhere, while in the adjacent photograph he held her hand very tightly while looking into her eyes.

She kept the letters in the drawer with his baby clothes, beneath the blue undershirts, in among Harry's booties, bibs, rattles, and short pants. (Sometimes she would put them in the wash as well, just to be able to iron them—they were the only things she ironed—and to be able to put them back in the drawer.) And all night long the letters lay next to her pillow, like a glass of water one does not drink but the thought of which refreshes. Without turning on the light, she would reach out with her hand and scratch the paper—a coarse, horrid sound in the night, like a gramophone needle stuck in the same groove of a song. She slept little or not at all. Instead of devouring her, sorrow nourished her: she had become twice as fat. She walked about on the farm, bareheaded, swearing like a man. At sunset her shadow, black and desperate, imprinted itself on the sky.

For a while no letters at all arrived. The days remained blank like the whitest paper, the house filthy, the tiles on the roof loose. The old man bored holes through his newspaper with a pin and stared at the seascape on the wall. The mother, lying in bed like a woman in childbed, on her back, naked, turned the pages of the calendar on the wall with her eyes. Then, one afternoon, a letter arrived again. Written as always in pencil. One phrase obscured all the others: "forty-eight-hour leave."

She dusted the furniture, washed the floors, spread naphtha over them, then wax, and rubbed them until they shone like mirrors. She ironed her dresses, cast off her black clothes, breathed fresh air into the house. The old man, driven into a corner, his hands resembling the oars of a boat that have been flung onto the mainland, sat speechless. His heart in his mouth, he would seldom light a cigarette, lest he dirty the house and unleash the tempest. The tempest lay in wait in every corner, armed with a ceiling broom capable of reaching up and piercing the roof to clean the sky, with a yellow kerchief pulled over her head like an angry sun, stout like a potato, light as a butterfly, gay and grim, merciless and mirthful, with her extra-wide duster that she waved to the east and to the west. Only the clock in the dining room maintained its composure, noting the seconds and the minutes with indifference until she felt the urge to seize it and tear out its hands. For three entire months she had brooded the day when Harry would be on furlough. Any moment now she expected to see him spring up, a chick in khaki.

The bus of the company line was late. She had walked hurriedly in the fields, gasping for breath. The distance seemed an eternity to her. The cars passed by, a chained caravan, puffing and blowing on the scorching highway. The dust choked her eyes, which she had disdained to protect with sunglasses. It left a thick, rough surface on her fingers, which had stayed awake all night next to the candle. (She had soaked a little cotton in the oil of the candle that, together with some holy bread, incense, and flowers from this year's holy ceremony of the burial of Christ, she had suspended from her son's neck—a small storehouse of love and tyranny.) "I wonder if he'll still be wearing them," she pondered, and the longer the bus was delayed, the more she despaired. Then she saw it coming, wrapped in hoarfrost, a gray beast with old pieces of iron hanging from its sides like scales that banged with every jolt and jingled like the bracelets of the popular song.

At first she didn't recognize him; he seemed a little thin to her. You might have thought the army clothes had robbed his body of its weight. She saw him advance gropingly, as if he were not already familiar with the place. He, in his turn, saw her standing dimly in the midday heat, taller than a fence, broader than a public square, in her black dress embroidered with little flowers, like a burnt field that had suddenly blossomed. They remained motionless for a few seconds and then, unrestrained, flung themselves at each other.

With the opening of the door the old man concealed the newspaper behind his back. The boy sensed relief in the father's eyes, and the old man sank into the azure gaze of his son as if into a wave. They sat down opposite one another, a vase of flowers between them. In order to converse they leaned sideways in the same direction. Afterward the old man very slowly took out his newspaper and again placed it like a shield in front of himself. The mother, unrestrained, was scurrying left and right, up and down, fetching water beforehand in case Harry was thirsty, food in case he was hungry, making up the bed in case he was sleepy. She knelt down and removed his boots one at a time; she wiped his forehead with a silk handkerchief; and when Harry removed the cigarettes from the pocket of his jacket, both the old lady and the old man, dumbfounded, stared at him. You might have thought they had never before seen a cigarette. They said nothing; but when Harry went to lie down, the mother took the cigarettes from his uniform and flung them out the window as if they were sin itself.

The house seemed fresh and shaded like a forest to him, the water ice-cold, the furniture like polished copper utensils, the rooms low-ceilinged and narrow, the bed made of fine down. He lay on the pillow and his cheek became silken. He touched the pitcher of water and it was as if he had touched the neck of a young girl. He sighed sweetly and turned to look out the window: the black backs of the workers were bent over the radishes, beans, and tomato plants, which were arrayed like troops inside the garden. Suddenly, without the warning of a bugle, a sharp pain, like a keen-edged knife, shot right through his flesh. All of a sudden he found himself back at camp—a camp without water, without shade, with mounds of helmets and Enfield 32's, with stripes shaded beneath the visor of a military cap—and he felt his hand ready to rise to his forehead in salute. He found himself back in the barracks on the first night, his head shaved, in civilian clothes, leaning against heads that might just as well have been feet. The darkness was woven with the smell of breaths, held respiration, mute silence. An occasional joke, thrown out here and there like fireworks that didn't go off, would fall and shatter on the damp slate. He found himself in the common bath, naked among the naked, in the yellow despair of the latrines, in the barracks with the national odor of soldiers' boots. He was back on sentry duty in the Command, with the searchlights that were scrutinizing the night in search of an imaginary enemy, the dogs that were fiercely inscribing their shadows behind mounds of discarded tin cans, the trucks that were roaming inside the camp, indiscriminately slashing with their wheels anything that passed by, any inkling of flight. He heard again the sea driving him mad with its cries, like a drowning woman. Yet he was unable to help her.

It was he himself who was drowning on the bed in his room, immersed in his own perspiration and fluids. The coarse sheet was pricking him, the cool pitcher with its thirst was burning him. And his mother, who kept moving about in the room, was a wasp that had come in through the open window. She counted twenty-two cigarette stubs in the ashtray. For twenty-two years he had been living under the yoke of a love that was on the verge of crushing him: "Harry in his cradle," "Harry on the farm," "Harry with his mother," Harry here, Harry there. He had grown tired of seeing his pictures hanging like flags on the walls, arranged on the shelves like a battalion in review. "What did you do, my little bird, in the army? Tell me too," his mother was asking him. "Did you fight bravely?" How was he to explain to her that military exercises are conducted with empty rifles on battlefields where, as soon as it gets dark, infantrymen and officers plank down behind the bushes the island's prostitutes? "Did you receive a medal, son?" In the army they called gonorrhea a medal. How was he to make her understand that he was too weak to lift the weight of the knapsack, that he was unable to take part in the final drills on the practice of arms, to jump over the water trench, to climb the seven-knot rope, to learn how to assemble and disassemble a submachine gun, to hit the black and red mark waiting to be riddled with bullets? His bullets had strayed to the right and to the left, spreading panic. The entire platoon had sunk facedown to the ground as the instructor, the veins of his neck swollen, kept repeating: "Incompetent... good-for-nothing..."

Incompetent—the word whirled round the cobbled streets when the company, off-duty in the evening, was besieging the island's brothels and he was wandering about reading his disgrace in the scornful looks of the girls. His head down, he walked past the cafés with the townspeople, the taverns with the workers, the public square where the notables were out strolling with their wives and their children, their watches looped through gold chains. Shame covered him like a shroud. He could scarcely wait to return to the base where there remained for him nothing other than a piece of paper and a pencil.

"Mother, I'm writing to you while the others are asleep. I'm worried you won't be able to make out my handwriting. I'm in good health. I've missed you both, I've missed you, mommy. I can see you opening the door and looking in to see if I'm all right, if I need anything. I think of you constantly, everywhere. Sometimes I turn to look at the sky—a small patch is visible from my bed—as others turn to watch the rain or sun, and then I see you silently waiting on the threshold of our house. I'm keeping my chin up and I'm being patient. All will pass. We're waiting for our furloughs. It seems strange to me, however, that everybody speaks about his fiancée or girlfriend. Nobody here speaks about his mother. This is why I've decided to stay clear of conversation. Forgive me..."

Sometimes he thought that his military service was an opportunity, a godsend, to break away from the nightmare at home. But the camp was without shade, the sun a black spot when one looked it in the eye, the bread dark and rare like a diamond. He felt like running and calling, "Mother, mother, mother," without knowing if it was his mother he was calling or that manna of old. Inside the house he was indecisive, outside it, incompetent. He saw again the school copybooks with their blue paper jackets and his mother's hand taking his fingers and guiding them. It was sweet to abandon oneself to other hands and ride on the wings of a butterfly, to hang onto their antennae like reins and swim in moonlit seas, in the lagoons of meditation and dream.

Thus, year after year he became more shut-up in himself, as if inside a shellfish, pressing his ear against its curved hollows, striving to understand the world through an echo. Every time some girl made an impression on him, he wanted to reach out with his hand and touch her. But each time, her hair was not shiny and dark, her eyes not almond-shaped, her body not solid and strong, not as blessed as his mother's. At bottom, the comparison tormented him. Still he had no other counterpart. No matter where he turned, the mirror reflected the same face, frontally, sideways, upright, upside-down. It was always his mother's face. He remembered that there were days when a sudden burst of light through the branches of an almond tree made him cry and become anxious. At such moments he was ready to come to a decision, to escape from the iron collar of tyranny. But every time his mother entered the room to bring him a freshly ironed and starched shirt, every time she offered him bitter orange and sour cherry, he felt his mouth drowning in the sweet torpor of the taste, his mind stopped, and his heart, tender like a little boy's, wanted to hug her... And the camp with the choking stench of soldiers' mess pots and the horrible sound of boot steps trampling on him died out and there remained only this sweet lulling contact with the sheet.

'The water's ready, come and wash," he heard her voice coming from the hall. "And don't smoke anymore," she said to him as she entered the room. "Where did you find cigarettes?" Whereupon she bit her lips from fear of letting on that she had already thrown away one of his packages. She opened the window to get rid of the smoke and then closed it again lest he catch cold lying down the way he was. "Come along, get up now," she said to him. His body was firm from maneuvers, as heavy to lift as military gear. The water was cool; it poured over him in ripples, and his fatigue gave way, abated, fell into the tub floating with insects and pine needles. Suddenly the tub was black and he was white. He could hear his mother pacing behind the drawn curtain that closed off the entrance to the kitchen, her voice asking him whether the water was too hot or too cold, whether he wanted the large, fluffy towel or the small, woven one. He was conscious of her voice, tender and caressing him, angry because she was unable to pass through the nylon wall to arrange things for him as only she knew how. She kept turning like a lioness in her cave, gathering up his discarded clothes from the floor, incapable of explaining the presence of a boot, a beret. Once the clothes, the accessories, had ceased to adhere to her son, they had again become clothes, accessories, alien and unrelated to everything that was and affected Harry. And all the while she kept urging him to use plenty of soap and to scrub hard because, as she said, one never knows what sort of people one comes in contact with away from home.

"Leave me alone, mother," he answered her, and instead of the soap he felt her voice flaying him savagely and imperiously. "Shall I rinse you off with a few buckets of water?" she asked him. "The water you have there won't be enough."

"Stop it, mother, I'm telling you. Just go and leave me alone." "You young scamp. I'm to blame for loving you and this is how you speak to me. Tell me, what would you do without me, tell me, what would my boy do without his mommy!"

And with a single movement of her arm, the dark arm in the photograph, she pushed aside the nylon wall, armed with a bucket of water, ready if necessary to fight. She spread her legs apart, steadied her body, stooped, took a run, and the water from the well reverberated on him like a sweet-sounding rattle. Harry in his tub, Harry in his cradle, whining, laughing, being tickled, shouting and waving his tender hands in all directions, sending forth bubbles and inarticulate cries from his mouth while she fed him more water—the way she used to feed him milk, by putting large morsels of bread in the milk, panadas that puffed up, burst, and settled at the bottom of the cup—scolded him, smiled at him, called him Harry, 'arry, little Harry, baby, cutie, sweetie, and all the time Harry, 'arry, little Harry screamed and splashed in the water while she threatened him with the index finger of her hand on which a gold wedding band sparkled—an unshakable circle that harmony, love, and large panadas which floated like life buoys around the ark of familial calm came to consolidate within him. And when the water in the bucket, a veritable tidal wave, emptied, she turned to look at her son, white and sweet-smelling from being washed, fed, ready to be wrapped in the white, fluffy towel.

She turned to look at him and confronted his infinitely thin body, legs that were dark from having forested in tropical vegetation, callouses like tiny, crumpled helmets on his toes; she ascended to the stomach, swollen from food and strewn with black grass, the navel that deepened like the mouth of a well, his chest a field intersected by a furrow planted with chicory, his armpits flower beds of spiders, his shoulders with the shoulder blades jutting out like the horns of a bull, his hands that fell like cataracts to his knees. She remained with the bucket in her hand, speechless: Harry when he was five, ten, fifteen, Harry at the age of twenty-two, and the numbers struck her head like a hammer. Inside his legs open windows of a house of ill-repute, the last thing she saw was a caterpillar which was coiling and uncoiling, struggling to stand on two large pine cones that propped it up. Amid her cries the bucket slipped from her hands and would have rolled down the stairs were it not for its rope, which at the last moment had managed to catch on the railing. She ran to escape, to see no more, but became completely entangled in the curtain that wrapped itself around her like a gigantic water lily made of nylon. She felt faint and nauseated. She ripped open the curtain, only to stumble against Harry. At the touch of him she was seized by a spasm. Her cries filled the house, knocked against the wall like bats, and flew out the windows. You could now see the workers waking from the torpor of work, lifting their heads, standing erect on tiptoe. Their stares entered through the windows, darkening the house. She ran into the hall in the hope that she would reach the dining room. Behind her the gigantic ape was spreading his legs, and if his hands were unable to reach her, nonetheless his shadow, wrought in relief on the wall, was holding her by the hair, making her scream and wail. She was about to close the dining room door, but with a single jolt the door wrenched itself free and went smack into the wall. She tried to backtrack, but her skirt became entangled in the pictures and with one sudden, abrupt movement she knocked them over. "Harry when he was one," "Harry with his mother," "Harry in his bath," and as each crystal glass fell it would burst on the waxed floor like a grenade, causing the windowpanes to rattle and her shouts to reach the sky. She escaped from him and through a second door sought shelter in the hall. All around her the open windows were gaping—never before had she realized how many windows the house had, how many eyes there were around her to undress her. Her every step was met with a flash of lightning accompanied by thunderbolts. She did not know whether this was a portent of a summer downpour or an echo of her own fright. He caught up with her outside his room and, in an attempt to restrain her, ripped part of her dress. A piece of shriveled yet firm flesh came and fell before him. His eyes received it like a starving dog. As her cries increased, sticking to the damp wall of the heat, he wanted at first to stop up her mouth. And as her whole body writhed in his hands, opening wide the door of his room, he threw her on the bed. Afterward he came out, closed the door behind him, and placed the key in his pocket. He could hear her all alone, thrashing about and beating her breast, but he merely took out the package of cigarettes and came and stood by the window, licking the cigarette paper. It was only then that the workers lowered their eyes, and that the rain, mixed with hail and pine needles, fell on the farm. Sky and earth had become bound by a thread and were struggling with infinite love and unsilenced hatred.

The old man, wrapped in his newspapers, was asleep face down on his bench, the ash of his cigarette growing longer next to him. A cloud of silence spread over the house.

NIKOS HOULIARAS

(1940-)

The Shoes

The shoe is divided into two parts: the upper part—the vamp—and the sole. There is also the heel.

Kostakis Frattas was holding his left shoe in his hands and looking at it. He admired beautiful things. Handsome clothes and shoes. Especially shoes. He had a weakness for them. Of all the parts of one's attire, he attached the greatest importance to the shoes.

It was Palm Sunday morning. Seated on the bench in his yard, he was deeply troubled..

He had picked up the shoes on the evening of the day before. After closing his shop, he had stopped by the shoemaker's, Ziabiras. They had placed them in a carton box for him, he had given them the money, and he had taken them.

They had not even exchanged a word. In any event, Kostakis Frattas had little to say. Ever since he was little, he had been like this. Taciturn and pensive.

He took the box and went out into the street. As he walked, he would lift it to his face from time to time and smell it. It smelled nice. Wax and leather. The familiar smell. They were first-quality shoes. Kid-leather.

And as he approached Nikolouzos', he was no longer able to

resist. He stood under the street lamp, quickly opened the box, and took them out. Holding them in one hand, he moved them once or twice in the light.

He had time enough to see them shining. He saw the counters, the uppers, and the welts. He saw the entire soles from one end to the other and the indentations. Everything was beautifully crafted. A light wind was blowing and tomorrow was Palm Sunday.

Kostakis Frattas partially retraced his steps and, after making sure that no one was watching him, put the shoes back in the box.

Not that it mattered much, only he had never given anyone any such right. What would people say if they saw him standing in the middle of the street staring at his new shoes? He had never given others the opportunity to comment on his behavior. No one had ever seen him happy or even troubled. Whatever happened to him was his concern and only his.

And the truth of the matter is that a great many things had happened to Kostakis Frattas of late. And all at once.

First, at the beginning of February, his mother died. Just like that. She had a tumor in her lungs and he lost her.

After that, his sister Aspasia's condition worsened. Her nerves were already on edge as a result of that engagement. Then came his mother's death and Aspasia shut herself in the upstairs room for good, coming downstairs only to eat or to go to the bathroom. His wife wanted nothing better. Now she was free to wander through the house with a face a mile long and to polish the floors all day long.

Kostakis Frattas had little commerce with his wife. Nor did he have any children. The two of them barely spoke to one another. An occasional exchange and even that was mumbled.

For some time now, she had been continuously telling him that she was going to leave. That she was going to return to her family. To her sisters and father. She would also make one or two remarks about the day's shopping.

This, however, didn't bother Kostakis Frattas very much. He had been accustomed to such ever since he was little. To life's being adverse to him.

At the age of fifteen, he had found himself fatherless and hedged in by events. Nor had he received many options. He had embarked on life unsmiling and was forced to bear his burden in this manner. From the shop to the house and from the house to the shop. For years now he had no recollection other than that of following the same itinerary.

This didn't mean, of course, that Kostakis Frattas didn't also have his small inventions. That he didn't harbor other things within himself.

Many times, particularly at night, while walking along in the street on his way home, he had thought of various ideas. What pleased him most, however, was the notion of changing the town plan. At least that of his district. Very often he demolished those small houses next to the girls' high school that divided the street in two. He demolished them and imagined in their place a square with small shrubs. Something well-defined. Still, other times he left these houses where they were, but visualized them differently. Tall and stately. With lovely balconies and many floors. He widened the street on both sides and visualized it paved with asphalt, with wide sidewalks and slender trees.

He also imagined another street, still wider, on the downward side. A large street, on the waterfront, with thick trees along its entire length. Manicured trees, acacias, for example, and beneath them benches sculpted in stone.

He also wanted a marble staircase that would descend as far as the water, bordered on either side with statues. Marble lions looking off in the distance, toward the mountain.

When he was young he had read about such things in a book and he remembered the people who traveled in carriages in these stories. They traveled on the wide street, in St. Petersburg, next to the river with the marble staircases and statues. Handsome, stately things. And people in their splendid coats that were looking off in the distance, thinking about their concerns.

It was somewhat like this that Kostakis Frattas imagined this street. He imagined it this way and told himself that perhaps he would live long enough to see these things. Perhaps they would tran-spire during his lifetime. For he had better things in mind for himself, even though he showed no such signs, and he was ready for every-thing. He wanted very much to be well-dressed, to go to some tea-room in the late afternoon and to sit there quietly. For there would undoubtedly be tearooms down there. There had to be. At least that's how he imagined things. Well-dressed and wearing new shoes that creaked, he would go there and sit. Because, deep down, Kostakis Frattas felt that he was very particular about such concerns and thus, without even knowing why, was fond of what others call elegance. He liked to be well-dressed. Not expensively or extravagantly. For that matter, the life he led wouldn't allow it. He wanted to have a handsome suit and an impeccable pair of shoes. The shoes especially he wanted to be perfect.

He felt this deep down. Ever since he was little he had felt it. It was as if it protected him from those around him. As if in this way he was raising a barrier so that they would respect him. So that they would leave him alone and tranquil and not meddle in his affairs. In any event, whatever he had, he wanted to be the only one to have it, to know it. And he wanted to endure it all by himself. The truth is that, regardless of what happened to him, Kostakis Frattas had never allowed anyone the opportunity to comment on it.

For that matter, he had few dealings with people. He never got involved in the affairs of others. Once in a while he ventured as far as Nikolouzos' café, but even there he indulged only in small talk. Just enough so that he wouldn't be considered unsociable.

Now, too, in spite of all his worries, he didn't want to avoid people. It was with people that he wanted to be, but with his own concerns kept secret, carefully protected.

This is why, even though business in the shop was going to hell like everything else, he went out and ordered the shoes. He saw in a catalogue a model that appealed to him, he selected the leather and the color, and they took his measurements. He also made some slight changes on the top part and told them not to make too many embellishments. To pay attention only to the indentations, and to make sure that the vamp was clear-cut, without a defect.

This is what he told them, and last night, on the eve of Palm Sunday, he had stopped by to get them.

He had taken them and was walking along in the street. Although he was very tired, he was unable to restrain himself. Right near Nikolouzos', under the street lamp, he stopped to look at them,

turned around once to see whether anyone had seen him, then quick-
ened his step and headed home.

He entered the courtyard through the back door and saw that the
light was on upstairs in Aspasia's room. The breeze stirred the leaves
of the quince tree outside in front of the dining room and suddenly
Kostakis Frattas felt sleepy.

He pushed open the glass door and entered the room. Everything
was neatly arranged and the light was on in the kitchen. He called out
his wife's name once or twice, but didn't receive an answer. He went
to the kitchen to see what she was doing, but didn't find her. He merely saw his plate with his dinner on the table and next to it a piece of
paper. She was gone! Hermione had said it and done it.

"I can't stand it in here any longer," the note said. "I'm leaving and
don't come looking for me. I'm going back home."

Kostakis Frattas was about to call his sister at once, but again
remained silent. He sat down at the table and ate the food. Afterward
he gathered up the crumbs and threw them in the sink. Then he took
the box with the shoes, went to his room, and lay down.

Outside his window, the rustling of the leaves from the trees
could be heard, and Kostakis Frattas saw in his mind the entire landscape receding and drifting toward Albania. Grasses and trees were
shriveling inside him and receding. He felt an emptiness in his stomach. So be it, he thought. Anyway, he would dress up tomorrow morning in his gray, striped suit, he would also put on his new, kid-leather
shoes, and he would go out. He would go to Nikolouzos' as though
nothing had happened. In any event, he was used to such things. Why
should he lose heart now? He wouldn't say anything to anyone. He
had never allowed anyone the opportunity to comment on his behavior. It was no different now. He would go. Calm and serious. With his
new shoes. Impeccably dressed.

This is what Kostakis Frattas thought. For a little while he smelled
the shoes next to him on his bedside table, then fell asleep.

❧

In the morning he was awakened by his sister Aspasia's footsteps. He
listened to her movements. She had gone down to the kitchen. He sat
up for a moment and was about to call her, but changed his mind and

stretched out again. He didn't let out a sound. He merely listened to her movements. She was drinking something down in the kitchen; afterward she went to the bathroom; then she climbed the stairs and returned to her room.

All this time Kostakis Frattas didn't budge. When she passed in front of his door, he pretended to be asleep. When he was certain that she was upstairs, he turned to look at the clock. It was ten o'clock. Palm Sunday morning. He had slept profoundly. A sleep heavy as lead.

He recalled yesterday's events briefly, then got up, went to the door that led to the courtyard and opened it. The odor of trees came to him and he heard children's voices out in the street. The sky was cloudy in places and a gentle wind was blowing.

Back inside, he made his way to the kitchen and splashed some water on his face. Next he drank a bowl of milk while standing. Afterward he went to the closet and took out his gray, striped suit. His best suit.

Anyway, he would get dressed up and go out. He would go to Nikolouzos' as he always did. To drink his ouzo.

In any event, everything is written, he thought. Just as what was happening to him was his again. It was his destiny. That's the way it was and he had to endure it. For everything is written up there in advance, then falls. Now on one person, now on another.

It was his turn again and Kostakis Frattas knew it. And he was enduring it. He wouldn't say anything to anyone. He would get all dressed up and go out. He would put on his new shoes and he would go to Nikolouzos' as though nothing had happened.

First he put on the trousers and the white shirt. Next came the vest. He pulled slightly on the pant pleats to smooth them out. Then he went and took the box with the shoes, taking the shoe-horn as well.

He sat down in the chair and opened the box, took out the shoes and put them on. Carefully. First the right foot, then the left. He stood up and took several steps as far as the mirror with the laces undone.

They were first-quality shoes. Kid-leather, extra fine, and they creaked as much as they were supposed to. The pant crease fell nicely on the brown shiny surface and Kostakis Frattas suddenly felt a wave of warmth rising in him. Like something enveloping him softly and protecting him. Everything was clear-cut. Impeccable.

The sole of his foot pressed gently on the sole of the shoe. The vamp clasped the foot without pinching it in the slightest.

He opened and closed his toes a little inside the shoe. He moved them around a little and saw the small waves formed on top by the leather. Pretty, rounded shiny surfaces. And the stitching on the vamp curving and descending, without a single defect, down to the indentations. Turning emphatically and fading out on the sole. Perfect.

Kostakis Frattas looked at them and felt that he was ready. Ready to go out again. Into the world. He was well-protected somewhere. He suddenly felt untouchable; this is why he lifted his foot to tie the shoelaces. So that afterward he could put on his jacket and go out.

Placing his right foot on the chair, he took hold of the shoelaces, leaned over to tie them and looked at the shoe closely.

He saw the counters, the uppers, and the padding, he saw the entire sole from one end to the other, he also saw the indentations. Everything was impeccable.

He slowly tied the laces on the right one, then lifted the left one. He lifted it and took hold of the laces, took hold of them and looked at the shoe closely, looked at it carefully when, suddenly, he felt a cold shudder run through him. From top to bottom. He felt a tightening in his stomach and let go of the laces. He immediately took off the shoe, took it in his hands, and looked at it again.

He remained motionless for a moment, then abruptly turned around and went out into the courtyard, limping.

He went quickly out into the light, holding the left shoe in his hand. He went over to the bench under the quince tree and looked at the shoe. He looked at it carefully in the daylight and saw it again, saw again that small cleft on the shiny leather. It was at the very front, where the vamp curved gracefully. On the left-hand side that covered his little toe. The cut of the shoemaker's knife was there, on the pretty shiny surface. A small, diagonal cut that wounded. That destroyed all this perfection and calm. It was at the very front, like a wound on the clear-cut vamp, the beautiful arc.

Kostakis Frattas looked at it again, examined it again. It was carefully mended. Skillfully and treacherously done so as not to be obvious. Yet it was the cut of a shoemaker's knife. An insignificant, brown cleft, but it shattered him. This small thing shattered Kostakis Frattas, and he remained there, seated under the quince tree, on this Palm Sunday, looking at it, looking at it, totally defenseless.

YIORGOS MANIOTIS

(1951–)

In the Depths of the House

W e lived our youth in the midst of indigence, war, and catastrophes. Untimely deaths, illnesses, hunger, and poverty. That was our youth. Entire years far from our homes. Entire years in mud and snow, with bullets buzzing all around us like hornets, with empty and ruined stomachs, with tattered and shattered nerves, with our heads and our armpits full of sores from lack of sanitation and squalor. Entire years far from our homes and our loved ones, with fever and without sleep, fighting on land and on sea for a better life. That was our youth.

War, harsh winters, indigence, and various epidemics were all destroying life and dispersing death everywhere. It was extraordinarily good luck and divine good will to be alive and reach forty in those times. Death and misery and the struggle for survival. That was our youth. As soon as we started getting back on our feet somehow or other, as soon as we started rebuilding something with great effort and pain, as soon as we started putting our lives in some kind of order— to see how we would go about living, my friend—and before getting completely back on our feet and enjoying the fruits of our toil and trouble, again WAR, again illnesses, again catastrophes, again hunger and poverty, again death, again fire. Whatever we had built up to that moment, whatever we had succeeded in building with great effort, pain, and privations, was becoming ASHES.

UNTIL we learned the tune. The last time things reached an impasse. Our land from one end to the other became filled with the corpses of small children, became filled with smoking black holes, mutilated men, and women dressed in black. We became desperate, my friend. What is the purpose of such destruction? For ideals, it seems, and for venerable objectives we were digging up and burning the country from one end to the other every ten years. For a better life and the like, it seems, we were pulling down and destroying whatever we had succeeded in building with our blood and tears. We were dying for a better life before barely turning twenty. But we learned the tune. Now things were as clear as daylight. Ideals and venerable objectives were the bait for dragging us into war, for breaking us, and for crushing us. AND ALL THIS...so that we would never ask questions and never find time to sit down, to reflect, and to assess our lives. Because everything backtracks in times of war—everything. The business you've begun goes to hell and your people leave never to return and you're unable to think properly about anything—anything at all. In the first place because you're concerned with coming out clean and surviving, and secondly because fanaticism and hatred don't allow you to see beyond the end of your nose. In peacetime it was work from morning until night so that you might have some security, at least somewhere to protect your head in an hour of need, and then suddenly, out of the blue, when war broke out, whatever you had succeeded in building with great effort and pain became ashes, smithereens...that is, NOTHING, nothing...that is precisely what our life was!

Finis, therefore, with wars and ideals and venerable objectives. They were a dead end. We were human beings and we wanted to live in peace and tranquility. *Finis* with wars that led nowhere. We couldn't kill each other off every ten years and tear down whatever we had built, foundations and all. Enough of that; we had grown weary. *Finis* with ideals and ideas that were dragging us into wild mountains to stand facing one another and to scatter our blood and flesh on the grass, mud, and snow. *Finis* with wars and hostilities. We wanted at long last to live in tranquility, my brother. We wanted a little peace, a little calm. That's what we were thinking as the war was coming to an end. And we were ready to blow everything sky-high if they failed to understand us and if they again put forth the game of heroism and fanfares. We were ready to blow everything sky-high because we could no longer bear it. We would tear down everything. Nothing would be left standing. Luckily, however, at that very moment the solution was found. What we had been awaiting for so many centuries, for entire years, was discovered at long last. What would bring happiness, joy, justice, wealth, and progress to the world was discovered at long last. It was machines. Yes, machines. With machines, all of us, without a single exception, would enjoy abundant and inexpensive goods, free time, amenities. All of us, without a single exception, would be happy and sweet-tempered. Peace would reign from one end of the world to the other. For there would no longer be cause for war. Goods would be abundant and all of us, without a single exception, would be satiated and happy.

Where were we? Ah, yes…precisely at the moment when the war was coming to an end and the new, great, and ardently awaited PEACE was beginning. At FIRST I was somewhat hesitant. But with time I turned things over in my mind and thought to myself: Hold on, John, I thought, you can see for yourself how things are changing, how life is improving; are you going to remain on the outside, then? Aren't you going to participate in the creation of the new world that's just now beginning? It would be sheer folly, I reflected, to remain on the brink just for a whim and a fear you aren't even able to define very well, nor are you really truly certain of feeling it. You fought so many years for justice and for the happiness of man, I reflected, and now that we've reached some kind of final result, now, my dear boy, you've decided to quit? What's come over you? Have you gone mad? I thought to myself. Don't procrastinate, time is passing, I reflected, sit down, concentrate, and figure out what you need in order to organize your new life perfectly so that you will not only live well yourself but will also be of help to others in some way. I sat down, therefore, deliberated, and realized that the first thing I needed in order to be somebody in the new world, which was just now barely beginning, what I needed first of all, I say, was a DEGREE. I had one. Fine. I forgot to mention that in spite of all the wars I was already, strangely enough, a graduate of law school. Let's move on, I thought to myself, you have a degree, what's the next step? The next step was to find a good little wife and to set up house, something akin to a base of operations, with two or three children as a source of joy and consolation. A simple matter. At least that's what I thought at first. I soon realized, however, that this was one of the most critical and difficult junctures in my life. The slightest mistake in the selection of my lifelong companion would be quite capable of transforming my life into a miserable failure. I had to find a woman who would be devoted to me, who would understand me, and who would be determined to stand by me like an unshakable rock, regardless of anything—anything whatsoever—that happened to me in the long and difficult journey of my life. After searching endlessly, I found Maria! She was a teacher and an orphan whose parents had died in the war and who had grown up in an orphanage. A beautiful, tall brunette with a fair complexion and green eyes. From the moment we set eyes on each other, we realized right away that we were perfectly matched. Maria had a zest for life and a love for others to the point of self-sacrifice! Because she had suffered a great deal when she was young, her dream was to have a family. She had, you see, been so deprived of one. We got married right away. I had opened an office that was doing quite well, and she was teaching in a very good private school. We had little in the way of economic difficulties. After returning from the village where we had gone on our honeymoon, we went out one afternoon and bought a large, bronze bed. One evening we stayed up all night on that bed, discussing our plans and dreams. "Listen, Maria," I said to her, "we won't rush, little by little…We'll work for three or four years, we'll put aside some money, and then we'll buy a house once and for all. We won't rush, little by little. For the time being these two rooms we're living in are more than adequate for us. When the children are born, then we'll see what we're going to do!"

Where were we? Ah, yes, on the BED.

Four years later our first child, Alexander, was born. It was a boy. Beside myself with joy, I made Maria a big surprise. I went out and bought this house. It was among the first apartment buildings, if not the first, to go up in our city. A tobacco manufacturer had built it and given it to his daughter as a dowry; this is also why the structure is extremely solid. His daughter, however, was unfortunate, and when her father died she started selling the apartments one by one at very reasonable prices because she was in dire need. I caught her at precisely one such difficult moment in her life and convinced her to sell me this apartment at a bargain. It has five rooms—three bedrooms, this living room, the dining room over there, a huge hall, a bathroom, a service room, a kitchen, and three large closets. When Maria left the hospital with Alexander in her arms, I brought her straight here, where the only furnishings were a cradle for the baby and our large, bronze bed. We didn't possess a thing and acquired all these belongings little by little. "Oh, John," Maria said, crying out of happiness, "oh John, what have you gone and done? Such extravagance, my love. It wasn't necessary, John, it wasn't necessary. I'm so touched, my love," she kept saying while crying and kissing the baby. "This is where we're going to live our lives, Maria. This is where our home will be, my love. This is where we're going to spend our lives," I said to her, kissing her hair. Soon I also started to cry and nothing could make me stop. Afterward Maria placed Alexander in his cradle and we then went up to bed like small children and cried without stopping and with all our love…so much so that our tears dried up. At last everything had entered into some kind of order, everything had found a direction. From now on we would be able to sleep in peace, without any apprehensions about TOMORROW. Several days later we threw a party for our friends. And what a party! It was magnificent! A party we would remember for the rest of our lives. I had purchased a hand-operated gramophone, a portable, among the first to be imported, and around thirty records so that we were able to go on dancing and singing until morning. All the men came dressed in military uniforms. The women wore multicolored dresses. At daybreak we men all shut ourselves in the dining room, took off our uniforms, and put on suits. Black, brand-new suits. After we were impeccably dressed, we opened the door and came out into this very living room. The women fell all over us, embracing us, kissing us, and loading us with presents—cologne, lighters, watches, and other such nice things, exactly the way they did when, dirty and fatigued, we had returned from the front and were entering the cities in the sub-prefectures. The party lasted until noon of the following day.

Over the next fifteen years, Thalia and Petros were born. We furnished our place and built a spacious country house where we spent the weekends, Easter, and several days during the summer. Those fifteen years were the happiest years of my life. My work was going exceedingly well. The house had become filled with the shouts of children. Maria had blossomed. On weekends and before building our country house, we would go on outings. On various short or long outings to the mountains or to the seashore where we knew all those kind, rustic folks—peasants, fishermen, shepherds—who treated us to all those marvelous and wholesome products one finds in the country. In return we took pictures of them and offered them all sorts of small gifts, which Maria always saw to that she had with her, such as flashlights, lighters, pens, costume jewelry, etc. All of us were extremely happy. We struck up friendships with them, baptized their children, and when they came to the city on business we even entertained them. The days, months, and years rolled by like waves. We bought furniture, lighting fixtures, kitchen appliances, the latest items to come out, the most modern. I worked like a slave. The children had started going to school. Everything, but everything, had finally found a direction. Oh my God, what relief and joy I experienced during those years! When we were about to buy this couch, we deliberated for nearly a week. We had become familiar with all the prices of all the couches in the city, with all the qualities of the fabrics and wood, with all the craftsmen. Every afternoon Maria and I, arm in arm, would make the rounds of the carpentry shops and stores and inquire about the quality of the materials. After a month of shopping around, we ended up with this one. When they delivered it, we were so happy that we would leap up from our sleep to come look at it, caress it, smell it, and sink into it, full of certitude and optimism about the future. The same occurred with our refrigerator, armchairs, table, china closet, and bookcases. It was five years since we had set foot in an entertainment center or theater. In the afternoon, when we weren't working, we would wander through the city searching, always searching. For the finest quality, the lowest price, the most modern lines. What scores of people we met during those five years. Thousands. Craftsmen, workers, engineers. All of them were happy and optimistic about the future, so industrious and so friendly toward us. In the evening when we returned home, the calm and relief we felt were such that they are indescribable. One or two of these craftsmen even became our children's godparents. The children were growing up. There were no problems with school. Maria proved to be a splendid mother. Two handsome, strong boys and a highly intelligent, charming little daughter allowed me to experience the greatest happiness in the world. Those years were truly unforgettable. The months and days rolled by like waves. After completing this house, we then tackled our country house, which, oddly enough and to our great disappointment, was completed in a very short while. This was to be expected both because the money was available and because, as a result of the experience we had acquired in the meantime from the previous house, we knew where to find the best materials and the best craftsmen and at the most advantageous prices with our eyes closed. This is also why the house in the country was completed, however unbelievable it may seem to you, within two years. The colors inside were not dark like these. The walls were painted pale green, a luminous color. The curtains were slightly cream-colored and also on the green side. This couch was upholstered in a blue, shiny fabric scattered with bouquets of flowers. The armchairs were upholstered in a bright, honey-colored satin. Everything then was more radiant, more pleasing, more cheerful. There were fancy laces on the table, the handiwork of Maria's patience and labor. The vases were full of flowers and the well-polished light fixtures glittered. Our carpets were multicolored like flowering fields. A riot of colors and flowers, the windows were always open and there was light everywhere, an abundant and strong light that made you dizzy. This happiness lasted fifteen years.

❧

Misfortune struck suddenly one summer afternoon. Maria and the children were in the country. I had returned from work, eaten something unprepared, taken a shower, and sat down on the couch, torpid and numb from exhaustion. The heat was unbearable and the house upside-down, full of dust and old newspapers. As I sat there relaxed and staring straight ahead at the radiator like an imbecile, I don't know how or why but something happened in my mind and I suddenly understood EVERYTHING! Everything in my head turned topsy-turvy. Everything in me became muddled...I was seized with short-ness of breath and panic. Alarmed, I stood up and stuck my head under the faucet. I thought I would go mad. Afterward I went and took a towel and started wiping myself for hours, pacing back and forth, up and down. Oh my God, I thought to myself, what a MISTAKE, what a dreadful MISTAKE! My God, what a trap! What a trap...But what could I do? Nothing, there was nothing I could do. Absolutely noth-ing. I had become paralyzed with fear and tension and was on the verge of going mad. Taking the picture album, I started leafing through it. I froze. It was the first time that I was seeing these things. Everything was lies. LIES. Maria, the children, this apartment—lies...lies. I thought I had gone mad. My head was about to explode. Everything was lies, lies, lies. What at first I had mistaken for joy and happiness in the photographs, yes...yes, now I could see clearly that it was pain, grief, terror, and anything but joy and happiness. I reflect-ed on my life. What was my life? My youth—combats, illnesses, war, and deaths. And after that, after that they imprisoned us, yes, they imprisoned us and appointed our wives, our children, our friends, and our parents as jailors, whatever was dearest and nearest to us. Maria must have seen through everything, this is why she always came out looking so distressed in the photographs. But she never once opened her mouth to make the least disparaging remark to me. She suffered in silence. Oh my God, what a MISTAKE, what a dreadful mistake! And the children, the children, my God, why did we bring up the children in this way? We brought them up like werewolves. No, no, I thought, such blackmail isn't possible. It's not possible, it must be my imagination, my imagination...Thoughts brought on by age, I'm going through a change of life. It's not possible, my God, my God, I thought, help me. Help me or I'll go mad. Are you by chance imply-ing that we were better off before, when the young didn't make it to twenty-five and died in various battles for a better life that never came? Were we better off before, when hunger and illnesses would wipe out the entire population? Were we better off before, my friend, when people were incapable of formulating a phrase, anything at all, and were like animals? Were we better off before? I somewhat calmed down as a result of these thoughts, but was unable to prevent my mind from continuing in the direction it had taken. Why, after all, are we better off now? Because we know precisely when our life will end? Or because we know precisely what we must do until it ends? Is this why we're better off? But I swear to you that this isn't in the least desirable, not in the least. Now we know that the young don't destroy their youth in the trenches, but on benches that are also a form of penal servitude. Now we know what we must do every hour and every minute of our lives. What people we must associate with, what individuals we must avoid, to whom we must offer our confidence and our friendship, to whom we must show our aversion and our hatred, today each of us knows very well how he must laugh in order not to be misunderstood, how he must think in order not to be carried away, what he must love, what he must ignore, what he must overlook, and in what precisely he must persevere. Now we know that what we ordinarily must do, what they force us to do, is not ordinarily what we also want to do. We know that by the time he's fifty-five, in order to be happy and respected by those around him, a man must have a house in the country, a house in the city, two children in college, one or two automobiles, money in the bank and a steady job. Because if he doesn't have all these things, those around him look at him askance and very often turn their back on him and refuse to speak to him. Because those around him realize that in some part of himself he is a traitor, that in some part of himself he didn't give himself with all his heart to the vision they brought forth all together after the war, they realize that in some part of himself he had misgivings and hesitated...and in so doing he fell behind and lost a little of his valuable time. They realize that in some part of himself he ultimately did what he really wanted to do; this is why...this is why those around him also point at him with their finger, because he didn't submit, because he didn't surrender body and soul and from time to time he did what appealed to him, this is why they all point at him like a leper. But we launched a new world, a world in which all would be free, satiated and happy—all.

We didn't launch a world that would be something like an illuminated dungeon, full of lunatics, neurotics, and unhappy people. We believed that people's problems would be resolved, and here we are more fettered than in the past. Because before, my friend, if you wanted to, you believed in something, and if you didn't want to, you didn't believe in it, and when all was said and done, you could pretend to believe in it if you were in some danger. Whereas now, now you're not given a choice. The small circumstances and events of your daily life give you no leeway, they prevail upon you, they lead you in an unmistakable and mathematical manner wherever they want, to something quite horrible and concrete. To a daily sacrifice without mercy, the sacrifice of yourself, of your desires, of whatever is most beautiful and dear to you. If you want to survive, if you don't want to do without the basic things in life, if you feel the need to be loved by those around you, in short, if you want to exist, you must pay with your life, with your blood, you must pay with your valuable time in order to accumulate useless objects around you, in order to provide your family with a comfortable life, in order not to deprive your children of the means to a bright future, you must pay with your health, with the sweat of your brow, with your life, so that you will be able, so that they will grant you the right, to breathe and see the sun, that is, in the end, nothing...nothing...A USELESS GIFT! And are you implying that we were better off before?

Ah yes, somehow we were better off, my friend. Because in combat you knew that you could receive a bullet at any moment and become a memory and you experienced a sensation of overexcitement, an oversupply of blood, a feeling of rage. You weren't made of paper. You weren't made of paper that can be ripped and feels nothing. Because we've reached the point where I'm banging my hand on the table and I don't feel a thing. So be it. At least before, the crime and the evil didn't last more than ten years, and you knew and said this is real, my friend, and this is phony. Whereas now the phony has, so to speak, donned the clothes and uniform of the real and you take it in your arms, place it in your house, put it in your bed, and when at some stage you're struck by calamity, you look around you like an imbecile without understanding a thing, and how could you, since you sacrificed half your life, your youth, in order to consolidate what you took for real and that in time turned out to be phony. You go mad and calm down. That's how you end up.

You mangle your sleep—you mangle your day—and it's hurry or I won't have time for this—hurry or I won't have time for that—this will go well—that will go well—what'll happen if I suddenly get sick?—everything will fall behind—what'll happen if I have an accident, my friend, what then?—you mustn't stop for even a second—tomorrow I have to see Mr. So-and-so—will he be a decent man?—I wasn't able to contact him—I must call him again—and what's Maria doing?—Alexander didn't do so well this quarter—where will we actually go this summer?—we're expecting guests tonight—make sure you're not late—come home early—we have to reupholster the couch—the children have grown—we must go shopping for the children—we're unpardonable—we have them looking like tramps! At least up there in the snow we were all brothers, for the moment we were all brothers, we would see people and roam from one place to the other. Danger and death lay in wait for us with every step we took, it filled us, brought us back to life, made us live with all our senses. We knew, we understood...what the purpose of a hand was, my friend, what the purpose of a leg was, the purpose of our chest, of our head. No, no, not like the present where we've all become like paper, as if we were biting a piece of iron all day long.

Fortunately Maria and the children were in the country and didn't see me in this state. The following day I requested an authorized leave of absence from my work and shut myself in the house for two weeks without giving a sign of life. Fine, I thought to myself, now what happens? Now that we've seen the light, what happens? How will we go on with our lives? Will we commit suicide or will we sink into debauchery? No, no, I thought to myself...nothing, nothing like that. We'll continue as if nothing has happened because we have obligations. We have children at a critical age and we mustn't leave them alone and abandoned in such a world. Anyhow we were accustomed to a hard life. Only we thought it was the best life we could make for ourselves and with the fewest sacrifices. We'll continue, therefore. We'll clench our teeth and continue. In any event we were accustomed to things being difficult, we weren't accustomed to their being easy. For forty years now we've had adversity at our fingertips. Only before we thought all these things around us were our salvation, whereas now...now we see them sort of like nightmares. What's going to happen? We'll continue as if nothing were the matter, we'll drink the poison without uttering a word and without revealing anything,

anything whatsoever, of our pain and grief to those around us. Only we'll be less intolerant of others, of those who failed, because now we know how they arrived at that stage; they were trying to stay alive. This is why they're paying. They showed great heart and courage. It is they who are heroes. We who lack the courage to shake off what is eating away at our flesh, we owe them our respect and all the help we can offer them.

From that point on the great MARTYRDOM began. Because I saw the MISTAKE in whatever I did. Everything had turned upside-down for me. When I scrutinized my authority over my children. When I bought various items. When I concluded a transaction, I saw the mistake everywhere, everywhere. But I had no alternative. None whatsoever. In the morning when I awakened I saw the mistake and the crisis everywhere. In the way women painted themselves, in the way they dressed, in the way they talked. In the houses, in the furniture, in the shop windows, in the songs I heard on the radio, in the conversations and harmless jokes of those around me and that my ear caught, everywhere there was HORROR, HORROR and SORROW. I saw the mistake, but could do nothing about it because...because somewhere inside me I wanted to LIVE...I longed to live! Maria had understood everything because once or twice while I was sitting down she had seen me grow pale and break out in a cold sweat for no reason at all. "John," she said, "what's wrong with you, my love, should I call the doctor?" "Relax, Maria," I replied, "there's nothing wrong with me, it'll go away, relax." It was then that I began to think seriously about an ACCIDENT! Isn't it possible, I thought to myself, my God, isn't it possible for me to have an accident? To be finished once and for all, I can't bear this martyrdom any longer, I can't. Unfortunately, however, not even the slightest thing ever happened to me. And this was my greatest torture! Everything went smoothly for me! One evening when I was suffering from insomnia and had come out and was sitting on this couch, Maria approached very softly and stood behind me. "John, I want to have a talk with you," she said. "Listen, John, I know that you've understood everything. I was never taken in, I knew from the start where we were headed all these years, but all that is irrelevant now. We've lived our lives, however well or badly, we've lived them. For us it really doesn't much matter any more. The problem lies elsewhere. It lies with the children. We must keep our lips sealed and must never, never reveal a thing, my love. The children are forming their character at this very moment and we mustn't in any way arouse their suspicions. Because if at their age they should get wind of what's happening, we may as well call it quits, we'll have lost them forever. We mustn't reveal a thing and must keep our lips sealed, my love. We mustn't harm them this soon, John. Once they've received their degrees, once they've set their lives in order, then, fine and dandy, they may do and think as they like. But now it's still too early. We must keep our lips sealed and guard our actions for seven more years because, I tell you, there is the danger that they will take things lightly, abandon school, and then we'll be in for it, John, one hears all kinds of things, you know what I mean. We'll pretend that nothing's happened. We'll be the way we were, cheerful, understanding, calm...as though things were going fine. Because you know what awaits us if we cease to be on our guard. Disintegration awaits us, my love, DISINTEGRATION! I don't want to see my children miserable, I don't want to see them deprived of the necessities of life, I don't want to see them become beggars or victims of fate, I don't want to see them become the scum of society, human wrecks as a result of drugs and dissipation. Do you understand, John?" Maria said to me, "the risks are very great, this is why you must be patient. If, however, you feel from time to time that you've reached the BREAKING POINT, that is, if you feel that you can't take it any longer, you have my permission, feel free to go out and let loose. I'll never call you to account, I'll always be here waiting for you to return, my love. It suffices that you bear up," Maria said to me, "it suffices that you bear up and not SNAP, John."

That's what Maria said to me that evening and I confess that she was absolutely right. Starting the very next day I held my tongue and pretended to be happy. It was not permissible that we poison the children at the precise moment when with the greatest of efforts they were building their characters. The slightest delay, the slightest vacillation could prove fatal to their lives. PESSIMISM is the greatest sin of our times. It is the path that without fail leads to suicide, mendacity, madness, and drugs. Our character was all set and we were no longer threatened; besides, our life was approaching its end; but how were these innocent creatures, who only now were beginning to stand on their own two feet, at fault? Why should we clobber them from above as well and destroy them altogether? Yes, in the end Maria was right. I held my tongue and pretended to be happy. Maintaining a neutral attitude, I never gave my children advice about any matter, however small. Nor did I ever even scold them. I simply buried myself in my work and saw to it that I was away from the house as much as possible. During those years I worked like a dog, as though I wanted to work myself to death. The result was that I became quite rich. It was all I managed to do. Fortunately the children didn't go astray. Maria made sure of this as did the American films they saw. Alexander is a nuclear research physicist in an American university. He's married and has two children. Thalia is a lawyer and very successful indeed. She took over my office. She's also married and has two children. Petros, the youngest, is a philosophy professor in the university. He is unmarried and worries me.

WHAT COULD I HAVE DONE? In the aftermath of wars, deaths, sacrifices and bloodshed, people had found a way of life they thought was right and had thrown themselves into work. Was I to say to my children, look children, everything around you is a big MISTAKE? What would I have accomplished? If they had not believed me, fine. If they had believed me, however, all I would have accomplished was to make my children the victims of others. Because if others suspect that you do and believe things that are far different from them, they won't rest until they see you miserable or dead. Thus I remained silent. That was when we painted the living room this color. Everything then was unbearable and false. The only truth was our fear that the children would catch on and an ABOUT FACE begin. Fortunately, though, everything turned out fine. The children completed their studies in proper fashion and they are all very well-established. At some point toward the end, Maria became ill with cancer. She was ill for two years before she died. The children got married and left. I received my pension and now live alone in this apartment. On that final evening, Maria, before closing her eyes forever, squeezed my hand and started speaking to me.

"I loved you, John," Maria said, "I loved you with all my soul. I never went with another man, my love, you may put your mind at rest.

I didn't love only you, John, that is, your appearance, your body, your eyes, or your nose. I loved you in a broader sense, I loved what you were, what you believed in, what you were attempting to accomplish. Your ideas, your dreams, your ambitions, I loved all these things in you, John, this is also why I stood next to you like an unshakable rock all my life, my love, without begrudging you. In the mornings when you left for work, John, and the children went off to school and I was left alone in the house, in the mornings around eleven and as soon as I had finished my chores, something akin to madness would seize me. Was it madness or was it fear? I don't know what it was exactly, my love. What I do know is that I felt the urge to run out into the street and to go off with the first person who came along, John. But I swear to you that this never happened because I always thought of you. I told myself that you, too, had not done what you really wanted to, my love, I told myself that you were putting up with everything for us. For me and the children. So that we would lack nothing and could live with dignity. Cooped up in your office, bent over your papers, you, too, my love, were paying with your life for our comfort and good times. Such thoughts took away any appetite for sexual passion and brought me back to my senses. I would then grab my bag and go out to do the shopping, or if we already had enough things and there wasn't any need for me to go out, then I would lose myself in my embroidery, John. All that I embroidered or knitted for you, my love, I did in order to remain faithful to you and to deserve being called your WIFE. Ah John, with what joy I waited for you to return from work, you from work and the children from school, because…because all morning long I had not laid eyes on a living soul, only the radio, John, and my knitting kept me company. Gradually, however, I became adept, I became so adept at this life that I would detect immediately the mistakes you and the children made. Not only the mistakes but also your mood and thoughts before you even decided to perpetrate your errors. This is why I was nervous, my love, because I could see that the rest of you had not yet given up. You hoped that something would happen, John. Something that would save you from all these things. This, however, filled me with fear and terror. For I knew very well where desertions of that kind lead. For example, I had often caught you, John, praying to yourself for WAR to break out.

Because, John, you believed that war would save you from many other things including me and the children. Admit it, my love, admit it. I had even caught you praying for an accident in order to escape from all of us for good and, other times, John, I could see in your eyes that you wanted to kill all of us and then die yourself, and I froze with fear. Petros likewise didn't look after himself at all, John, he was always sick with a cold for no other reason than to stay home from school and remain in bed with fever all day long. That's why I was nervous, my love," Maria said to me, "and often stern with the rest of you. I wanted to strike at the root of the evil before it became gigantic and destroyed us all. Forgive me. I believe that we lived well. I have no regrets. It is for you I feel sorry, you who will be left alone now in your old age."

Thereupon she turned her head to the side and went to sleep forever.

I know now that the end is near.

Today, tomorrow, at any moment what we all dread so in life can take place...DEATH.

No, I'm not at all terrified. Nor afraid. Nor even panicked.

What I feel is entirely different.

For the first time I feel complete. Yes...COMPLETE.

I feel a wave of life swelling within me. I want to live. To run. To jump...high up in the air. I want to sing...to fall in love...to participate...to help.

An awesome life force is unfurling within me.

It is swelling in my chest and is seeking an outlet.

It is knocking against my entrails like a typhoon wave.

The blood is tingling in my veins. I feel numb from pleasure and joy.

I want to live. To live. To live.

Alas, however, I am but a useless old man.

My body, my appearance...provoke disgust.

No one will approach me. I am a wretched and pitiful old man.

I feel such a drive and lust for life...as if I had never LIVED at all, all these years that passed by. As if I am about to live now at the end...all that I deprived myself of.

I AM DROWNING! In order not to go mad I sit and think about all these things...that occurred.

What is happening to me, my God? I am not calm! No!

I want to live! TO LIVE! Empty I go on, empty I proceed...

I AM AFRAID! I AM AFRAID!

BIOGRAPHICAL NOTES

C. P. Cavafy (1863-1933), one of the greatest poets not only of Greece but of the entire modern world, was born in Alexandria. As an adolescent he lived first in England, then in Constantinople. In 1885 he returned to Alexandria where, except for occasional trips to Paris, London, and Athens, he lived for the rest of his life. He worked as a common clerk in the Department of Irrigation until his retirement in 1922. The rest of the time Cavafy devoted himself entirely to his poetic production, writing only three or four poems yearly, which were published in broadsheets for private use. During his lifetime he brought out only one slim volume of fourteen poems in 1904, reissued with seven additional poems in 1910. His complete poetic opus, amounting to 154 poems, was collected and published after his death. It falls into three categories: historical, erotic, and philosophical. The poems of Cavafy, a mixture of demotic and ancient Greek, are short and epigrammatic dramatic narratives that relate facts and events in a detached, ironic, and nearly prosaic manner. All the while emotion is intentionally concealed behind this anti-rhetorical and anti-lyrical language. "In Broad Daylight" is the only short story Cavafy ever wrote. A striking example of the fantastic tale, it reveals that the author had the makings of a great short-story writer.

DINOS CHRISTIANOPOULOS, born in Thessaloniki in 1931, is a poet who writes intimately about sex and love. He blends lyricism with realism, his graphic evocations concealing a vulnerable sensibility. Simplicity and brevity further characterize his poems, many of which consist of only a few lines. Here, for instance, is the way he describes the heat of desire: "let your saliva dribble down on me / making me mud / how long must I remain / dry earth?" He describes thus the distinction between love and lust: "the kiss / unites more / than the body / / this is why most / avoid it." Thus the elusiveness of love: "every time I think I have you well in hand / I see that love is not made by hand." Thus the precariousness of love: "everything hangs by a thread / only love hangs by a hair." Thus the end of love: "new snow falls / on the old / / as other snowflakes hurry / to become mud." Christianopoulos appeared on the literary scene as early as 1950, when he published a slim volume of verse, Season of Lean Cows. In 1985 all his poems were published in a single volume, Poems. (A second edition in 1992 includes new pieces.) He is the author of numerous essays and in 1958 he became the editor of Diagonal, a provocative literary journal which he founded and which has been responsible for introducing many new authors to the public. He has also published two collections of short stories, The Downward Path (1980) and The Rembetes of the World (1986), which were subsequently published as a single collection, The Downward Path (1991). "Rosa Eskenazi" is based on the life of an actual singer of folk songs.

MARIOS HAKKAS (1931-1972) was born in Makrakome, a village in the province of Phthiotida. He was a gifted and original writer who died of cancer at the height of his powers. Although he did not begin to write until he was in his thirties, he managed within the brief space of seven years to produce a small yet impressive corpus. Most significant are three volumes of short stories. One already finds many of the elements of his later mode of expression—brevity, wit, satirical intent, and the unexpected linking of the most heteroclite of phenomena—in his first book of short stories, The Enemy's Infantryman (1966). By the time Hakkas published The Bidet and Other Stories (1971), his second collection of short stories, his manner of writing had become disarmingly direct. The intimate, tautly written first-person confession is devoid of characters, plot, and time sequence. The author returns repeatedly to the same themes: love, friendship, the failure of ideals, the struggle involved in poetic expression, and the life of the political prisoner. (He served a four-year prison term from 1954 to 1958 and later was detained for a month by the military junta because of his leftist activities.) In his third and final collection of short stories, *The Commune* (1972), he concerns himself with sickness and death. This creation—his last—is a moving testimony to the courage of a man dying yet determined to record his final thoughts about life. He thus transformed death into art. Hakkas died a few days before the book was published.

DEMETRIS HATZIS (1913-1981) was born in Ioannina. A newspaper editor and member of the Communist Party, he was forced to go into exile in 1948, following the defeat of the Communists in the Greek Civil War. He studied in East Berlin, then in Budapest, where later he taught modern Greek literature and Byzantology at the university. With the fall of the dictatorship in 1974, he returned to Greece after having lived in exile for more than twenty-five years. Hatzis is best known for his short stories, particularly those that make up the volume entitled *The End of Our Small City* (1963), of which "Maria Perdikari" is the concluding piece. Writing in a realistic manner but from a Marxist point of view, he depicted a class society whose traditions have been undermined by recent social and economic changes and which is about to disappear. His realism, however, is deceptive, concealing a stylist who combines terseness with vision. In his best works, ideological demands are subordinated to those of literary creation, as external reality becomes permeated with poetic emotion. For beneath both realism and ideology, and despite the optimistic endings of his stories, prompted by his deep political beliefs, he the temperament and sensitivity of an exile who knew from experience the dreariness of life in a provincial city and whose own life was fraught with injustices and struggles. His works, relatively few in number, include *The Double Book* (1976), a novel, as well as *The Undefended* (1965), *Studies* (1976), and *Military Service* (1979), collections of short stories.

NIKOS HOULIARAS, a man of diverse talents, was born in Ioannina in 1940. He studied at the School of Fine Arts in Athens and is an artist of high repute. His works have appeared in many exhibitions and have been bought by private collectors throughout the world. In the sixties he also pursued a successful career as a musician, composing songs that were interpreted by him as well as by other singers. In the seventies Houliaras embarked upon a literary career, gaining wide recognition for *Loussias* (1979), a novel in which the world is seen through the eyes of a slightly retarded orphan. This was followed by *Bakakok* (1981), a collection of short stories whose marginal characters—failures and lonely individuals—also view existence with a childlike innocence. A disciple of surrealism, the author repudiates realism in order to transcend existing reality and express the uncontrolled flow of the subconscious mind, the immediate manifestation of the poetic imagination. He refuses to explain or analyze the exact nature of the relationship between his characters, which always remains vague; he prefers instead to capture the magical power of people, objects, and events from his past, the strangeness and enchantment of certain remembered moments. His works include *Painting-Texts* (1978), essays on painting; *The Snow 1 Knew* (1983), a collection of short stories; and *Life Another Time* (1985), a novel. *Loussias* and many of his short stories have been adapted for television.

GEORGE IOANNOU (1927-1985), born in Thessaloniki, was a teacher for many years. His short stories—poetic narrations—represent perhaps the most significant writing in Greece since World War I. After having brought out two slim volumes of verse, he published *For a Sense of Honor* (1964), which bore the subtitle *Prose Writings*. It was followed by several works similar in style and content: *The Sarcophagus* (1971), *The Sole Inheritance* (1974), and *Our Own Blood* (1978). Narrated in the first person, the twenty-two brief, plotless, and laconic texts that constitute *For a Sense of Honor* are a blend of the personal, confessional tone with objective, critical observations of the outside world. The hero of these prose writings is essentially the same person—an intelligent, sensitive, disoriented young man who experiences economic hardships, suffers from erotic deprivation, and is restless and not content. The seeds of his distress are found in the author's adolescence. The son of refugee parents from eastern Thrace, Ioannou grew up among the poor, populous Jewish communities of Thessaloniki during the German Occupation, in the midst of hunger, mass executions, and the extermination of the Jews. It is clear that he was tragically scarred by these horrors, as he was by those of the Greek Civil War. Later, in his mature years, he remained an "outsider," exploring the land and frequenting the company of common workmen and social outcasts—of those who, burdened with a harsh destiny, were for him closer to the heartbeat of existence. Even when Ioannou writes in the third person and relies more heavily on plots and characters, as in *Epitaphios Threnos* (1980), a collection of short stories, his writing remains poetical.

M. KARAGATSIS (1908-1960), pseudonym of Demetrios Rodopoulos, was born in Athens. One of the most prolific of modern Greek writers, he was primarily a novelist who was known also for his short stories. The inventiveness of his plots earned him the reputation of being the best "storyteller" of his generation. His first novel, *Colonel Limpkin*, appeared when he was only twenty-five, and by the time of his premature death his literary works totalled twenty-one. He returns almost obsessively to the same subject—man's dominant sexual instinct, his gravitation toward woman, the inevitable attraction between the sexes. For Karagatsis, as for D. H. Lawrence, all of man's attributes are subsidiary to this elemental force. Unlike Lawrence, however, he sees this impulse as capable of reducing man to the level of a beast, thus rendering his destiny tragic. Despite his affinities with Freud, Karagatsis does not write in an analytical, but in a naturalistic, sometimes almost journalistic style. He describes in detail the setting and atmosphere in which his characters move, after which, rather than concentrating on the inner workings of their mind, he allows their psychology to emanate from their acts and the evolution of their external behavior. Regardless of how pessimistic and scoffing in tone his writing may be, it is not lacking in exuberance and lyricism. His works include *Chimera* (1936) and *The Big Sleep* (1946), novels; and *The Man with the Flemoni* (1935), *Litany of the Profane* (1940), and *Fever* (1945), collections of short stories.

ANDREAS KARKAVITSAS (1865-1922) was born in Lehaina, a small Peloponnesian town. As a doctor for a coastal navigation company, he had the opportunity to witness life on the sea, and later, as an army surgeon, to know life in the villages as well. He returned to these two subjects repeatedly in his short stories, the genre in which he excelled. Karkavitsas began publishing his tales in periodicals as early as 1885, collecting them in a single volume, *Stories* (1892). This was the only book by him that was written in Katharevousa.* Everything else he wrote was in the language of the people. His later stories appeared in two volumes: *Words from the Prow* (1899) and *Old Loves* (1900). He is also the author of several novellas, including *The Archaeologist* (1903), after which he ceased to write. Karkavitsas drew his inspiration from folk tales and from simple people, especially sailors. He wrote in a realistic vein (though he often used colorful epithets) and was a pessimist who saw man as a victim of fate. Essentially a narrative poet, he was at his best when writing about the sea. In addition to his literary production, he was also active in such progressive movements as the National Language Society, which advocated the use of demotic as the national language, and the Educational Association, which sought to reorganize Greek education.

GEORGE KITSOPOULOS(1919-1996) was born in Athens and resided in Thessaloniki until 1935. He was for many years co-editor and contributor to *Kohlias*, an avant-garde literary magazine, and later he served as director to the National Theater of Northern Greece. Kitsopoulos brought out his first book, *A Selection: 19 Short Stories* (1968), relatively late in life. Written between 1943 and 1965, the short stories contained in this volume range in style from the traditional to the modern, yet even those that belong to the former category are highly original. Whereas many modern writers believe that an elliptical and elusive style suffices for the creation of a work of art and often neglect the nucleus of literary activity which is, after all, the human being, Kitsopoulos succeeds in combining both elements in his fiction. In his works, which are free of unnecessay details and

---

* The official language in Greece from the beginning of the nineteenth century until 1976, Katharevousa was a form of Greek whose vocabulary, morphology, and syntax resembled Classical Greek more than present-day Greek, known as demotic.)

images, objects and events are fraught with symbolism. The author, however, gives preference to the individual, whom he sees as trapped by fate and ineluctably bound to his dreams, to the search for love, to the futility of life, and to death. His works include *The Unnailing* (1972), a novella; *The Stage Curtain of Marvels* (1986), a novel; *Sacred Company* (1971), a play; and *Alexander the Great* (1981-1986), a three-volume biography.

IOANNIS KONDYLAKIS (1861-1920) was born on the island of Crete and took part in the Cretan revolution of 1878-79. He spent most of his adult life working as a journalist in the capital, living alone and without a family. Under the pseudonym "Wayfarer," he wrote countless newspaper chronicles in which, with cultivated irony, he denounced society of his day, particularly the weaknesses and faults of the ruling class. The same qualities that distinguish these chronicles characterize the rest of his literary production, nearly all of which first appeared serialized in newspapers. *Les Misérables of Athens* (1894), a naturalistic novel, describes the underworld of Athens. *Down with the Tyrant in '62* (1895), a historical novel, is about the military revolt that deposed King Otto from the throne. His finest works, however, are those which grew out of his recollections of Crete: *Patouhas* (1916), a novel depicting life in a Cretan village; *When I Was Master of a School* (1916), a collection of short stories based on his personal memories as a teacher in the Cretan town of Modi; and the lyrical novella *First Love* (1920), the last work he wrote and the only one in which he used demotic. His Katharevousa is characterized by liveliness, succinctness, precision, wit, and humor.

MENIS KOUMANTAREAS, born in Athens in 1931, was employed for many years by maritime insurance companies. He launched his literary career with a volume of short stories, *Pinball Machines* (1962), which explores the lives of adolescents or young men at odds with themselves or with society. It is a subject to which the author often returned in the numerous short stories and novels that followed. Another persona on whom he concentrates is the older woman. The heroine of the novel *Glass Factory* (1975), for example, is a middle-aged, attractive woman who still possesses a passionate and sensuous love of life. As she races against time both to save her shop from bankruptcy and to find personal fulfillment before it is too late, she becomes increasingly aware of the futility of the struggle against Time. A graceful style, skillful use of ellipsis, and poignancy of subject matter make of *Glass Factory* the author's most accomplished work to date. In *Player Number Nine* (1986), a best-selling novel that was made into a film, Koumantareas shifts his focus to the sports arena and professional rugby as he follows the rise and fall of a gifted rugby player of humble origins. His works include *The Navigation* (1967), *The Burnt Ones* (1972), and *Seraphim and Cherubim* (1981), collections of short stories; *Madam Kovla* (1978), a novel that was adapted for television; and *Itinerant Trumpeter* (1989), a book of essays. Koumantareas has also translated such authors as Melville, Faulkner, and Fitzgerald.

YIORGOS MANIOTIS was born in Athens in 1951. After first studying law, he pursued a literary career and became one of Greece's finest playwrights. His plays have been staged by the National Theater of Greece and the National Theater of Northern Greece, as well as by commercial theaters. They have also been performed on both stage and radio in Germany and on the New York stage. Maniotis confronts the spectator with a metaphor of the horror of the modern world—a dehumanized world in which society is based on technology, the lure of profit, and the search for prestige. His plays are metaphysical farces whose dark humor exposes the absurd and grotesque aspects of contemporary man's customs and habits. Despite their direct language and the dreary realism of their settings, they are imbued with poetry. In his novels and short stories, the author further depicts the isolation of the individual who, regardless of his efforts to resist, is at the mercy of a world that crushes him, whether by his own illusions, as in *The Unknown Soldier* (1986), by the social mechanism, as in the allegorical *Dark Fairy Tales* (1987), or by a mother's power, as in *The Awesome Protection* (1990). His numerous theatrical works include *The Match* (1978), *The Pit of Sin* (1979), *Common Sense* (1980), *Order and Disorder* (1985), and *Vacation in Heaventown* (1988). Maniotis has also written for Greek television and radio.

Stratis Myrivilis (1890-1969), a pseudonym for Eustratios Stamatopoulos, was born on the island of Mytilene. He took part in the Balkan wars and World War I. For many years he was a journalist and editor. Later he became general program director of the Greek National Broadcasting Institute and the director of the Greek Parliament Library. He launched his literary career in 1915 with his *Red Stories*. These were followed in 1924 by *Life in the Tomb*, an account of trench warfare on the Macedonian front during World War I. It is an anti-polemical novel of epic proportions that combines harsh realism with soaring lyricism. With the 1930 edition it became one of the most widely read books of its period. War, now joined to a love story, was also the subject of his second novel, *The Schoolmistress with the Golden Eyes* (1933). In time Myrivilis tempered his liberal attitude, remaining a descriptive lyricist and great stylist whose work is unusually rich in images. His later literary productions include a series of short stories collected into volumes that were each entitled with a different color: *The Green Book* (1935), *The Blue Book* (1939), *The Red Book* (1952), *The Crimson Book* (1959); *Vasilis Arvanitis* (1943), a novella which was the author's own favorite and which is generally thought to be his masterpiece; and *The Mermaid Madonna* (1949), a novel. Myrivilis has been widely translated.

Alexandros Papadiamantis (1851-1911) was born on the island of Skiathos. His father was a priest, and both his life and his work were profoundly religious. Before going to the University of Athens to study literature, he spent several months on Mount Athos but without taking religious vows. And throughout his life he chanted in church. Not only was the literary genius of Papadiamantis never given the recognition it deserved during his lifetime, but he also experienced severe material hardships, barely eking out a living as a translator and proofreader in Athens. He never severed his bonds with his native island, to which he returned periodically for extensive stays, and it was there that he lived the final years of his life. Papadiamantis first brought out several historical novels. Then in 1885 he turned to the short story, devoting himself almost exclusively to this genre until his death and writing some two hundred tales, many of which are truly remarkable. In them he describes the lives of the villagers from the island of Skiathos, infusing his descriptions with psychological analysis and profuse lyricism. While the author assails an iniquitous society in which the wealthy exploit the poor, he also suggests that society is imperfectible. For as a Christian Papadiamantis believed that all men after Adam have been doomed to suffer and that salvation lies only in Christ and self-abnegation. Like others in his generation, he wrote in Katharevousa but often introduced demotic elements to forge an entirely personal style that combines realism with symbolism.

EMMANUEL ROIDIS (1836-1904), who was born on the island of Syra to an aristocratic family, was brought up and educated mainly abroad. At the age of twenty-one he returned to live permanently in Athens where, as a dashing young nobleman, he led a cosmopolitan existence devoted to the arts. As a result of bad investments, he lost the large fortune he had inherited from his father and in the last years of his life was forced to earn his livelihood as director of the National Library. Still another misfortune, the loss of his hearing, excluded him from social life and crushed the arrogance for which he was known in his youth. He first appeared on the literary scene in 1860 as a translator of *Chateaubriand*. His sole novel, *Pope Joan* (1866), satirized religious prejudices both past and present. This work, which has been translated into English by Lawrence Durrell, was censured by the Church because of its scandalous theme. Roidis was in direct opposition to the romanticism of his times by his rationalism, irony, and consummate Katharevousa. As a literary critic, Roidis played a crucial role in the development of Greek letters, condemning Katharevousa (in which he wrote!) as barbarous and urging the return of the spoken language as the written one. Toward the end of his life he turned to the writing of short stories inspired by his childhood in Syra. Writing in the first person with acute psychological penetration and a very elegant style, he describes provincial social life during the last decade of the nineteenth century.

GALATIA SARANTI, born in Patras in 1920, originally studied law. She became a prominent figure in the Greek literary world immediately after World War I. Nearly all her novels, the genre in which she excels, are set in provincial cities and concern middle-class families who have withstood the onslaught of war and who now continue their sorrowful lives almost as though the war had never occurred. External situations and events barely interest the writer. She prefers instead to concentrate on the psychology of her characters, who are solitary individuals living in the past. In fact, the true protagonist in her fiction is Time, the author choosing to depict her characters at the very moment when they become conscious of its inexorable passage. Psychological truth, moreover, is shrouded in an atmosphere of poetic realism, metaphysical nostalgia, low tones, and feminine tenderness. Her works include *The Book of Joy* (1947), a novella; *Lilacs* (1949), *Return* (1953), and *Our Old House* (1959), novels; and *Colors of Confidence* (1962), *Remember Vilna* (1972), and *Helen* (1982), collections of short stories. Saranti is also the author of children's books.

COSTAS TAKTSIS (1927-1988), who was born in Thessaloniki, grew up and resided in Athens. He lived in Western Europe, Australia, and the United States from 1954 to 1964. *The Third Wedding*, his sole and remarkable novel, was published in 1963 at his own expense. It went unappreciated by both critics and public in Greece until 1970, and then only after it had been well received in England and France, where it had appeared in translation, did it win an audience in Greece. Since that time it has become the only steady "best seller" in Greece, with the exception of the works of Nikos Kazantzakis, and has been translated into many other languages. The novel, which spans the political and cultural history of contemporary Greece from the Balkan wars to the Civil War, is a brilliant demonstration of feminine psychology. Woman, energetic and creative, generates a sense of being by exploiting the male as a source of existential energy. Female dominance, male passivity, and homosexuality are also the themes of *Small Change* (1972), a collection of short stories. Narrated from the point of view of a child or adolescent, these autobiographical stories represent scenes from the life of a boy growing up in a poor Athenian neighborhood and stifled by the adults around him. The author's two other major works are *My Grandmother Athens* (1979), a book of essays, and *The Awesome Step* (1989), his unfinished and posthumously published autobiography. Taktsis, who openly practiced transvestism, was brutally murdered in his Athens apartment.

STRATIS TSIRKAS (1911-1980), pseudonym for Yiannis Hatzeandreas, was born in Cairo, but his father was from Imvros, a small Aegean island. After studying at the Ampateio Merchant School, he worked for ten years as an accountant and then as a director in the cotton industry in Egypt. As of 1963 he took up residence in Greece. Tsirkas began his literary career by publishing *Fellahs* (1937), the first of several volumes of poetry, though in time he wrote only prose. A leftist writer, he recounted with literary skill and historical precision the events of World War II in his novels and short stories. In three novels grouped under the same title, *Drifting Cities* (1961-1965), he evoked the war in the Middle East, describing the mutineers in the Greek expeditionary force and the role of the imperialists at the expense of the Greek people. The trilogy was banned by the military junta. Most postwar writers who were anxious to write about the Occupation and Resistance from a political point of view ended up writing chronicles. Unlike them, Tsirkas created real characters who live and move in a real social climate and who reflect the anguish of their times. As with André Malraux, a major difficulty in reading his fiction is that it assumes on the part of the reader a detailed knowledge of the political happenings to which he alludes. His works include *Lyrical Journey* (1938), a volume of poetry; *Strange People* (1944), a collection of short stories; and *The Lost Spring* (1976), a novel. Tsirkas has also translated such authors as Erasmus, Stendhal, and Malcolm Lowry.

ELIAS VENEZIS (1904-1973), pseudonym for Elias Mellos, was born in Aivali, a town in Asia Minor. At the age of eighteen he was conscripted by the Turks into compulsory work camps during the Asia Minor catastrophe* and was dispatched with other Greeks into the interior. While not experiencing war directly, he was brought face-to-face with man's inhumanity and barbarity. In 1923 he managed to

* The burning of the city of Smyrna and the massacre of the Greek population of Asia Minor in 1922.

escape and went to live in Athens. There he was active in the Resistance movement during World War II and eventually became a director of the National Bank of Greece. Venezis took his themes from life on the shores of Asia Minor—both before and after the catastrophe. *Number 31328* (1931), his first novel, chronicles his captivity with documentary realism. *Peace* (1939), his second novel, depicts the plight of the refugees and their difficulty in adapting themselves to their new country. In this work, however, realism makes way for a lyrical sensitivity and a profound love of humanity—characteristics henceforth of all that he wrote. *Aeolian Land* (1943), the last of his three major novels, is a nostalgic and dreamlike evocation of his childhood and homeland. His works include *Beyond the Aegean* (1941), *Winds* (1944), and *Hour of War* (1946), collections of short stories, as well as *Black C* (1946), a play. Venezis, like Myrivilis, has been widely translated.

GEORGE VIZYINOS (1849-1896) was born of a humble family in a village of Thrace. After a penurious youth in Constantinople and Cyprus, he was able, with the assistance of an affluent Greek living abroad, to study philosophy and psychology in Germany, receiving a doctorate at Leipzig in 1881. Afterward he lived on the Continent, with brief visits to his native country, until 1884, when he became an assistant professor at the University of Athens. He continued to suffer from economic hardships throughout his life and was denied a university chair. As a result of some mysterious illness and an unrequited love, he went insane in 1892 and was committed to a mental institution, where he died four years later, his work uncompleted. Vizyinos published his first collection of poetry, *First Poems* (1873), in Constantinople; his second, *Kodros* (1873), in Athens; and his third, *Breezes of Attica* (1883), in London. He then applied himself to the short story and within two years published the majority of his tales. More successful than his poetry, they are studies of customs as well as subtle psychological studies. Their appearance in 1883 heralded the publication during the next five years of the first short stories by major Greek writers. While Vizyinos believed theoretically in the necessity of writing in demotic, most of his poetry and all of his short stories were written in Katharevousa (though his use of demotic enlivens the dialogues). "My Mother's Sin," which is considered the first modern Greek short story, is based on a tragic event in the life of the author's own mother.

GREGORIOS XENOPOULOS (1867-1951), who was born in Constantinople, was brought up on the island of Zakynthos, the home of his father. His knowledge of and affection for the islanders later became an inexhaustible literary wellspring. In Athens he studied natural sciences and mathematics at the university, but soon committed himself to literature. Influenced by Zola's naturalism and by socialism, he portrays contemporary Greek life, both in the capital and in Zakynthos, in his numerous novels, short stories, and plays (some of which continue to be produced on the Greek stage). Xenopoulos deplored the barriers that existed in his time between a decadent aristocracy and the common people (or even the rising middle class) and that prohibited marriage between the two. He saw love, however, as an overwhelming force that transcends the barrier of class. Writing with narrative facility, he was a faultless observer of details and a creator of lively dialogue. Only his first novel, *Margarita Stefa* (1893), was written in Katharevousa. The rest of his work, which was read by a wide public, was in demotic. It includes: *Rich and Poor* (1909), *Honest and Dishonest* (1921), and *Fortunate and Unfortunate* (1924), a trilogy that explores social problems; and *Photini Santri* (1908) and *Stella Violanti* (1909), two of his best-known plays. He was also the editor of *Education of Children*, a children's magazine, and the founder of *Nea Estia*, still one of the leading literary magazines of Greece. The cruelly satirical intent and nightmarish at-mosphere of "The Madman with the Red Lilies" suggest the influence of Poe.

ABOUT THE TRANSLATOR

PROFESSOR NICHOLAS KOSTIS taught French cinema and Proust at Boston College from 1965 until 2000. He has translated several modern Greek literary works including Dinos Christianopoulos *Poems*, Odysseas Publications, 1995; Ersi Sotiropoulou *Selected Poetry and Prose* and *A Three-Day Holiday at Yiannena*, Greek Institute of Massachusetts, 1991; and, *Two Thrillers* by Giorgos N. Maniotis, Kedros, 1996. He travels frequently to France and Greece.

A CENTURY OF GREEK POETRY 1900-2000

Selected and edited by

Peter Bien, Peter Constantine, Edmund Keeley and Karen Van Dyck

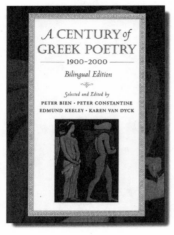

DE LUXE EDITION
HARDCOVER WITH DUST JACKET
PAGES 1.024
17 x 24 cm

This bilingual anthology presents the achievements of Greek poetry in the 20th century. Included are 109 poets and 456 poems, with the Greek original and the English translation on opposite pages. Many of the poems and their translations are published for the first time, most notably Kimon Friar's own unpublished corrections/modifications to his original translations.

"...If Homer, Sappho and Euripides live on as household names, Seferis and Elytis, both Nobel laureates, are still little known to the wider public. The poet and scholar Constantine A. Trypanis refers to Greek poetry as that 'with the longest and perhaps noblest tradition in the Western world,' and concludes that 'in the last hundred years greater and more original poetry has been written in Greek than in the last fourteen centuries which preceded them.' With the exception of Cavafy, whose poetry earned him international recognition as one of the most important poets of the twentieth century, no other major Greek modern poet has been able to attract more than a limited readership. Yet modern Greek poetry is neither marginal nor minor. It is the constituent part, and a very important one, of the literature of modern Europe. The 20th century poets, including the two Nobel prize winners, that appear in this anthology will be bringing to light a massive and splendid achievement of modern European literature and will underline its continued vitality and originality."

—Haris Vlavianos

www.greeceinprint.com

LIFE IN THE TOMB

By Stratis Myrivilis

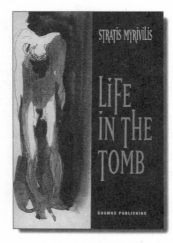

PAPERBACK
SIZE 14 x 21 cm
PAGES 356

Life in the Tomb, a war novel written in journal form by a sergeant in the trenches, has been the single most successful and widely read serious work of fiction in Greece since its publication in serial form in 1923-1924, having sold more than 80,000 copies in book form despite its inclusion on the list of censored novels under both the Metaxas regime and the German occupation.

Published in nearly a dozen translations, it is the first volume of a trilogy containing *The Mermaid Madonna* and *The Schoolmistress with the Golden Eyes,* both of which have been available in a variety of languages.

"Life in the Tomb *has moments of great literary beauty and of more than one kind of literary power. In 1917, Myrivilis was twenty-five. 'Before I entered the trenches I had not the slightest inkling of life's true worth. From now on, however, I shall savour its moments one by one...' This... truthful fiction... [makes] one see... It is antiheroic and completely convincing."*

—Peter Levi

"*[Peter Bien] has turned a Greek masterpiece into something not much less than an English one."*

—C.M. Woodhouse, Times Literary Supplement

THE COLLECTED POEMS OF NIKOS KAVADIAS

Translated by Gail Holst-Warhaft

PAPERBACK
PAGES 240
14 x 21 cm

"*Modern Greeks dominate the world's merchant marine; ancient Greeks like Homer's Odysseus sailed the Mediterranean and beyond. But what do we know about shipboard life? Not much. Reading Kavadias fills this emptiness. He spent his adult life sailing world-wide and writing poems about monsoons, cats dying on shipboard, masts snapping in two, dream-girls or disgusting whores on shore, and fleas jumping off one's pubic hair. "In this fo'c'sle," he laments, "I ruined my calm self / and killed my tender childhood soul. / But I never gave up my obstinate dream, / and the sea, when it roars, tells me a lot." Scrupulously translated, these accessible poems will tell landlubbers a lot about life on the winedark sea.*"

—Peter Bien, Translator of Nikos Kazantzakis and Stratis Myrivilis

"*It is from the open sea's horizon that he draws his inspiration. The anchor, the fo'c'sle, the marabou and brothels in various exotic countries, excite his imagination to the point that the world of the sea becomes a metaphor for his poetic philosophy. "A mad dog's howl. / So long shore and farewell tub. / Our soul slipped out from under us. / Hell has got a brothel too". (Fata Morgana). His erotic ideal is Fata Morgana, a beautiful woman in Celtic myth, heralding disaster; just like the sea that seduces and drowns. Kavadias turned his profession into poetry. Does this explain the unique charm of his poetry? It certainly suggests the added difficulty that it must have presented for the translator, Gail Holst Warhaft. The translation is very successful.*"

—Katerina Anghelaki-Rooke, Poet

www.greeceinprint.com

THE PASSPORT AND OTHER SELECTED SHORT STORIES

Translated by Andrew Horton

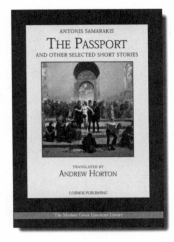

PAPERBACK
PAGES 112
14 x 21 cm

Antonis Samarakis (1919-2003) was modern Greece's most widely translated writer after Nikos Kazantzakis. He published four collections of short stories and two novels beginning in 1954. His novel, *To Lathos (The Flaw)* has been translated into over twenty languages. Graham Greene called this novel, "A real masterpiece. A story of the psychological struggle between two secret police agents and their suspect told with wit, imagination and quite outstanding technical skill." Arthur Miller wrote that, "*The Flaw* is a powerful work. I only wish some people who profess democracy would read *The Flaw* and see what it is they actually support. We are living in a time when words and their substance are very unrelated-to the point of meaninglessness. And this is not only in the question of Greece."

Samarakis's short stories were equally well received at home and abroad, and this collection brings together eight of his finest stories including "The Last Participation", "Mama", "The Knife", and "The Passport" which he wrote during the period of the Dictatorship of 1967-75 when he was denied a passport to travel abroad.